Throughout his life, Johan Theorin has been a regular visitor to the Baltic island of Öland. His mother's family – sailors, fishermen and farmers – have lived there for centuries, nurturing the island's rich legacy of strange tales and folklore.

Johan's first novel, *Echoes from the Dead* (originally published in Sweden as *Skumtimmen*), won the CWA John Creasey Dagger for Best Debut Crime Novel 2009, was a top ten bestseller in Sweden, and has been sold all over the world. His second novel, *The Darkest Room* (originally published in Sweden as *Nattfåk*), won the CWA International Dagger 2010 and was a Swedish number one bestseller.

A journalist by profession, Johan is currently working on the final novel in his Öland quartet of books, all of which are set on the island that means so much to him.

JOHAN THEORIN'S ÖLAND NOVELS

ECHOES FROM THE DEAD

Winner of the CWA John Creasey Dagger for Best Debut Crime Novel of the Year 2009

Voted Best First Crime Novel by the Swedish Academy of Crime

When a child's sandal arrives in the post, Julia Davidson knows it belongs to her son who went missing on the Swedish island of Öland twenty years previously. It soon becomes clear that someone wants to stop Julia's search for the truth behind her son's disappearance. And that he's much closer than she thinks . . .

'An evocative and haunting thriller, with a subtle sense of menace that grows with each page'
Simon Beckett

THE DARKEST ROOM

Winner of the 2008 Glass Key Award for Best Nordic Crime Novel, and a number one bestseller in Sweden

It is bitter mid-winter on Öland, and Katrine and Joakim Westin have moved with their children to the boarded-up manor house at Eel Point. But their remote idyll is soon shattered when Katrine is found drowned off the rocks nearby. As Joakim struggles to keep his sanity in the wake of the tragedy, the old house begins to exert a strange hold over him . . .

'A powerful study of grief, loss and vulnerability, with a commendably earth-bound solution'
Guardian

THE QUARRY

Johan Theorin

Translated from the Swedish
by Marlaine Delargy

BLACK SWAN

TRANSWORLD PUBLISHERS
61–63 Uxbridge Road, London W5 5SA
A Random House Group Company
www.transworldbooks.co.uk

THE QUARRY
A BLACK SWAN BOOK: 9780552777049

First published in Great Britain
in 2011 by Doubleday
an imprint of Transworld Publishers
Black Swan edition published 2012

Copyright © Johan Theorin 2011
English translation copyright © Marlaine Delargy 2011

Johan Theorin has asserted his right under the Copyright, Designs
and Patents Act 1988 to be identified as the author of this work.

This book is a work of fiction and, except in the case of historical fact,
any resemblance to actual persons, living or dead, is purely coincidental.

A CIP catalogue record for this book
is available from the British Library.

This book is sold subject to the condition that it shall not,
by way of trade or otherwise, be lent, resold, hired out,
or otherwise circulated without the publisher's prior
consent in any form of binding or cover other than that
in which it is published and without a similar condition,
including this condition, being imposed on the
subsequent purchaser.

Addresses for Random House Group Ltd companies outside the UK
can be found at: www.randomhouse.co.uk
The Random House Group Ltd Reg. No. 954009

The Random House Group Limited supports The Forest Stewardship
Council (FSC®), the leading international forest certification
organization. Our books carrying the FSC label are printed on FSC®
certified paper. FSC is the only forest certification scheme endorsed by
the leading environmental organizations, including Greenpeace.
Our paper procurement policy can be found at
www.randomhouse.co.uk/environment.

Typeset in 11/13pt Giovanni Book by
Kestrel Data, Exeter, Devon.
Printed and bound by
Clays Ltd, St Ives plc

2 4 6 8 10 9 7 5 3 1

THE QUARRY

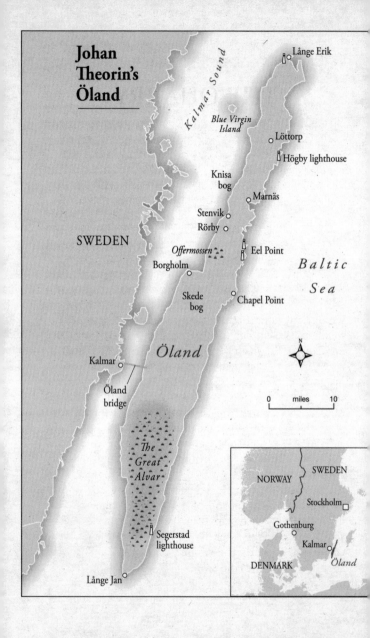

1

It was March in northern Öland, and the sun was shining on small, dirty-white snowdrifts as they slowly melted on the lawns at the residential home for senior citizens in Marnäs. Two blue flags fluttered in the breeze by the car park – the Swedish flag with its yellow cross, and the flag of Öland with its golden stag. Both were flying at half-mast.

A long, black car moved slowly towards the home and stopped in front of the main entrance. Two middle-aged men in thick winter coats climbed out and went around to the boot of the car, where they slid out a metal trolley. They lowered the wheels and set off, pushing it up the wheelchair ramp and in through the glass doors.

The men were undertakers.

Retired sea captain Gerlof Davidsson was sitting drinking coffee in the dining room with his fellow residents when they emerged from the lift. He watched them move along the corridor, pushing the trolley in front of them; on top of it lay yellow blankets and broad straps which would be used to secure the body. The men plodded silently past the dining room and continued towards the service lift, which would take them down to the cold store.

The murmur of conversation among the elderly residents had temporarily died away as the trolley passed by, but now it began once more.

A couple of years earlier, Gerlof recalled, everyone in the home had been asked to vote on whether they wanted the undertakers to park at the back of the building and make their way in discreetly through a side door when they came to collect someone who had passed away. Most had voted against the suggestion, Gerlof included.

The old people in the home wanted to see a dead neighbour's final journey. They wanted to say goodbye.

The person being collected on this cold day was Torsten Axelsson, and he had died in his bed – alone and late at night, as was often the case when death came. The staff on the morning shift had found him, called a doctor to certify the death, then dressed him in his best dark suit. They had fastened a plastic bracelet with his name and ID number around one wrist, and finally they had wound a bandage around Torsten's head to keep his jaw closed when rigor mortis set in.

Gerlof knew that Torsten had been well aware of exactly what would happen to him after his death. Before he retired he had worked as a churchwarden and gravedigger. One of the many coffins he had buried belonged to a murderer by the name of Nils Kant, but most of the graves Torsten had dug were for ordinary islanders.

He had dug graves in the churchyard all year round, except when there was a great deal of snow and the temperature below zero reached double figures. It had been particularly difficult to dig in the spring, he had explained to Gerlof, because the frost was so slow to leave the ground on Öland. But the physical exertion hadn't been the worst thing, Torsten had added: he had found it extremely hard to get out of bed on those days when he knew he had to make his way to the church-yard to dig a grave for a child who had passed away.

Now he would soon be lowered into his own grave. In an urn – Torsten wanted to be cremated.

'I'd rather burn than have my bones left in the ground, to be tossed here and there,' he had said.

Things were different in the old days, Gerlof thought. When he was young and some relative died, there were no undertakers or funeral directors to take care of the practicalities. In the old days you died in your bed at home, then some relative would make a coffin.

This thought reminded Gerlof of an old family story. As a newly married couple living in a renovated cottage down in Stenvik at the beginning of the twentieth century, Gerlof's father and mother had been woken one night by strange noises coming from the attic; it had sounded as if someone was hurling around the leftover planks of wood his father stored up there. But when he went up to see what was happening, everything was silent and there was nothing there. His father came down and went back to bed, and the crashing and banging began again. Gerlof's parents lay there in the darkness listening to the terrifying noises, not daring to move a muscle.

When Gerlof had finished his coffee, the undertakers came back with the trolley. He could see that there was a body on it now, hidden beneath a blanket and secured with the leather straps. They moved silently and quickly towards the door.

Farewell, Torsten, he thought.

When the outside door closed, Gerlof pushed back his chair.

'Time to go,' he said to his companions.

He got slowly to his feet with the help of his stick. He gritted his teeth against the rheumatic pains in his legs and went into the corridor, heading for the supervisor's office.

For a few weeks now Gerlof had been thinking something over, ever since his birthday, when he suddenly realized he would be eighty-five in just a couple of years. Time was passing so quickly – a year now that he was old was like a week when he was young. Today, following Torsten's death, Gerlof had made up his mind.

He knocked tentatively on the supervisor's door, and pushed it open when Boel answered. She was sitting at the computer, filling in some kind of report. Gerlof stood in the doorway, saying nothing. Eventually she looked up.

'All right, Gerlof?'

'Yes.'

'What is it? Is there some kind of problem?'

He took a deep breath. 'I have to get away from here.'

Boel started to shake her head. 'Gerlof . . .'

'I've already made up my mind,' he broke in.

'Oh?'

'I'm going to tell you a story . . .' Gerlof noticed Boel raising her eyes wearily to the ceiling, but he carried on anyway. 'My father and mother got married in 1910. They took over an old croft where no one had lived for several years. On that first night when they went to bed, they heard strange noises from the attic . . . It sounded as if somebody was sorting through the planks of wood my father had stored up there. They could find no explanation for the noise, but the following morning a neighbour called round.' Gerlof paused for effect, then went on: 'The neighbour told them that his brother had died over on his farm the previous evening. Then he asked if they could spare him some wood to make a coffin. My father let him go up into the attic alone to choose some planks, and as my parents sat there in the kitchen listening to the banging and crashing from above, they recognized the noise . . . It was exactly the same as they had heard the previous night.'

Silence fell in the room.

'And?' said Boel.

'It was a sign. A sign of impending death.'

'Well, that was a very nice story, Gerlof . . . But what exactly is your point?'

He sighed. 'The point,' he said, 'is that if I stay here, it'll be my coffin they're making next. I've already heard the planks of wood being moved around. And the rattle of the trolley as it comes to collect the body.'

Boel appeared to give up. 'So what are you intending to do, then? Where will you go?'

'Home,' said Gerlof. 'Home to my cottage.'

2

'Dying? Who said you were dying, Dad?'

'I did.'

'But that's ridiculous! You've got years and years left . . . lots of springs to look forward to,' said Julia Davidsson. 'Besides, you've made it out of an old people's home alive – how many manage that?'

Gerlof said nothing, but he was thinking about the steel trolley with Torsten Axelsson's body on it. He remained silent as his daughter drove on down towards the coast and into the village of Stenvik.

The sun was shining through the windscreen, making him long for butterflies and birds and everything else the warm weather would bring. His zest for life raised its sleepy head within his breast and blinked in surprise, and he had to make a real effort to sound gloomy when he eventually spoke.

'Only God knows how much time I have left, and He is allowing it to pass all too quickly . . . but if I'm going to die, I want it to be here in the village.'

Julia sighed. She stopped the car on the deserted village road and switched off the engine. 'You read too many obituaries.'

'Correct. They keep the newspapers going.'

Gerlof's last comment was meant partly as a joke, but Julia didn't laugh. She simply helped him out of the car in silence. They walked slowly towards the gate of the family's summer cottage, which lay in a grove of trees in Stenvik, just a few hundred metres from the sea.

He would be alone here most of the time, Gerlof was well aware of that, but it meant he would avoid all the illness back at the home. The residents with their pills, their oxygen cylinders and their constant harping on about what was wrong with them had started to get on his nerves. His former girlfriend, Maja Nyman, had become increasingly unwell, and now spent most of her time in bed in her room.

It had taken almost a month to persuade Boel and the rest of the management team at the home to agree to let him move back to Stenvik, but eventually they had realized that Gerlof would be making room for somebody else who actually *did* want to live in the Marnäs residential home for senior citizens. Of course, Gerlof would still need help with cleaning, medical care and the provision of meals, but that could be organized through visits from the community nursing team and the home-care service.

Gerlof's mind was perfectly clear, even if he could barely move sometimes. There wasn't much wrong with his head or his teeth – it was just his arms, legs and the rest of his body that could do with a makeover.

This day at the end of March was the first time this year he had been back to the village on the coast where he had been born and had grown up. He was back on the land the Davidsson family had owned and worked for centuries, and back at the cottage he had built for himself and his wife Ella some fifty years earlier. Stenvik was the place he had always come back to during his years at sea.

The snow had almost disappeared from the garden, leaving a sodden lawn that needed raking.

'Last year's grass and last year's leaves,' said Gerlof. 'Everything that has been hidden by the winter is re-appearing.'

He held tightly on to Julia's arm as they walked across the pale-yellow grass, but when she stopped at the bottom of the stone steps he let go and made his way slowly up to the door, leaning on his chestnut stick.

Gerlof was able to walk, but was glad of his daughter's help; he was glad too that Ella was no longer alive. He would have been nothing but a burden to her now.

He took out his key and unlocked the door.

The musty smell of the cottage rushed towards them as he opened the glass door: cold, slightly damp air, but no hint of mould. It seemed that the slates on the roof were still in good condition. And as he stepped inside he noticed that there were no little black deposits on the wooden floor. The mice and shrews liked to spend the winter in the foundations, but they never came into the rooms.

Julia had come over to the island for the weekend to help him move into the cottage and get it sorted out. Spring cleaning, she called it. It was Gerlof's cottage, of course, but it had been used as a holiday home for his two daughters and their families for many years. When the summer came they would somehow have to rub along together in the little rooms.

Plenty of time to worry about that, he thought.

When they had taken Gerlof's things inside, switched on the electricity and opened the windows to air the cottage, they went back out on to the lawn.

Apart from the screaming of a few gulls down by the shore, the village had seemed completely deserted on this Saturday morning, but they suddenly heard thumping noises from the far side of the village road, echoing across the landscape like loud hammer blows.

Julia looked around. 'There's someone here.'

'Yes,' said Gerlof. 'They're building over by the quarry.'

He wasn't surprised, because last summer when he was down in the village he had noticed that all the bushes and undergrowth had been cleared from two large plots over there, and a Caterpillar tractor was busy flattening the ground. He presumed somebody was building even more cottages that would stand empty for most of the year.

'Do you want to have a look?'

'If you like.'

He took his daughter's arm again, and Julia led him out through the gate.

When Gerlof built his cottage at the beginning of the 1950s, he had had a view of the sea to the west and had just been able to see the tower of Marnäs church in the east, but at that time there were plenty of cows and sheep grazing the land. Now the animals were gone and the trees had come back, their crowns forming an increasingly dense canopy around the cottage. As they crossed the village road, Gerlof caught only a brief glimpse of the ice-covered Sound to the west.

Stenvik was an old fishing village, and Gerlof could remember a time when rows of gigs and skiffs lay drawn up out of the water along the gently curving shore, waiting to be rowed out to the fishing nets further out in the Sound. Now they were all gone, and the fishermen's cottages had been converted into holiday homes.

They turned off on to the gravel track leading to the

quarry, where a new white sign proclaimed ERNST'S ROAD.

Gerlof knew who it was named after: Ernst had been a quarryman and a friend of his, and the last of the villagers to work in the quarry before it closed for good at the beginning of the sixties. Now Ernst was gone too – only his road remained. Gerlof wondered whether anything might be named after him some day.

As they approached the quarry, which lay behind a grove of trees, he saw that Ernst's red-brown cottage was still there right by the edge, all closed up. Some second cousin and his family had inherited it when Ernst died, but they had hardly ever been there.

'Goodness,' said Julia, 'I see they've been building here as well.'

Gerlof tore his gaze away from Ernst's cottage and noticed the two new houses she was talking about. They were on the eastern side of the quarry, a couple of hundred metres apart.

'They only cleared this last summer,' said Julia. 'They must have built them during the autumn and winter.'

Gerlof shook his head. 'Nobody asked my permission.'

Julia laughed. 'They don't bother you, do they? I mean, you can't see them, because of the trees.'

'No, but even so. They could show a bit of consideration.'

The houses were built of wood and stone, with shining picture windows, whitewashed chimneys and roofs made of some kind of black slate. The scaffolding was still up at one of them, and a couple of joiners in thick woollen sweaters were busy nailing wooden panels in place. Outside the other house a large white bath stood in the garden, still wrapped in plastic.

Ernst's cottage, to the north of the new houses, looked like a little woodshed in comparison.

Luxury homes, thought Gerlof. Hardly what the village needed more of. But here they were, almost finished.

The abandoned quarry lay like a wound in the ground, five hundred metres wide and filled with large and small lumps of reject stone that had been broken off and cast aside in the quest for the fault-free stone deeper down.

'Do you want to take a closer look?' asked Julia. 'We could go over and see if anyone's home.'

Gerlof shook his head. 'I already know them. They're rich, irresponsible city folk.'

'Not everybody who buys a house comes from the city,' said Julia.

'No, no . . . But I have no doubt they're rich and irresponsible.'

3

'Do you want me to open the window?' said Per Mörner.

His daughter Nilla nodded, her back to him.

'Are there any birds out there?' she asked.

'Loads,' said Per.

That wasn't true; he couldn't see a single one outside the hospital. But there were trees by the car park, and maybe some little birds were sitting in them.

'In that case you can open the window,' said Nilla, and explained: 'My nature studies homework this week is to count different species of birds.'

Nilla was in Year 7, and all her school books were on the table next to her hospital bed. She had placed her favourite cuddly toy and lucky stones by her pillow, then climbed on the bed so that she could hang a big piece of fabric with NIRVANA on it on the wall above her head.

Per opened the window, and the faint sound of chirruping drifted into the room. But it was mixed with the whine of revving engines, and no doubt the birds would soon fall silent anyway; it was almost evening, after all, and shiny cars were leaving the car park as doctors and nurses set off for home. His own brown

18

Saab was down there too, but it was nine years old and definitely not shiny.

'What are you thinking about?' said Nilla behind him.

Per turned his head. 'Guess.'

'You're thinking about the spring.'

'Spot on,' said Per, even though he'd actually been thinking about his old car. 'You're getting better and better at this.'

Mind-reading, that was his daughter's latest project. Before that she'd spent several months practising until she could write just as well with her left hand as with her right, but over Christmas she had seen a television programme about telepathy and had started experimenting with her twin brother Jesper and her father, sending thoughts to them and attempting to read theirs. It was Per's task to send a special thought to Nilla every evening at eight o'clock.

He stood by the window, watching the setting sun glinting on the car windows.

It was probably spring now, in spite of the cold, but Per hadn't really had time to notice. The birds were returning home from the Mediterranean and the farmers were beginning to sow their crops. Per thought about his father, Jerry, who had always looked forward to the spring. That was when his work really took off. Didn't people say that spring was the time of youth? Youth, and love.

But Per had never had any real feeling for the spring. Not even when he and Marika had got married on a sunny day in May, after meeting at a marketing seminar fifteen years ago. It was as if he had sensed even then that she would leave him, sooner or later.

'Did Mum say when she was coming?' he asked over his shoulder.

'Mm-hmm,' said Nilla. 'Between six and seven.'

It was almost five o'clock now.

'Do you want me and Jesper to wait until she gets here?'

Nilla shook her head. 'I'll be OK.'

That was the answer Per had been hoping for. He had nothing against seeing Marika, but she was only coming to visit her daughter, and there was a risk that she would have her new husband with her – Georg, with his substantial income and his expensive presents. Per had got over Marika, but he had a problem with the fact that she had met a man who spoiled both her and the twins.

Nilla was in a private room, and seemed to be well looked after. A young male doctor had been in half an hour earlier, and had explained which tests they would be doing over the next few days, and in what order. Nilla had listened with her eyes lowered; she hadn't asked any questions. She had glanced up at the doctor occasionally, but not at Per.

'See you soon, Pernilla,' the doctor had said as he left.

She had two long, hard days of tests and medical examinations ahead, and Per couldn't come up with anything encouraging to say.

She carried on arranging her things, and Per helped her. It was never possible to make a hospital room look cosy – it was too bare and full of tubes and call buttons – but they tried. Along with her own pink pillow, Nilla had brought a CD player and some Nirvana CDs, a couple of books, and more trousers and tops than she really needed.

She was dressed in jeans and a black top, but soon she would be in the usual hospital garb: a white suit that was easy to fold back for all the examinations.

'Right,' said Per. 'We'll be off, then, but Mum will be here soon . . . Shall I go and get Jesper?'

'OK.'

His son was sitting on a sofa in the waiting room. There were some books and magazines on a shelf, but Jesper was bent over his Gameboy, as usual.

'Jesper?' Per said loudly.

'What?'

'Nilla wanted to say goodbye.'

Jesper paused the game. He went into his twin sister's room alone, and closed the door. Per wondered what they were talking about. Did Jesper find it easier to talk to Nilla than to his dad? Did they talk about her illness? He hardly spoke to Per at all.

When they were small, just a few years old, the twins had had their own language that nobody else could understand. It was a sing-song language, consisting almost entirely of vowels. Nilla in particular had found it difficult to start speaking Swedish; she preferred this secret language she shared with Jesper. Until Per and Marika found a speech therapist who was able to sort out the problem, it had sometimes felt as if he had fathered two aliens.

A door opened further down the corridor. The doctor who had spoken to Nilla earlier emerged, and Per went over to him. Per had always admired the medical profession – when his mother had refused to tell him what his father did for a job, Per had got the idea that Jerry worked abroad as a doctor. He had believed that for several years.

'I'd like to ask a question,' he said. 'About my daughter, Nilla.'

The doctor stopped. 'What would you like to know?'

'She looks a bit swollen,' said Per. 'Is that normal?'

'Swollen? Where?'

'Her face – her cheeks, and around her eyes. It started on the way here. Does it mean anything?'

'Maybe,' said the doctor. 'We'll have a good look at her. ECG, ultrasound, a CAT scan, X-rays, blood tests . . . The works!'

Per nodded, but Nilla had already had so many tests for her mysterious pains. The results just seemed to lead to more tests, more waiting.

The door to her room opened and Jesper came out. He headed for the waiting room with his Gameboy, but Per raised a hand to stop him.

'Don't start playing again,' he said. 'We're going up to the summer cottage now.'

When they drove off the Öland bridge quarter of an hour later and turned north on the flat island, the countryside around them was a kind of yellowish brown, a landscape on the borderline between winter and spring. The evening sun was shining across the ditches by the roadside where wood anemones and coltsfoot were beginning to raise their heads, but there were still drifts of sparkling snow on both sides of the road. The snow that had melted in the sun had begun to form large pools out on the alvar, with narrow spring streams bubbling along as they searched for a way to the sea.

A world of water. There wasn't a soul in sight out there, just flocks of lapwings and bullfinches.

Per loved the emptiness and the clean lines of the island, and when the traffic thinned out once they had passed Borgholm he put his foot down.

The Saab hummed northwards through the open landscape, past forest groves and windmills – it was a little bit like driving through an oil painting. A painting of the spring. The green and brown fields, the vast crystal dome of the sky, the Sound over to the west. The sea was still covered in dark-blue ice, but it looked thin, and there were black rifts further out. Soon the waves would be set free.

'Isn't it beautiful?' said Per.

Jesper, who was sitting next to him, looked up from his Gameboy. 'What?'

'All this,' said Per. 'All this, the island . . . everything.'

Jesper looked out through the windscreen and nodded, but Per couldn't see the fire in his son's eyes that he himself felt here on the island. He tried to tell himself it was because of Jesper's age; young people didn't appreciate nature for its own sake. Perhaps it required a certain maturity, or even a deep sorrow, to become interested in the soul of the landscape.

Or maybe the problem was Jesper. Would Per rather have Nilla sitting beside him, healthy and full of anticipation? Would he rather Jesper was the one waiting for tests?

He pushed the thought aside and focused on the spring instead. Spring on the island.

Per had first started coming to the island as a little boy at the end of the 1950s, along with his mother, Anita. It was the summer of 1958, two years after her divorce, and she didn't have much money for holidays. Jerry was supposed to pay maintenance every month, but he had coughed up only occasionally – although Anita did say that Jerry had once driven past her terraced house in his big flashy car, chucked a bundle of notes at the door and disappeared.

The shortage of money meant brief, cheap holidays not too far from Kalmar. But Anita had a cousin called Ernst Adolfsson, a quarryman who lived alone in a little cottage on Öland, and she and her son had always

23

been welcome to catch the ferry across to the island in the holidays and stay as long as they wanted.

Per had loved playing in the abandoned quarry down below Ernst's house. It was a world of adventure if you were nine years old.

Ernst had no children or siblings, and when he died a few years ago, Per had inherited the cottage. He had cleared it out the previous summer, and now he was intending to spend the next six months living there – perhaps he might even stay all year round. He couldn't afford to keep two properties going, so he had rented out his apartment in Kalmar until the end of September.

The plan had been for his two children to come over to Öland as often as they wanted. But Nilla had started Year 7 as a tired, listless child, and had grown increasingly exhausted as the autumn went on. The school doctor had put it down to puberty, or growing pains, but after New Year she had started to complain of pains in her left side. The situation had grown worse and worse during the winter, and none of the doctors seemed to know why.

Their summer plans had suddenly become uncertain.

'Do you want to ring Mum when we get there?'

His son didn't look up from the game. 'Dunno.'

'Would you like to go down to the shore?'

'Dunno,' Jesper said again.

It felt as if he were as distant as an orbiting satellite – but that's probably what it was like to be a thirteen-year-old these days. When Per was that age, his greatest wish had been for his father to come and visit and talk to him.

Suddenly he spotted a sign showing a petrol pump by the side of the road, and slowed down. 'Would you like an ice cream? Or is it too early in the year?'

24

Jesper looked up from his game. 'I'd rather have sweets.'

'Let's see what they've got,' said Per, pulling into the car park.

They got out. It was freezing cold in spite of the sun. Per had thought it would be warmer on the island at this time of year, but the layer of ice out in the Sound probably made the air cooler. The wind cut straight through his padded jacket, and a little swirl of sand blew up and into his mouth, crunching between his teeth.

Per walked quickly past the petrol pumps and sheltered by the kiosk. The front window was dark, but he knocked a few times anyway, until he spotted a note stuck inside, faded by the sun:

> *Thank you for your custom this summer –*
> *we re-open on June 1st!*

April was too early – the island hadn't yet woken from its winter slumbers, and the number of shops that stayed open in the winter no doubt matched the demand. Per had worked in market research for fifteen years, and understood perfectly.

Jesper was sitting on a wooden box with SAND written on it, next to the car park. He was playing on his Gameboy again. As Per walked over to him he heard the sound of an engine in the distance. A white HGV was fast approaching from the north.

He took out the car keys and shouted to Jesper, 'No sweets, sorry. They're shut.'

Jesper merely nodded, and Per went on, 'There are some more shops further north. We can . . .'

Then he stopped, because he suddenly heard a muted thud out on the road and the sound of tyres screeching across the Tarmac. To the south he could see the dazzling reflection of the sun on a car.

It was an Audi, and the driver had lost control; the car veered across the carriageway, right in front of the on-coming truck.

Per could only stand and watch. The car must have collided with something; the bonnet was spattered with red, and the windscreen was covered in blood.

Whose blood?

The truck driver sounded his horn at the car. A male figure was just visible behind the smeared windscreen, leaning over the wheel and struggling to regain control of the car.

Per started to move just as the harsh sound of the truck's horn died away. It had moved to the right, out on to the verge. Per saw the Audi straighten up for half a second, then veer off the other way.

The vehicles missed one another, because the car had skidded into the car park. The wheels locked and the car slid across the gravel, still travelling at speed. It was moving sideways across the Tarmac, heading straight for the sand box.

'Jesper!' Per yelled out.

His son was still sitting on the box, pressing the buttons on the Gameboy with his thumbs. He didn't even look up.

Per shot forward, hurtling across the Tarmac.

'Jesper!'

Now he looked up. He turned around, open-mouthed.

But the Audi was moving faster, the tyres spraying gravel and sand all around as it headed straight for Jesper.

4

Vendela Larsson had been sitting meditating next to Max when the accident happened. She had disappeared inside herself, eyes half-closed, perceiving the fields and meadows and all the stone walls like a film rolling past outside the car window. A familiar landscape, yet alien at the same time. Max had been here on a couple of occasions during the autumn and winter when the house was being built, but for Vendela it was the first time for many years.

Was it thirty years, or thirty-five? She couldn't remember.

As she started to calculate in her head, something hit the front of the car with a thud.

'Fuck!' yelled Max, and Vendela was suddenly wide awake.

There was a brief slurping sound, then the windscreen was covered in red.

The car was no longer whizzing along smoothly. It was swerving and skidding as if it were on a slalom course, veering back and forth across the carriageway with screeching tyres – first to the left, heading straight for a truck bearing down on them from the opposite direction, then suddenly to the right, lurching towards a wide entrance of some kind. It was a petrol station with a shop and an empty car park.

Not completely empty. There was a car, and she could see people. A man running across the Tarmac, and a boy sitting on a big box.

'Fuck!' Max yelled again.

Vendela heard her dog Ally yapping. She opened her mouth, but no sound emerged. She was a body moving with the car, and there was nothing she could do.

Max wrenched the wheel to one side. There was a bang and a screech, and the car came to an abrupt halt. Vendela was thrown forward, but the seatbelt held her.

The engine sputtered and died.

'Shit . . .' said Max. He sat there, his eyes staring straight ahead, his white fingers clamped around the wheel.

They weren't moving. The front of the Audi had driven into the box of sand, smashing it to pieces.

And there was no sign of the boy who had been sitting on the box. Where was he?

Vendela undid her seatbelt and leant forward, pressing her forehead against the windscreen. She saw a little hand sticking out to the right of the car.

The boy seemed to be lying next to the box, with his legs underneath the car. The tall man had reached him; he placed a hand on the bonnet of the Audi and bent down.

Max fumbled with the door and flung it open. He staggered out, his face bright red. 'Don't touch my car!'

It was the shock, Vendela could see that; Max was totally wound up, and had no idea what he was doing. He took two steps forward, raising his hands towards the other man.

Two seconds later he was on the ground, with his

nose pressed firmly against the Tarmac a couple of metres from the car. The man had flattened him.

'Calm down.' He bent over Max with gritted teeth, his fist raised. He seemed to be focusing on the back of Max's neck.

His heart. Vendela grabbed the door handle and somehow managed to get the door open; she stepped out into the wind and yelled the first thing that came into her head: 'No! He's got a bad heart!'

The man looked up at her, still angry. But the fury in his eyes suddenly died. He breathed out, lowered his shoulders and looked down at Max. 'Have you calmed down?' he asked quietly.

Max didn't reply. He gritted his teeth and struggled to free himself, but eventually he appeared to relax. 'OK,' he said.

Vendela stood motionless next to the car. The man let go of Max and straightened his back. He gently took hold of the boy's upper body and pulled him out cautiously, away from the car.

'Are you OK, Jesper?'

The boy gave some kind of answer, too quietly for Vendela to hear, but thank God, he didn't seem to be hurt.

'Can you move your toes?' said the man.

'Yeah.'

The boy started to get up. The man helped him, and led him over to their own car. They didn't look back, and Vendela had a feeling that she was somehow being excluded.

Max grabbed hold of the Audi's radiator grille and pulled himself to his feet. He blinked and noticed Vendela.

'Get back in the car,' he said. 'I'll take care of this.'

'OK.'

29

Vendela took a deep breath and turned back to the car. She sat down, saw the blood running down the windscreen and almost thought it was beautiful. No, in fact she could admit to herself that it *was* beautiful. The blood had been smeared across the glass by the windscreen wipers, forming sweeping lines. It looked like two little rainbows in pale pink and dark red, glowing like a neon sign in the sun.

A faint breeze from the sea made the feathers that had stuck to the car dance around and adhere to the windscreen. They were brown and dirty white.

Perhaps they had hit a pheasant, or a wood pigeon.

Whatever kind of bird it was, it had suddenly appeared in front of the car, its big wings flapping, and it had exploded like a balloon on impact. The body had hit the radiator grille hard, bounced up towards the windscreen in a blood-red explosion, then disappeared over the roof. It had left broad lines behind.

The sound of whimpering was coming from the floor next to her seat.

'Quiet, Ally!' shouted Max.

Vendela swallowed. It was bad enough when Max shouted at her, but it was even worse when he started on their dog.

'It's all right, Aloysius,' she said quietly.

She opened the door. 'Are you OK, Max?'

He nodded. 'I'm just going to wipe the car,' was all he said.

He was breathless and red in the face, but that was probably just because he was so angry.

The previous summer, Max had experienced a sudden pain in his chest while he was on stage in Gothenburg, giving a talk about his latest book, *Self-Confidence to the Max*. He had to stop and leave the stage, and his voice was full of panic when he called Vendela. He had taken

30

a taxi to A & E, where he had been examined and given oxygen.

It had been a mild heart attack, according to the doctor, with the emphasis on mild. There was no need for an operation – just rest. And Max had rested more or less right through the autumn, when he wasn't overseeing the building of the house on Öland and planning his new book. This was to be a different kind of book, less about psychology and more about living the right way and eating well. A cookery book by Max Larsson. Vendela had promised to help him.

There were tissues and a bottle of mineral water in the glove compartment, and she took a couple of gulps before winding down the window.

'Have some of this, Max.'

He took the bottle without speaking, but didn't have a drink; instead he poured the water over the windscreen, rinsing the blood away so that it ran down over the bodywork in red stripes. He leant over the bonnet, his jaw tightly clamped, scrubbing away at the glass.

Vendela wanted to forget the dead bird. She looked over to the right, through the clean side window and out across the alvar. A flat world of grass and bushes and rocks. She longed to be there. If Max wasn't in too bad a mood after the collision, she might be able to go for a run this evening.

Vendela's family came from the island; she had grown up on a farm outside Stenvik, which was partly why she had persuaded Max to buy a plot of land here.

Her husband really would have preferred a summer retreat closer to Stockholm, he had said so several times. But when Vendela showed him the location of Stenvik, right on the coast, and allowed him to choose exactly what kind of house they would build by the quarry, he had given in. Their house was an architectural dream by the sea, a fairytale palace of stone and glass.

Aloysius was still hobbling around on his stiff legs, shifting position down on the floor; his anxiety transmitted itself to Vendela, making her feel slightly unwell.

'Lie down, Ally . . . we'll be off soon.'

The greyish white poodle stopped howling, but he continued to whimper, pressing himself against her legs. His big eyes gazed up at her, pale and unfocused. Aloysius was thirteen years old – more than eighty in dog years. He could no longer bend his right front leg, and his sight had deteriorated over the past year. Their vet in Stockholm had explained back in the autumn that Ally would soon be able to distinguish only between light and darkness, and in less than a year he would probably be completely blind.

Vendela had stared at him.

'But isn't there anything you can do?'

'Well yes . . . there's always something we can do when it comes to an old dog. And it doesn't hurt at all.'

But when the vet had started to talk about how a dog is put to sleep, Vendela had swept Ally up in her arms and fled.

It took about twenty tissues to get the car anything like clean. Max poured water and wiped, then threw them in the ditch next to the car park, one after another.

Vendela watched the dripping red tissues tumbling down into the ditch. No doubt they would lie there like dry leaves all through the spring and summer, and the islanders would mutter darkly about tourists leaving their litter. And the inhabitants of the alvar would see the mess too.

Max threw away the last tissue and leant forward – he seemed to be checking that he hadn't got any blood on his suede jacket or his jeans. Then he got back in the car, without looking Vendela in the eye.

'All right?' he said when he was settled.

She nodded, thinking, *Absolutely. It's just that some days are a little crazier than normal.*

She looked over towards the other car, where the man and the boy were sitting. 'Are you going to have a word with them?'

'What for?' said Max, starting the engine. 'Nobody got hurt.'

Except the bird, thought Vendela.

There was a screeching sound as Max reversed away from the sand box. It had split down one side; Vendela could see a thin stream of sand pouring out on to the Tarmac. No doubt the front of the Audi was also cracked.

Aloysius stopped whimpering and lay down again.

'Right,' said Max, shaking his head as if he wanted to shake off what had happened. 'Off we go, then.'

He put the car into first gear and squirted water over the windscreen. Then he accelerated out of the car park.

Vendela turned to see if she could spot the bird's broken body by the side of the road. But it wasn't there; perhaps it was lying in the ditch.

'I wonder what kind of bird it was,' she said. 'Did you see it, Max? I didn't have time to notice if it was a pheasant or a grouse or—'

He shook his head. 'Just forget it.'

'It wasn't a crane, was it, Max?'

'Forget about the bird, Vendela. Think about the new house.'

The road was completely empty now, and Max put his foot down. Vendela knew he wanted to get to the house to carry on with his cookery book. After the weekend a photographer was coming to take pictures of him in the new kitchen. Of course, the actual food would be prepared by Vendela.

The Audi picked up speed. Soon they were zooming along just as quickly as before, as if the collision and the quarrel had never taken place, but Aloysius was still trembling when he pressed himself against Vendela's leg. He almost always trembled when Max was around.

If he had been younger and fitter, Ally could have gone with her on relaxing outings on the alvar, but as it was he would have to stay at home. Max didn't enjoy going walking or running either. Vendela would have to venture out on to the alvar alone.

But perhaps not completely alone. After all, the elves were out there.

5

'Are you OK?' asked Per for the sixth or seventh time.

Jesper nodded.

'No broken bones?'

'Nope.'

They were back in the car. Ten metres away, the Audi was disentangling itself from the broken sand box. Per could see that the spoiler was cracked, as was the right headlight.

The Audi swung around and pulled out on to the main road. The driver kept his gaze fixed straight ahead, but the woman beside him caught Per's eye for a second before looking away. She had a narrow, tense face, and she reminded him of someone. Regina?

He looked at his son again, his arm around his shoulders. Jesper seemed calm, but the muscles at the back of his neck were trembling.

'No pain anywhere?'

'Just bruises,' said Jesper, with a fleeting smile. 'I threw myself out of the way of the wheels, but it was really close.'

'It was *horribly* close . . . It's a good job you're so quick.'

Per's smile was tense. He removed his arm from his

son's shoulders, placed his hands on the wheel and exhaled. The anger was gone now, but just a few minutes ago he had knocked another man off his feet, and had been quite prepared to punch him. He would have happily thumped just about anybody, to be honest. As if that would make anything better.

It also occurred to him that Jesper had just smiled at him, the first smile for ages. A sign of spring?

He saw the Audi pick up speed, shining traces of blood still showing on the bonnet. It shot off northwards.

The big car made Per think about all the flashy cars his father had driven – a long series of vehicles Jerry had imported from the USA. In the mid-seventies he had driven Cadillacs, switching to a new model almost every year. People had turned their heads when Jerry came roaring along, and he'd loved every minute of it.

'What was that move?' asked Jesper.

'Sorry?'

'That judo throw?'

Per shook his head and turned the key in the ignition. He had trained in judo for less than two years and had only got as far as an orange belt, but Jesper seemed impressed nevertheless.

'That wasn't judo . . . I just pulled him down, like tripping someone up,' he said. 'You could have done that too if you'd carried on training.'

Jesper didn't answer.

'Well, you've packed it in as well,' he said eventually.

'I haven't got anybody to train with,' said Per, pulling out of the car park. 'I'm thinking of taking up running instead.'

He looked out at the flat landscape beyond the road. The ground looked lifeless, but there was a lot going on beneath the surface.

'Where will you run, Dad?' asked Jesper.

'Just about anywhere.'

6

Burn them, Gerlof, Ella Davidsson had said when she was lying in hospital like a skeleton. *Promise me you'll burn them.*

And he had nodded. But his late wife's diaries were still here, and this Friday he had found them.

The sun had returned to the Baltic, just a week before Easter. Now all that was lacking was the warmth, then Gerlof would be able to spend whole days sitting in the garden. Resting, thinking, and building his ships in bottles. Slender blades of green were beginning to appear among the brown leaves around him. The grass wouldn't need cutting until May.

The sunshine in the middle of the day was beginning to entice the butterflies out. For Gerlof they were the most important sign of spring. Even as a little boy he had waited to see the first butterflies appear, and to see what colour they were. At the age of eighty-three it was difficult to be filled with the same sense of anticipation as when he was a child, but Gerlof still waited eagerly for the first butterfly of the year.

He was alone at the cottage now; everyday life had resumed after the move, and he ambled around the small rooms, his stick in one hand and a cup of coffee in the other. The wheelchair waited silently in the bedroom, ready for the day when his rheumatic problems, caused by Sjögren's syndrome, would take a turn for the worse. At the moment he could still get up and down the stone steps without any problem.

The previous week his furniture had been delivered – the small number of pieces he had wanted to keep from his room at the home – and all the mementoes from his thirty years at sea: the ships in bottles, the maritime charts, the name plates from some of the ships on which he had sailed, and beautiful examples of rope work, dark brown and still smelling of tar.

Gerlof was surrounded by memories.

It was when he had opened the cupboard next to the fridge in the kitchen to put away the log books and charts that he had come across the diaries.

They had been tied up in a bundle on a shelf behind Ella's little jewellery box and old books by Karl May and L. M. Montgomery. Each one had a number in black ink on the cover, and when he undid the string and opened them, he saw densely written pages in his wife's ornate handwriting.

Ella's diaries – eight altogether.

Gerlof hesitated briefly. He thought about the promise he had made Ella. Then he picked up the top book and went out to the wooden seat in the garden, with a feeling that he was doing something dishonourable. He had seen her writing in her diary on the odd occasion, but she had never shown him what she had written, and had only mentioned her diaries on that one occasion, when she was dying.

Burn them, Gerlof.

He sat down, wrapped a blanket around his legs and placed the book on the table beside him. It was twenty-two years since Ella had died of liver cancer in the autumn of 1976, but here in the garden he often had the feeling that she wasn't gone at all, that she was in the kitchen making coffee.

Ella had always set clear boundaries. For example, she had never allowed her husband in the kitchen, and of course Gerlof had never tried to change her mind. When their daughters Lena and Julia became teenagers at the beginning of the sixties they had made determined attempts to get him to help with the housework, but Gerlof had refused.

'It's too late for me,' he'd said.

For the most part he had been afraid and unsure of himself in the kitchen. He had never learnt to cook or do the washing, although he could do the dishes. These days Swedish men seemed to do just about everything; times had changed.

Gerlof turned his head. He saw a small fluttering movement in the long grass beyond the garden. It was the first butterfly of the year. It came flying towards him with the same jerky movements as every other spring butterfly he had seen over the years, flitting here and there with no apparent goal.

It was a Brimstone Yellow. A perfect sign of spring.

Gerlof smiled at the bright butterfly as it reached the lawn in front of him – but stopped smiling when he spotted another butterfly over in the long grass. This one was dark, almost black, with grey and white stripes; he didn't know the name of it. Camberwell Beauty? Or did they call it the Mourning Cloak? This one was flying in a straighter line, and reached the lawn at almost the same time as the Brimstone Yellow. They fluttered around each other for a few seconds in a spring dance before flitting past Gerlof and disappearing behind the cottage.

A yellow butterfly and a dark-grey one, what did that

mean? He had always regarded the first butterfly as a sign of what the rest of the year would be like: bright and hopeful or dark and gloomy, but now he wasn't so sure. It was as if he had hoisted a flag that had got stuck at half-mast before continuing to the top.

When he opened the diary he heard the sound of a car engine. A big shiny car came along the road and turned off on to the gravel track leading to the quarry.

Gerlof caught a glimpse of a middle-aged man and woman in the front.

Probably some of the new neighbours who had built houses by the quarry. Summer visitors. No doubt they would be here only when it was light and warm; they were hardly likely to spend time here when it was freezing cold, chopping down the last of the trees along the coast as his own relatives had once done.

Gerlof wasn't interested in the couple in the car. He looked down at the diary and began to read.

7th May 1957

Tonight Gerlof will set off on his first voyage of the year to Nynäshamn for oil. He was in Kalmar today getting some measurements done on the ship because he has altered the cover of the hold. Lena and Julia are on board with him.

Today has been sunny. Got to the cottage at six this evening and opened the windows to air the rooms. There was a faint smell of mould, I thought; I tried to get some fresh air in, but in fact it was a pot of juniper berries in syrup that had started fermenting and had exploded into a thousand pieces. Had to start cleaning rancid, sticky purple syrup off the floor, only just managed to cook something (meatballs). The children and Gerlof will be home the day after tomorrow.

Gerlof realized these were holiday diaries. He knew that when he had been away at sea, Ella had often gone up to the summer cottage with their two daughters. Later, when they were older and wanted to go with Gerlof to Stockholm or stay at home in Borgholm, she had come here alone. That was probably why he had rarely seen her writing in them.

He read on:

15th May 1957
Sunny, but a little chilly in the wind from the north-east. The girls went for a long bike ride along the coast road this afternoon.

A strange thing happened while they were away. I was standing out on the veranda watering the pelargoniums – and I saw a troll from the quarry.

What else could it be?

It was a two-legged creature at any rate, but it moved so fast I was quite taken aback. Just a shadow, a snapping twig out in the pasture, a rustling among the bushes, and it was gone. I think it laughed at me.

'The pasture' was Ella and Gerlof's name for the over-grown area beyond the summer cottage where the cattle used to graze before the war.

But what did Ella mean by a troll?

Suddenly Gerlof heard the sound of another car behind the trees. The engine died away, then the gate creaked. He quickly hid the diary under the blanket. He didn't know why – a guilty conscience, perhaps.

A short, powerfully built man in his seventies was heading up the path. It was his friend John Hagman, dressed in the worn blue dungarees and the pale-grey peaked cap he wore winter and summer. He had been

Gerlof's first mate on the Baltic cargo ships once upon a time; these days he ran the campsite at the southern end of the village.

He came over with a heavy tread and stopped on the grass; Gerlof smiled and nodded at him, but John didn't smile back – a cheerful, happy expression was not his style.

'So,' he said. 'I heard you were back.'

'Yes. You too.'

John nodded. He had been up to visit Gerlof at the home a few times during the winter, but otherwise he had been staying in his son's small apartment down in Borgholm. He had seemed almost shame-faced when he explained that the village had begun to feel too cold and lonely during the winter. He couldn't cope with it any longer, and Gerlof understood completely.

'Anyone else here?'

John shook his head. 'There hasn't been anybody around in the village since New Year, apart from the odd weekend visitor.'

'What about Astrid Linder?'

'She gave up as well in the end, and closed up the cottage. I think she went to the Riviera in January.'

'I see,' said Gerlof, remembering that Astrid had been a doctor before she retired. 'I should think she's got a fair bit of money tucked away.'

They fell silent. Gerlof couldn't see any more butterflies. He listened to the faint soughing of the wind over in the trees and said, 'I don't think I'll be here much longer, John.'

'Here in the village?'

'No, I mean here,' said Gerlof, pointing to his chest, where he presumed the soul and therefore the source of life was located.

It didn't sound quite as dramatic as he'd expected,

43

and John merely nodded and asked, 'Are you ill, then?'

'No more than usual,' said Gerlof. 'But I'm very weary. I ought to do something useful, a bit of carpentry, paint the cottage like I used to do . . . but I just sit here.'

John looked away, as if the conversation was hard work. 'Start with something small,' he suggested. 'Go down to the sea and clean up the gig.'

Gerlof sighed. 'It's full of holes.'

'We can fix it,' said John. 'And there's a new millennium in two years, a new era. You want to be around for that, don't you?'

'Maybe . . . we'll just have to see what this new era is like.' Gerlof wanted to change the subject, and nodded in the direction of the fence. 'So what do you think of the neighbours, then? Across the road.'

John said nothing.

'Don't you know them?'

'Well, I've seen them. But they've hardly been here up till now, I don't really know much about them.'

'Me neither. But I'm curious – aren't you?'

'They're rich,' said John. 'Rich folk from the mainland.'

'Definitely,' said Gerlof. 'You need to let them know you're around.'

'What for?'

'So you can do some jobs for them before the campers arrive.'

'That's a good idea.'

Gerlof nodded, leaning forward slightly. 'And make sure they pay you well.'

'Good thinking,' said John, looking almost cheerful.

7

'So you'll be staying here for a few weeks now?' asked the young estate agent as he handed over the keys and the last of the paperwork to Vendela Larsson. 'Enjoying the spring sunshine?'

'That's what we're hoping,' said Vendela with a laugh.

She often laughed nervously when she was talking to people she didn't know. But she was hoping the habit would disappear now she was on the island. A lot of things were going to be different now.

'Good, excellent,' said the agent. 'That means you'll be helping to extend the tourist season, like real pioneers . . . Showing people on the mainland that it's possible to enjoy the peace and quiet of Öland for more than just a few weeks in the summer.'

Vendela nodded.

Enjoy the peace and quiet? That depended on whether she would be able to relax, of course, and whether Max would settle and be able to get his cookery book finished.

Right now he was in the heated garage washing the car. Every drop of blood must go. Since they had arrived at the summer house Max hadn't said a word about what had happened on the way, but fury surrounded him like a sour smell.

Vendela had been left to deal with the agent, and she was trying not to shiver in the cold wind. It was evening; the sun had set over the Sound and taken every vestige of warmth with it. She really wanted to go back indoors.

The agent looked around in the twilight, over at the large house next door and the small cottage a few hundred metres to the north.

'This is an excellent area,' he said. 'Absolutely top-notch. The neighbours are just in the right place – not too close, not too far away. And no other properties between you and the shore . . . All you have to do is walk around the quarry if you fancy a morning dip.'

'Once the ice has melted, of course,' said Vendela.

'It won't be long now,' said the agent. 'It's quite rare for it to be here this late . . . but we had a hard winter this year. Minus fifteen some nights.'

A stocky man in blue dungarees was standing next to the agent. He was the local builder, and nodded to Vendela.

'Any problems, give me a ring,' he said.

Those were his first and last words to Vendela this evening. Both he and the agent made a move.

'Don't fall out with your neighbours,' was the agent's final piece of advice to Vendela as they shook hands. 'That's the golden rule for house-owners.'

'We haven't met the neighbours yet,' said Vendela, laughing again.

As she walked back into the house, little Aloysius hauled himself laboriously out of his dog basket on his stiff legs and barked. He didn't seem to be aware that it was his mistress who had come into the room – perhaps his sense of smell was failing too.

'It's only me, Ally,' said Vendela, patting him.

She had felt a little exposed out in the windswept garden, but in here nobody could get to her. She loved the clean surfaces in the new house. Everything was pristine, there was no rubbish hidden in cupboards or attics. There was no cellar waiting to be cleared out and cleaned.

She remembered what the agent had said about the neighbours, and suddenly had an idea: perhaps she and Max ought to organize a party for everyone in the village, some time this week, so that they could get to know people. It would also be a way for her to practise relaxing when she was in company.

A party would definitely be a good idea.

Although it wasn't actually the neighbours she wanted to meet, it was the elves.

Once upon a time, long, long ago, a hunter went out on to the alvar, her father had told Vendela one evening. *The hunter was after hares and pheasants, but instead he met the great love of his life out there. And he was never the same again.*

She had been six or seven years old when her father, Henry, started to tell her a story about the elves out on the alvar. Vendela had never forgotten that story. She often pondered on it and everything else she had learnt about the elves over the years.

She started to write down Henry's story, exactly as she remembered it:

The hunter went far out on to the alvar, but there were no birds or small wild animals to be seen that day. The only thing he saw was a tall, slender deer in the distance, a deer that remained where it was, as if it were waiting for him to come closer, before turning and setting off towards the horizon.

The hunter followed across the grass, his gun at the ready. His pursuit of the deer lasted for several hours, but the hunter never got any nearer to his quarry. The sun went down and the evening came, and slowly the hunter drew closer to the deer. He raised his gun.

Then suddenly the sun was shining brightly once again, and the hunter saw that he was standing on the alvar where the grass was fresh and green, with little streams babbling around him. The deer had vanished, but in its place a tall, beautiful woman dressed all in white was coming towards him.

The woman smiled and told him she was the queen of the elves; she had seen him many times out on the alvar, and had fallen in love with him. Now she had lured him into her own domain.

Vendela looked up and studied the wide Sound beyond the window. In the darkness the ice looked grey and dirty.

If she moved close to the glass she could see the house next door, which made her think about the party again. Yes, she would definitely get that organized.

She leant back and continued to write:

When the hunter saw the queen of the elves standing before him, he lowered his gun and sank to his knees. And the queen took out a silver goblet and bent down to a murmuring brook. She filled the goblet to the brim, and when she stood up and offered it to the hunter, he tasted the sweetness of white wine. He felt free and happy, and did not want to return to the world of men. So he stayed with the queen all evening and all through the night, and fell asleep in her arms.

The hunter woke as the sun was rising, but he was back in his bed in the cottage on the edge of the alvar, and the beautiful woman was gone. And even though he searched and searched out on the alvar, he never found the gateway to the kingdom of the elves again.

Vendela paused. She heard a dull roar, and looked out of the window. A car was coming slowly up the gravel track, and Vendela recognized it immediately.

It was the Saab from the car park.

The car passed their house on its way to the old cottage by the north-eastern end of the quarry. Behind the wheel sat the fair-haired man who had flattened Max. His teenage son was sitting next to him.

When Vendela saw the man in profile, she realized who he reminded her of: Martin. He bore a slight resemblance to her first husband.

Perhaps that was why Max had been so angry with him. Vendela had bumped into Martin by chance one day five years ago and had lunch with him, and she had been stupid enough to tell Max about it. He still brought the matter up from time to time.

So she had already met a couple of the neighbours, in fact. But did she really want to invite these people to a party? She was going to have to discuss it with Max.

She bent over her book and wrote a final paragraph, the end of the story:

The hunter lived in his cottage for many years after the encounter on the alvar, but he never fell in love again and he never married, for no human woman could match the queen of the elves. He never forgot her.

'That was a story about the elves,' her father had said, getting up from the edge of the bed. 'Time to go to sleep now, Vendela.'

Henry had told her stories about the elves on several occasions after that. He never mentioned his late wife, but the queen seemed to fascinate him. And the story of the elves had remained in Vendela's thoughts. It made her begin to dream of doing as the hunter had done, setting off for the place where she could meet them.

Öland 1956

It is spring when Henry Fors shows his daughter Vendela traces of the elves and trolls, the year before she goes to primary school.

First of all they go to the elves. Henry takes Vendela with him out into the meadow behind their little smallholding to fetch the cows in for milking.

Henry has three cows, but even Vendela can see that he doesn't really want to be a farmer. Not in the least. He runs his little farm simply in order to survive.

'This is where they dance,' he says as they stand on the grass, the cows lumbering towards them with their udders full to bursting.

Vendela looks out over the meadow, which is enclosed by a high stone wall. Beyond the wall the world of the alvar begins, with its grass and juniper bushes. Nothing is moving out there.

'Who?' she asks.

'The elves and their queen. You remember her, don't you?'

Vendela nods, she remembers the story.

'You can even see the traces they've left behind,' says

Henry, pointing with his right hand, dry and cracked from working with stone. 'Look, a fairy ring.'

Vendela looks at the meadow and sees a circle of paler grass, perhaps three feet in diameter, in the midst of all the green. It looks as if someone has trodden on the blades of grass and broken them. Only the centre of the ring is fresh and green.

As Henry gathers the cows ahead of him, he takes a wide sweep around the ring in the grass. 'You mustn't walk across the places where the elves dance – it brings bad luck,' he says. Then he raises his hand and gives the cows a gentle push to hurry them along.

A few days later, Henry takes his daughter down to the coast to look at the quarry. That's where he'd really like to be.

Vendela is supposed to go and fetch the cows from the meadow, but Henry says they can stay out for a while longer today.

He sings all the way down to the sea in his deep baritone voice; he likes to sing songs about Öland.

There is both sorrow and longing in his voice, and Vendela thinks it is because her mother Kristin no longer exists.

Dead, she has been dead for several years. She became ill, and then the quiet noises in the house grew louder, the walls creaked more, there were rustling, cracking noises. And then she died, and everything fell silent once again.

'Consumption,' Henry said to Vendela when he came home from hospital for the last time.

It was the old name for a condition that meant a person had simply faded away, someone who had grown tired of everything and no longer had the strength to live.

Consumption. For several years Vendela wonders if it runs in the family, until her Aunt Margit tells her that Kristin died of a burst appendix.

As they reach the quarry, Henry stops singing. He halts at the edge, a few metres above the wide hollow in the ground. It is dry and cold here.

'People have cleared away the earth and dug out stone for five hundred years. Stone for palaces and castles and churches. And for graves, of course.'

Vendela stands beside her father, gazing out over a grey landscape that has been smashed to pieces and stripped of all life.

'What do you see?'

'Stone and gravel,' says Vendela.

Henry nods. 'It's a bit like the moon, isn't it? I feel like an astronaut when I walk around here, all I need is a rocket . . .'

Her father laughs; he has always been interested in space.

But his laughter dies away when they reach the gravelled surface.

'There were lots of people here just a few years ago,' he says. 'But they've given up and gone home, one by one . . .'

Vendela looks over at the other quarrymen. There are only five of them, and they are spread out along the bottom of the quarry, their backs weary, their clothes powdered with limestone dust.

Henry waves and calls out to them. 'Hello there! Hello!'

None of the men wave back. They are holding drills and hammers, but have lowered them to stare at the visitors to the quarry.

'Why aren't they working?' whispers Vendela.

Henry looks at his colleagues and shakes his head,

as if he has given up on them. 'They're standing here wishing they were somewhere else,' he says quietly. 'They're asking themselves why they never took the opportunity to travel to America.'

Then he shows her the spot where he works at the southern end of the quarry, where he has piled up reject stone to form a makeshift shelter from the wind.

'This is the kelpie!' he says.

He invites Vendela inside, and they sit down on two stone stools. Henry has brought a flask of coffee, and drinks two cups.

'Look out down below!' he says, tipping the last of the coffee out on to the stones.

Vendela knows he is warning the trolls in the under-world, giving them time to get away.

The dust from the limestone is tickling her nose. She looks around; there is so much crushed stone here. It's everywhere, and she gazes at the piles, trying to see if anyone is hiding behind them.

'What are you looking for?' says Henry. 'Trolls?'

Vendela nods, but her father laughs.

'There's nothing to worry about, the trolls keep away during the day. They can't tolerate sunlight. They only come out when the sun has gone down.'

He glances around and goes on, 'But before the people came, this was the kingdom of the trolls. They lived here by the sea. And the elves, who were their enemies, lived further inland. There was just one occasion when the elves came down to the trolls. They met here at the quarry, and the blood flowed that day. The ground was stained with red.'

He points towards the rock over in the east. 'The blood is still there . . . Come and see.'

He leads Vendela down into the quarry and across to the vertical rock face. He bends down and points to a reddish layer running through the pale stone, just above the ground.

She looks more closely and sees that the layer is full of dark-red clumps.

'The place of blood,' says Henry, straightening up. 'That's all that remains of the battle between the trolls and the elves . . . petrified blood.'

Vendela realizes that the queen of the elves must have led the battle against the trolls, but she doesn't want to look at the blood any more.

'Do they still fight, Daddy?'

'No, I think they've called a truce now,' says Henry. 'Perhaps they've decided that the trolls will stay underground beneath the place of blood, and the elves will stay on the alvar – that way they don't have to meet.'

Vendela looks up at the top of the quarry and thinks they ought to build a palace up there, with tall windows and walls made of stone. She would like to live there, between the kingdoms of the trolls and the elves.

Then she looks at her father. 'Why were they enemies, the trolls and the elves? Why did they fight?'

Henry merely shakes his head. 'Who knows . . . I suppose they each thought the others were just too different.'

8

Per and Jesper had to travel several kilometres to find a shop where they could buy food on Friday evening. When they finally reached Stenvik, they drove through a village full of dark, closed-up summer cottages.

Per turned on to Ernst's Road by the quarry, and saw that at least there were lights showing in the windows of the two newly built luxury houses. Each house had a big shiny car parked in front of it. Suddenly he recognized one of them as the Audi that had almost run Jesper over. The damage to the car was still clear to see, but all the blood had been washed away.

So the man and woman he had met in the car park had built a house here in the village. They were his new neighbours.

'A new car,' he said. 'That might not be a bad idea . . . both for us and for the environment.'

Jesper turned his head. 'Are you going to get a new car, Dad?'

'In a while. Not right now.'

His own Saab had worn-out shock absorbers, and it squealed and creaked over the potholes and hollows on the gravel track. But the engine was pretty good, and Per had no intention of being ashamed of his car.

Nor of Ernst's cottage – even though it resembled nothing so much as an abandoned builders' hut this evening, with its low roof and small, dark windows. The cottage had stood in the sun and wind by the quarry for almost fifty years and really needed scraping down and painting, but that could wait until next summer.

Per had last visited the island to check on the cottage at the beginning of March, and the alvar had been covered in snow. The snow was almost gone now, but the air still wasn't much warmer – at least not after the sun had gone down.

'Do you remember Ernst, our relative?' he asked Jesper as he pulled up in front of the house. 'Do you remember coming to visit him here?'

'Sort of,' said Jesper.

'So what do you remember?'

'He worked with stone . . . he made sculptures.'

Per nodded and pointed in the darkness towards a little shed to the south of the cottage. 'They're still in his workshop . . . some of them. We can have a look.'

He missed Ernst, perhaps because he had been the complete opposite of Jerry. Ernst had got up early every morning to work with hammers and chisels down in the quarry. He had worked hard – the resounding clang of steel on stone was one of Per's childhood memories – but when Per and his mother had come to stay, Ernst had always had time for him.

His old doormat bore the word WELCOME.

When they opened the door of the summer cottage they were met by the faint aroma of soap and tar, traces of the former owner that had not completely faded away. When he switched on the light, everything looked just as Per had left it in the winter: flowery wallpaper, rag rugs with brown coffee stains, and a worn, shiny wooden floor.

57

In the main room was a seaman's chest that Ernst had made, with a carving on the front showing a knight on a horse chasing a scornfully grinning troll into his mountain hideaway. On a block of stone behind the knight a fairy princess sat weeping.

The chest could stay, but when Per got some money he intended to start changing the furniture.

'We'll get some air in here,' he said to Jesper, 'and let the spring in.'

With the windows ajar, the rooms were filled with the soughing of the wind. Fantastic. Per tried to feel pleasure in the cottage he had inherited, both as it was now and as it would one day be.

'It's only a couple of hundred metres to the shore on the far side of the quarry,' he said to Jesper as they carried their cases into the little hallway. 'We'll be able to swim there a lot in the summer, you and I and Nilla. It'll be cool.'

'I haven't got any swimming trunks,' said Jesper.

'We'll get some.'

The twins each had a small bedroom to the left of the kitchen, and Jesper disappeared into his room with his rucksack.

Per stayed in the little room behind the kitchen with a view over the northern section of the quarry and the ice-covered Sound. This could be his study over the summer.

If he lived another twenty or thirty years he would still have this house, he was sure of it. And the children could spend as much time here as they wanted.

A telephone started ringing while Per was in the bedroom unpacking his clothes. For a few seconds he couldn't remember where the old phone was, but the sound seemed to be coming from the kitchen.

The phone was on the worktop next to the cooker; it was made of Bakelite, and had a dial. Per picked up the receiver.

'Mörner.'

He was expecting to hear Marika, or the confident voice of a doctor with news about Nilla, but he heard nothing but a rushing noise on the line, a poor connection with the mainland.

Eventually somebody coughed, then came a quiet, weak voice – an old man's voice.

'Pelle?'

'Yes?'

'Pelle . . .'

Per took his time before answering. Since his mother had died, there was only one person who called him Pelle, and besides, he recognized his father Jerry's hoarse voice. Thousands of cigarettes and too many late nights had worn it out. And last spring, after the stroke, his voice had become slurred and lost. Jerry could still remember names – and telephone numbers; he rang Per at least once a week, but much of his vocabulary was gone.

Per had redirected the phone line from his apartment in Kalmar through to the cottage, despite the risk that Jerry might ring.

'How's it going, Jerry?' he said eventually.

His father hesitated, and Per could hear him inhaling cigarette smoke. Then he coughed again and lowered his voice still further.

'Bremer,' was all he said.

Per recognized the name. Hans Bremer was Jerry's colleague and right-hand man. Per had never met him, but it was obvious that Bremer had a better relationship with his father than he had ever done.

'I can't talk to you today,' said Per. 'Jesper's here.'

His father said nothing. He was searching for words, but Per didn't wait. 'So I'll speak to you soon,' he said. 'Bye now.'

He hung up calmly without waiting for a response, and went back to his bedroom.

Two minutes later, the sound of the telephone reverberated through the cottage once more.

He wasn't surprised. Why had he redirected it?

When he picked up the receiver he heard the same hoarse voice: 'Pelle? Pelle?'

Per closed his eyes wearily. 'What's the matter, Jerry? Can you tell me why you're ringing?'

'Markus Lukas.'

'Who?'

Jerry cleared his throat and said something that sounded like 'that bastard', but Per wasn't sure. It sounded as if Jerry had a cigarette in his mouth.

'What are you talking about, Jerry?'

No reply. Per turned towards the kitchen window and looked out over the quarry. It was completely deserted.

'Have to help Bremer,' his father said suddenly.

'Why?'

'Help him with Markus Lukas.'

Then there was complete silence at the other end of the line. Per looked out of the window, towards the water and the narrow strip of black that was the mainland. *Markus Lukas?* He thought he'd heard the name before, a long time ago.

'Where are you, Jerry?'

'Kristianstad.'

Jerry had been living in Kristianstad for the last fifteen years, in a stuffy three-room apartment by the railway station.

'Good,' said Per. 'Stay there.'

'No,' said Jerry.

60

'Why not?'

No reply.

'So where are you going, then?' asked Per.

'Ryd.'

Per knew that Ryd was a small village in the coniferous forests of Småland where Jerry had a house; Per had given him a lift out there once a few years earlier.

'How are you going to get there without a car?'

'Bus.'

Jerry had relied on Hans Bremer for more than fifteen years. Before his stroke, when he spoke in full sentences, his father had made his relationship with his colleague very clear to Per: *Bremer takes care of everything, he loves his job. Bremer fixes everything.*

'Good,' said Per. 'Go and spend a few days there. Give me a ring when you get back.'

'Yes.'

Jerry started coughing again, and broke off the conversation. Per put the phone down, but remained standing by the window.

Parents shouldn't make their children feel lonely, but that was exactly what Jerry did. Per felt totally alone, without family or friends. His father had frightened them all away. Jerry had even ruined Per's first experience of falling in love, with a smiling girl called Regina.

Per exhaled slowly and stayed where he was. He ought to go for a jog on the track along the shore, but it was too dark now.

Jerry's persecution mania had simmered inside his head like a bubbling soup for as long as Per could remember. There had been a joyous lust for life too, but after the stroke that had completely disappeared. In the past Per had got the impression that Jerry needed these real or imagined conflicts to spice up his life, that they gave him fresh energy in his role as an entrepreneur, but the voice he had heard on the phone today was confused and weak.

For as long as Per could remember, his father had imagined that people were after him: usually the Swedish government and its tax inspectors, but sometimes the bank or a rival or a former employee from Jerry's company.

Per couldn't do much about his father right now. He probably needed some kind of supervision, but for Per it was more important to be a father to Nilla than a son to Jerry.

And Jesper, too. He mustn't forget Jesper.

His son's door was closed, but Per was a good father, he cared. He knocked and popped his head around the door. 'Hi there.'

'Hi Dad,' Jesper said quietly.

He was sitting up in bed with his Gameboy, even though it was really too late to play.

Per chose to ignore it. Instead he told Jesper about a plan that had occurred to him as he was looking out of the window: why not build a shortcut down to the shore?

'Shall we do some work tomorrow?' he asked. 'Build up our muscles and make something worthwhile?'

Jesper thought about it. Then he nodded.

They slept in until nine the next morning, and made a start on the flight of steps after breakfast.

Ernst had left only a rickety ladder leading from the cottage down to the quarry, and Per wanted something more stable. A flight of steps he and the children could use when they went down to the shore on sunny summer days.

At the southern end of the Mörners' stony plot the

edge of the quarry was several metres lower, and that was where Per had chosen to construct the steps. One by one he and Jesper threw some of Ernst's tools down on to the gravel at the bottom of the quarry: crowbars, spades and pickaxes. Then they lowered the old wheelbarrow down, pulled on their thick gloves and climbed down after it.

It was cold at the bottom of the rock face, and there wasn't a soul in sight. Nor were there many plants, just grass and the odd little bush determinedly clinging to the gravel or growing in crevices. Gulls were standing on top of some of the piles of stone, screaming at each other, their beaks stiff and wide open.

At about knee height in the rock face a strange layer of dark-red clumps ran through the pale limestone. Per remembered it from his childhood. *The place of blood*, Ernst had called it, but he had never explained why. It was hardly likely to be real blood.

'What are we going to do, Dad?' asked Jesper, looking around.

'Right . . . first we're going to collect some gravel.' Per pointed over at the piles.

'But is it OK just to pinch it?'

'We're not *pinching* it,' said Per, realizing that he hadn't a clue who owned the quarry. 'We're *using* it. I mean, it's just lying here, isn't it?'

Time to start work. Not too hard and not too fast – he had to think about his back – but hard enough to build a flight of steps up from the quarry.

For over an hour they pushed the wheelbarrow back and forth between the piles of gravel in the middle of the quarry and the rock face below their garden, and slowly they constructed a steep ramp leading upwards.

It was already half past ten, but Per had warmed up

now, and besides, he had spotted a big stack of long, narrow blocks of stone about fifty metres away.

'Shall we start with those?' he said.

They went over to begin loading the limestone blocks into the wheelbarrow. Per avoided the biggest ones, but the medium-sized ones were heavy enough. He grabbed hold of the nearest block and got Jesper to take the other end. The surface of the stone was dry and smooth.

'Always lift with your legs, Jesper, never with your back.'

They lifted together, and placed three blocks at a time in the wheelbarrow.

By the time they had unloaded the blocks by the rock face and placed them in position as steps, Per was panting – this was hard, heavy work. How had Ernst managed to work here day after day, year after year?

By about twelve o'clock they had finished the lower section of the steps, and Per's back, neck and arms were aching. Despite the protective gloves, the skin on his fingers was badly chafed, and he had blisters. And the steps still reached less than halfway up to the top.

He smiled wearily. 'Only the rest to go, then.'

'We could do with a crane,' said Jesper.

Per shook his head. 'That's cheating.'

They hauled themselves over the edge of the quarry and went back into Ernst's house.

Their house, thought Per, and wondered about a name. Casa Grande?

No. Casa Mörner: that would do nicely.

That same evening, the wind started to blow ferociously across the island, and by the time darkness came, a gale was howling across the rooftops.

The telephone on Nilla's hospital ward had been

engaged all evening, but at eight o'clock Per had done what Nilla wanted and sent her a thought.

Love, he thought, and sent it away with a mental picture of the sunset over the Sound.

No thoughts from his daughter popped into his head in return; it felt completely empty. He didn't really believe telepathy worked, but they had nothing to lose.

Per went to bed and fell asleep to the sound of the howling wind; he dreamed that he had found a pale little wooden doll in the quarry. He put it in a cloth bag and brought it into the cottage, for some reason. The doll was angry, and because the bag was torn, he got some tape and tried to repair it so that the fingers wouldn't stick out. The doll struggled inside the bag and Per kept on trying to tape the bag up; he could hear his father laughing at him.

No, it wasn't Jerry's hoarse laughter that was reverberating through his dream, it was a dull roar that was making the ground shake.

Per stopped fighting with the bag. He looked out of the window towards the quarry and discovered something unbelievable: a volcano had begun to form out in the Sound between the island and the mainland. The water was boiling, the air was full of grey smoke, and a crater a hundred metres wide was rising towards the sky, higher and higher.

Lava poured down the sides, starting to fill the quarry.

Then he woke up, disorientated and confused, fumbling in vain for the doll in his bed.

The gale was still blowing over the house, but the dull roar had stopped. It didn't come back, and eventually he fell asleep again.

*

Sunday morning was sunny, with a strange rushing noise in the wind. Per got up at about half past seven, and noticed something different as soon as he looked out of the window to the west: the Sound was no longer greyish white, it was dark blue.

He realized what had happened. The roaring din that had woken him during the night was the noise of the ice being broken up by the strong wind. Now there were just odd ice floes drifting around out on the water, and a grey patch of slushy ice bobbing up and down among the rocks by the shore. The rushing noise was coming from the newly liberated waves.

The ice had left the Sound – hundreds of tons of frozen water had been released, and Per had heard their thundering roar.

Terrific.

But last night's dream had been strange and unpleasant. He didn't want to think about it.

9

As Max sat pondering his cookery book, Vendela wandered around the new house thinking about not eating. She had decided to do two things here on the island: jog more and eat less. Not to lose weight – she weighed fifty-two kilos on the bathroom scales at home – but as a way of cleansing her body and getting closer to nature. So on the first morning in the new house she drank only a glass of water for breakfast, alone with Aloysius in her big new kitchen.

The idea of throwing a party for the neighbours was still in the back of her mind. She had decided to invite everyone she could find in the village. On Ash Wednesday – people didn't normally give dinner parties on that day, did they? To be on the safe side, she had tapped on the door and run the idea past her husband.

Max was in his study – one of them.

He had driven a furniture van to the new house the previous week. Max needed *three* desks when he was writing his books: a work desk where he sat and thought, a desk where he wrote, and a desk where he did his editing, and in order to have space for everything, he had to have two rooms all to himself, side by side.

He had a rowing machine, some weights and a

skipping rope in one of the rooms as well. No tread-mill.

When Vendela knocked on the door he was sitting at the thinking desk, which was completely empty. She told him about her idea of inviting the neighbours to a party. He listened, then nodded in the direction of the cottage to the north.

'Including them?'

She knew who he meant – the father with the son Max had almost run over.

'We could leave them out,' said Vendela, but he shook his head.

'No, invite them too. Do you need any help?'

'It's fine, I'll sort out the food, but you could welcome the guests.'

Max sighed. 'I can play the host, but I've no intention of handing out advice.'

'No, of course not.'

'People are always asking me for help with all kinds of problems . . . but I have to be free while I'm here.'

Max closed his eyes and Vendela left the room.

She would go for a walk soon, but first she went into the bathroom. She hadn't unpacked her toilet bag yet. She placed it on the cistern and started taking out her tablets and arranging them in the medicine cabinet. Her allergy tablets with the Latin names went on the bottom shelf. She had several boxes, but this morning her nose and eyes felt quite good. Then she put away the box of tranquillizers, plus the small packs of Vistaril, which she had started to take at night a few years ago; sometimes she took them first thing in the morning as well.

But that was in Stockholm. Here on the island she would be more careful, and today she was going to take only two tablets. Something new. It was called Folangir, and had arrived by post from Denmark last week. It was a kind of diet pill that was supposed to suppress hunger and anxiety – but it also contained nutrients. Extract of calendula and several important vitamins, according to the label.

She washed them down with a glass of water.

There. Time for that walk.

The new tablets were unusually strong, and she felt slightly dizzy as she stepped outside. The sun was shining, and a chilly spring breeze swirled around the house, but neither warmth nor cold affected her now. She had found her balance. Everything was lovely.

The sky was immense here; there wasn't a single mountain to stop the light flooding the island. That was why the elves were happy here.

The countryside was so silent as Vendela crossed the narrow track. No cars, no voices. Just birdsong all around her, and the tranquil lapping of the waves from the open Sound.

On the other side of the gravel track was an even narrower path. Two wheel ruts with a line of grass running up the middle; it could lead anywhere. She set off, jogging along with her eyes closed for a few seconds.

When she looked up, she saw a closed gate in an old stone wall. Behind it was a small garden, with someone sitting on the pale-yellow lawn. A man in a deckchair.

As Vendela crept closer she could see that the man was very old, wrinkled and almost bald, with a fringe of white hair at the back of his head. He had a thick scarf knotted beneath his chin, a blanket over his legs and a slender book on his knee. His eyes were closed, his chin resting on his chest, and he looked completely at ease, like a man who had finished his work here in this life and was satisfied with everything he had achieved.

It could have been her father sitting there – but of course Henry had always been too restless to sit in the garden.

Vendela thought the man was asleep, but as she stopped by the gate he raised his head and looked at her.

'Am I disturbing you?' she called out.

'No more than anybody else,' replied the man, tucking the book beneath the blanket.

He had a quiet yet powerful voice, the voice of someone who was used to being in charge. A bit like Max.

The tablets made Vendela more courageous than usual; she opened the gate and went in.

'I'm sitting here looking for butterflies,' said the man as she walked towards him. 'And thinking.'

It wasn't a joke, but Vendela still laughed – and regretted it immediately.

'I'm Vendela,' she said quickly. 'Vendela Larsson.'

'And my name is Davidsson, Gerlof Davidsson.'

An unusual name. Vendela didn't think she'd come across it before.

'Gerlof . . . is that German?'

'I think it was Dutch originally. It's an old family name.'

'Do you live here all year round, Gerlof?'

'I do now. I suppose I'll be here until they carry me out feet first.'

Vendela laughed again. 'In that case we'll be neighbours.' She pointed back the way she'd come, trying to keep her hand steady. 'We've just moved in over by the quarry, my husband Max and I. We'll be living here.'

'I see,' said Gerlof. 'But only when the weather's warm. Not all year round.'

It wasn't a question.

'No, not all year round . . . just in spring and summer.'

She was going to add *thank God*, but stopped herself. It probably wasn't very polite to mention that it was too cold and desolate to live on the island in the middle of winter. She'd done it when she was little, and that was quite enough.

Neither of them spoke. There were no butterflies to be seen, but the birds were still singing in the bushes. Vendela closed her eyes and wondered if their nervous twittering was a warning of some kind.

'Have you settled in?' asked Gerlof.

Vendela looked up and nodded energetically. 'Absolutely, I mean it's so . . .' She searched for the right thing to say, '. . . so close to the shore.'

The old man didn't speak, so Vendela took a deep breath and went on: 'We were thinking of having a little get-together for everybody in the village. This Wednesday at seven, we thought . . . It would be nice if you could join us.'

Gerlof looked down at his legs. 'I'll come if I can move . . . it varies from day to day.'

'Good, excellent.'

Vendela laughed nervously once more and walked back towards the gate. She was hungry now, and the new tablets were making her feel sleepy. But it felt good to be moving across the grass, drifting along like an elf towards the wind and the white sun.

'Max? Hello?'

Vendela was back home, her voice echoing across the stone floor. There was no reply, but she was so excited by her encounter with Gerlof that she simply carried on calling out, 'I met this man, an old villager . . . he's just fantastic! He lives in a little cottage on the other side of the track. I invited him to our party!'

There was silence for a few seconds, then Max opened

the door of his thinking room. He looked at his wife for a few seconds, then asked, 'What have you taken?'

Vendela met his gaze and straightened up. 'Nothing . . . Just a couple of slimming pills.'

'Nothing to perk you up a bit?'

'No! I've just got spring fever, what's wrong with that?'

She wanted to turn and walk away, but remained where she was, shaking her head. She tried to stand up straight without swaying, even though the stone floor was moving slightly beneath her feet.

'Vendela, you were going to cut the dose when we came here. You promised.'

'I *know*! And I'm going to go jogging.'

'Good idea,' said Max. 'It's better than pills.'

'I'm just feeling really happy,' Vendela went on, keeping her tone as serious as she could, 'but it's nothing to do with any pills. I'm happy because spring is in the air, and because I met this wonderful old man . . .'

'Yes, well, you always did like old folk.' Max rubbed his eyes and turned back to his thinking room. 'I must get back to work.'

10

The smell of limestone and seaweed, sea and coast. The wind over the shore, the sun shining on the Sound, winter and spring meeting in the air above the island.

It was Sunday morning, and Per was standing out on the patio with a broom, wishing that the spring sunshine could reach into all the dark corners of his body. Ernst had built two stone patios along the front and back of the house, one facing south-east and the other north-west, which was clever, because you could either follow the sun from morning until evening, or sit in the shade all day.

He straightened his back and looked out over the rocky shoreline. He knew he should feel happier to be standing here by the sea than he actually did. He wanted to feel peaceful and calm, but his anxiety about Nilla was too strong. Anxiety about what the doctors would find.

There wasn't much he could do about it; he just had to keep going.

The old patio was made of limestone; it was uneven and full of weeds growing between the slabs, but it was sturdily built. Once Per had swept all the leaves away, he walked to the edge and looked down into the quarry.

Nothing was moving, and the stone steps they had built yesterday stood firm, halfway up the rock face. Then he looked over at the new houses to the south, thinking about the new neighbours and their money.

It was certainly worth thinking about. He estimated that the two plots and the houses on them must have cost a couple of million, at least. Perhaps even three, including all the overheads. His new neighbours weren't short of money, and that was really all he knew about them.

Time to get out Ernst's garden furniture. It was made of cane, like something you might find on a plantation veranda in the jungle.

The telephone in the kitchen started ringing as he was standing in the doorway with the first chair in his hands.

'Jesper?' he shouted. 'Can you get that?'

He didn't know where his son was, but there was no response.

The telephone rang again, and after the fourth ring he put the chair down and went to answer it.

'Per Mörner.'

'Hello?' said a slurred voice. 'Pelle?'

It was his father again, of course. Per closed his eyes wearily and thought that Jerry could have afforded to build one of those luxury villas by the quarry. Well, ten or fifteen years ago, anyway. But Per had never seen any of his money, and since the stroke Jerry's finances were uncertain, to say the least. He was no longer able to work.

'Where are you calling from, Jerry? Where are you?'

There was a hissing noise on the line before the answer came: 'Ryd.'

'OK, so you've arrived. You were going to go up to the studio, weren't you?'

74

'To see Bremer,' said Jerry.

'I understand. You're at Bremer's now.'

But Jerry hesitated, and Per went on, 'Haven't you seen Hans Bremer? Wasn't he going to pick you up?'

'Not here.'

Per wondered if Jerry was drunk and confused, or merely confused.

'Go home then, Jerry,' he said firmly. 'Go the station and hop on the next bus back to Kristianstad.'

'Can't.'

'Yes you can, Jerry. Off you go.'

There was a silence once more. 'Fetch me, Pelle?'

Per hesitated. 'No. It's impossible.'

Silence at the other end of the phone. 'Pelle . . . Pelle?'

Per clutched the receiver more tightly. 'I haven't got time, Jerry,' he said. 'I've got Jesper here, and Nilla will be coming soon . . . I have to check with them first.'

But his father had put the phone down.

Per knew where the village of Ryd was. Two hours by car – that was how long it would take from Öland. Too long, really. But the conversation with Jerry had left him uneasy.

Keep an eye on him, his mother had once said.

Anita had never referred to her ex-husband by name. And it was Per who had kept in touch with Jerry and told her what he was up to, year after year. The trips he had made, the women he had met. It was an obligation he had never asked for.

He had promised Anita that he would keep an eye on Jerry. But the promise had been made on certain conditions, one of which was that he never saw his father alone.

Per decided: he would go down to Ryd.

Jesper could stay here. He and Nilla had only met

75

their grandfather on a handful of occasions, for a few hours each time, and that was no doubt for the best.

Not letting his children associate with Jerry had been one of Per's best decisions.

11

Vendela quickly realized that her curiosity about their new neighbours in the village was not mutual.

When she went round to invite people to the party, she started by trying to find houses in the rest of the village that were actually inhabited. It was hopeless. She walked along the coast road that swept around the deep inlet, but didn't see a soul. There was nothing but closed-up houses with shutters covering the windows – and when she rang the bell at those without shutters, no one answered. From time to time she got the feeling that somebody *was* at home, but didn't want to show themselves.

It wasn't until she reached the southern end of the village and knocked on the door of the little house next to the kiosk that somebody answered. A short, white-haired man with sooty hands, as if he were busy with a chimney or a boat engine. Vendela decided not to shake hands.

'Hagman, John Hagman,' he said when she introduced herself.

When she told him about the party, he merely nodded. 'Fine,' he said. 'So you live up by the quarry?'

'That's right, we've—'

'Do you need any help in the garden? I can dig and weed and rake. I can do most things.'

'That sounds good,' said Vendela with a laugh. 'That might be just what we need.'

Hagman nodded and closed the door.

Vendela looked around and thought that John Hagman ought to take care of his own garden first. It had grown wild.

She headed north again, back towards the quarry, with a faint yearning for her medicine cabinet. But she wouldn't open it today.

She turned off towards the neighbours' house. It was about the same size as theirs, but the walls were made of pale wood, and the windows were tall and narrow. The garden looked closer to being finished than theirs too; fresh topsoil had been spread and raked where the lawn was to be, and someone had found the time to sow grass seed.

The owners were at home. A youngish woman in blue dungarees opened the door when Vendela rang the bell. She had short blonde hair and greeted Vendela politely, but, just like John Hagman, she didn't seem particularly pleased to have a visitor.

The woman's name was Kurdin, Vendela learnt. Marie Kurdin.

'Am I disturbing you?' she said with a nervous laugh.

'No, but I was working on a wall.'

'Are you wallpapering?' asked Vendela.

'Painting.'

As Vendela asked her to the party, Marie Kurdin's mind seemed to be elsewhere, perhaps on her drying paint.

'Fine,' she said quietly, her tone neither friendly nor unfriendly. 'Christer and I and little Paul will be there; we'll bring some wine.'

'Excellent. Look forward to seeing you.'

Vendela turned away, feeling as if she'd failed. Not that there had been anything wrong or embarrassing about the conversation, but she had hoped to be made more welcome. At times like these she longed more than ever to be out on the alvar – just to head out there. To the elf stone, in spite of everything that had happened there.

But she forced herself to stay, and walked over to the last house by the quarry. The little cottage at the northern end. The Saab was parked outside, and Vendela stopped, wondering if she really ought to knock on the door. In the end she did.

The door was opened immediately by the man who had been driving the car, the man who had flattened Max. He looked more friendly now.

'Hi there,' said Vendela.

'Hi,' said the man.

She held out her hand and introduced herself, and found out that the man was called Per Mörner. She laughed nervously. 'I just want to explain something about that business in the car park, my husband got a bit—'

'Forget it,' said Per Mörner. 'We were all a bit worked up.'

He stopped speaking, so Vendela went on: 'I'm just going round saying hello to people.' She laughed again. 'I mean, somebody has to make a start.'

Per just nodded.

'And I had an idea,' said Vendela. 'I thought we could have a bit of a get-together.'

'Right . . . when were you thinking of?'

'Wednesday,' said Vendela. 'Would that be OK for you and your wife?'

'That's fine, but I don't have a wife. Just two children.'

'Oh, I see . . . Are you around on Wednesday?'

Per nodded. 'I have to go to the mainland now, just for the day. My son Jesper will be staying here. Do you want us to bring something?'

Vendela shook her head. 'No, we'll provide the food, but feel free to bring something to drink.'

Per Mörner nodded, but didn't seem to be looking forward to the party.

Perhaps he hadn't forgotten the quarrel with Max, whatever he might say. Or maybe he just had other things on his mind.

When Vendela got home, Aloysius had settled in his basket again. She stroked his back quickly and went into the living room to carry on writing in her notebook.

Max was out at the back of the house, dressed in a country-style tweed suit. A photographer had come over from Kalmar that morning and was staying for a couple of days to take pictures of Max for the cookery book – which had now acquired the title *Good Food to the Max* – and Vendela had helped groom her husband.

Before she had time to start writing, the outside door suddenly flew open and the young photographer dashed into the hallway. He seemed excited and went over to his camera bag in the kitchen, with only a passing glance at Vendela.

'Need my wide-angle lens.'

'What for?'

'Max has killed a snake!'

Vendela watched him disappear from the kitchen and remained sitting in her armchair for a few seconds before she got up. Behind her Aloysius sat up in his basket and whined at her, but she didn't have time to attend to him now.

She went outside into the cold.

The sun was shining over the flattened-down earth in the garden. Max was standing by the old stone wall with a spade in his hand, studying something that was lying on it.

Vendela moved slowly towards him. It was a snake with black diamond-shaped markings – an adder. She couldn't see the head, because the slender body had twisted itself into a large, shapeless knot, and seemed to be trying to tie itself even tighter.

'It was lying here in the sun when I came over to stand by the wall with the spade,' said Max as she reached him. 'It tried to crawl under a stone when it saw me, but I got it.'

'Max,' said Vendela quietly, 'you do know that adders are protected?'

'Are they?' He smiled at her. 'No, I didn't know that. Neither did the snake, eh?'

Vendela just shook her head. 'It's still alive,' she said. 'It's moving.'

'Muscle memory,' said Max. 'I smashed its head with the spade. It's just that the body hasn't caught on yet.'

She didn't answer, but she was thinking about her father, who had warned her about killing adders when she was little. They weren't protected in those days, but they were magical creatures. Particularly the black ones – killing a black adder meant a violent death for the person who committed the deed.

At least the one Max had killed was grey.

'We must bury it,' she said.

'No chance,' said Max. 'I'll chuck it away, and the gulls can take care of the body.'

He went towards the quarry with the spade held out in front of him.

'Just one picture!'

The photographer had his camera at the ready now. He started clicking away with Max posing happily, smiling broadly as he displayed his prize on the spade.

'Fantastic!' shouted the photographer.

Max went round to the front of the house with the adder. When he reached the edge of the quarry he gave the spade a flick, and the snake's body flew through the air like the punctured inner tube of a bicycle tyre.

'There!'

The snake had landed at the bottom of the quarry, but Vendela could see that it was still struggling and writhing in the limestone dust. It made her think of her father, who had always come home from the quarry with white dust all over his clothes and his cap.

The photographer walked to the edge of the quarry and took a few final pictures of the snake's body.

Vendela looked at him. 'Are those going in the cookery book?'

'Sure,' he said, 'if they turn out well.'

'I don't think so. Snakes aren't food.'

Vendela decided never to go down into the quarry. Never, right through the spring. The alvar was her world.

12

Gerlof received two visits every day. They were both from the home-care service, and although a temporary helper sometimes turned up, it was usually Agnes who brought him a meal at half past eleven, and her colleague Madeleine who came at around eight in the evening to assess his chances of surviving the night. At least, that's what Gerlof assumed she was there for.

He quite enjoyed their visits, even though both women were stressed and sometimes called him by the wrong name. But it must be difficult for them to remember all the old men they called on out in the villages during the course of a day. The visits were usually short. Now and again they had time to stay and chat for a while, but on other occasions they were so rushed they hardly had time to say hello. They just put the food down in the kitchen and disappeared.

A third visitor who came less regularly was Dr Carina Wahlberg. She swept into the garden with her long black coat over her white doctor's coat. If Gerlof was indoors, her knock was firm and demanding.

Sometimes she came on Thursdays, sometimes on Tuesdays, sometimes even on Sundays. Gerlof never got to grips with Dr Wahlberg's schedule, but he was always pleased to see her. She checked that he had enough medication, took his blood pressure, and from time to time she did a urine test.

'So what's it like being over eighty, Gerlof?'

'What's it like? It doesn't involve a lot of movement, I just sit here. I should have gone to church today . . . but I couldn't get there.'

'But how does it feel, in purely physical terms?'

'You can try it for yourself.' Gerlof raised a hand to his head. 'Stick some cotton wool in your ears, pull on a pair of badly soled shoes and a pair of thick rubber gloves . . . and smear your glasses with Vaseline. That's what it's like to be eighty-three.'

'Well, now I know,' said the doctor. 'By the way, do you remember Wilhelm Pettersson? When I said I was coming to see you today, he sent his best wishes.'

'The fisherman?' Gerlof nodded, he remembered Wille from the village of Tallerum. 'Wilhelm got blown up by a mine during the war. He was standing in the stern of a fishing boat when the prow hit the mine, and the boat flew thirty metres in the air. Wille was the only one who survived . . . How is he these days?'

'Fine, but he's getting a bit deaf.'

'I expect that's because of his unexpected flight through the air.'

Gerlof didn't want to think about all the minefields that had lain off Öland during the war, but they were on his mind anyway. They had sunk many ships. He had worked as a pilot guiding cargo ships past the mines during the war years, and he still had nightmares about running into one of them. Some were still down there in the depths of the sea, rusty and covered with algae . . .

The doctor had asked him a question.

'Sorry?' said Gerlof.

'I said, How's your hearing these days?'

'Not bad at all,' said Gerlof quickly. 'I can hear most things. Sometimes I get a rushing noise in my ears, but that's probably the wind.'

'We can check it some time,' said Dr Walhberg. 'You said you'd got cotton wool in your ears . . . perhaps you need a hearing aid?'

'I'd rather not,' said Gerlof. He didn't want yet another little gadget to worry about.

'So how are you feeling otherwise?'

'Fine.'

That was the only reply Gerlof was willing to give – if he told the doctor he didn't think he had all that long to live, she might send him back to the home. Instead he said, 'Of course, it's a bit strange to have no future.'

'No future?'

Gerlof nodded. 'If I was younger I'd probably buy a boat, but at my age you don't want to go making too many plans.'

He thought Dr Wahlberg looked a little concerned, and when she opened her mouth he went on quickly, 'But it doesn't matter. Quite the reverse, I feel free.'

'Well, you have a lot of memories,' said the doctor with a smile.

'Exactly,' said Gerlof, but he didn't smile back. 'I spend a lot of time with my memories.'

When the doctor had gone, Gerlof remained in his chair for a few minutes. Then he got up and went to the cupboard in the kitchen to fetch one of Ella's books.

I spend a lot of time with my memories, he had said to Dr Wahlberg – but that was just a way of dressing up the fact that he was reading the diaries when he shouldn't be. He felt ashamed of himself while he was doing it, and yet it was difficult to stop. If Ella really did have something to hide, shouldn't she have burnt the books herself before the cancer took her? She had left them to Gerlof, in a way.

He opened a new page and began to read:

3rd June 1957
There was a market up in Marnäs this morning; the weather was lovely, and there were lots of people there. And unfortunately the first wasps of the year were out too.

Gerlof travelled down to Borgholm last night and has loaded up 30 tons of limestone to go to Stockholm. He sets sail tomorrow, and the girls are on their summer holidays, so they're going with him.

The place feels so empty without Gerlof and the girls. We used to cycle up to the market together when they were little, but they're big now, and I felt a bit lonely today. I daren't cry because that will make me ill, but when I think about Gerlof out on the Baltic until November, it's like being stabbed with a knife.

But I'm not completely alone, because I have the little changeling, my little troll.

He scuttles along by the stone wall, crouching down, and creeps out from the juniper bushes for some milk and biscuits. But only when I'm alone in the middle of the day, when there aren't so many people out and about. Perhaps he senses that's the safest time to be out.

13

The sun had come out by the time Per left Öland to go and sort out his father. He had called Jerry's home number and mobile several times on Sunday morning, but with no luck. The silence increased his anxiety.

As he and Jesper were eating an early lunch, Per explained quietly, 'I think your grandfather could do with some help . . . He sounded confused when he rang me, so I need to go down and check he's all right.'

'When will you be back?' asked Jesper.

'Tonight. It might be late, but I'll be back.'

The last thing he did was to redirect the telephone from the cottage through to his mobile so that Jesper wouldn't have to answer if Jerry rang again.

His son was playing games in front of the TV when Per left, but he waved in the general direction of the hallway. Per waved back.

Jesper would be fine, there were meatballs in the fridge and there were no cars around the quarry to run over him. Per was not an irresponsible father, and he was definitely *not* worried as he left Stenvik and headed south.

The sun was shining, spring had arrived. He could

put his foot down; there weren't many cars out and about today.

He passed Borgholm at about one o'clock and drove across the Öland bridge to the mainland half an hour later. As he was driving past Kalmar he saw a red cross on a road sign, and tried not to think about Nilla in her hospital bed. He would call in to see her on the way home.

After Nybro the forest closed in around the main road, with the odd break for a meadow or lake. The fir trees made Per think about Regina again, and the drive out into the forest with her one beautiful spring day.

The prospect of seeing his father gave him no pleasure whatsoever. Two hours to get to Ryd, then perhaps another two hours to drive him home to Kristianstad. Four or five hours in Jerry's company, that was all – but it still felt like a long time.

After a couple of hours' driving through the forest he reached Ryd, by which time the sun had disappeared behind thick cloud cover. The spring suddenly felt like autumn.

Ryd wasn't a big place, and the pavements were empty. Per pulled up by the bus station and looked for Jerry in vain. Either he was already sitting on a bus heading south, or he was wandering around somewhere by himself.

He took out his mobile and called his father's number again. The phone rang three times, then someone pressed the answer button. But nobody spoke. All Per could hear was a rushing sound, followed by two thuds.

Then there was silence.

Per looked at his phone. Then he went into the newsagent's and asked about Jerry.

'An old man?' said the girl behind the counter.

Per nodded. 'Seventy-three. He's broad-shouldered, but he looks kind of worn out and small.'

'There was some old bloke waiting outside about an hour ago . . . he was standing there for quite a while.'

'Did you happen to notice where he went?'

'Sorry.'

'Did he get on a bus?'

'Not that I saw.'

'Did anyone pick him up?'

'Maybe . . . He disappeared.'

Per gave up. He went back to the car and decided to drive out to Jerry's house – to the studio. It was a few kilometres west of Ryd, near a village called Strihult. Jerry had bought and equipped the place when the money started pouring in in the mid-seventies. Through all the years while he was still driving, Jerry had commuted from Kristianstad on a weekly basis to make films, first with various freelance operatives, then with Hans Bremer.

Per had been there only once; he had given Jerry a lift three or four years ago. At that time his father had still been in good health and was going to Ryd to edit a film – one of the last he and Bremer made together. Per had been on his way home to Kalmar and had just dropped Jerry off outside the house, refusing to go inside.

Strihult was nothing more than a collection of houses with a petrol station and a grocery shop. Per drove straight through without seeing a single person.

Beyond the village the road grew even narrower, the forest thicker – and after about a kilometre he saw a sign pointing to the right, a white arrow with the words MORNER ART LTD on it. That was the name of one of Jerry's businesses.

He was close to his destination now, and gripped the steering wheel a little harder. Although Jerry rang him at least once a week, they hadn't seen each other since December, when Per had called round and spent a few hours at his father's apartment. Jerry had celebrated Christmas all alone.

After five hundred metres of forest without a single house, Per suddenly came upon a dense cypress hedge. He had arrived.

A red sign by the entrance warned visitors to BEWARE OF THE DOG!, despite the fact that Jerry had never owned a dog.

Per turned in, followed the driveway around a garage next to the large wooden house, and pulled up on a huge, deserted gravelled area. He switched off the engine, opened the door and looked at the house. It was big and wide, L-shaped and two storeys high. Jerry, Bremer and their actors had stayed here when they were working, so he assumed it consisted of a smaller residential section and a larger work area.

He didn't feel welcome, but he was going to knock on the door anyway. Even if his father wasn't here, perhaps Hans Bremer was.

Per had never met Bremer, but now they needed to talk – about the future. Jerry wasn't well enough to run a business; it was time to wind up Morner Art and sell this place. Bremer would just have to look for a new job, but he'd probably worked that out already.

A wide flight of concrete steps led up to the door, which was flanked by shiny windows with the curtains drawn.

Per got out of the car and looked at his watch. Twenty past four. It was at least a couple of hours until sunset, but the sky was overcast and the fir trees towering up beyond the garden shut out the daylight.

His shoes crunched on the gravel as he went towards the steps.

The front door was imposing, made of oak or mahogany – and it was only when Per started up the steps that he noticed it was ajar. It was open an inch or so, and the hallway inside was pitch black.

He pushed open the heavy door and peered inside.

'Hello?'

There wasn't a sound. He reached in and found a switch, but when he flicked it down the light didn't come on.

He glanced back quickly to check that the area in front of the house was still deserted, then he stepped inside.

Two ghostly figures were waiting for him on the left in the hallway. Per stiffened – until he realized they were nothing more than two dark raincoats hanging beneath a hat stand.

On the floor below the shelf stood a row of slippers and Wellington boots, along with an umbrella. There was an ebony sculpture in a dark corner, a tiger almost three feet tall who seemed ready to pounce.

Per took a couple of steps into the hallway. There were four doors leading off to the sides, but they were all closed.

For some reason he had been expecting a stale or sour smell in the air, but he was aware of only a faint aroma of old tobacco smoke and alcohol. Had someone had a party here?

There was something lying on the rug – a black mobile phone. Per picked it up and saw that it was switched off.

Was it Jerry's? It certainly looked like his father's, with big buttons that were easy to press with a shaky finger. He put the phone in his pocket and called out, 'Hello? Jerry?'

No reply. And yet he still had the feeling that there

91

was someone in the house, someone who was moving cautiously across the floor to avoid being heard.

He went over to a door on the left and tentatively pushed down the handle. Behind it was a large kitchen, a long room with several windows letting in grey light which fell on a sturdy dining table, several sinks and two large ovens. It reminded him of a restaurant kitchen, and there were a number of empty wine bottles and a pile of unwashed plates on the worktops.

Per turned around; he thought he had heard something. A shout from inside the house?

He stopped just inside the kitchen door and jumped when a bell suddenly started ringing. A telephone. It was coming from the wall on the far side of the kitchen, and from somewhere else in the house.

Per wanted to shout *Can someone get that?*, but he remained silent.

The telephone rang out three times, four, five.

No one answered, but when he finally moved towards it with his hand outstretched, it fell silent.

He moved slowly backwards, out of the kitchen. He stepped back into the hallway and turned around. The smell of alcohol was still there, perhaps it was even stronger now, and the black tiger was still lurking in the shadows, waiting for him. He walked past it and tried a door on the other side of the hallway.

The room behind the door was pitch black. When Per stepped inside he saw that the windows were taped shut, but he had the impression of a large, long room with plastic flooring, movable walls and spotlights on the ceiling. This must be Jerry and Bremer's studio.

He spotted a light switch by the door and pressed it, but nothing happened. The power must have gone off in the whole house. Or somebody had turned it off.

There was no point in groping blindly across the room. He was just about to turn around when he heard a faint sound in the darkness.

A sigh, or a groan? Yes, there was somebody groaning in the room in front of him. And it sounded like a man.

Per moved forward into the darkness. He bumped into something large and hard on the floor, a big leather sofa, and slowly felt his way around it.

The smell of alcohol was stronger in here – or was it something else?

Then he saw something moving on the other side of the sofa, a few metres away, and took another step forward. It was a shadow with arms, its head raised.

'Pelle?' said a voice in the darkness.

It was low and hoarse, and Per recognized it.

'Jerry,' he said. 'What's happened?'

The figure stirred. It was lying on the floor, but it turned its head in his direction. Slowly, as if it had difficulty moving. Per bent down towards it, towards a pale head with greasy strands of grey hair and a body covered with a crumpled overcoat.

'You weren't easy to find, Jerry. How are you doing?'

Per saw his father's yellow-white eyes flash in the darkness. They were blinking at him, but Jerry didn't seem surprised to see his son.

'Bremer?' he said, coughing.

Per shook his head. He spoke quietly, as if someone were creeping up on them.

'I don't know where Bremer is . . . Is he here in the house?'

He sensed that his father was nodding.

'Can you get up?'

He reached out to him, but felt something cold and heavy across Jerry's chest. Some kind of lighting stand or metal rig had fallen on top of him. Per lifted it out of the way – and at the same moment he heard a loud thud from the ceiling, and looked up.

There was somebody upstairs, he realized.

'Up you get,' he said quietly to Jerry, moving the stand out of the way. 'There you go . . .'

He got his father up on to his knees, then his feet. Jerry groaned and seemed to be reaching out for something lying on the floor.

It was his old leather briefcase. Per let him take it. 'Come on,' he said.

His father's body was substantial and heavy, bearing witness to long, lazy dinners and plenty of wine. Jerry moved slowly across the floor, leaning on his son.

'Pelle,' Jerry said again.

Per could smell a mixture of sweat, nicotine and unwashed clothes emanating from his father. It was a strange feeling, being so close to him. It had never happened when he was a little boy. No reassuring pats from Jerry, no hugs.

When he had managed to get him halfway to the door, he heard a brief clicking sound in the darkness. Then something hissed.

Per turned his head. Over his shoulder he saw a glow on the floor further inside the room, and a small flame flared up.

It was thin and weak, but quickly grew bigger; the fire reached up from the floor, illuminating a peculiar device standing by the wall. It looked like a car battery with wires, standing next to a plastic box.

The smell in the air wasn't alcohol, Per realized. It was petrol.

The box was a big green can, and somebody had drilled little holes in the side. The petrol had already run out and formed a pool on the floor.

Per stared at the fire, watching it grow and creep closer to the can, and he saw the danger.

'We have to get out of here.'

He pulled Jerry across the room.

Once they were out, Per quickly closed the door behind them, and almost immediately heard a dull, sucking roar from inside the room as the petrol ignited, rattling the door.

Jerry raised his head, and Per noticed that his father had a red lump on his forehead.

'Pelle?'

'Let's go, Jerry.'

He staggered through the hallway with his arm around his father. They could hear a muted crackling noise through the door behind them as the fire spread through the room.

Per blinked as he stepped out into the daylight, supporting Jerry as they made their way down the steps and over to the Saab.

When they reached the car he let go of Jerry, took out his mobile and quickly made a call. A female voice answered after two rings.

'Emergency services.'

Per cleared his throat. 'I want to report a fire.'

'What's the location?'

Per looked around. 'It's in a house outside Ryd, it's arson . . . the ground floor is burning.'

'Can you give me the address?'

The woman on the other end of the phone sounded very calm; Per tried to calm down in turn, tried to think. 'I don't know the name of the road. It's near Strihult to the west of Ryd and there's a sign that says Morner Art . . .'

'Is everyone out of the house?'

'What?'

'Has everyone left the house?'

'I don't know . . . I just got here.'

'And your name?'

Per hesitated. What should he say? Should he make up a name?

He had nothing to hide. Jerry might have, but he hadn't. 'My name is Per Mörner,' he said, and gave his address and home number on Öland. Then he switched off his mobile.

Jerry was leaning against the car. In the grey daylight Per could see that his father had on the same crumpled brown coat he had been wearing day in and day out for the past few years; the seams were coming apart, and several buttons were missing.

Jerry sighed and gritted his teeth. 'Hurts,' he said.

Per turned to face him. 'Are you in pain?'

Jerry nodded. Then he turned back his coat and Per suddenly saw that the shirt below Jerry's ribcage was wet and torn.

'What have you done? Have you . . . ?' Per fell silent as he lifted up his father's shirt.

A couple of inches above the navel a long, bloody wound ran across Jerry's pot belly. The blood had begun to coagulate; it looked almost black in the gloom.

Per lowered the shirt. 'Who did this, Jerry?'

Jerry looked at his bloodstained belly as if he'd only just noticed it. 'Bremer,' he said.

'Bremer?' said Per. 'Were you fighting with Hans Bremer? Why?'

Quick-fire questions made his father's brain shut down. He merely stared and blinked at his son, but said nothing.

Per looked over at the big house on the other side of the parking area. The front door was still open, and he thought he could see a thin cloud of smoke drifting out.

'So where's Bremer now? Is he still in there?'

Jerry remained silent as he laboriously clambered into the Saab's passenger seat.

'Wait here,' said Per, closing the car door.

He ran back to the house. Up the steps, into the hallway. It wasn't without risks; he could hear the fire roaring and crackling behind the closed door of the studio. The air inside the house also felt warmer, like an oven heating up. He didn't have much time.

And he needed a weapon, given that there might be somebody with a knife in the house. He grabbed the furled umbrella from the hall. Holding it in front of him with the point raised, he opened one of the middle doors and saw a steep staircase leading downwards.

The cellar. It was pitch black, he didn't want to go down there.

Behind the fourth and final unopened door there was another staircase, this time leading upwards.

Per set off up the stairs, which were covered in white fitted carpet that completely deadened the sound of his footsteps. At the top of the stairs was a corridor which ran along the upper floor, with closed doors along both sides; Per felt as if he had landed in a hotel.

He set off, holding the umbrella like a sword.

'Bremer?' he shouted. 'It's Per Mörner!'

The stench of petrol or some kind of accelerant was just as powerful up here, and suddenly he heard a low crackling sound. He couldn't see any flames, but he realized there was a fire somewhere up here too. There was a grey mist of smoke forming around him in the corridor, rapidly growing thicker and drying out his windpipe.

But where was the fire?

Per quickly walked over to the nearest door and opened it, only to discover a cupboard full of cleaning

97

materials. He opened the next one: a small bedroom with bare walls and a made-up bed.

The third door on the left was locked, but curls of smoke were rising from a narrow gap at floor level.

'Bremer? Hello? Hans Bremer?'

No reply. Or was that a noise? A whimpering sound?

Per had never kicked a door open, he'd only seen people do it in films. Was it easy? He took a couple of steps back; unfortunately he couldn't give himself any more of a run at the door, as his back was against the opposite wall. Then he lunged forward and kicked hard.

The door shuddered, but it was made of pine, and didn't open.

He looked around. There was a key in one of the doors on the other side of the corridor, and he took it out. He tried it in the locked door; it fitted, and he was able to turn it.

The door opened smoothly to reveal billowing white smoke. The air in the corridor sucked it out of the room, straight at Per.

He blinked and felt tears spring to his eyes. The smoke was dense, like autumn fog, but he walked into it anyway and suddenly recognized a particular smell beyond the smoke. The smell of burnt flesh.

The room was small and dark. Per blinked and groped around with his hands, but was unable to find the light switch; he had to crouch down at floor level where the air was fresher.

He took a couple of steps into the room. To the right he could see flames running up the wallpaper. There was an unmade bed with a pile of blankets on it, burning fiercely. He took another step forward, but the heat brought him to a standstill.

He blinked at the smoke and tried to see. Was there a burning body beneath the blankets? Per imagined he

98

could see outstretched arms, legs in trousers, a charred head . . .

His eyes were streaming, his lungs seared with pain. And that was when he heard the cry behind him.

There were no words, just a long drawn-out scream. It sounded like a woman's voice, and it was terrified.

Per dropped the umbrella and turned around, half-blind. He went back into the corridor. The cry had come from somewhere on this floor, but it was muted, as if it came through a wall.

All the doors were still closed, but at the far end of the corridor he saw something new: a patch of bright flames that had taken hold of the carpet. He realized that the whole of the upper floor was burning. He was surrounded by fire.

'Hello!' he yelled.

He heard a cry from the woman in response, even more muted.

He stood still, indecisive, then moved towards the closest doors. They were locked, and he banged on them.

Door after door, but no response.

'Hello? Where are you?'

He wanted to kick down the doors, find the woman. But the smoke was quickly growing thicker around him; darkness was falling in the corridor. The fire was coming from two directions, burning and crackling, and the air was like a sauna. Per realized the whole of the ground floor was also ablaze by this time; he couldn't get back down the stairs.

The walls seemed to be pressing in on him, he couldn't get any air.

There was no time.

He had to turn back, groping his way through the smoke until he found himself back in the room with the burning bed. As he turned around he felt a cooling breeze against his face, and saw that one of the windows was half-open, letting in the light. The curtains were open and a wooden chair stood below the window.

He could get to the window if he stayed on the left, where the air was a little cooler. But the flames from the bed were creeping across the floor and the smoke was growing thicker.

He could no longer breathe, he had to get out, fast.

He took three steps towards the window, climbed up on the chair and looked out. He could see fields and dense forest. And two or three metres below this was the garage, with a tarred felt roof.

The cool of the evening struck his chest and face while the heat of the fire pressed against his back, pushing him out of the room. It was like standing with his back towards the oven in a crematorium. He couldn't stay where he was, and eventually he stepped out into the air and jumped.

He landed on the garage roof with a crash; the wood shuddered beneath his feet, but it held.

From the garage he jumped down on to the gravel. Three metres – a short, dizzying fall, with the grey gravel coming closer and closer – and then his shoes hit the ground. His knees gave way.

He coughed, got to his feet and inhaled the cold, fresh air. He was at the back of the house and could see a low fence in front of him, with a deserted field of yellow grass beyond it, then the dense forest of firs.

On a track leading between the trees, perhaps two hundred metres away, someone was standing staring at the house. Per thought it looked like a man dressed in dark clothes, but he had no time to see anything else before the figure turned and disappeared into the forest.

The fire had begun to crackle and roar above him, but he thought he heard the sound of a car engine. A car starting up, its engine revving as it quickly disappeared among the trees.

14

When the windows of Jerry's house began to shatter with the heat of the fire, raining down like shards of ice, Per was suddenly overcome by nausea, even though he was quite safe on the far side of the drive. He kept drawing deep breaths of cold air into his lungs, painfully dry from the effects of the smoke; he rubbed his smarting eyes and tried to stand up straight.

Black smoke billowed out through the gaping windows, whirling around the house like a thick shroud. No one could have survived in there.

A veil seemed to fall between Per and the rest of the world, and he could hear the sound of sirens in the distance. What had he actually seen with his tear-filled eyes? A body on a bed and someone fleeing into the forest? The more he tried to remember, the more unclear the images became.

The sirens were getting closer. Two fire engines, their blue lights flashing, turned into the drive and stopped in front of the house. The fire-fighters leapt out, dressed in black protective suits.

Per moved backwards across the gravel. He bumped into something solid, turned around and saw that it was his own Saab. Flakes of dirty white ash had begun to accumulate on its roof.

A burning bed, a body in the smoke. And the frightened cries of a woman.

He looked around.

Jerry? Where was Jerry?

Oh yes, he was still sitting in the car.

He looked back at the house. The flames were shooting out of the windows on both floors now.

The fire-fighters were moving around their vehicles, dragging out bulky hoses and starting to connect them up. One of them, dressed in a red jacket, strode over to Per and leant close to make himself heard through the roar of the fire: 'What's your name?'

'Per Mörner.'

'Are you the owner of this property, Per?'

He shook his head. He took a deep breath and tried to explain, but his windpipe felt as if it had disintegrated in the dry heat.

'Are you all right?'

'Yes, it's just . . .'

'The ambulance is on its way,' said the fire-fighter. 'Do you know where the fire started?'

Per swallowed. 'Everywhere,' he whispered. Then he took another deep breath and tried to give a sensible answer: 'There was fire upstairs and downstairs . . . and I think someone might still be inside. Perhaps more than one person.'

'What?'

'I think I saw a person inside the house. And I heard cries.'

He had raised his voice; it sounded better now. The fire-fighter blinked and looked at him. 'Where exactly was this, Per?'

103

'Upstairs, in the rooms upstairs. It was burning inside the rooms, so I . . .'

'OK, we'll search the place. Are there any LPG bottles in the house?'

Per shook his head. 'I don't think so,' he said. 'It was a . . . a film studio.'

'Any hazardous liquids?'

'No,' said Per. 'Not as far as I know.'

The man nodded and went back to the fire engines. Per saw that three of his colleagues were pulling on suits with breathing apparatus on their backs. The specialist search team. Two of the others turned on the water from their tank and directed the stream of water up towards the broken windows.

The search team moved slowly towards the front door, and at the same time a red car with the words EMERGENCY RESCUE TEAM on the side pulled into the drive. A man in a yellow jacket got out, holding a two-way radio in his hand. He switched it on and started reporting to someone.

Per coughed and drew more air into his lungs. Then he went back to the car and opened the door. His father was slumped in the passenger seat, his briefcase on his knee.

Per showed him the mobile phone he had found in the hallway. 'Is this yours?'

Jerry looked and nodded. Per handed it over. 'How are you feeling now?'

Jerry's only response was a cough. Per could see him clearly for the first time that day, and he looked pathetic – tired and grey in his crumpled coat. When Per was little and his father used to come and visit him and Anita, Jerry's hair had been black and slicked back. He had always worn expensive fur coats in the winter and Italian suits in summer. Jerry had earned a lot of money, and liked to show it off.

When Per was fifteen, his father had suddenly changed his name from Gerhard Mörner to Jerry Morner, possibly in order to appear more international.

'You stink,' Jerry said suddenly. 'Stink, Pelle.'

'So do you, Jerry . . . We stink of smoke.'

Per looked over at the burning house. The men with breathing apparatus were making their way up the stone steps now. The one in front opened the door wide and took a step inside, straight into the thick smoke, and disappeared. The other two remained outside.

Half a minute passed, then suddenly the first man reappeared in the doorway and shook his head at the other two. He raised his hand.

They went back down the steps.

Per realized there was no hope for anyone inside the house.

'Go, Pelle?' said Jerry behind him.

It was a tempting thought, simply to start the car and set off for Öland – but of course it was impossible.

'No,' Per said. 'We have to wait here.'

Several more sirens could be heard in the distance. An ambulance swung in and parked between the fire engines and the Saab. The siren was switched off and two paramedics climbed out. They stood looking at the burning house with their arms folded; there wasn't much else they could do.

'Come with me,' said Per, helping his father out of the car. They went over to the ambulance, and Per pointed at Jerry. 'My father's got an injury to his stomach, and he's had some kind of blow to the head . . . Could you take a look at him?'

The paramedics nodded, without asking any questions. They simply opened the back doors of the ambulance and helped Jerry inside.

Per himself was starting to feel a little better; he just

needed lots and lots of fresh air. He left Jerry and walked over to the fence running along one side of the house. He stood there for a minute, deep in thought, looking over at the forest. Then he climbed over the fence.

He had stared so much at the burning house that he hadn't noticed that the sun had gone down. It was almost dark now, and as he crossed the field he glanced at his watch: it was ten to seven.

He thought about Jerry, who always wore two watches when he was working: one stainless steel, one gold.

The forest rose up ahead of him. Per searched for the opening among the fir trees, and found it after a few minutes. It was a forest track, deserted but not overgrown. There was a strip of grass down the middle, with a broad rut along each side. He bent down. The ground was hard and stony, but with patches of wet mud here and there, and in the fading light Per thought he could see fresh tyre marks.

He straightened up and looked along the track, which wound through the trees and disappeared round a bend. Where did it end? Perhaps it led to a road north of Ryd.

A good escape route.

Ten minutes later he was back at the house. He stayed away from the fire-fighters, but stopped by the ambulance.

The paramedics had cleaned up Jerry's wound. Now the blood had gone, a long, red slash was visible across his pale, fat belly.

'It looks like a knife wound,' said one of the paramedics as he applied a dressing. 'Pretty superficial – I think the knife must have slipped.'

'Slipped?' said Per.

'Slipped across the skin . . . He's been lucky, it should heal in a week or so. Then you can go to a clinic and ask them to remove the dressing, or do it yourself.'

Per helped Jerry back to the car. They sat beside each other in the front seats, gazing over at the house.

Eventually Per broke the silence. 'There was a body in a bed upstairs,' he said. 'At least I think it was a body, but I could hardly see anything with all the smoke . . . and I thought I heard cries.'

He sighed, leant back in his seat and thought about the open window. Who had opened it?

His father was mumbling something beside him. His brain seemed to have shut down again.

Per made a fresh attempt. 'What did you and Bremer talk about?' he asked. 'What did he say when he called and wanted you to meet him here?'

'Can't remember,' said Jerry.

'But why did you have a fight?'

Jerry just coughed and leant back. Per sighed, placed his hands on the steering wheel and gazed at the dark-grey sky. 'I have to go home soon,' he said. 'Nilla, my daughter, she's in . . .'

He stopped speaking as a white Volvo turned into the drive. It was moving slowly as it swung around the fire engines, then pulled up facing Per's car. When it had stopped directly in front of him, a man and a woman got out. They were dressed in civilian clothes, but he suspected he knew who they were.

The man went over to the ambulance; the woman came over to Per's car, and he opened the door.

'Good evening.'

'Good evening,' said the woman, showing him her ID. She was from police headquarters in Växjö. 'Was it you who called the emergency services?'

'Yes,' said Per.

The officer asked for his name and address, and he gave them.

'And who are you?' she said to Jerry, who stared sullenly back at her.

Per knew that his father had never been fond of the police. Police officers and traffic wardens were two of his bugbears.

'This is my father, Jerry Morner,' said Per. 'He owns the property.'

'I see,' said the police officer, glancing over at the fire. 'Well, let's hope you're insured. Are you, Jerry?'

No response.

'My father's had a stroke,' Per explained. 'He has some speech problems.'

The officer nodded. 'So you were both here before the fire started?'

'Something like that,' said Per. 'Jerry was here . . . I arrived just after.'

'Can you tell me what you saw?'

Nothing to hide, Per thought again. Then he began to tell her about going into the house, discovering Jerry and the petrol can, helping his father out and going back inside.

The officer took out a notebook and started to write down what he said. 'So you saw somebody upstairs? And you heard cries for help?'

'I think so.'

'Did you see anyone else in or near the house?'

Per was silent, considering what he had seen. A figure fleeing into the trees? And tyre tracks from a car?

'I didn't see anything clearly . . . But someone had knocked my father down, and slashed him with a knife.'

'Oh?'

'Bremer,' said a voice behind Per.

'Bremer?' said the police officer. 'Who's that?'

'Hans Bremer, he's my father's associate,' said Per. 'He might be the person inside the house.'

All three of them gazed silently at the blaze, which was still defeating the efforts of the fire-fighters. Sparks were shooting up into the sky, and the heat could be felt right across the drive.

'OK,' said the police officer, looking around. 'My colleagues and I will make a start on cordoning off the area.'

'So you're treating this as a crime scene?' said Per.

'It could be.' She turned away.

'Is it all right if we leave?' Per said to her back. 'I mean, there's nothing more we can do, is there?'

She shook her head. 'We'll soon be done here,' she said over her shoulder, 'and then you can follow us up to Växjö in your car.'

'What for?'

'We'd just like to do another interview back at the station. It won't take long.'

Per sighed. He looked up at the darkening sky, then down at his watch. It was quarter to eight.

He felt very tired. The plan had been to drive Jerry back to his apartment in Kristianstad, but then he wouldn't have time to get back to Öland tonight. And Jesper would have to spend the night alone in the cottage.

He turned around. 'Jerry, I won't have time to drive you home tonight. You're going to have to come to Öland with me.'

His father looked at him. 'Öland?'

He looked doubtful, and Per had his doubts too. After all, he had promised himself that he would keep Jerry away from Nilla and Jesper.

'Yes . . . well, I mean, you are my father, after all. Part of the family.'

'Family?' Jerry didn't seem to understand the word.

'My family,' said Per. 'So you can come and celebrate Easter with me and Nilla and Jesper in our summer cottage – on one condition.'

Jerry waited, and Per went on: 'That you keep quiet.'

'Quiet?'

Per nodded. Asking someone who couldn't manage a whole sentence to keep quiet was quite funny, of course, but he wasn't laughing.

'I want you to keep quiet, Jerry. You are not to tell your grandchildren what you and Bremer used to do here.'

15

Vendela was wearing a white cap and a windproof red tracksuit as she bent down to the dog basket in the hallway and kissed Aloysius on the top of his head. Then she went to the front door. 'I'm going for a run!' she called out. 'See you in an hour or so!'

There was no reply from Max, just a whimper from Aloysius. He was uneasy; perhaps he sensed there was going to be a party. Since he had lost his sight, Ally always found strange voices around him quite stressful.

It looked as though there were going to be about ten people at Wednesday's get-together: she and Max, the Kurdins and their baby, Per Mörner and his two teenage children, plus Gerlof Davidsson, the elderly man from across the road, and his friend John. She wouldn't need to prepare too much food, although of course it was important to work out how much they would need. She would go down to Borgholm tomorrow and fill the car with supplies, including dog food.

Then all she had to do was get everything ready for Wednesday, and she wouldn't get any help from Max. But she wasn't going to think about that now, she was going to go for a run.

Vendela had taken up jogging ten years ago. She had

actually started when she married Max, who didn't run and couldn't understand why she wanted to do it. Last winter she had stayed fit by jogging on a running machine, but she had missed nature and the chance to be out in the open air.

She spent a couple of minutes stretching on the steps outside before heading off northwards, in a wide semi-circle around the edge of the quarry.

Vendela noticed a strange kind of gateway to the north of the quarry – two substantial hazel bushes growing a couple of metres apart. She ran between them. Hazel was always special; it was used for both magic wands and divining rods.

It felt as if she was in a new world now. Her goal was to return to her childhood home after almost forty years – if she could find her way. A great deal had changed since then. Houses had been built, Tarmac roads had appeared, meadows and fields had become overgrown.

She increased her speed and ran out on to the coast road above the shore. It was late afternoon and the sun was low in the sky, just as in October, but its light was sharper in the spring. The narrow strips of snow still remaining on the grass and in the ditches were melting fast.

The rocky landscape was silent and still. The only thing that was moving was Vendela herself, her arms and legs swinging back and forth. Slowly she began to find her rhythm, and was able to relax. When she came to a fork in the coast road she turned right, inland. The air she inhaled was fresh and cool. There was no sign of her allergy.

It took about twenty minutes to run to the place where her childhood had begun and ended. She ran virtually straight there, without getting lost. First of all along the wide Tarmac road, then on to a narrower gravel track which she thought she recognized, past a grove of ash trees that had grown tall and dense over the years since she had left the island. In the middle of the grove was a short, narrow track, and Vendela turned on to it. She was hot and sweaty by now, and tense with anticipation.

When she had run another fifty metres she reached the end of the track, and there was the farm. She breathed out and tried to compose herself.

It was slightly set apart at the edge of the alvar, a couple of kilometres north of Stenvik. There were two new white-painted iron gates in front of the stone path leading into the garden. Vendela couldn't see anyone moving about, so she opened the gates.

The sun had slipped lower in the sky to the west, and the garden lay in shadow. But the sun's rays were still shining on the house, and the windows gleamed at her. Vendela had been afraid that the place would be deserted and falling apart, with broken windows and the doors hanging off their hinges, but the house was well maintained and had recently been painted yellow. Someone with time and money had bought the place.

There was a lawn below the house, and to the left a slight rise in the ground was visible, a long rectangle. Forty years ago a little barn had stood there, but it was gone now. Grass and moss had crept up and covered the foundations.

For appearances' sake Vendela walked up the path to the house and knocked on the kitchen door, but no one answered. The farm had become a summer residence, like so many others, the lawn uncut and the blinds lowered. Presumably the place was empty and deserted from autumn through to spring.

She thought about the family who would soon arrive and quickly clear away all traces of winter. On the very first evening they would be busy raking up the leaves and cutting the grass. Young, carefree people; perhaps they had children. But could they feel echoes of the unhappiness that had existed in this house?

Vendela walked through the garden. At the far end, there were still fragile patches of snow and the ground was sodden, like a marsh. She looked over at a thicket of bushes and spotted an old shed. It was standing in the shadows, and didn't fit in with the rest of the well-cared-for holiday idyll at all. It was scruffy and unpainted and was leaning slightly to one side, as if it were in the process of sinking down into the ground. The shed looked hidden and forgotten, and Vendela suddenly remembered that her father had used it as his tool shed. He had left some tools down in the quarry at the end of the day, but the rest he had brought home and locked up here.

She went over and tugged at the rickety door, and it opened reluctantly on stiff hinges. There was no unpleasant smell. Just a faint aroma of earth. It was dark inside, dark and cramped. Old tools and bags were piled up on top of one another. In the corner nearest the door stood a slender stick made of chestnut, with the bark scraped off. Vendela recognized it at once. She hesitated, then picked it up.

The cow stick.

It was hers. Her father had given it to her when she was responsible for tending the cows. The stick was shiny and well used.

Öland 1957

The flies are buzzing lazily and sleepily above the path, woken by the spring sunshine. The wind is soughing in the trees, and Vendela raises her stick and hits the three cows, over and over again.

'Go on! Get a move on!'

She is walking barefoot along the path, wearing a white dress, and she hits the cows as hard as she can. Three blows each. She measures the distance and swings the stick sideways at their flanks, just above the back legs. When she hits them there, it goes *smack*! Further forward on their bodies the sound is duller, *smock*!

The blows can be heard in long, rhythmic sequences along the path between the meadow and the farm, where she and Henry and the Invalid live.

'Go, go, go!'

The bell on a strap around the leading cow's neck clonks rhythmically. It is hot, and hitting the cows is tiring. Vendela is only nine years old and the stick is heavy. She is sweating. Her dress is stuck to the skin under her arms, her hair hangs in her eyes and bluebottles circle around her and the cows. She blows her nose on some grass and raises the stick once again. 'Get a move on!'

When she turned eight, Vendela was given the responsibility of moving the cows between the farm and the meadow. It was a proper job, but there was never any mention of Henry paying her – he doesn't even have enough money for electricity, even though the cables were brought as far as the farm several years ago. Her only reward was to be allowed to name the cows, and she called them Rosa, Rosa and Rosa.

That made her father laugh. 'We might as well just give them each a number,' he said.

The cows' names mean nothing to him; he has marked them with a clear snick in the ear so that anyone who comes across them on the alvar can see that they belong to him. But he must have found the idea amusing, because the names stick.

Rosa, Rosa and Rosa.

Vendela is not in the least amused. It doesn't matter what the cows are called, because she can't see any difference between them. To her they are merely three brown and white things that have to be driven back and forth between the meadow and the barn. It's a daily obligation that begins with the start of the spring farming and the arrival of the sun in April. That is when Henry, in keeping with tradition, gives each cow a herring dipped in tar for its first meal outside the barn. Then he lets them out on to their spring grazing land and tells his daughter to take care of them.

The cow stick is smooth and beautiful, slender and flexible. Henry removed all the bark before he gave it to her. *Use this to guide the cows*, he said. *Walk behind them and prod them in the side occasionally, just to make sure they're heading in the right direction.*

The cows are as big as great lumps of rock, and Vendela prodded them tentatively when she first started driving them between the meadow and the farm. For the first

116

few days she was afraid they would turn on her, but the cows didn't react at all. It was as if she didn't exist. So she prodded harder and harder, and after a month or so she started hitting them with the stick.

Finally she took to beating them.

By now, hitting the nearest cow as hard as possible with the stick has become a habit. Rosa, Rosa and Rosa have such thick brown and white hide, as hard as leather, and she wants to penetrate it and see it bleed; most of all she wants to *frighten* the cows. But the Rosas just carry on lumbering along, their great heads swaying as Vendela's stick swishes through the air. Occasionally the blows make them give a little skip or two along the gravel track. The cow bells lose their rhythm, then they settle back to their normal, lumbering gait.

The lumbering along, the swaying heads, the brown eyes with their indifferent expression – Vendela regards all this as part of the daily struggle. Rosa, Rosa and Rosa try to show her that she is of no significance, but they are wrong.

Last summer Henry gave her responsibility for the henhouse as well, and she thought she would start hitting the hens and chickens too, or at least kicking out at them when they got in her way. But the cockerel went mad when she tried. He crowed and flapped his wings and stabbed at Vendela with his beak, chasing her out of the henhouse and halfway across the farmyard.

She wept and screamed for help, but she had to look after herself. Henry was down in the quarry, the Invalid was in his room, and of course her mother, Kristin, was gone.

Henry no longer talks about his late wife, and Vendela barely remembers her – not her face, not even her perfume. All that remains is a gravestone in the churchyard at Marnäs, an oval photograph of her that hangs in the kitchen, and a box of jewellery in Henry's bedroom.

There is an ache inside Vendela's body too, but that is probably just a result of all the times she has raised the arm holding the stick.

Since her mother died, Henry always seems to be on the way out, both mentally and physically. In the mornings he sings on the steps as he sets off for the quarry; in the evenings he often stands gazing up at the stars.

He leaves most of the work on the farm to Vendela. She has to do the cleaning, and she washes her own clothes so that she doesn't smell of cows when she's at school. She has to carry food between the earth cellar and the kitchen, because they can't afford electricity and a fridge. She grows potatoes, French beans and sugar beet. And she milks the Rosas and drives them back and forth along the track.

Every single day she walks along behind them, back and forth, before and after her lessons at the village school down in Stenvik. But before that she has another job to do: she has to go upstairs and give the Invalid his food.

That's the worst job of all.

Vendela doesn't remember exactly when the Invalid came to the house, just that it was an evening in late autumn when she was six or seven years old and Henry could still afford to run a car. He had been pacing up and down in the kitchen all afternoon, then suddenly he went out and drove off, without any explanation. Vendela went and lay down in her little room behind the kitchen.

Several hours later she heard the car coming back. It drove right up to the steps in the darkness and stopped. The front doors opened, first one, then the other. Vendela lay in bed listening as her father helped someone out, *carried* someone out of the car, marching up the front steps in his boots, opening the door and stomping upstairs with something heavy in his arms.

He was up there for quite a while, and Vendela could hear him talking quietly to someone. And she heard someone laughing.

Then he came back down and went out to the car again. He struggled with something large in the boot, and eventually managed to get it out and bring it into the kitchen. Vendela could hear squeaking noises, like some kind of heavy machinery.

She got out of bed, opened the door and peeped out. Her father was pushing a wheelchair across the kitchen floor. He had a blanket over his arm, and there was a transistor radio on the seat of the wheelchair.

He set off up the stairs, pulling the chair behind him. After a couple of steps he stopped to rest, and met Vendela's gaze.

He looked embarrassed, as if he had been caught out, and mumbled something.

Vendela took a step towards him. 'What did you say, Dad?'

Her father looked at her and sighed. 'He couldn't stay in that place,' he said. 'They tied them down with leather straps.'

That was the only explanation he gave. He doesn't tell her who this relative is, this person he has brought to the farm.

And Vendela dare not ask. It doesn't matter, because from now on Henry refers to the new resident upstairs only as the Invalid. Most of the time he doesn't even say that, he simply nods up at the ceiling or rolls his eyes. But that first evening, when Vendela heard muted laughter from upstairs and glanced at the ceiling, her expression fearful, he asked her a question across the kitchen table: 'Would you like to come up and say hello?'

Vendela quickly shook her head.

The new duties quickly become routine; there is no need to spell them out. Vendela has to look after the Invalid, just as she looks after the cows, but the difference is that the Invalid never shows himself. The door of his room upstairs remains closed at all times, but the sound of music and news bulletins on the radio can be heard through it from morning to night. She sometimes wonders if the Invalid has locked himself in, but she is never brave enough to reach out and check.

All she does before she sets off for school each morning is to walk slowly up the dark staircase with his breakfast tray and place it on the little coffee table outside the door.

Always knock when you bring the food, Henry said.

Vendela knocks, but never waits for an answer. She hurries back down the stairs.

It takes time for the door to open. Vendela has often managed to put on her outdoor shoes by the time the hinges up above her begin to squeak. Sometimes she remains standing in the porch, holding her breath; she hears the door open, followed by the sound of heavy breathing as the Invalid emerges from his room. Then comes the clink of china as the tray is picked up.

At that moment Vendela is always afraid that something will go wrong up there, that she will hear a crash as the tray lands on the floor. Then she would have to go upstairs and help.

The crash never comes, but with each passing day during those first months with the Invalid, Vendela grows more and more afraid that the door to his room

120

will be open one day when she gets home. Wide open.

But it doesn't happen; every afternoon, once the cows are in, she comes home and finds the empty tray back on the table. There is usually a chamber pot there too, which she has to empty.

From the room behind the door she hears the sound of quiet laughter.

Henry has few friends, and there are only two regular visitors to the farm each year: two days before Christmas, Aunt Margit and Uncle Sven arrive from Kalmar in their big car, the boot filled with food and presents. Vendela and Henry have cleaned and scrubbed the kitchen and put a fresh cloth on the table, but that's about it when it comes to housework.

Henry makes coffee and tries to make small talk, then he and his sister go upstairs to see the Invalid, Aunt Margit carrying a number of small, wrapped packages.

Vendela stays at the kitchen table and hears them open the door of his room, then close it. Aunt Margit's voice sounds shriller and more spirited than ever as she talks to the Invalid and wishes him Merry Christmas.

Vendela doesn't hear any response.

The door is open only once when Vendela walks past, a few months after the Invalid moved in. It is standing ajar. She slows down, stops and cranes her neck to look inside. It is dark, but she is aware of a sour, closed-in smell, and she can see a cramped room with a bed and a small table. And an old blanket on the floor.

Someone is sitting on the blanket: a thin, shrunken person with uncombed grey or white hair sticking out in all directions. The figure is sitting there motionless, in a stooping position. Suddenly the shadow straightens up. It turns its head towards her and opens its mouth. And it begins to giggle.

Vendela hurries quickly past the room, as if the Invalid does not exist. She dashes down the stairs and straight out on to the grass.

She understands why the Invalid closes the door – of course you can't let people see you when you are so old, and so ill. But still. Spending all your time in a room upstairs, never coming out into the sunlight? She can't imagine what that would be like.

The winter passes and it is March, and the snow is melting out on the alvar. For a few weeks big pools form on the yellow grass, spring lakes, and when school is over and the cows have been shut in, Vendela sometimes sets off to explore. She sees the water reflecting the clouds in the vast, open sky, and she feels free, far away from the farm.

One sunny afternoon on the alvar she suddenly sees a large, unusual object among the juniper bushes on the horizon. It is a block of stone. It looks like an altar, leaning slightly to one side, and it is perhaps two or three kilometres from the farm. It is tall and wide, and it can be seen from some distance away. The juniper bushes stand in a circle around the stone, but seem to be keeping their distance.

Vendela doesn't actually go up to it, because she is further out on the alvar than ever and is afraid of getting lost among the spring lakes. She turns around and runs home.

Spring passes and the school year ends, and Vendela doesn't go back to the isolated stone out on the alvar. But one summer evening she mentions it to her father and asks if he has ever seen it.

'The elf stone?' Henry is sitting at the kitchen table polishing a round lamp stand. He has carved it from a piece of limestone, and as his emery cloth moves across the surface, it shines like polished marble. 'The one on the way to Marnäs? Is that the one you mean?'

Vendela nods.

The elf stone. Now she knows what it's called.

'It's from the Ice Age,' says Henry. 'It's always been there. And people have always gone there to leave offerings.'

'Who for?'

'For the elves,' says Henry. 'It's called the elf mill. Back in the old days, people believed the hollows in the stone were formed when the elves milled their grain to make flour. But these days, people go there to ask for things . . . you leave a gift for the elves and make a wish.'

'What do you wish for?'

'Anything you like. If you've lost something you can ask the elves to help you find it . . .' Henry says, glancing out of the window towards the barn, '. . . or maybe you can ask for a bit more good fortune in life.'

'Have you ever done it, Dad?'

'Done what?'

'Have you ever left a gift for the elves?'

Henry shakes his head and carries on polishing the limestone. 'You shouldn't wish for things you don't deserve.'

16

Vendela weighed the cow stick in her hand. Was it really the same one? It looked shorter now than when she was little, but it was still unpleasantly long. She thought she could hear the faint sound of cow bells in the distance.

Go, go, go!

After forty years she can still remember the swishing sound of the stick, but not why she had hit the cows so hard. Was she a sadistic child?

She put the stick back in the shed and walked through the empty garden, in amongst the trees next to the house.

A narrow path led to an open space. Now she was standing in the pasture where the cows used to graze in the summer, but it was no longer a meadow; it was overgrown with tangled bushes. There were no cowpats in the grass. No cows had grazed here for many years.

Rosa, Rosa and Rosa, she thought, and started to run.

The alvar began beyond the stone wall on the other side of the pasture. It had been almost completely devoid of trees and bushes when Vendela was little, but now she could see low-growing birches and spindly hawthorns in front of her. The bushes were in the way, but she managed to maintain as straight a line as possible as she moved across the flat ground.

When she could no longer see the farm behind her, she focused on a bush straight ahead and kept on running, increasing her speed. The sun would not remain in the sky for more than a couple of hours now, and she had no wish to be out on the alvar in the dark.

Ten minutes later she was out in the wilds – the distance seemed shorter than in her childhood. A couple of hundred metres ahead of her she could see a tall, dense group of juniper bushes and slowed her pace. Her legs were shaking; she inhaled the cold air and concentrated. Then she made her way through the thicket and stopped in the little glade inside. Any visitor was completely hidden from view in here.

The stone was still there.

It was rough and unpolished, just as she remembered from childhood.

It's all about being in the right place at the right time, she thought.

She moved slowly closer to the rectangular stone. It was solid, sunken firmly in the ground.

The elf mill, where the elves once milled their grain in the twilight. The gateway to their kingdom.

The stone seemed a little smaller now; perhaps it had sunk further down over the past forty years. But it was probably just that Vendela had grown up.

There were things in the hollows.

No, not things, money. Old coins.

Made of bronze or gold? She wasn't brave enough to pick them up and take a closer look, but now she knew that other islanders believed in the power of the elves too.

She remained a few feet away from the stone, listening. The wind soughed in the trees, and far away she could hear the faint roar of traffic from the main road.

But there were no rustling noises. No footsteps.

Vendela walked up and placed her hand on the stone. It was just as cool as she remembered, even though the sun was shining.

She lay down behind the elf stone, where it was less windy. The ground was cold but not damp, and she closed her eyes. She could feel the big stone beside her, emanating solidity and a protective sense of calm.

When Vendela was thirty she had travelled to Iceland, where people still believed in elves. She had met elderly people who said they had seen them, and had accompanied a group of tourists up to Snaefjellsjökull, the glacier north of Reykjavik where the elves evidently appeared from time to time. She had spent one bitterly cold night sitting waiting in a cave by the glacier, but she hadn't seen them.

Five years earlier she had seen an advertisement in a magazine about a course on the island of Gotland, where you could learn to see and communicate with elves. Vendela secretly booked a place on the course, and flew to Visby one sunny Friday at the beginning of May. (She told Max she was going to do a pottery course.)

The course leader was about thirty, and had long brown hair in a pony tail. His name was Adam Luft, and he lived in a crofter's cottage south-west of Visby; the area was flat, but with plenty of trees, and several elf paths met there. Adam did not cut the grass around his house, because he said it was important to leave nature untouched as far as possible.

'The paths often lead between hazel or juniper bushes,' he said. 'That's where we find the gateways into their world.'

Adam could sit cross-legged talking about elves for

126

hours on end. He was particularly interested in their private lives, which according to him were free and open. Vendela wasn't quite so sure about that, and sometimes when he talked about sex between elves and people, she had the feeling it was more a case of wishful thinking on Adam's part – but when he left that particular topic alone, he often said sensible things. Such as: 'It's important to embrace new ways of thinking. When the Europeans first came into contact with white tufts of cotton during the Middle Ages, they had no idea what kind of material it was, or where it came from. They guessed that the cotton came from small flying sheep and lambs, who built their nests up in the trees.'

Adam had paused to let his students finish laughing.

'So when today's scientists hear that people have met elves,' he went on, hands outspread, 'what are they to think? How do they interpret this information? Just like almost everyone else, the scientists are helpless when faced with the inexplicable.'

Adam told her so much about elves. For Vendela the weekend course had been a fantastic experience. The little group had gone for long walks in the spring countryside, and had sat down to sing to the elves when the sun went down. After a while, several of the participants said they began to see them. One of the youngest, a twenty-year-old girl from Stockholm who also worked as a medium, saw elves so frequently and so clearly that she started to recognize them and gave them beautiful names, such as Galadriel and Dunsany.

Vendela was slightly envious, because she never saw any elves, but the course was still brilliant. The land-scape on Gotland seemed timeless and tranquil, just like Iceland. She had returned home with a new-found belief in elves, and a powerful desire to find them on

Öland, the island of her childhood. And now here she sat by the elf stone. Nobody knew where she was. Out here the rest of the world was of no importance.

Adam Luft had said it was easier to see the elves if you had faith but lacked hope. Then you were ready for them. And you could only glimpse them out of the corner of your eye. Elves didn't like it if you stared straight at them, according to Adam; they couldn't cope with our intense scrutiny.

The countryside had suddenly grown still around her; not a twig was moving on the juniper bushes around the stone. Vendela slowly opened her eyes and thought that the alvar, with its vernal yellow grass, looked frozen, faded like an old photograph. If she looked at her watch now, she knew the hands would be standing still.

The kingdom of the elves.

She suddenly heard a rustling sound in the grass beyond the bushes, as if someone was moving along, light as a feather. She got up cautiously, but saw no one. And yet she still had the feeling that someone was watching her through the bushes.

Her tracksuit was damp, and she shivered. All her energy was gone, chased away by a sudden sense of anxiety. She wanted to go up to the dense thicket of bushes and look on the other side, perhaps ask if anyone was there, but she remained standing by the stone.

They're creeping up on me, she thought. *The elves . . . or the trolls?*

She didn't dare go over and look. Her legs were taking her in the opposite direction; she moved backwards around the elf stone so that it was between her and the muted noises.

Then everything fell silent once more. The rustling stopped.

The wind began to blow, and Vendela breathed out.

She felt stiff and cold, but had one thing left to do. She rummaged in her jacket pocket and placed a coin, a shiny new ten-kronor piece, in one of the empty hollows on the stone.

It was risky to wish for things in this place; nobody knew that better than her. But she needed help.

She was going to ask for one thing, no more.

Please don't let Aloysius go blind, she thought. *Give him a few more healthy years . . . That's all I wanted to ask.*

She put the coin down and backed away from the stone.

As she left the glade tucked away among the juniper bushes, she felt time begin to move once more. Her watch was ticking, and it was evening. The sun in the west had lost its yellow glow and was sinking down towards the horizon, the light reflected as red stripes in the spring lakes around her.

17

'Pelle?' Jerry asked, waking up in confusion. 'Pelle?'

As they left Växjö after being interviewed by the police, his father had fallen asleep. He had slept deeply, mumbling inaudible words, then woken up as they drove into a deserted Kalmar. Per had parked next to the hospital entrance.

'Pelle?'

'Everything's all right, Jerry. We're in Kalmar.'

He opened the car door. Fresh evening air poured into the car, soothing his lungs. He coughed and turned around. 'You stay here . . . I'm just going up to see Nilla. My daughter – do you remember her, Jerry?'

When he saw his father looking at the hospital signs, he went on: 'She's just in for some tests. I won't be long.'

It was half past ten, and every window in the hospital was glowing against the dark sky. Per's legs were stiff as he got out of the car; he'd been sitting in the same seat for most of the day.

The main entrance was still unlocked, and the glass doors opened silently. He took the lift up to Nilla's ward without meeting a soul.

The corridor was also deserted, and the door to the ward was closed. He rang the bell and was admitted by a night nurse. She didn't smile at him, but perhaps she was just tired. It didn't necessarily mean that Nilla's condition had worsened.

The door to her room was ajar, and he could hear two voices inside: Nilla talking to her mother.

Per coughed one last time. He had hoped that Marika wouldn't be there. He knew, of course, that his ex-wife spent every evening with Nilla, but with a bit of luck she might have been somewhere else when he arrived. For a couple of seconds he considered walking away, then he pushed the door open.

Nilla was sitting up in bed with a pillow behind her back. She was wearing a white hospital gown, and a drip had been inserted in her arm. She looked just the same as when he had left her; a little paler, perhaps.

Marika was sitting on a chair next to the bed. The television up on the wall in one corner of the room was switched on, showing a man and a woman screaming and waving their arms at one another in a kitchen, but the sound was turned down.

'Hello, you two,' said Per, smiling at mother and daughter.

The conversation had stopped when he came in. It seemed as if Marika had just been joking with Nilla, because she was smiling at her, but the smile died away as soon as she saw Per. It was as if her mask slipped, and she looked very tired.

'Hi Dad.' Then Nilla sniffed, her expression surprised. 'You smell of smoke!'

'Do I? Really?'

Per's smile was tense, and he was trying not to cough again. He couldn't come up with anything sensible to say.

'What's happened, Per?' said Marika. 'Are you hurt?'

'No, I'm fine . . . There was a house fire in Småland. I

131

saw it from the car, so I called the fire brigade. And they came and put it out.'

'Was there anyone in the house?' said Nilla.

'There was nobody living there,' said Per, and quickly went on, 'So how are you two, anyway?'

'We're waiting for the evening rounds,' said Nilla. 'And we're watching TV.'

'Good.'

Marika got up. 'I'll go out, then you two can have a chat.'

'There's no need,' said Per, 'I was just going to . . .'

'It's OK, I'll go.'

She walked past him with her eyes lowered and disappeared into the corridor.

Father and daughter looked at one another, and Per realized he should have turned up with something other than smoke-damaged clothes. Chocolate maybe, or a CD.

'Has Mum been here all the time?'

'She's here during the day, but not when she's sleeping.' She looked at him. 'I'll be going home soon. Won't I?'

Per nodded. 'I'll come and pick you up on Wednesday,' he said. 'Then we can celebrate Easter on Öland with loads of eggs. Boiled eggs and chocolate eggs.'

Nilla looked pleased. 'Chocolate eggs would be good.'

Per went over and gave her a hug, rubbing his cheek on her forehead. It was cool. 'See you soon.'

As he left the room he realized how stiff his smile had been.

Marika was standing down the corridor a little way off as he gently closed the door. She crossed her arms as he walked towards her, and he stopped three steps away.

'She seems to be feeling pretty good,' he said.

132

Marika nodded. 'Is Jesper still on Öland?'

'Yes.'

Per had no intention of going into what had happened during the day, or of mentioning that he had gone to help his father and had brought him back with him. Particularly the latter; Marika wasn't fond of her ex-father-in-law.

'I'll be back on Wednesday,' was all he said. 'When's the doctor due?'

'I don't know . . . Before lunch, I think.'

'I'll be here then.'

'Georg is coming too,' said Marika quietly. 'Is that OK?'

'Of course,' said Per, adding a lie: 'That'll be nice, I like Georg.'

Jerry had got out of the car when Per reached the car park. He was standing with his briefcase under his arm and a cigarette in his right hand. How could he smoke tonight?

'Don't light that,' said Per, 'we're going now.'

He opened the car door and got in. All Jerry could do was put the cigarette away and get in beside him. He was coughing.

Jerry didn't breathe, he wheezed. Since the fire it was worse than ever, but he had always coughed and wheezed. Wrecked lungs and too many cigarettes made him sound more and more like a leaking balloon.

His father had abused his body all his life, thought Per as he drove away from the hospital. But it was Nilla who got sick.

Per pulled up in front of the cottage at half past eleven on Monday night. Casa Mörner was in almost complete darkness; Jesper had switched on only a couple of lights in the hallway and the kitchen.

'Home?' said Jerry, looking around.

'Yes, this is home now,' said Per, looking over at the cottage. 'This is where Anita and I used to come in the summer, Jerry, after you left her. Mum couldn't afford to take us on a proper holiday for a good few years after that. You must know that, surely?'

Jerry shook his head, but his eyes had narrowed. Per knew he had recognized his ex-wife's name, at least.

He turned off the engine and sighed to himself in the silence. He was very tired, but there was one last meeting to get through this evening. He carried Jerry's old briefcase into the cottage, and his father followed slowly behind.

'Hello?' Per shouted as he walked into the hallway. 'Jesper?'

The door to his son's room was open; Jesper was sitting up in bed, absorbed in his Gameboy.

'What?'

'Turn that off now. Come and say hello to your grandfather.'

Per sniffed the air. Did his clothes still smell of smoke?

Jesper showed no sign of noticing. He simply got out of bed and walked slowly into the hallway. Per could understand his hesitation; Jerry hadn't seen his grandchildren for almost ten years. He had never shown any interest in meeting them, and Per hadn't gone out of his way to arrange it.

'Hi, Granddad,' said Jesper, holding out his hand.

Jerry seemed slightly hesitant, then he shook the boy's hand. 'Jesper,' he said quietly. He let go of his grandson's hand and looked around.

'Would you like a drink?' said Per.

Jerry nodded quickly, so Per went into the kitchen and poured him a glass of milk.

When he had settled Jerry in an armchair in front of the television, he went outside to get a last dose of clean air into his lungs. He went over to the edge of the quarry – and stopped dead.

A half-moon was shining over the Sound and the quarry was full of shadows, but Per could still see that the flight of steps he and Jesper had built didn't look right. The blocks of stone near the top had gone.

He fetched a torch and shone it down over the steps.

He was right – the wide blocks had collapsed. A couple had crashed into one another in the fall, and were smashed to pieces.

But the steps had felt perfectly stable yesterday. Who had destroyed them?

18

On the Tuesday of Easter week Gerlof had two new visitors – a father and son who didn't appear to like each other.

After warming up his lunch and eating it, he settled down in his chair out in the garden to read the newspaper and listen to the birds, waiting peacefully for the evening.

Then he caught sight of a grey-haired man in a crumpled coat, walking along the road with a cigarette dangling from the corner of his mouth. A young man, at least compared with Gerlof, though he might have been in his seventies; he didn't look all that well.

The man appeared to be lost. First of all he stood by the gate for a little while, smoking his cigarette and looking around, then he opened it and walked in. He stood on the lawn looking around, as if he couldn't remember where he was or how he had got there. His left arm was dangling straight down from the shoulder; it looked paralysed.

Gerlof stayed where he was, without saying anything. He wasn't particularly keen on having any visitors apart from the home-care service today.

However, the man eventually walked up to the lawn

in front of the house. He carried on staring around him in a slightly odd way, before suffering a violent coughing fit and stubbing the cigarette out on the grass. Then he stared straight at Gerlof and said, 'Jerry Morner.'

His voice was hoarse and rough, and he had a Skåne accent. It sounded hardened and experienced.

'I see,' said Gerlof.

The man took two steps closer and sat down heavily on the other chair.

'Jerry,' he repeated.

'In that case, we have similar names. I'm Gerlof.'

Jerry took out a fresh cigarette, but merely held it in his hand, staring at it. Gerlof noticed that oddly enough the man had two watches on his left wrist, one gold and one stainless steel. Only one of them was showing Swedish time.

'Is everything all right?' asked Gerlof.

The man looked at him open-mouthed, as if the question was too complicated.

'Jerry,' he said eventually.

'I understand.'

Gerlof realized that the man in front of him was lost in more ways than one, and asked no more questions. Silence fell in the garden, but Jerry seemed happy in his chair.

'Do you have a job?' asked Gerlof.

There was no reply, so he went on: 'I'm a pensioner myself. I've done my bit.'

'Jerry and Bremer,' said Jerry.

Gerlof had no idea what he was talking about, but Jerry smiled contentedly and lit his cigarette with a lighter adorned with the American flag.

'Jerry and Bremer?' said Gerlof.

The man coughed again, without answering Gerlof's question. 'Pelle,' he said.

'Pelle?'

Jerry nodded.

'I see,' said Gerlof.

Silence.

'Jerry!'

They heard a shout from the road. A youngish man was standing there; he owned one of the houses over by the quarry.

Was this the son? He opened Gerlof's garden gate and walked in. 'Jerry . . . I've been looking for you.'

Jerry didn't move at first, as if he didn't recognize the man who had shouted to him. Then he straightened his back. 'Pelle,' he said again.

'You need to tell me where you're going, Jerry,' said the younger man.

'Bremer,' said Jerry, getting to his feet. He looked anxious. 'Bremer and Markus Lukas . . .'

He set off towards the gate. The younger man lingered and nodded to Gerlof, who suddenly realized he had met him before, many years ago.

'You're related to Ernst Adolfsson, aren't you?' he said. 'Per . . . ?'

'Per Mörner.'

'That's it, I remember now,' said Gerlof. 'You used to stay with Ernst sometimes when you were little.'

'Me and my mother,' said the man. 'We stayed with him quite often. Were you and he friends?'

'We certainly were. My name is Gerlof.' He nodded towards Jerry. 'Is that your father?'

'Jerry? That's right.'

'He doesn't talk much.'

'No, he finds speech difficult. He had a stroke last year.'

'I see. And why does he wear two watches on one arm?'

'You might well ask,' said Per, looking away. 'One shows American time . . . Jerry's always been fond of the USA.'

'So who are Bremer and Markus Lukas, then?'

'Has he been talking about them?' Per glanced over at his father and went on, 'Hans Bremer was his work partner. And Markus Lukas . . . I don't really know.' He stopped. 'I'd better get him home.'

He set off, but stopped when Gerlof asked, 'So will you be living here now?'

Per nodded. 'Well, I will anyway . . . along with my children. I inherited Ernst's cottage last year.'

'Good. Look after it.'

Per nodded again and caught up with his father, who had stopped by the gate. 'Come on, Jerry.'

Gerlof watched them disappear behind the stone wall, a father and his son who were definitely a little bit tired of each other.

It was strange, this business of people and their children. They were close to each other, but the relationship was often strained.

The older man reminded Gerlof of some of the more senile residents in the home at Marnäs; it was just as impossible to conduct a conversation with them over coffee as it would be with someone who was roaring drunk. They lived mostly within their own memories, making only brief visits to the real world. But from time to time they came out with unexpected things. Ideas, stories, sometimes shameless confessions.

Two expensive watches on one arm . . . He wondered how Jerry Morner had made his money.

19

When Per was little he had enjoyed watching the sun go down over Kalmar Sound, and on Tuesday evening he stood by the window for a while. He had settled Jerry in front of the TV, and shortly he would ring Nilla to arrange a time to pick her up, but first he wanted to see the sunset.

It was just after eight. The sun had lost its heat much earlier in the evening, but it was still dazzling as it hovered just above the water line in the west, bright and golden. It was only when it had slipped halfway below the horizon that it lost its glow, staining the clouds dotted over the mainland dark red, like blood-filled arteries.

Then all of a sudden it was gone. The sky in the west continued to glow, as if a fierce fire were burning beneath it, but the darkness quickly moved in across the shore and the quarry.

Per leant closer to the window and studied the compact shadows down there. He thought about the steps that had been destroyed. Perhaps it was his imagination, but he thought some of the shadows might be creeping and crawling around the piles of reject stone.

The police had not been in touch since the initial interview, and Per hadn't called them. On Wednesday morning he drove into Kalmar to collect Nilla. In the hospital cafeteria he came across an evening paper from the previous day. He flicked through it quickly, and found a short news item:

MAN MISSING AFTER HOUSE FIRE

A man is missing after a devastating fire which started on Sunday evening in a large house in the forest outside the village of Ryd, sixty kilometres south of Växjö.

When the police and fire brigade were called to the scene at approximately 18.00, the wooden house was already burning fiercely, and the fire-fighters concentrated on ensuring that the fire did not spread. The damping-down operation continued until midnight.

The house was completely destroyed, and as we went to press it was unclear whether anyone had lost their life in the blaze. The owner of the property managed to escape and has been questioned by the police, but was unable to shed any light on the cause of the fire.

A witness has stated that at least one person was seen inside the burning house. An employee of the owner, who used the house as an office and for overnight accommodation, is still missing, and the police fear that he could have perished in the blaze.

Forensic technicians will be examining the remains of the property as soon as possible in order to clarify whether anyone could have been inside, and to establish the cause of the fire.

Per closed the paper. 'The owner of the property', that was his father, and 'the missing employee' must have been Hans Bremer. Per himself was only 'a witness', which made him feel better. If and when the press found out that it was Jerry Morner who owned the house, they might well write more.

There were no answers yet, but they would no doubt come in time.

He headed for the lift.

Nilla had put on her outdoor clothes and was waiting for him in the day room. She had brushed her hair and was smiling at him, but she looked even thinner than before. Her shoulders felt narrow and bony when he gave her a hug.

'Did it go OK?'

She nodded. 'They said they've finished now. Mum went to talk to the doctor this morning, before she left.'

'Good, I'll give her a ring. Shall we make a move, then? Jesper is waiting for you at the cottage, and Jerry's there too.'

'Jerry?'

'Yes, Jerry . . . your grandfather.'

Nilla blinked. 'Why?'

'He's going to celebrate Easter with us.'

Nilla nodded, and didn't ask any more questions. 'I need to bring that with me,' she said. 'Have we got room?' A folded wheelchair was leaning against the wall further down the corridor.

Per looked at it. The wheelchair made him go cold – why did Nilla need it right now? He wanted to ask someone, but there was no sign of a doctor.

'Of course,' he said. 'I'm sure we can fit it in the boot.'

*

142

They reached the quarry about an hour later.

'Do you remember the cottage?' said Per as he pulled up.

Nilla nodded. 'You said you were going to paint it last summer . . . Have you done it?'

'I didn't get round to it.'

'And what about the repairs?'

'When I get time,' Per said quickly. 'And we're going to build a flight of stone steps too. But tonight we're going to a party.'

'What kind of party?'

'A get-together with the neighbours.'

Per got out of the car to avoid further questions. Then he helped Nilla out on to the gravel, and over to the door.

'I can walk by myself,' she said, but she clung to his arm as they moved into the hallway and then on to a small bedroom.

'This is your room,' he said. 'It's nice and clean, and I've aired it for you.'

Nilla sat down cautiously on the bed, and Per went to fetch her luggage and the wheelchair.

Jesper was on the computer in his room, but Per couldn't find Jerry.

He went out on to the patio in the sunshine. His father was slumped in one of the chairs, with a sunhat tipped down over his forehead and his eyes closed. His briefcase was lying at his feet like an old brown dog.

'Hi Jerry.' Per sat down in front of him and placed the newspaper on his knee. 'Read this.'

But Jerry wasn't looking down at the paper, he was looking at something over Per's shoulder.

Per turned and saw Nilla standing in the doorway. Her arms were dangling wearily by her sides, but she was smiling at Jerry. 'Hi Granddad,' she said. 'How are you?'

Jerry just nodded. He raised a hand slowly in her direction, and cleared his throat. 'Hi,' he said.

Per was holding his breath. His first instinct was to protect his daughter from Jerry in some way, but that was hardly necessary.

'Granddad doesn't say much,' he said to Nilla. 'I'll be in soon . . . we'll have something to eat.'

Nilla nodded and went back inside.

Per leant forward and pointed to the newspaper article. 'Jerry, it seems as if Hans Bremer was in the house. He's still missing, according to the police.'

His father was listening, but there was no reaction. 'Bremer,' was all he said. Then he pulled up his shirt to reveal the large plaster on his stomach.

Per didn't need to look, he just shook his head. 'Jerry, why would Bremer want to harm you?'

Jerry's mouth worked as he struggled to find the word, and at last it came. 'Frightened.'

Per nodded. He didn't want to leave his father, but he was wondering if it was a good idea to take him over to the neighbours' party.

20

Party time. Other people might have neighbourhood disputes, but the families around the quarry were going to have a neighbourhood party, thanks to Vendela Larsson. There was no need to thank her, but without her it wouldn't be happening.

At six o'clock she was out on the veranda setting the long festive table with wine glasses and plates. Over in the west, above Kalmar Sound, the sun glowed in shades of red and gold, like a dying fire. In a couple of hours it would be gone. Vendela knew it would be a chilly evening on the veranda, and decided to bring out some thick blankets so that everybody could wrap up warm. And of course they could always turn on the halogen heating.

Max had emerged from his study at the end of his working day, wearing his dressing gown and heading for the sauna. He crossed the stone floor in the main living room quickly on his bare feet, but stopped in the doorway.

'How did it go?' she asked.

'Pretty well,' said Max. 'I've almost finished the beginning . . . you can have a look at it soon.'

'No problem,' said Vendela, who had actually written

the outline for the introduction and given it to him the previous evening.

'And after that it's mostly recipes and pictures,' said Max. 'I'm sure we can get it done.'

He was always more amenable when he'd been able to spend a few hours in peace at his desk, particularly when he could have a sauna afterwards.

'Not too hot, Max,' she shouted as he went into the sauna. 'Think about your heart!'

Vendela had spent most of the day in the kitchen. There was an assortment of quiches warming in the oven, and the table was ready.

By half past six everything was done. Max was out of the sauna and dressed, and she had managed to get him to carry all the chairs out on to the veranda, and to light the lanterns and candles on the table. Then she had sent him off to fetch the old sea captain from across the road.

He came back after quarter of an hour with Gerlof Davidsson in a wheelchair. Gerlof was wearing a smoking jacket – the fabric was shiny, and it looked at least fifty years old. John Hagman was walking beside him, dressed in a black suit with brown protective patches on the elbows.

Max pushed the wheelchair along the path, but when Vendela opened the door, Gerlof got up slowly and walked in, his back straight. When he stood up he was almost a head taller than Max, Vendela noticed.

'I can walk. Now and again,' said Gerlof. Then he handed Vendela a small package. 'For you – I made it myself this morning.'

'Oh, thank you!'

Vendela opened the package and was struck by the acrid smell of tar. Inside was a piece of brown rope-work, cleverly knotted to form a small mat.

'It's a Turk's head knot,' said Gerlof. 'It will bring happiness and good fortune to your home.'

The smell of tar made Vendela feel slightly dizzy, almost as if she'd taken some kind of strong medication, but she smiled at Gerlof.

The other neighbours were quite punctual. The Kurdins, who were an attractive couple, arrived first, with their baby fast asleep in his pram. Christer smiled at Vendela and said they had a beautiful house; he seemed a little more friendly than his tall, ice-cold wife, who was wearing a dark-grey linen dress. Marie Kurdin merely nodded briefly at her hostess, then marched in with her chin in the air.

The Mörner family arrived five minutes later: Per, the father, with his teenage twins. Nilla was holding on to her brother Jesper's arm. She was small and pale, and took very small steps. Vendela smiled, but she was concerned; was the girl anorexic?

When Per Mörner held out his hand to Max, Vendela saw her husband stiffen. They hadn't met since the encounter in the car park on Friday. Neither of the men smiled.

'OK?' said Per.

'Sure,' said Max, quickly shaking hands with him and nodding at the son, to show that everything was fine.

The Mörners had a fourth person with them, someone Vendela hadn't seen before: a stooping, elderly man with grey, slicked-back hair. He stumbled as he crossed the threshold, and Per Mörner quickly grabbed hold of him. Then he nodded to their hosts.'This is my father, Jerry Morner.'

Jerry's tired eyes stared dully at Vendela's body as he shook hands; he didn't say a word, and didn't really seem to be with them. Under the other arm he was clutching an old briefcase.

Then he shuffled straight through the hall and out on to the newly cleaned floor, without removing either his shoes or coat. Vendela bit her tongue and said nothing. She hurried into the kitchen to fetch the last of the quiches.

Max went over to the drinks table in front of the picture window and offered his guests whisky, dry Martini or fruit juice.

The conversation between hosts and guests slowly but surely got under way, mostly involving comparisons between the various houses. The men did most of the talking, particularly Max and Christer Kurdin, who were keen to compare their newly built houses. Both wanted to have the last word, and Vendela listened to their interweaving voices:

'Well, yes, I can see you've gone for a lot of glass, but I think you'll find our stone walls will be cooler in summer . . .'

'A basement? Well, of course that increases your surface area . . .'

'Formica has had its day, it's well out of date now . . .'

'Harmonious proportions are important, not only the design . . .'

After ten or fifteen minutes Vendela brought out the last of the food, and Max encouraged all their guests to move out on to the veranda. In the west the sun was hovering just above the black line of the horizon, like a painting in red and yellow. The sea was dark blue and shining.

Max switched on the halogen heating and the metal tubes suspended around the veranda began to glow faintly. The cold evening air was soon almost as warm as in summer.

'Is everyone here?' he said, looking around.

'I think so,' said Vendela.

Max nodded, tapped his wine glass and raised his voice. 'Sit down, everyone! Anywhere you like!'

The murmur of conversation died away, everyone made their way to the table and Max smiled at them.

Vendela could see that he had slipped into the role of party host, like a real entertainer. He loved the role; it was his confidence when he was the centre of attention that had made her fall for him, once upon a time.

'Welcome, everyone.' Max raised his glass and went on: 'My dear wife and I have spent all day in the kitchen, and many of the recipes are taken from my new cookery book . . . so we hope you enjoy what we have to offer!'

21

Gerlof had decided to keep his distance from the new neighbours, but after a couple of glasses of whisky, it was actually rather pleasant on their big wooden veranda.

They had brought out a leather armchair and settled him at one end of the table like a patriarch. Vendela Larsson, their little hostess, had placed a blanket over his legs and he didn't need to reach for anything – everyone kept passing him food and drink. He leant back comfortably, sitting next to John on the oiled decking.

Two large glasses of whisky were actually one too many for him, and he hoped someone would offer to push him home in the wheelchair – and preferably not too late. It was already half past eight and the drink was starting to make him feel sleepy, but nobody seemed to be in any hurry to finish eating. They hadn't even got to the pudding.

'So, Gerlof . . . did you and John work with the stone down here?' asked Per Mörner, nodding in the direction of the dark quarry.

'Only in the summer when we were little,' said Gerlof.

'Before we went to sea,' John added.

'Were you quarrymen?' asked Max Larsson.

Gerlof shook his head. 'We weren't strong enough.'

'Really? Was it hard work, then?'

Gerlof didn't say anything. He was wondering whether these families from the mainland realized that the quarry was an old workplace, or whether they saw it only as some kind of artistic creation, built up above the shore for their amusement, with charming piles of stones here and there and little pools of rainwater in which they could bathe.

He knew they would never understand the hard work that had been necessary in order to win the struggle against the rock face, hacking out the limestone day after day with nothing but chisels and hammers and crowbars. His friend Ernst had once said that during his forty years in the quarry he must have hacked out more than fifty thousand metres of kerbstones for flights of steps, roads and pavements in the towns all around the Baltic Sea.

And then there were the gravestones. There had always been a need for gravestones, of course, even when times were hard.

'No, we never became quarrymen.' Gerlof looked at John. 'But we were good errand boys, do you remember that? We fetched tools and cleaned up the kelpie hut, and so on.'

'The kelpie hut?' said Per.

'That's what we called the place where the workers took their breaks.'

It struck Gerlof that he and John might well be the last people in the village who remembered that name. The quarrymen were gone, after all.

Gerlof took a sip of whisky and went on: 'In the old

days people believed that the trolls lived down in the quarry, but I came across quite a different creature when I was little . . .'

He saw John's shoulders slump; he had heard this story many times before. But he carried on anyway.

'When I was eight or nine I found a crane down here, one evening when all the workers had gone home. It was a youngster, lying on the gravel. I don't know where it came from, but it was too small to fly, and there was no sign of its parents. Perhaps the fox had got them . . . So I carried it home to our outhouse and laid it down on some hay, and started feeding it with old potatoes. And when it was big enough I let it out – but it refused to fly away. It had grown attached to me.' Gerlof smiled to himself. 'It followed me around all summer, like a two-legged dog. And if I got tired of it and tried to sneak off, it flew up in the air and circled around over the village until it found me again. So I had a pet crane for a whole summer, until the autumn came and it flew south with the others.'

Everybody around the table smiled at the story.

'And when you went to sea,' said Per, 'was that a full-time job?'

'No, because in the winter the cargo ships froze in the sea down in the harbour, so we couldn't work then,' said Gerlof. 'We came ashore in December and took it easy for a few months, when the sea was covered in ice. We would carry out repairs to our ships, check the engine and mend the sails. For the rest of the time we sat waiting for the spring with the other skippers.' He looked over at the empty quarry. 'But of course they carried on quarrying the limestone all through the winter, piling it up down by the harbour. Thousands of tons. Then in the spring the sun came and melted the ice out in the Sound, and it was time to go to sea again.'

'Out at sea in the spring breeze,' said Marie Kurdin. 'That must have been a fantastic feeling.'

Gerlof shook his head. 'It wasn't quite that romantic.'

'Were there many accidents?' said Per. 'Ships running aground, that sort of thing?'

'Not for us,' replied John. 'We never ran aground.'

'No, not in thirty years,' said Gerlof. 'One of our cargo ships sank in a fire, but we never ran aground . . . But it was hard work being at sea, hard and lonely. I tried to take my wife and daughters along sometimes in the summer holidays, but most of the time John and I were alone on board, day after day. The family had to stay at home.'

He glanced sideways in the direction of the quarry, and thought about his late wife. Obviously he didn't believe in trolls. But who was the visitor Ella had seen when he was away at sea?

22

Vendela had drunk a couple of glasses of wine, and was at last beginning to relax at her own party, when she suddenly heard a loud voice from the other side of the table. It was probably also under the influence of quite a lot of wine, and sounded particularly sure of itself.

'No, I don't pay tax in Sweden,' said Max. 'My company isn't registered here, it would be too expensive . . . Besides, I don't believe in the Swedish tax system. All it does is oppress people.'

Max smiled across the table, but Vendela felt compelled to smooth over the situation. 'Of course you pay tax here, Max.'

He looked at her and stopped smiling. 'When I have to, yes. But as little as possible.'

Then he raised his glass, as if everyone around the table was a member of the same financial club, until an equally loud voice chipped in: 'I'm quite happy to pay tax.'

It was Christer Kurdin.

'Really?' said Max. 'And how do you earn your money?'

'Internet security,' said Kurdin tersely.

He had also drunk a fair amount of wine; there was

an almost empty bottle of white Bordeaux next to his plate, and he was having some difficulty focusing as he looked at Max.

'I'm sick and tired of people like you,' he went on.

'I'm sorry?' said Max.

'People like you who try to get out of paying your taxes . . . I'm sick and tired of all the fiddling.'

Max lowered his glass. 'I don't fidd—'

'I mean, you drive on the roads in Sweden,' Christer Kurdin broke in.

'What?'

'I presume you drove across the Öland Bridge to get here?'

Max frowned. 'What's that got to do with anything?'

'Well, our taxes paid for the bridge,' said Christer. 'And the roads. And everything else we all use. Schools. Hospitals. Pensions . . .'

'Pensions?' said Max. 'As far as I'm concerned, pensions are just a joke in this country. And health care.'

'Health care is no joke,' said a voice further down the table. 'Those who work in the health service do a fantastic job.'

Vendela saw that it was Per Mörner.

'Exactly, we get a good service for our money,' said Christer. He looked at Max and went on: 'Anyway, if everything's so terrible in Sweden, why stay here?'

Max stared in silence at his neighbour, as if he were trying to work out exactly what kind of people he'd ended up with here on the island. 'The summer makes it worth staying,' he said, emptying his glass.

'More wine, anyone?' said Vendela.

Nobody answered, nobody seemed to have heard her, so she drank a little more and listened to the hum of conversation. If she closed her eyes it could almost be music, a series of soloists singing around the table.

155

For a moment she thought she caught a strange smell coming off the alvar, a burnt smell like rubber or sulphur, but it was probably just her imagination. It was dark out there now. It was dark everywhere. Only their veranda was lit up.

Sitting above the quarry this evening was like sitting by the edge of a pitch-black crater. A slumbering volcano.

Suddenly she heard a loud male voice from across the table. 'Do any of you newcomers know northern Öland? Anyone lived here before?'

It was their young neighbour again. Christer Kurdin was holding his wine glass and looking up and down the table, as if he didn't mean any harm with his question. Of course he didn't mean any harm, he just looked curious.

'Vendela comes from this area,' Max said tersely.

Not every conversation died away, but several faces turned towards her. All she could do was nod. 'I used to live here when I was little.'

'Here in the village?' said Marie Kurdin.

'To the north-east . . . We had a little smallholding.'

'That sounds lovely. With cows and geese and cats?'

'Just hens . . . and a few cows,' said Vendela. 'I used to look after them.'

'How lovely,' Marie Kurdin reiterated. 'The children of today ought to get the chance to look after animals in the country too.'

Vendela nodded. She didn't want to think about the three Rosas. Such frustration, such a longing to escape. Where had it come from?

Rosa, Rosa and Rosa had been dead for many, many years. Everyone she had known here on the island was dead.

She took another swig of her wine.

Gerlof Davidsson was sitting motionless on the other side of the table, diagonally opposite her. He was smiling and seemed happy, and Vendela leant a little closer and said quietly, 'My father was a quarryman here, his name was Henry. Did you know him, Gerlof?'

His expression was kind as he looked at her, but he didn't appear to have heard what she said. She raised her voice. 'Did you know Henry Fors, Gerlof?'

He heard her this time. But the name made him stop smiling.

'I did know Henry Fors . . . he was one of the last men working down in the quarry. He was very good at polishing the stone. Were you related?'

'He was my father.'

Gerlof looked grim, or perhaps sorrowful. 'I see. I'm sorry . . .'

Vendela understood what he was talking about, and lowered her eyes. 'It's a long time ago.'

'I used to see Henry coming along on his bike in the mornings,' said Gerlof. 'Sometimes he would be singing so loudly it echoed out across the alvar.'

Vendela nodded. 'He used to sing at home as well.'

'Henry was widowed quite early on, wasn't he?'

She nodded again. 'My mother died just a few years after I was born. I don't remember her . . . but I think my father missed her all his life.'

'Did you ever go with him to the quarry?'

'Only once. He said it was dangerous there – women and children shouldn't be down in the quarry, it brought bad luck.'

'They were a bit superstitious,' said Gerlof. 'They used to see different signs in the stone, and they believed in ghosts and trolls. The trolls in particular used to cause the quarry workers a lot of trouble. They used to steal their hammers and hide them underground, or make them disappear . . . but of course it was easier to blame mythical creatures than their workmates.'

'They used to steal from each other, you mean?'

'No,' said Gerlof, smiling at her. 'I'm sure it was the trolls.'

'Trolls,' said a voice beside them. It was the other old man at the table, Per Mörner's father. Vendela couldn't remember his name: Billy or Barry or Jerry? He had been lost in his own thoughts with a cigarette between his yellowing fingers, but now he looked up and gazed around, his expression full of anxiety.

'Markus Lukas,' he said. 'Markus Lukas is sick.'

23

It was half past ten and Per was sitting in the shadows on the neighbours' veranda listening to his father's laboured breathing. He sounded worse than usual tonight – like a man who didn't have long to live, but who intended to enjoy himself right to the very end.

Jerry actually seemed to be quite happy at the party. Sometimes he disappeared into himself, staring down at his paralysed arm. Then he would come back to life and raise his glass. Sometimes he looked frightened, sometimes he would smile to himself. He seemed to have already forgotten that his business partner Hans Bremer was missing, and that their entire film studio – the whole of Morner Art, in fact – had gone up in smoke three days earlier.

His father's hacking cough had been heard across the table all evening, but the number of his smiles increased in direct proportion to the amount of wine he drank. Per thought he must have knocked back four or five glasses since they sat down to eat; he was drunk, but that shouldn't be a problem. Jerry had been drunk before, usually in restaurants.

It was pitch black beyond the veranda now, with thick clouds covering the night sky. Per felt something cold touch his cheek, and realized it had started to drizzle. Soon it would be time to go indoors, and for everyone to head home.

Nilla was probably already asleep over in the cottage. Per turned his head, and could see only one isolated light in the living room. He had pushed her home in the wheelchair after she had been at the table for about an hour; she had whispered to Per that she couldn't cope any longer. Had she eaten anything? He wasn't sure.

Jesper had stayed for another hour or so before he too headed back to Casa Mörner, hopefully to get an early night. Per was also intending to leave soon, taking Jerry with him. He had met the neighbours now; they seemed like decent, reliable people, but he had no desire to become friends with them. He only had to compare his own shack with their newly built luxury houses to see how different they were.

Suddenly a question came across the table: 'So what do you do, Jerry?'

Max Larsson.

Jerry put down his wine glass and shook his head. He could find only two words: 'Not working.'

'OK, but what is it you do when you're not sitting here?'

Jerry looked at his son in confusion. Per shifted forward: 'Jerry's retired . . . He ran his own business for many years, but he's recently downsized.'

Max nodded, but didn't give up. 'So what kind of business was it? Jerry Morner . . . I've been sitting here pondering, and I'm sure I recognize the name.'

'Media,' Per said quickly. 'Jerry worked in the media. So do I.'

'Oh,' said Max, suddenly more interested. 'Are you on television, then?'

'No . . . I work in marketing surveys.'

'Right,' said Max, looking disappointed.

'I do a fair amount of jogging too,' said Per, glancing around the table, 'although that's more of a hobby. Does anyone else go jogging?'

'I go running,' said a voice in the darkness. 'I've done it for years.' It was Vendela, their hostess. She had large, beautiful eyes.

'Good,' said Per, smiling at her.

He wanted to round off the evening now, to say thank you and leave this enormous house – but at that moment Jerry straightened up and looked at Max Larsson. His gaze was suddenly completely clear and focused. 'Films!' he said.

Max turned his head. 'Sorry?'

'Films and magazines.'

Max laughed a little uncertainly, as if Jerry were teasing him, but Jerry looked annoyed at not being taken seriously. He raised his voice and went on, 'Me and Bremer and Markus Lukas . . . films and magazines. Girls!'

There was complete silence around the table now; the last word had made all the guests stop talking and turn to look at Jerry. Only Per kept his eyes downcast.

Jerry himself seemed very happy with the attention, almost proud, and he pointed across the table with a steady finger; Per knew there was no escape.

'Ask Pelle!'

Per gazed into the distance and tried to give the impression that he wasn't listening, as if there was no point in listening to Jerry. Eventually he did look at his father, but by that time it was too late.

Jerry had already picked up his old briefcase; he had refused to leave it at home. He quickly undid the straps and pulled something out. It was a brightly coloured magazine, Per saw, made of thick, glossy paper.

161

His father threw it into the middle of the table, smiling proudly.

The title on the cover was written in red: BABYLON. Beneath the name a naked woman lay sprawled on a sofa, her legs spread wide apart.

Per stood up. The magazine seemed to lie there for an eternity before he reached over and picked it up. But of course everyone had seen it by then; he noticed Vendela Larsson leaning forward to study the picture, her eyes wide with surprise.

At the same time his father's voice echoed across the entire veranda: 'Girls! Naked girls!'

24

Per didn't want to wake up the morning after the party, but it happened anyway. It was quarter to nine. He lay there blinking at the ceiling.

It was Maundy Thursday. It was almost the Easter weekend, or had it already started? And how were they going to celebrate it, with the way things were?

He supposed they would just have to celebrate as best they could, as he had promised Nilla. With eggs – fresh eggs and chocolate eggs.

Then Per remembered that his father was in the house, and what had happened at the party the previous evening.

Jerry's hoarse laughter. Vendela Larsson, smiling nervously at her guests. And the porn magazine, lying there in the middle of the table.

The cottage was silent, but inside his pounding head he could hear echoing voices and shouts. He had drunk too much red wine yesterday, he wasn't used to it.

'Markus Lukas,' Jerry had said several times.

That name and the memory of Vendela's smile made Per think of Regina, the girl he had met one warm, sunny spring day many years ago. She too had had a quick, slightly nervous smile and a pair of big blue

163

eyes framed by short brown hair, and high cheekbones dusted with freckles.

Had Regina been the first real love of his life? She had certainly seemed much more exciting than the girls at his school. Older, more worldly-wise. They had sat next to each other for several hours in a car one day when he was thirteen years old.

An outing in the car in springtime with a pretty girl should have been straightforward, but not for Per. Regina had been sitting in the back doing her make-up when Jerry and a friend turned up at Anita's in the Cadillac to pick him up. For once Jerry was on time. They were going to hang out together for the whole of the Easter weekend, father and son.

And how old had Regina been? Several years older than Per, maybe sixteen or seventeen. She had laughed and patted him on the head when he sat down beside her on the leather seat, as if he were just a little boy.

It was Jerry's fault; as soon as they got in the car he started referring to Per as 'my lad'.

'Regina,' said Jerry, exhaling cigarette smoke as he turned his big black sunglasses towards the back seat and touched the girl's cheek, 'this is my lad . . . Pelle.'

Per wanted to touch the girl's cheek as well, in the same confident way as his father.

'My name is Per,' he said.

Regina laughed and ruffled his hair with her slender white fingers. 'So how old are you, Per?'

'Fifteen,' he lied.

He felt quite grown up, sitting there in Jerry's car, and he grew bolder and bolder; he ventured a smile at Regina, and realized she was the prettiest girl he'd ever seen. Her quick smile was beautiful, and he became more and more smitten. He kept on stealing glances at her, admiring the sunburnt legs disappearing under her short skirt, the slender hands protruding from her leather jacket. Her fingers fluttered like eager butterflies as she talked to Jerry and the man who was driving. Per could see only the back of the man's head; he had broad shoulders and thick, black hair, but he was bound to be a friend of Jerry's. His father had a lot of friends.

They set off, and Per sat next to Regina, feeling his legs and back grow; he didn't look back to see whether Anita was waving to him, or whether she had gone indoors. He had already forgotten his mother; he was sitting next to Regina, and they were smiling at one another.

The car smelled of cigarettes, as Jerry's cars always did.

They drove out into the country, and afterwards Per had no idea where they had been – just that they had driven and driven and eventually reached a gravel track surrounded by dense fir trees. A southern Swedish forest.

'This all right?' asked the man behind the wheel.

'Sure,' said Jerry, coughing. 'Fantastic, Markus.'

The car pulled up among the trees.

'Pelle,' said Jerry when they had all got out, 'Regina, Markus Lukas and I are going off into the forest for a while.' He gripped Per firmly by the shoulder, his expression serious. 'But I have an important job for you here by the car. I want you to keep guard, and I'm going to pay you. That's the most important thing about jobs – getting *paid* for them.'

Per nodded – this was his first job. 'And what if anyone comes?'

Jerry lit a fresh cigarette. He went over and opened the boot. 'Tell them it's a military exercise,' he said with a smile. 'Tell them we're shooting here, so nobody is allowed in.'

Per nodded as Jerry and Markus Lukas looped several bags over their shoulders and set off into the trees with Regina. His father waved to him. 'See you soon. Then it'll be time for a picnic.'

Per was suddenly alone next to the car. The spring sunshine made the red bodywork gleam, and flies buzzed across the grass.

He took a few steps along the track and looked around. There was no sign of anyone, and not a sound to be heard. When he listened carefully he thought he could hear Regina laughing in the distance, just once. Or was it a scream?

Time passed more and more slowly. The forest surrounding Per felt dark and dense. He thought he heard Regina crying out, several times.

Eventually he left the car. He followed Jerry and the others, without really knowing where they had gone.

A little path wound its way through the trees. He followed it up a steep slope, over a little rise among moss-covered rocks, and down a small hill. He increased his speed, took a few more steps, then suddenly heard male voices, and Regina's cries. She was screaming deep in the forest – loud, long-drawn-out screams.

Per started to run.

The trees thinned out and he hurtled into a sunlit glade.

The sun was shining down like a spotlight into the middle of the glade. Regina was lying there naked on a blanket on the grass; she was wearing a long blonde wig. She was sunburnt, Per noticed, but her breasts were chalk-white.

Markus Lukas, the man who had been driving the car, was also naked. He was lying on top of her.

And Jerry, who was standing next to them holding a big camera, didn't have any clothes on either. He was snapping away all the time, *click click click.*

Regina gave a start as Per cried out; she looked at him, then quickly turned her head away.

Jerry lowered the camera and glared at Per. 'Pelle, what the hell are you doing?' he shouted. 'Go back and keep a lookout – stick to the job I gave you!'

Per turned and fled through the forest.

Twenty minutes later his father and the other two came back to the car, with their clothes on. Regina had taken off the wig.

Jerry laughed at his son all the way home.

'He thought we were going to kill her.' Jerry had turned to face the back seat. 'Regina, he thought we were murdering you out there in the forest! He was coming to your rescue!'

Per wasn't laughing.

He looked at Regina, but she refused to meet his eye.

Regina and Markus Lukas.

Per could still remember those two names. His head was full of old memories, and felt very heavy this morning. He lifted it and looked out of the bedroom window towards the two new houses. Nothing was moving over there, but the Larssons' veranda looked empty. No trace of the party remained.

It had ended fairly soon after Jerry had thrown the magazine on the table. The Kurdins had gone home with their baby, Gerlof Davidsson and John Hagman had also left, and Vendela Larsson had started gathering up the remains of the food. It might have been his imagination, but Per had the feeling his neighbours wanted to see the back of him and Jerry as soon as possible.

He knew more or less what to expect from now on. The neighbours hadn't said anything yesterday as he thanked them and took his leave, but he knew the questions would come.

The curiosity, the constant curiosity. And the meaningful smiles each time some new acquaintance found out he was the son of the notorious Jerry Morner.

'So have you ever been in a porn film then, Per?'

'No.'

'Not even one?'

'I've never had anything to do with Jerry's activities.'

'Never?'

'No. Never.'

He had become adept at it as an adult, distancing himself and swearing that he was nothing like his father. But why had he kept in touch with Jerry? And why had he been stupid enough to bring him to Öland?

Per would have preferred to stay in bed, but he got up anyway. He wished the sun wasn't shining quite so brightly this morning. He didn't want to think about Regina any more.

He didn't want to think about the neighbours either.

Nobody else in the cottage seemed to be awake. The doors to the twins' rooms were closed, and when he went into the kitchen he could hear his father's long-drawn-out breathing from the spare room. It was a mixture of snoring and wheezing.

Per had heard the same sound each time he visited his father in the small apartment Jerry had rented in Malmö in the mid-sixties, before the really big money started pouring in.

The sound was particularly noticeable when he brought women home. Per would lie on his mattress in front of the TV listening to Jerry wheezing in the room next door, interspersed with regular groans and irregular cries or bouts of weeping from the women. He could never sleep on those nights when Jerry was taking photographs or filming, but he didn't dare get up and knock on the door. If he disturbed his father, Jerry would shout at him, just like that day in the forest.

The bedroom had been Jerry's workplace during the autumn and winter months when it was too cold to work outside. That was where he took photographs and did his filming, and it also served as his office. He had bought a water bed that filled half the room, and kept the company's money in a fat envelope underneath it. The bed was both his office and his playroom; he had two telephones next to it, plus a Facit calculator, a drinks cabinet and a projector that he could use to show films on the white walls.

The Swinging Sixties, thought Per. *But that's all over now.*

He knocked on the door of the spare room. 'Jerry?'

The snoring stopped, only to be replaced by coughing.

'Time to get up, Jerry – breakfast.'

Per turned and saw a black mobile phone lying on the table in the hallway. It was Jerry's. He noticed that it was switched on, and that someone had called at around seven o'clock that morning. Everybody had been asleep, of course.

He picked up the phone to see if he recognized the name of the caller, but the display showed only NUMBER WITHHELD.

Jerry shuffled out on to the patio quarter of an hour later wearing a white dressing gown he had borrowed from Per. The twins were still asleep, but that was fine – Nilla in particular needed her rest. Besides,

Per wanted to talk to his father without the children eavesdropping.

They nodded at one another in the sunshine.

'Pelle?' said Jerry, looking at the glass in front of him.

'No alcohol today,' said Per. 'Orange juice.'

As his father sat down, Per caught a glimpse of the white dressing on his stomach. He helped him to butter a slice of toast, and Jerry took a big bite.

Per looked at him. 'You should have played things a bit cooler yesterday, Jerry.'

His father blinked.

'You shouldn't have told the neighbours what you used to do. You shouldn't have shown them the magazine.'

Jerry shrugged his shoulders.

Per knew that his father had never been ashamed of anything. Not Jerry, he just did whatever he wanted. He had loved his job and had fun all his life.

Per leaned across the table. 'Jerry, do you remember a girl called Regina?'

'Regina?'

'Regina, who worked with you back in the sixties . . . She used to wear a blonde wig.'

Jerry pointed to his own thinning hair, and shook his head.

'Yes, I know you turned all your girls into blondes . . . But do you remember Regina?'

Jerry glanced sideways, as if he were thinking.

'What happened to her? Do you remember?'

Jerry said nothing.

'Got old, I suppose,' he said eventually, and started coughing.

Per let him finish, then picked up his father's mobile to show him the missed call.

'Somebody's trying to get hold of you, Jerry.'

25

Vendela woke up at about eight o'clock on Maundy Thursday with a dry mouth and a blocked nose. It was probably her imagination, but when she opened the blinds she thought the air outside was yellow with whirling pollen.

Aloysius was sleeping at the foot of the bed, and Max was completely wrapped up in his duvet on the other side of the double bed. His face was turned away, but he was snoring loudly, with his mouth open. It was the wine, of course. He had knocked back glass after glass of red wine last night, despite all the talk of thinking about his heart and cutting back on the alcohol.

He would be like a bear with a sore head when he woke up, so she let him sleep for a while longer.

Today would be the photographer's final visit to the island, which meant she would have to cook and bake bread before the morning's photo shoot.

She threw the covers aside, blew her nose as quietly as possible and got up.

When Max lumbered out of the bedroom in a sad-looking dressing gown an hour later, Vendela had taken an antihistamine tablet and was waiting for it to take effect. She had set the dough for two different kinds of artisan bread to rise, and was mixing melted butter and rye flour for another kind. Ally had eaten some chicken-flavoured kibble and was lying under the kitchen table.

'Good morning!' she said to Max.

'Mm-hmm.'

He poured himself a cup of coffee and surveyed her efforts. 'You've started on the bread too early,' he said. 'It's supposed to look freshly baked, so that steam comes out when I cut it.'

'I know, but the problem is that the loaves cool really quickly,' said Vendela, wiping her forehead. 'But I'm just going to use these as decoration in the background . . . I'll make some more when the photographer arrives.'

'OK. Have you had breakfast?'

She nodded eagerly. 'A banana, three slices of bread and cheese, and a yoghurt.'

That was a little white lie; breakfast had consisted of nothing but a cup of lemon tea.

'Well done,' said Max. He headed for the bathroom and locked himself in.

Vendela looked over at the front door, longing to be out on the alvar and to see if the coin had gone. She picked up the butter that was left over from her baking and began to form it into curls.

The golden-yellow butter looked good in photographs, but she had nothing but bad memories of real butter, however delicious it might be. She had had to churn it by hand when she was a little girl; Henry had made whisks from birch twigs and taught his daughter how to make butter from cream. It took eight litres of cream to make a tub of butter, and it had been bloody hard work, to say the least. It had given Vendela blisters on her hands.

An hour later, the young photographer from Kalmar turned up. He was met on the steps by a smiling Max, dressed in appropriately rural clothing in shades of grey, brown and blue, picked out for him by Vendela. The two men disappeared into the kitchen to discuss the composition of the pictures and various camera angles, and Vendela went out into the sunshine and walked up the road to fetch the newspaper. The mailboxes belonging to the summer cottages were arranged in a long row, to make life easier for the postman.

As she approached them she saw a tall man in a green padded jacket coming towards her, a newspaper under his arm. It was Per Mörner.

Vendela straightened her back and smiled instinctively. There had been a brief astonished silence at the party when Jerry Morner got out his magazine, but it had quickly passed.

That was when she had recognized him from various interviews and television documentaries. In the seventies Jerry Morner had been a high-profile figure, frequently seen in night clubs and exclusive bars. He had been one of the porn film directors who had taken the image of Swedish sinfulness out into the world, making the Americans and Europeans regard Sweden as a dreamland where every woman wanted sex all the time.

Before that, when Vendela was young, pornography was banned and couldn't be sold. Then it became legal, but it was still something dirty. These days there were no moral rules; one day the newspapers were writing about the horrors of the sex industry, the next they were listing the best erotic films.

She nodded at Per Mörner, intending to walk past him, but he stopped, which meant she had to do the same.

'Thank you for last night,' he said.

'You're welcome,' Vendela said quickly. She added, 'So now we all know each other a little bit better.'

'Yes . . . quite.'

There was a silence, then Per went on: 'That business my father was talking about . . .'

Vendela laughed nervously. 'Well, at least he was honest.'

'Yes, and the work he did was all above-board,' Per said. 'But he's given all that up now.'

'I see.'

Vendela was about to ask how Per could be so certain, when her kitchen window was flung open and Max yelled, 'Vendela, we're ready now! We're about to photograph the bread, are you coming?'

'Just a minute!' she called back.

Max gave her and Per Mörner a quick glance and nodded briefly without saying anything, then he closed the kitchen window.

Vendela felt as if her husband had passed judgement on her and given her a black mark for conduct, but she was only chatting to a neighbour.

In a sudden burst of defiance she turned to Per. 'So you're a jogger too?'

He nodded. 'Sometimes. I'd like to do more.'

'Perhaps we could go out for a run together one evening?'

Per looked at her, slightly wary. 'OK,' he said. 'If you like.'

'Good.'

Vendela said goodbye and went back to the house.

That was good, she had been sociable, perfectly normal. And she had got herself a running buddy.

Of course, she wouldn't run to the elf stone with Per Mörner. That was her place, and hers alone.

Öland 1957

Vendela sees the elf stone once again when she has left the village school and started at the bigger high school in Marnäs on the other side of the island, almost four kilometres away.

It's a long way to walk six days a week, at least for a nine-year-old, but Henry never goes with her, not once.

All he does is take his daughter to the edge of the meadow, where the cows are chewing the cud beneath the open sky. Then he points east, towards the treeless horizon.

'Head for the elf stone, and when you get there you'll be able to see the church tower in Marnäs,' he says. 'The school is just past the church. That's the shortest route . . . but if we get a lot of snow in winter, you'll have to go along the main road.'

He hands over a packet of sandwiches for break time. Then he sets off for the quarry, humming some melody.

Vendela heads off in the opposite direction, straight across the burnt brown grass. Summer is over but its dryness remains, and dead flowers and leaves crunch beneath her shoes as she walks towards the church tower. She is terrified of adders, but on all those walks to and from school she encounters only nice animals: hares, foxes and deer.

She sees the elf stone again that very first day. It is still there in the grass, isolated and immovable. Vendela walks past it and continues on her way to Marnäs church tower.

School begins at eight thirty, and the children are met by Eriksson, the headmaster, who stands in front of the blackboard looking strict, and Fru Jansson, whose hair is in a bun; she looks even stricter. She calls the register, reading each name in a loud, harsh voice. Then she sits down at the pedal organ to lead morning worship with a hymn, and lessons begin after that.

At half past one the first school day is over. Vendela thinks it has gone well. She felt lonely and a little bit scared of Fru Jansson at first, but then she thought that the class was just like a herd of cows, and everybody else was afraid too; that made her feel better. Besides which, they had needlework after break, and music and movement at their desks every hour. If she can just make some friends, she will be happy at the high school.

On the way home she passes the big, flat elf stone once again, and stops. Then she walks over to it.

When she stands on tiptoe she can see that there are little hollows in the top of the stone, at least a dozen of them. They look as if they have been made deliberately then polished, like little round stone bowls.

She looks around, but there is no one in sight. She remembers what Henry told her about gifts to the elves and she wants to linger here, but in the end she leaves the stone and sets off home, back to the cows.

From then on hardly a day passes when Vendela does not stop on her way home from school to see if people have left any gifts on the elf stone. She never sees anyone

177

else visiting the stone, but sometimes there are small gifts in the hollows, coins or pins or pieces of jewellery.

There is a strange atmosphere around the stone; everything is so quiet. But when Vendela closes her eyes, thinks of nothing and screws her eyes up so tightly that the light coming through her eyelids turns dark blue, she gets pictures inside her head. She sees a group of pale, slender people standing on the far side of the stone, looking at her. They become clearer and clearer the longer she keeps her eyes closed, and the clearest of all is a tall, beautiful woman with dark eyes. Vendela knows that she is the queen of the elves, who once upon a time fell in love with a huntsman.

The queen does not speak, she merely stares at Vendela. She looks sorrowful, as if she were missing her beloved. Vendela keeps her eyes closed, but thinks she can hear the sound of jingling bells in the distance; the grass beneath her feet seems to disappear, and the ground becomes hard and smooth. Fresh water is splashing from cool fountains.

The kingdom of the elves.

But when she opens her eyes, everything has vanished.

She goes home to the farm and looks up at the middle window upstairs, in spite of the fact that she doesn't really want to.

The Invalid's room. As usual the window is dark and empty.

Vendela goes into the porch and continues straight through the kitchen into Henry's bedroom, where unwashed clothes, invoices from wholesalers and letters from the authorities are lying all over the place. She has no money to offer the elves, but in a dark-brown cupboard next to her father's bed is her mother's jewellery box.

Henry won't be home from the quarry for several

hours, and of course the Invalid can't disturb her either, so she kneels down in front of the cupboard and opens it.

The white jewellery box is on the bottom shelf. It is lined with green fabric, and contains brooches, necklaces, earrings and tie-pins – perhaps twenty or thirty pieces in total, both old, inherited items and things that were bought after the war, everything that her mother and her family gathered over the years and left behind.

With her thumb and forefinger, Vendela carefully picks up a silver brooch with a polished red stone. Even here in the darkness the stone has a glow about it, almost like a ruby.

A ruby in Paris, Vendela thinks.

She listens, but the house is silent. She takes the brooch and tucks it down her dress.

On her way home from school the next day, Vendela takes the brooch out of the inside pocket of her coat when she reaches the elf stone. She looks at the brooch, then at the empty hollows.

It's funny, but she can't think of anything to ask for. Not today. She is almost ten years old and there ought to be lots of things to wish for, but her head is completely empty.

A trip to Paris?

She mustn't be greedy. In the end she just wishes for a trip to the mainland – to Kalmar. She hasn't been there for almost two years.

She places the brooch in one of the hollows and runs home.

It is Saturday. For once the school is closed, because new stoves are being installed in the classrooms.

'Hurry up with the cows this morning,' her father

179

says at breakfast. 'And get changed when you come home.'

'What for?'

'We're going to Kalmar on the train, and we're going to stay overnight with your aunt.'

A coincidence? No, it was the elves.

But Vendela should have stopped wishing for things at that point.

26

Per was going to ring the police about the fire, but if the family was going to eat, he had to get some work done as well. So after breakfast, when he had settled his father on the patio, he shut himself in the kitchen with a list of numbers and his questionnaire. He placed his finger on the list and called the first number.

Three rings, then a male voice answered with his surname. The name matched the one on Per's list, so he straightened up and took a deep breath in order to fill his voice with energy.

'Good morning, my name is Per Mörner and I'm calling from Intereko; we're involved in market research. I wonder if you have time to answer a few questions? It will only take a couple of minutes.'

(In fact it was more like ten minutes.)

'What's it about?' said the man.

'I'd just like to ask you some questions about a particular brand of soap. Do you use soap in your household?'

The man laughed. 'Well, yes . . .'

'Good,' said Per. 'I'm going to say the name of this soap, and I'd like you to tell me when you last saw it.'

He said the name, slowly and clearly.

'I do recognize it,' said the man. 'I've seen adverts for it in town.'

'Great,' said Per. 'Can you describe in three words what you felt when you saw these adverts?'

He was well under way now. Marika had looked amused last year – or scornful, Per thought – when he told her he was interviewing people over the phone. When they met they had both been working in marketing, but Marika had become a team leader while Per had decided to quit after their divorce. It was a decision he had arrived at gradually, partly because of Jerry. His father had been hungry for money and success, and he didn't want to follow him down that road.

But interviewing was a job he could do wherever there was a telephone. It was all about checking what image a particular item had, finding out people's dreams and hopes about the product, so that future sales and marketing campaigns could build on that knowledge.

By shortly after ten o'clock he had called twenty-five of the numbers on his list, and had got answers from fourteen of them. When he put down the phone after the last interview, it rang immediately.

'Mörner.'

He couldn't hear a voice, just a strange, echoing noise. It sounded as if someone was yelling in the background, a few metres from the phone, but it sounded metallic. Recorded.

'Hello?'

No reply. The yelling continued.

Wrong number – or perhaps another telephone interviewer. Per hung up.

He carried on working through his list, but at about eleven o'clock he took a break to go and fetch the Kalmar newspaper from the mailbox. It was supposed to be a morning paper, but it arrived much later in Stenvik.

He walked back to the cottage, flicking through the news pages, and stopped dead when he saw the headline:

BODIES FOUND AFTER HOUSE FIRE

The badly burnt bodies of a woman in her thirties and a man in his sixties were found on Wednesday in a house outside Ryd, to the south of Växjö.

The property was completely destroyed in a fire on Sunday night, and an employee who was believed to be in the house was reported missing. The police searched the remains of the house and discovered a body which has been identified as that of the missing man. Another person was also discovered in a different part of the house, a younger woman who has yet to be identified.

The cause of the fire is not yet known, but after interviewing a witness, police believe it was started deliberately. A preliminary investigation into arson has begun.

Per folded up the paper and went back to the cottage. So he really had heard a woman screaming in the burning house, and no doubt the police would soon be in touch. He sat down in the kitchen and called them himself.

He rang the number for the station in Växjö and asked for the woman who had interviewed him after the fire, but she wasn't at work and he was passed on to an inspector by the name of Lars Marklund, who demanded both Jerry and Per's personal ID numbers before he said anything at all; even then he wasn't particularly talkative.

'This is a case of arson involving two deaths, and the

183

preliminary investigation is ongoing. That's all I can say.'

'One of the dead is a woman, according to the paper,' said Per. 'Do you know who she was?'

'Do *you* know who she was?' asked the inspector.

'No,' Per said quickly.

The inspector didn't say anything, so Per went on: 'Do you have any suspects?'

'I can't comment on that.'

'Is there any way I can help?'

'Yes,' said the officer. 'You can tell me about the scene.'

'The scene . . . Do you mean the house?'

'Yes – our technicians have been wondering what the house was actually used for. There were several small bedrooms upstairs, and parts of the house were set out like a classroom, and a bar or a pub, and then there was some kind of prison cell . . .'

'It was a film studio,' said Per. 'The guest rooms were for the actors who came to work there. Other rooms were set up for filming a variety of scenes. I was never involved, but according to my father they had every possible scenario.'

'Oh, so they made films there,' said the inspector. 'Anything we might have heard of?'

Per sighed to himself before replying. 'No. They made films that went straight to video, films that were made very quickly.'

'Mysteries?'

'No. They made . . . erotic films.'

It was like a production line, he thought. Hans Bremer had worked fast as a director; Jerry had said that he sometimes made an entire full-length film in two days.

'Erotic films . . . Do you mean porn?'

184

'Exactly. They took male and female models out there and made porn films.'

Marklund paused.

'I see,' he said eventually. 'Well, that isn't necessarily illegal, as long as no minors are involved. Were they?'

'No,' Per said quickly, although he wasn't absolutely certain. How old had Regina actually been?

'So you were part of this . . . activity?'

'No, not at all. But my father has told me a certain amount.'

'Has he said anything about why his companion burnt down their studio?' asked the inspector. 'Or do you have any idea why he did it?'

The question revealed how the police were thinking. They believed Bremer was behind the fire.

'No,' said Per. 'But I don't think the business has been going all that well for the last few years. My father fell ill, and I think perhaps competition from abroad has increased in . . . in this particular industry. But that's no reason to kill yourself, surely?'

'You never know,' said Marklund.

Per wondered whether to tell him about the figure he had seen on the edge of the forest, but decided to keep quiet. He'd already mentioned it in an interview; that would have to do.

He looked out of the window at the patio, where Jerry was fast asleep on a sun lounger. 'Are you going to talk to my father?'

'Not before Easter,' said Marklund. 'But we'll be in touch.'

Per put down the phone. That was that.

If Jerry hadn't been fully retired before this weekend, he had no choice now – his workplace was gone. Per would drive him back to his apartment after Easter, and he could live a peaceful life there. Sit in front of the TV and live on his pension. If he had one.

Per went out on to the patio. 'I've just been speaking to the police, Jerry. They've found two bodies in your house . . . Hans Bremer and a woman. Did you see a woman there?'

Jerry looked up at him and shook his head.

Per sat down opposite him. 'The police seem to think it was Bremer who set fire to the place,' he said. 'And that does seem like the logical explanation, doesn't it?'

But Jerry was still shaking his head. Eventually his mouth formed just one word: 'No.'

'Yes, Jerry. They think he wanted to destroy the studio.'

His father appeared to abandon the attempt to speak. He bent down to his briefcase and opened the worn straps. He rooted through a pile of papers and pulled out a magazine. It was the same old copy of *Babylon* he had whipped out at the party.

'I don't want to look at that,' said Per curtly.

But Jerry started flicking through the pages anyway, as if he were looking for something. Then he found a particular double-page spread, and held it up to Per. 'Markus Lukas,' he said.

Per sighed, he didn't want to look. But he leant forward anyway.

The pictures Jerry was holding up showed nothing more than yet another sex scene between a well-built man and a young blonde woman – the same scenario his father had published in one magazine after another over the years. The female model was lying underneath the man, but her face was turned away from him and towards the photographer, and the couple seemed to be making every effort to touch each other as little as possible. There could be no hint of love or tenderness.

'Markus Lukas,' said Jerry, pointing at the man.

'OK, Markus Lukas. So that was the name of your male model?'

Jerry nodded.

Per contemplated the naked back of a muscular, broad-shouldered man aged between thirty and forty. He had thick, curly black hair, visible in one picture that showed the back of his head; most of the pictures revealed him only from the waist down.

He thought about the man who had been driving the car that spring day, with Per and Regina in the back seat. Jerry had called him 'Markus Lukas'. Was this the same man?

'You can't see his face,' said Per.

Jerry nodded, but pointed at the man again. His stiff mouth was working. 'He . . . ang—'

'Angry? Is he angry?' said Per.

Jerry nodded.

'Who is he angry with? You and Hans Bremer?'

Jerry looked away. 'Cheated,' he said.

'That doesn't surprise me . . . you and Bremer cheated him out of some money?'

Jerry shook his head, but said nothing more.

Per picked up the magazine and leafed through it. There were plenty of pictures of different girls, page after page of close-ups and full-length shots, but the male models with whom they were having sex were only partly visible in the photographs. The camera focused on the women; the men were completely anonymous.

'Are there *no* pictures of Markus Lukas's face?' he asked.

Jerry shook his head.

Per sighed, but he wasn't surprised. There was no need to show the men's faces – only one small part of their body was important.

'So what's Markus Lukas doing now? Do you know where he lives?'

Another shake of the head.

'But he's not involved in porn any more?'

Jerry didn't say anything. Per thought he understood why; in a way Jerry no longer worked in the porn industry, although of course it hadn't been a voluntary decision.

'And I don't suppose he was actually called Markus Lukas, was he?' Per went on. 'I imagine it was made up, just like all the names you gave the girls?'

Jerry nodded.

'So what was his name?'

Jerry's gaze was blank.

'You don't remember what Markus Lukas was called?'

A brief shake of the head.

'In the contract,' said Jerry.

'OK, so he had a contract of employment, and his real name is on that?'

Jerry nodded and pointed across the water, in the direction of the mainland. 'Home,' he said.

'Good, you've got it at home,' said Per. He looked down at the pictures in the magazine, at the naked man.

'Angry,' said Jerry.

Per looked at the magazine one last time. He remembered the year after his meeting with Regina, when he finally realized why his father took women out into the forest and photographed them: it was to earn money from a magazine he published, a magazine called *Babylon*. Per had cycled to a newsagent's on the other side of Kalmar and sneaked in to buy a copy.

BABYLON, it said on the cover in dark-red letters, above a picture of a smiling girl who resembled Regina.

He stuffed it under his jumper, took it back to his room and hid it under the mattress. Late that night when Anita was asleep, he sat there looking through the pages by the light of a torch. He saw page after page of smiling, naked girls, their white skin glowing in the sunshine or under the studio lights. They were all blonde, but several of them looked as if they were wearing a wig.

On one of the pictures he noticed a thin curl of cigarette smoke drifting across from the left – and he knew that Jerry was standing there smoking just a few metres away. Inside his head Per could hear Jerry coughing and encouraging the model to arch her back and show as much as possible. He could hear his voice.

'Come on, darling, you're not shy, are you?'

The girl in the picture reminded him of Regina, and Per knew that looking at her ought to give him a warm feeling in his body, but nothing happened. All he could think about was the cigarette smoke.

Per shivered in the spring breeze, and he was back by the quarry.

'So the only thing we know for certain about Markus Lukas,' he said, closing the magazine, 'is that he's got big muscles.'

He held out the magazine between his thumb and forefinger and passed it to his father, without looking at it.

'Hide that now, or throw it away. I'm going to wake up the twins.'

27

It wasn't until six o'clock on Thursday evening that Vendela was able to change and set off for a run across the alvar again. She thought about the elf stone and the coin she had placed in a hollow on the top of the stone, but, just as before, she visited her childhood home first.

The allergy affecting her nose and throat eased slightly as she started to jog, and after a few hundred metres she found a comfortable rhythm. It took her quarter of an hour to run north-east and reach the old farm.

She walked into the garden and stopped.

There was a red car on the grass in front of the house, a big Volvo with a roof rack. The boot and two of the doors were open, as was the door of the house.

The family who owned the place had obviously arrived to spend Easter on the island. But Vendela couldn't help herself, she still had to move closer, walking towards the open door in the glass veranda.

Suddenly a woman appeared in the doorway. She stepped out into the sunshine and caught sight of Vendela.

'Oh,' she said.

She was perhaps ten years younger than Vendela, and looked frightened.

'Hi,' said Vendela with a tense laugh. 'I just wanted to stop and rest for a minute, I'm out jogging and . . .'

'Yes?'

'. . . and I grew up here. My family used to own this place.'

'So you used to live here?' The woman looked more friendly. 'Well, come in and have a look around, if you like. I should think it's changed quite a bit!'

Vendela nodded and stepped on to the veranda without saying anything; she walked through the porch and into the kitchen. She recognized the rooms, but they appeared to have shrunk since she was a child. The kitchen had been repainted and kitted out with trendy bench seating and a tiled stove. The aromas were different too; the smell of her father and his unwashed clothes was gone.

From the kitchen a staircase led up to the first floor. She went over to it and stopped. 'Is it OK if I go up and have a look?'

'Of course, but there's not much to see.'

Vendela went up the stairs, and the woman followed her. 'It was almost four years before we could face making a start up here,' she said, with a weary laugh. 'But we're really pleased with it now.'

Vendela nodded without speaking or smiling. She couldn't find the words; this was very difficult for her. But she moved up the last step and stood on the landing. It was bright and clean now; when she was a child it had been brown with ingrained dirt, and there had been dust everywhere.

And there it was on the right, the shiny door. It led to a little bedroom. There had been a small table by the door, where Vendela had always placed a tray of food before she left for school in the morning.

The door was half-open now; she could see toys and pieces of Lego on the floor, and she could hear a little boy laughing.

She turned to face the woman. 'Are you staying long?'

'No, just over Easter. We'll be going home on Monday.'

'I'll be here until the middle of May,' said Vendela, trying to sound calm. 'I could keep an eye on the house, if you like. I come past here sometimes when I'm running anyway, so . . .'

'Would you do that?' said the woman. 'That would be really kind; there have been quite a few break-ins here on the island.'

Vendela looked around. 'Are you happy here?'

'Oh my goodness, yes, we love it here,' said the woman. 'It's really cosy here.'

Vendela doubted that. The farm was in the way of the elves – she realized that now. Living here could bring nothing but misfortune.

Patches of snow were still hiding beneath the thickest bushes, and the lakes formed by melting ice and snow on the alvar were wider than ever, but were evaporating in the sunshine. By the time May came, they would be gone.

Vendela was finding her way more easily now, and after running for quarter of an hour she had reached the big stone once more. She saw immediately that the elves had been there.

The old coins were still there in the hollows, but the ten-kronor piece she had offered as a gift for Aloysius was gone.

She wasn't surprised, just delighted that they still gathered at the elf stone after all these years.

She sat down on the grass with her back against the eastern side of the stone and breathed out. She had had her doubts, but now she knew this was where she needed to be; every other place she had ever visited or yearned for disappeared beyond the horizon. Here by the stone there were no demands on her; the Vendela Larsson that Max and the rest of the world constantly watched did not exist here.

She closed her eyes, but continued to see pictures inside her head. She could see all the way across the alvar to the water, and she thought she could even see the quarry and her own house beside it. Max was sitting there at one of his desks working on the penultimate chapter of *Good Food to the Max*. He was describing his day-to-day life, in which he was responsible for most of the cooking in the home, simply because 'the greatest joy in life lies in sharing your own happiness with another person'. So in order to see a happy face in the morning, Max would wake his wife – 'my beloved V' as he referred to her in the book – 'with a groaning breakfast tray laden with freshly baked bread, fruit and freshly pressed juices'.

Vendela knew that at that moment Max was utterly convinced that this was the case, despite the fact that she was almost always the one who made their breakfast. He had treated her to breakfast in bed or had made dinner on the odd special occasion, and she had hoped that if she praised him enough he might help her in the kitchen more often. But cooking had never become part of Max's everyday life.

That didn't matter now, out here on the alvar.

She could see their neighbours' house to the north, the old house built by one of Henry's workmates, and the family who were living there now. Per Mörner was sitting on the patio with his elderly father. His children were there too. Everything looked very peaceful and festive, but Vendela knew that appearances could be deceptive.

Per was a stressed and tortured soul. It would do him good to get out here on the alvar for a run.

Then she stopped gazing into the distance and her thoughts returned to the place where she was sitting now, to the stone and the little glade among the juniper bushes. For a brief moment everything was bright and shiny, but suddenly she saw the image of a tall man in her mind, dressed in a white robe. He was standing completely still, unaffected by her gaze. He was smiling at her.

The king of the elves? No, Vendela sensed that this was their messenger, a servant indicating that they were aware of her presence. This man was of a lower rank – he actually reminded her of Max to a certain extent.

He remained there inside her head, still smiling, as if he were trying to say: *It is you who must take the first step, not me.*

But Vendela was not ready to take that step, not yet.

She opened her eyes and looked around. The glade was empty, but she could hear the sound of rustling over in the bushes.

She shivered, just as she always did when she dragged herself back from the world of the elves. She got up and took three coins out of her pocket. She placed them in a row on top of the stone, each in its own hollow.

One coin for Max and herself, one for Aloysius's health, and one for the neighbours by the quarry. Per Mörner and the others.

Then she turned and set off across the alvar again, loping between the gleaming pools of water. The evening

194

sun was shining in the west, a warm lighthouse guiding her down towards the coast.

It was only seven o'clock when she got home. Time had passed slowly, as it always did in the world of the elves.

28

Gerlof was sitting in the garden. It was Good Friday, the day that Jesus had died on the cross. When he was a little boy, Gerlof had been forced to mark the day by doing absolutely nothing. You were not allowed to play, or listen to the radio, or talk loudly, and you were most definitely not allowed to laugh. All you could do, in fact, was sit still on a chair. As an old man he marked the day in more or less the same way, but now it felt pleasantly restful.

He was waiting for his children and grandchildren to arrive from the west coast. There were things he could be doing; he had customers waiting for ships in bottles, and he was paid well for making them. But it was a holiday, after all, and in any case his thoughts kept returning to the pile of Ella's old diaries.

He should never have started looking at them.

In the end he got up and went to fetch the diary for 1957. He settled down in his chair, opened the diary somewhere around the middle, and began to read Ella's neat handwriting.

16th June 1957
Last night we had a storm, and the children and I

got up to watch the lightning. It struck three times out in the Sound – we could hear the water crackling. Gerlof slept through the whole thing, but I suppose he's used to noise out at sea.

Yesterday he cycled up to Långvik, bought a new fishing net and cycled back to lay it out, then he got up at five this morning to check it – there were twenty-five flounder and six perch. So today we had fish in white sauce – delicious.

This morning Lena and Julia saw a young deer run across the road into the forest.

Today that poor widower Henry Fors who lives to the north of the village sold his last two calves for slaughter, the wagon came from Kalmar to fetch them at two o'clock, so now he just has the three cows that his daughter Vendela helps him with. It's sad, but I suppose he needs the money.

Ella was right about Vendela Larsson's father, Gerlof thought; he had never had much money. A few skinny cows grazing on meadows that were anything but lush, and his job in the little village quarry that could no longer compete with the big companies. It wasn't easy.

He turned to the next page:

27th June 1957

It's been a while since I wrote; time goes so quickly and I've got so much to do that the days just disappear. And I don't always feel like writing, anyway.

It's hot and sunny – summer has definitely arrived.

Gerlof has sailed down to Kalmar to measure the ship; he went yesterday and took the girls with him – they're on holiday from school. I'm perfectly happy up here in the village on my own, though – I mean, there's the sewing group down in Borgholm, but I don't really miss it. It's mostly talk and gossip about whoever hasn't turned up that evening, so I expect they'll be busy talking about me right now.

There are cock pheasants all over the place in the evenings; I expect they're attracted by the hen pheasants down on the farms. The owners of the hens have no intention of letting them get together!

The little changeling from the pasture crept up to the cottage again today, and I gave him some oatcakes and lemonade. He's full of life, he never stands still, but he doesn't say much, and he won't tell me who he is or where he comes from.

He needs a wash. And his hair is really long and matted – I've never seen anything like it.

Suddenly Gerlof heard the sound of a car engine, and almost jumped out of his seat. A car was coming along the village road; it slowed down and turned in.

He quickly closed the diary and hid it under the blanket; he was sitting quietly and calmly in his chair when the gate was opened and the Volvo rolled slowly down the path, bringing his two daughters and their families. The car doors were flung open.

'Hello Granddad! Here we are!'

'Welcome!' Gerlof shouted, waving cheerfully. 'Happy Easter!'

They all climbed out: Lena and her youngest daughter, then Julia and her two youngest stepsons, along with their suitcases and rucksacks.

The family had arrived, and that was the end of his peace and quiet.

The grandchildren gave Gerlof a quick hug, then raced into the cottage and switched on the TV or the radio – whatever it was, the volume was turned up high and loud music came pouring out of the windows.

Gerlof stayed in his chair on the lawn, thinking about what Good Friday had been like when he was a child.

'How are you, Dad? Is everything nice and quiet here?'

It was Julia. She gave him a kiss on the cheek.

'It's nice and quiet here at the cottage,' said Gerlof. 'I think the whole village is pretty quiet . . . but the people by the quarry have moved in.'

'What are they like?'

'Quite pleasant.' He thought about the magazine Jerry Morner had suddenly thrown down on the table the other night. 'And slightly odd, in some cases.'

'Shall we go over and see them?'

'No, I was at a party over there on Wednesday. That's quite enough.'

'So it'll be just us for Easter?'

Gerlof nodded. He had a young relative up in Marnäs, his brother's granddaughter Tilda, but she had found a new man back in the autumn and was fully occupied with her new life.

'So what else have you been up to, then?'

'I spend a lot of time just sitting here thinking.'

'What about?'

'Nothing.'

Julia held out her hands. 'Do you want to get up?'

Gerlof smiled and quickly shook his head. He didn't want to get up right now. 'I'm fine here.'

Sooner or later he was going to have to talk to his daughters about Ella's diaries, and find out what they knew about her visitor.

29

Up to the point when Nilla collapsed and started coughing up blood at the table, the Mörner family's Easter lunch had been going very well.

Per had managed to fool himself, and hadn't realized how ill she was. But he should have sensed something, because she had seemed tired on Saturday morning. She had helped him prepare the vegetables after breakfast, but progress had been slow, and sometimes she just stood there staring at the chopping board.

'Are you tired?' he asked.

'A bit . . . I didn't sleep very well last night.'

'Would you like to go back to bed?'

'No, it's OK.'

'Well, you could go out for a bit later on,' he said. 'You could go for a walk along the coast – try to get Jesper to go with you.'

'Mm-hmm,' said Nilla quietly as she carried on chopping tomatoes with slow strokes.

Per kept an eye on her and tried to relax.

He had repaired the lower section of the stone steps on Tuesday, and had got into the habit of going to the edge of the quarry every morning and evening to check if it was still standing. He did the same on the morning of Easter Saturday, and the stones were untouched. He would carry on building soon, until the steps reached all the way to the top of the quarry.

The pools of water were starting to dry up down below. In the summer, when the gravel was completely dry, he and Jesper would be able to have some fun down there, playing football perhaps.

Nilla too, of course.

He turned away from the quarry and walked around the house, stopping outside Ernst's workshop. It was a square wooden box, two metres high, with traces of Falun red paint still visible on the weathered planks. There were small dusty windows on the shorter sides, and a black, creosoted door.

A heavy chain ran from the door to a ring on the wall, but the only thing holding it in place was a large, rusty nail. Per pulled it out and opened the door.

The air inside was dry because of all the limestone dust covering the floor. He had been in here three years ago, when Ernst's family had come to collect the things they wanted to keep from the workshop. The finished sculptures standing by the door had disappeared that day: sundials, bird baths and lampstands. All that remained were the unfinished sculptures, or pieces that were such an odd shape nobody could quite work out what they were meant to be.

They were clustered together at the back of the workshop. Blocks of stone formed into swollen, headless bodies or heads with deep eye sockets and gaping mouths. Some of them didn't even remotely resemble people.

Per didn't go inside to take a closer look; he simply closed the door and went to fetch the paper.

*

'So your father is the famous Jerry Morner?' said Max. 'I didn't know him, but I do remember the name.'

Per hadn't spoken to Max Larsson since the party, but they had bumped into one another by the mailboxes.

'Really?'

He took a couple of steps away from the mailboxes with the newspaper in his hand, but Max didn't take the hint. He just smiled, one neighbour to another. 'Oh yes. Jerry Morner, he was a bit of a celebrity in the seventies. He sometimes gave interviews and appeared on those noisy debates about porn on TV . . . and of course when I was doing my military service we all read those magazines of his.' He winked at Per. 'Well, I say read, but of course they were mostly pictures.'

'Yes,' said Per.

'One of them was called *Babylon*,' said Max. 'Now, what was the other one called? *Sodom*?'

'*Gomorrah*.'

'That's it, *Babylon* and *Gomorrah*. They were pretty upmarket . . . But you had to ask for them in the newsagent's, they never had them out on display.' He coughed and added, 'Of course, I don't read them these days. Are they still going?'

'No, they're not around any more.'

'I suppose videos took over, and now there's the internet too,' said Max. 'Things move on.'

Per didn't respond.

'So how did he find the models?' Max went on.

Per shook his head. 'I was never involved.'

'You have to wonder what kind of girls would be willing to do that sort of thing,' said Max.

'Haven't a clue,' said Per, but a picture of Regina's smile came into his mind.

'I mean, you could see their faces quite clearly, and some of them were really pretty.'

Per shrugged his shoulders and set off towards the quarry. He had been nice for long enough now.

'I suppose they were well paid,' Max persisted behind him. 'And it must have been an experience.'

Per stopped and turned around. He decided to go for the Children Test. He'd done it several times before.

'Have you got children?' he asked.

'Children?' Max looked bewildered, then replied, 'Yes, I've got three from my first marriage.'

'Daughters?'

Max nodded. 'One. Her name is Annika.'

'Max,' said Per, lowering his voice, 'what would you say if you found out Annika had worked with my father?'

'She hasn't,' Max said quickly.

'How do you know? Do you think she'd tell you?'

Max didn't speak. Per allowed the silence to continue, and set off again. He had gone several metres by the time Max hissed behind him, 'You bastard!'

Per just kept on walking. He was used to that reaction when he tried to make people see Jerry's models as people.

But of course, that meant that good relations between the neighbours by the quarry had been destroyed once more.

You bastard.

The comment was in Per's mind as he prepared the Easter lunch.

Jerry, Per, Nilla and Jesper – three generations celebrating Easter together. It was too cold to sit out on the patio, so he laid the table in the living room, in front of Ernst's wooden chest. As he set out the plates he stared at the drawings on the chest; he wondered why the troll running into its cave was smiling, and why the princess was sitting weeping. Had the knight not arrived in time to defend her virtue?

'Pelle?' said a voice behind him. His father had come into the room.

'We'll be eating soon, Jerry. You can sit down . . . You like Easter eggs, don't you?'

Jerry nodded and sat down.

'You can have as many as you like,' said Per, and carried on setting the table.

Before he went to fetch the children, he turned back to Jerry and added, 'But no magazines on the table, thank you.'

Jerry kept quiet during the meal. The twins didn't say much either. Everybody ate their eggs and sat there in a world of their own.

'Did you go out today?' Per asked.

Nilla nodded slowly. She looked pale and tired, and her voice was quiet. 'We went down to the quarry. And Jesper found a skeleton.'

But Jesper shook his head. 'It was only a little piece of bone . . . I think it was part of a finger.'

'A finger?' said Per, looking at him. 'A human finger?'

'I think so.'

'Where did you find it?'

'At the bottom of a pile of stones. It's in my room.'

'I'm sure it'll be part of some animal, we can have a look at it later,' said Per, peeling an egg. 'But you shouldn't really pick up bits of bone you find on the ground, there could be germs and—'

But Jesper didn't seem to be listening; he was staring past Per, his eyes full of fear. 'Dad!' he shouted. 'Nilla!'

Per looked to his right and saw that Nilla had dropped her egg and was leaning over the table beside him; her head was drooping and she was about to topple side-ways.

There were red splashes of blood on the tablecloth. When she coughed, more appeared.

Per moved fast. 'Nilla!' He grabbed her just before she fell.

She looked at him, but her eyelids were heavy. 'What? What is it?' she said, as if she were talking in her sleep. 'Shall I . . .'

Then she fell silent and slumped against him.

Per held her tightly. 'It's OK,' he said quietly. 'Everything's OK.'

But it wasn't fine – his daughter's face was suddenly bright red. Per could feel the blood pulsing in her arm, and suddenly there was no strength in her thin body, it was completely limp. She had fainted.

The meal had come to a complete standstill. Jerry was sitting on the opposite side of the table with an egg in his hand, staring blankly at the red drops on the table. Jesper was on his feet, gazing wide-eyed at his sister.

Per carried Nilla over to the sofa. When he had laid her down on her side, she coughed and opened her eyes.

'I'm cold,' she said.

Per remembered the doctor in Kalmar saying that the new medication could leave her open to infection, and he looked over at Jesper. 'Nilla will be fine,' he said. 'But I need to take her back to hospital. Will you be OK here with Granddad?'

Jesper nodded.

'And can you ring Mum?'

The hospital was silent and empty on Easter Saturday, but of course the emergency department was open. Nilla was wheeled off down the corridor on a trolley. All Per could do was go up to her old ward and wait.

He sat down on a chair in the corridor; he was used to waiting, after all. He waited and waited.

After almost an hour, the door opened and Marika and her new husband came in. Georg was tanned and was wearing a dark suit, just as he had been on the two previous occasions when Per had met him.

'We've come to see the doctor,' said Marika.

Per didn't recognize the doctor who was on duty this evening. His name was Stenhammar and he was younger than Nilla's previous doctor, but his expression was serious as he took them into his office and sat down at the desk.

'Well, I have good news and bad news.'

Nobody said anything, so the doctor went on: 'The good news is that we've managed to bring down her temperature; Pernilla will be coming back from intensive care shortly.'

'Can we take her home this evening?' said Marika, in spite of the fact that this was Per's weekend.

Dr Stenhammar shook his head. 'That's the bad news,' he said. 'Pernilla won't be coming home . . . she needs to stay here.'

'How long for?' asked Marika.

The doctor didn't speak for a few seconds. Then he began to elaborate at length on the thorough examination they had done, on Nilla's test results, and on what they had found. He talked and talked, and he kept using long words.

'Epithelioid . . . what was it again?' said Per.

'The usual abbreviation is EHE,' said Dr Stenhammar, 'and it's very rare, an extremely uncommon type of cancer that usually affects the soft tissues. I know it's no consolation to you, but as a doctor I—'

'What does this mean for Nilla?' Marika interrupted.

The doctor started to speak again. Afterwards Per

could remember only two words: *malignant tumour.*

'. . . so it's best if she stays here until the surgery,' said Stenhammar, linking his hands on the desk.

Surgery. Per could feel the floor swaying beneath his feet.

'So you're going to operate?'

The doctor nodded. 'We have to, radiotherapy alone won't be enough, unfortunately . . . We're on the way to a vital indication.'

Per didn't ask what the final words meant, but they didn't sound good.

'When?' Marika asked quietly.

'Soon, very soon.' The doctor paused. 'And I'm afraid it's not a straightforward operation.'

'What are the odds on her recovery?' asked Per. A terrible question – he wanted to take it back. But Dr Stenhammar merely shook his head.

'We don't bet in here.'

They walked out into the corridor in silence. Georg went to get some coffee. Per had nothing to say to his ex-wife, but Marika suddenly looked around.

'Where's Jesper?'

'Back at the cottage.'

'Alone?'

'No, my father's with him.'

'Jerry?'

Marika had raised her voice in the empty corridor. Per lowered his: 'Gerhard, yes. He came to us a few days ago . . .'

'Why?'

'He's sick,' said Per. 'He's had a—'

'He always has been, hasn't he?'

'. . . and he needed some help,' Per went on. 'But I'll be taking him home soon.'

'Well, don't bring him here,' Marika snapped. 'I don't want to risk meeting that dirty old sod ever again.'

'Dirty old sod? Well, he might be,' Per said quietly, 'but as far as I recall you were very curious about Jerry and his activities when we met. You thought it was exciting, or so you said.'

'I thought *you* were exciting at the time,' said Marika. 'I soon got over that as well.'

'Good,' said Per. 'That's one problem less.'

'It's not me who has a problem with you, Per. It's you who has a problem with *me*.'

He took a deep breath. 'I'm just going to say good-bye to Nilla.'

Marika stayed in the corridor while Per went in to see Nilla before setting off for home. The room was quiet. She was lying in bed beneath a white sheet, and of course the drip was back in her arm. He bent down and pressed his cheek against hers. 'Hello, you.'

'Hi.'

She was pale now, her chest trembling with shallow breaths.

'How are you doing? How do your lungs feel?'

'Not too bad . . .'

'You're looking good.'

She shook her head. 'I can't find my black stone, Dad.'

'What black stone?'

'My piece of lava from Iceland . . . Mum bought it, it's my lucky stone. It was in my room. I thought I put it in my pocket, but it's not there now.'

Per remembered; it was a smooth, coal-black stone, and Nilla had let him hold it; it fitted perfectly into his palm.

'I'm sure it's in the house somewhere,' he said. 'I'll find it.'

*

208

When he got back to the cottage half an hour later, Jerry and Jesper had cleared away the food and removed the stained cloth. But the dishes were piled up in the kitchen, and Per had to deal with them.

His father and son were sitting on the sofa in the living room watching some American sitcom. Jerry seemed captivated, but Jesper turned his head as his father walked in.

'How did it go, Dad?'

Per rubbed his eyes. 'Well, Nilla has to stay in Kalmar tonight, but she's feeling better now.'

Jesper nodded, and turned his attention back to the TV.

Later, thought Per. *I'll tell him about the tumour later.*

He turned away.

'What are you going to do now?' asked Jesper.

'I'm going to look for a stone, a lucky stone.'

Then he remembered something, and turned back. 'By the way, what was it you found, Jesper? A piece of bone?'

'Mmm. It's in my room, on the bookshelf.'

Per went into his son's room. He tried to ignore the mess, but opened the window to let a bit of air in. Then he looked at the bookshelf.

The piece of bone lying there amongst Jesper's books and games was very small, just four or five centimetres long. It was greyish-white and felt rough to the touch, as if it had been lying out in the open for many years and had become dry and fragile.

And Per could see that Jesper and Nilla were right; the piece of bone did actually resemble a broken-off human finger.

30

As their parents were dead and they had no children together, Max and Vendela would be celebrating Easter alone in their new summer home. It didn't really matter, Vendela felt. Easter wasn't that important.

Her grown-up daughter Caroline had phoned from Dubai to wish them Happy Easter, but she wouldn't be home until midsummer. Max had three children with his first wife, but his daughter had fallen out with him after Max had made some comments about her mother a couple of years earlier. Then she had got her two brothers on her side, so at the moment none of them were in touch with their father.

And of course the children were particularly poisonous towards Vendela as their stepmother, she knew that. Things had always been the same.

She had brought some birch twigs from the old farm, and although they triggered her allergy she took them into the house to use as her Easter decoration. Nothing more was needed to create a festive atmosphere.

Then it was time for dinner. Vendela was tired of cooking – both the fridge and the freezer were full of leftovers from the party – but she still had to come up with some kind of celebratory Easter meal. Some eggs, some herring and potatoes, a little wine. A Bordeaux – she had already opened the bottle and poured herself a glass.

The door of Max's study was closed; he had been sitting at his thinking desk all day, and didn't wish to be disturbed. He was charging his batteries before a small book tour which he was due to undertake after Easter, and the first hundred pages of proofs for *Good Food to the Max* had just arrived from his publisher. Yesterday they had sent the final recipes to the editor, so the project was almost finished. Sooner or later Max would no doubt emerge and ask her to proofread the pages.

The fan was whirring away as the eggs and potatoes simmered on the hob. Vendela thought about Max's children; they hadn't even called to wish him Happy Easter.

The kitchen timer started buzzing behind her; the eggs were done. She lifted the bubbling pan off the hob and ran cold water into it.

There were twelve hard-boiled eggs, but Vendela wouldn't be eating any of them. She had won the struggle against hunger since she came to the island, and as long as she boiled enough eggs, Max wouldn't be able to keep track of whether she'd eaten any or not.

Vendela saw a small movement out of the corner of her eye, and turned her head. 'Hello Ally,' she said.

Aloysius had come into the kitchen – without bumping into the door frame with his nose, as he often did. He shuffled across the floor towards her, slowly but in a straight line.

'How's my boy?' said Vendela, smiling at him. 'Happy Easter, little one.'

The poodle sat down slowly, his stiff front leg extended to the side.

'There'll be something nice for you tonight – you'll like that, won't you?'

The dog licked his nose and looked over at Vendela.

It was unbelievable, but Aloysius actually seemed to be *looking* at her. His gaze seemed to be focused, he could see it was her. She stepped quickly to one side, and watched his eyes follow the movement.

Vendela dropped her pen and whirled around. She rushed over to Max's thinking room, ignoring the fact that the door was still closed.

'Max, his eyes are better!' she shouted, hammering on the door. 'Ally's eyes are better, Max, come out and see!'

31

The grandchildren had spent the whole of Easter Saturday painting hard-boiled eggs. There were yellow eggs with blue stripes and red eggs with green spots – but most of them had so many layers of colour they had ended up black.

Gerlof ate a couple with plenty of salt and fish roe, but he preferred spiced herring with potatoes and crispbread. He had a couple of glasses of schnapps too, flavoured with wormwood picked down by the shore, and noticed that no one else at the table was drinking spirits. Good. (From time to time over the years he had been worried about his younger daughter Julia, but this evening she had only milk in her glass.)

After the eggs and the schnapps Gerlof felt so good that he started talking about how miserable life on the island had been back in the old days.

'*Saturday slops*, do you know what that was?'

The grandchildren shook their heads.

'It was a very special dish,' said Gerlof. 'The recipe was simple . . . you just collected a whole week's worth of leftovers in a wooden bowl, then you put plenty of salt in, boiled the whole thing up in a pan and ate it. The whole family!'

Julia shook her head. 'You've never eaten Saturday slops, Dad. You weren't that poor!'

He frowned at her. 'I'm talking about my grandfather, he used to have it when he was little. Things were bad enough when I was little, mind you . . . We had no running water, we had to pump the water into a bucket out in the yard.'

'I remember that pump,' said Lena. 'It was still there in the sixties . . . and I thought the water from the well tasted better than tap water, anyway.'

'Well, yes,' said Gerlof, 'but sometimes it was all brown, and you had to pump until it ran clear again. And of course we didn't have a proper toilet, just the outhouse with a big bucket that had to be emptied into a hole when it was full. It all splashed up your legs if you weren't careful, and if you slipped you got—'

Lena put down her fork. 'We are still eating, Dad.'

'Yes, yes,' said Gerlof, winking at the grandchildren. 'But in the spring it was the opposite way round, we had far too much water. Sometimes there would be great big lakes out on the alvar . . . I can remember swimming in them now and again. And once my brother Ragnar and I found an old tin bath; we made a sail from a sheet and launched it in the spring floods.' He laughed. 'It got up such a good speed that it capsized – it was my first shipwreck!'

'Were there cars then?' asked one of the children.

'Yes,' said Gerlof, 'there have been cars as long as I remember. They came to the island quite early on, long before electricity. There were cars up here before the First World War, but some farms didn't get electricity until the forties. And some people didn't want it – it cost too much. They carried on using paraffin lamps as long as they could.'

'At least you didn't have any power cuts if you were using paraffin lamps,' said Julia.

'Yes, and with the electricity everybody was terrified whenever we had a thunderstorm. People would go into each other's houses, or go and sit in the car until it was over . . . We just weren't used to electricity.'

When almost all the eggs had been eaten, the grandchildren left the table. It was much quieter, and Gerlof stayed there with his daughters.

He had something to tell them. Something that felt like a confession. 'I've started reading your mother's diaries.'

'They're in the attic, aren't they?' said Julia.

'No, they were at the back of a cupboard. Do you want to read them too?'

'I'd rather not,' said Julia.

Lena shook her head. 'I've seen them lying there, but I've never touched them . . . It felt too private. Wasn't she going to burn them? I've got a feeling she—'

'Burn them? Not that I know of,' Gerlof broke in. He didn't want to feel any worse than he already did, and carried on in his firmest captain's voice. 'Well, *I'm* reading them anyway. It's not illegal to read another person's diaries.'

Silence fell around the table. He picked up the last black-painted egg and started to peel it, then added in a quieter voice, 'She saw strange people around the house, did you know that? She wrote about it in the diaries.'

His daughters looked at him.

'You mean she saw little goblins?' said Julia. 'I know Granny did.'

'No, not goblins. Ella writes about a "changeling" who came to the cottage sometimes, when she was on her own up here. At first I thought she had some suitor

215

from the village coming to call when I was away at sea . . .'

'No chance,' said Julia.

'I don't think so either.' Gerlof looked thoughtfully out of the window, over towards the grass and bushes beyond their garden. 'But I do wonder what it was she actually saw. She never mentioned it to me. Did she say anything to you?'

Julia shook her head. She scooped out her last boiled egg and said, 'Mum was a bit secretive . . . she was good at keeping quiet.'

'Perhaps it was a troll from the quarry,' said Lena with a smile. 'Ernst used to talk about them.'

Gerlof didn't smile back. 'There are no trolls there.'

He started to get up from the table. Both his daughters quickly moved to help him, but he waved them away. 'I can manage, thank you. I think I'll go to bed soon. You won't forget the Easter service tomorrow morning?'

'We'll get you to the church, don't worry,' said Lena.

'Good.'

Gerlof still had his own bedroom at the cottage. He closed the door behind him and changed into his pyjamas, even though it was only nine o'clock. He knew he would sleep well, even if all the others were still up and watching TV. He could hear their laughter and loud voices, and closed his eyes.

The grandchildren's constant rushing about from morning till night wore him out. What would it be like when the summer holidays started? He'd better enjoy the peace during the spring, while it lasted.

32

'Ally?' Max called. 'Ally, look at me.'

Max was leaning forward in his armchair in the living room. The little poodle was sitting on Vendela's knee on the other side of the room, and turned his nose towards the voice.

'Aloysius? Can you see me?'

Vendela whispered in his ear, 'Ally, can you see Daddy?'

The dog whimpered faintly and seemed to be sniffing, but in different directions all around the room.

Max sighed. 'He can't see me, Vendela. He can hear and he can smell, but he can't see a thing.'

Vendela stroked the dog's back. 'He can,' she said. 'He's much better than he was . . . he doesn't bump into the furniture any more.' She scratched the back of his neck. 'And he looks at me, he really does. Don't you, poppet?'

Ally stretched up and licked her throat.

Max shook his head. 'Eyes don't heal themselves, I've never heard of that happening. I don't think sight can just come back . . .'

'Yes, it can,' said Vendela. '*Here* it can. Here on the island.'

'Really?'

Vendela put the poodle down on the stone floor. 'It's healthy here,' she said. 'I think it's the water and the earth . . . There's so much lime in the ground.'

'Right,' said Max, getting up from his chair and heading towards the hallway. 'I'm going to put the summer tyres on the car. Can you make me a snack to take with me later – some pasta salad?'

Vendela went into the kitchen and put the water on to boil. In a couple of hours she would be alone in the house. She was looking forward to it.

But the Easter weekend had gone well; they had eaten good food, and Vendela had helped Max with the proofreading of his cookery book. Now, on Sunday evening, he was getting ready to leave the island for a five-day promotional tour of southern Sweden; he would be away until Friday. He would talk about his previous self-help books and, of course, would give as much publicity as possible to his forthcoming venture, *Good Food to the Max.*

'Anticipation,' he said. 'You have to create the anticipation.'

He was stomping around the house, excited one minute and irritated the next, but Vendela knew he was always like that when he was due to go off and meet the public. There was so much that could go wrong; perhaps nobody would turn up, or his microphone might not work, or the organizers might have forgotten to order his books or arrange the venue. He was always more relaxed when he came home from his tours.

In the beginning Vendela had gone with him and they had enjoyed intimate dinners in various city hotels, but now they had an unspoken agreement that she would stay at home.

Once the pasta started boiling she went back into the

living room, and stopped dead. There was a milky-white puddle on the dark stone floor. Vendela realized what had happened and hurried off to fetch some kitchen roll before Max saw the puddle, but it was too late.

His call came as she stood by the sink: 'Vendela!'

She went back, her expression blank. 'What is it, darling?'

'Have you seen what he's done on the floor? Your dog?'

Now he was *her* dog.

'Yes, I've seen it.' She hurried in with kitchen paper in both hands. 'He's just got a bit of an upset tummy.'

She knelt down. Max stood behind her, his back ramrod straight as he watched her clean up the mess. 'It's not the first time.'

'No. But he does eat grass sometimes, it could be that,' said Vendela. 'But he's been much better this last week.'

Max said nothing, he just turned away. Vendela wiped up the last of the mess and got to her feet. 'There, all gone!'

The front door slammed; Max had gone out. Ally had crept under the kitchen table and was lying with his paws over his nose as if he were ashamed of himself, and she bent down. 'Don't do that again, poppet.'

Max had enjoyed spending time with Ally through all the years he could take the dog for long walks, or throw sticks and balls for him to fetch. But now Ally wasn't very well, he was obviously worthless.

She would go out to the stone with another coin this very evening. She would stay and pray – not only for Aloysius to get better, but also for Max to start liking the dog as he was, young or old, cute or ugly, healthy or sick. He was their Ally, after all.

'We're not finished yet, poppet,' she said, straining the pasta through a colander. 'We'll show him!'

Öland 1957

When the winter storms come, the fresh snow drifts to form metre-high frozen waves out on the alvar. Vendela can no longer walk across it, so for several months she has to take a long detour in order to get to school.

At the end of March the sun comes back and her father gives her a pair of boots made by the old village cobbler, Shoe-Paulsson. The stitching is poor and they let the water in, but she can walk across the alvar again between the melting snowdrifts.

She can go to the elf stone.

That spring Vendela takes her mother's jewellery, piece by piece, and on her way to school she leaves each item as an offering to the elves. Her father doesn't seem to notice that things are going missing; when he isn't working in the quarry, he's too busy looking at the starlit sky and working out the orbits of the man-made satellites. The farm is going to rack and ruin, and he seems to have forgotten the Invalid, but none of this bothers him.

Vendela places the pieces of jewellery in the hollows on the stone, and they disappear. Sometimes they stay there for a few days, but sooner or later they vanish. She never sees them again.

When she makes a wish it is almost always granted, sometimes in the strangest ways.

She wishes for a best friend in her class, someone who is hers alone and who doesn't care about the farm-yard aroma surrounding her. Two days later, Dagmar Gran asks if Vendela would like to come to her house after school. Dagmar's family is rich; they have a big farm near the church with several tractors and more than forty cows – so many that they are known only by a number rather than a name. Vendela can't go, because she has to see to Rosa, Rosa and Rosa, but she asks if she could perhaps come over a bit later on. Dagmar says that's fine.

The following week Vendela asks the elves if they could sort out something other than boiled eel for dinner; Henry has discovered cheap eels from the east coast, and has cooked them for ten consecutive days by this stage.

'We're having chicken tonight,' says Henry that same evening. 'I've just wrung the neck of one of them.'

Once she and Dagmar Gran have become best friends, Vendela asks if she can move to an empty seat next to Dagmar, but Fru Jansson says that she is the one who decides where her pupils will sit, and Vendela is to sit by the window, next to Thorsten Hellman, who needs someone who has a calming influence on him.

So the next day Vendela stops at the elf stone and places a fine gold chain in one of the hollows. Then she wishes for a new teacher, someone nicer and kinder than Fru Jansson.

Three days later Fru Jansson catches a cold and stays at home. The cold turns into a chest infection which almost kills her, and she has to go to a sanatorium on the mainland. She is replaced by Fröken Ernstam, a young supply teacher from Kalmar.

The pupils pick spring flowers by the roadside and give them to Fru Jansson's husband, who is the school caretaker. Vendela curtsies extra deeply and says quietly that she hopes Fru Jansson will soon be better.

On her way home that day she dare not even look at the elf stone.

33

Jerry Morner's belly was large and white and not remotely muscular. It had swollen with the consumption of wine and cheese and Cognac, year after year. And for the last week it had had a long dressing across it, but Per pulled it off on Easter Sunday morning. With one quick yank.

Jerry grunted on the kitchen chair, but didn't move.

'There,' said Per, folding up the dressing. 'Does that feel better?'

Jerry grunted again, but Per thought the wound in his stomach looked as if it had healed. It had knitted together, and now there was just a pink line.

'Do you remember what happened?' he asked.

There was a long pause, then Jerry answered, 'Bremer.'

'Bremer was holding the knife? He stabbed you and hit you?'

Jerry nodded. 'Bremer.'

'OK. But I mean, you were friends . . . Do you know why he did it?'

Jerry shook his head. He was sticking to his story – perhaps that made it more credible, Per thought, but it was still very odd. Why would Hans Bremer attack his colleague with a knife, lock himself and some woman in the house and then set fire to it?

Per could only hope that the police would go through the film studio, find some answers soon, and pass them on to him.

There were several mysteries to puzzle over. He had searched for Nilla's lucky stone both last night and this morning, but it just wasn't in the house. He also searched the car, but with no luck. He tried to stay out of sight of his father, because as soon as he showed himself the hoarse cries started up: 'Pelle? Pelle!'

When he had removed Jerry's dressing, Per straightened up. 'Now you're better, I thought it was time we got you home. I'll drive you down to Kristianstad this evening. What do you think about that?'

His father said nothing.

'OK, that's decided then. You can sit here and rest, and we'll have something to eat in a little while.'

An hour or so after lunch Per went out for a run, partly to clear his head and partly to get away from Jerry for a while.

Easter Sunday was chilly and bright, with just a few wispy clouds visible over the mainland. He ran north along the coast, and when he'd gone so far that he could see the little island of Blå Jungfrun as a black dome out in the Sound, he stopped and took in the view. The rocks, the sun, the sea. For a few seconds he was able to forget everything else. Then he turned around and ran back.

When he was almost home he caught sight of another runner, wearing a white cap and a red tracksuit. He or she was coming from the east, along the track that wound its way inland. A slender figure, approaching rapidly. It was Vendela Larsson.

Per stopped a few hundred metres from the quarry and allowed her to catch up with him. He smiled at her. 'Hi – how far?'

It was strange, but he thought she looked slightly embarrassed as she came up to him, as if she had been caught out somehow.

'How far? You mean how far have I run?' She seemed to be thinking it over. 'I don't really work it out . . . I ran out on to the alvar and back again. That's my usual circuit.'

'Great. I usually run up the coast. Two kilometres north, then back again.'

She smiled. 'I go for a jog almost every evening. We did say we might go together . . . how about tomorrow?'

'Sure,' said Per. Vendela didn't say anything else, so he turned and jogged towards the cottage. She joined him, and asked, 'How are the kids?'

Per glanced sideways at her. How much did she know? Did she know how sick Nilla was? He just didn't have the strength to start telling her all about it.

'Up and down,' he said. 'Jesper's fine, but Nilla's . . . she's lost her lucky stone.'

'Oh dear, is she upset?' asked Vendela. 'I thought she looked a bit pale at the party, as if she—'

'A bit,' Per interrupted. 'She's a bit upset.'

Vendela looked over at the cottage. 'Did she lose it indoors?'

'She thinks so.'

Vendela suddenly stopped dead and closed her eyes for a few seconds.

Per looked at her. 'Are you all right?'

She opened her eyes and nodded. She started to jog again, heading for her own house. Over her shoulder she said briefly, as if it were obvious, 'I think you'll find the stone now – it's probably in her room.'

And it was.

When Per got in he looked in the little room where Nilla had slept over Easter, and there it was on the bed. A little round piece of polished lava, clearly visible on the white duvet.

But he'd looked there, hadn't he? He'd looked for Nilla's lucky stone everywhere, surely?

34

'The one from the party,' said Jerry.

He was standing outside the cottage pointing south with a trembling index finger.

'What are you talking about?' said Per, putting Jerry's suitcase in the car.

'Filmed her,' said Jerry.

'Who?'

'Her!'

He was still pointing. Per looked over at the neighbours' house, where a couple of figures were moving about on the drive.

'Do you mean Marie Kurdin? The woman you saw at the party?'

Jerry nodded.

'She was in your films?'

Jerry nodded again. 'Slag.'

Per gritted his teeth; he'd heard Jerry use that word before. 'Don't say that.'

'But fresh,' said Jerry slowly, as if he liked the word. 'Frresh slag.'

'Stop it,' said Per. 'I'm not interested.'

But he couldn't help looking over at the house.

Marie Kurdin was standing outside, packing the

family car with a dozen suitcases, changing mats and bags of toys. The Easter break was over, and the Kurdin family were evidently on their way home.

How old was she? Thirty, perhaps. A tall, slender mother with a baby. She was heaving the suitcases energetically into the car, shouting something inaudible to her husband indoors. It couldn't be true, surely? Marie Kurdin couldn't have been in Jerry's films? He suddenly saw images in his head, images he hadn't asked for: Marie Kurdin lying on a bed like all the others, with Markus Lukas bending over her and Jerry standing slightly to one side, smoking . . .

No. Per shook his head and looked at his father. 'You're imagining things.'

Before they left, Per went over to Vendela Larsson's house to say thank you for helping him to find Nilla's lucky stone – and to ask his neighbour how she could have known where it was.

He knocked on the door, but there was no answer. He scribbled a quick note:

> *Thanks a lot for the stone!*
> *Per*

Then he folded it up and tucked it into the doorframe.

There were three of them in the car this time; Jesper was with them as they left the island and drove across the Öland Bridge. He was going back to his mother, and back to school after the Easter holidays.

Marika lived in north Kalmar and Per dropped his son off outside the house; he didn't want to run the risk of Marika meeting Jerry.

'Can you find your way from here?' he asked as Jesper got out of the car.

Jesper nodded without cracking a smile at the joke, but leant over to give Per a quick hug.

'Good luck with school,' said Per, 'and say hello to Mum from me.'

When Jesper had gone inside, he turned to Jerry. 'Did you see that hug, Jerry? Some daddies get hugs.'

Jerry said nothing, so Per went on, 'OK, let's get you home.'

'Home,' said Jerry.

A couple of hours later they drove into the centre of Kristianstad, but by that time Jerry had fallen asleep. He slept leaning back in his seat, his face tipped up towards the roof of the car and his mouth wide open between hollow cheeks. His snoring drowned out the sound of the engine, and Per switched on the radio, which was playing a sentimental old song:

> The little girl lay pale and wan
> In her narrow hospital bed,
> She looked for hope to the doctor,
> But he grimly shook his head.

He quickly turned it off again.

Per wasn't familiar with the area, but eventually he found his way and parked ten metres away from the door to his father's apartment block. It was closed.

When he switched off the engine, Jerry gave a start and woke up. He blinked and looked confused. 'Pelle?'

'You're home now.'

'Kristianstad?' Jerry coughed and looked down the street. He shook his head slowly. 'No.'

He'd changed his mind again. Per sighed. 'Yes, Jerry – you'll be safe here.'

Jerry shook his head again. He raised a trembling finger and pointed.

'What is it?' Per was still looking over at Jerry's door. 'Wait here,' he said, getting out of the car. 'I'll go and have a look, then I'll come back for you. Have you got the key?'

Jerry fumbled in his pocket and handed it over. 'Prince,' he said.

Jerry wanted cigarettes, but Per's only response was to close the car door.

He walked slowly towards the building. Jerry's apartment was fairly central, but it wasn't in the most upmarket area of Kristianstad. The turn-of-the-century block was in need of renovation. Just below the metal roof, four floors up, small carved stone heads gazed down at him. They looked like deformed owls.

He unlocked the outside door and stepped into the darkness.

He thought back to the day a week ago when he had walked into Jerry's house. He thought about the smoke and flames shooting up from the ground floor. About Bremer in the burning bed, and a girl screaming for help.

At least there was no smell of smoke in here. The stairwell was filled with nothing but echoes. The stone staircase wound its way upwards in a spiral around a cylindrical lift shaft, but the circular lift looked at least eighty years old and was far too small; it would close around him like a steel cage if he stepped inside.

Per preferred to walk up the three floors to Jerry's apartment. He passed two floors with closed doors, and carried on to the third. He stopped before he got to the top of the stairs.

Jerry's door was ajar.

At first Per thought he'd made a mistake, but when

230

he counted the floors again, he knew he was in the right place.

He could just see the hallway inside, but it was dark and silent. There was no movement inside.

He stayed where he was, on the landing a few steps below the open door. He listened again. There wasn't a sound, apart from the odd car passing by.

Per thought about the front door of Jerry's house, which had been half-open.

Why was this door open as well? It shouldn't be. *You'll be safe here*, he'd said to Jerry, but now he had his doubts.

Are you scared?

Yes, he was scared. A little bit.

Per took a deep breath, thought about his judo training and tried to find the balance within his body, from his feet upwards. Slowly he set off up the stairs again. Now he had the feeling somebody was standing in Jerry's hallway, waiting for him. Someone who was holding their breath, listening to him coming closer, however slowly he was moving, however quietly his heart was beating.

Cautiously he approached the open door.

He took the last three steps in a single, decisive movement, grabbed the handle and pulled the door wide open.

The stink of cigarette smoke rushed towards him, but it was probably just an old smell left behind by Jerry.

It was dark in the hallway; Per reached in and switched on the light. Then he peered inside.

At first everything looked normal. Normal? He hadn't been in Jerry's apartment for over three years, and then he'd only stayed for half an hour. But there were still lots of clothes hanging in the hall – suede jackets, yellow jackets, and down on the floor black patent shoes which Jerry presumably hadn't worn in years.

Per took two steps inside and listened. Silence.

There was a fine Persian rug in the big living room, and at the edge of the rug a large suitcase lay open.

It was empty, but there were several more bags behind it. Moroccan carpet bags, plastic bags and shabby briefcases lay scattered across the floor – and it looked as if they had been opened by someone who had searched through them, because there were piles of clothes and papers all over the floor as well.

Per was frightened now, but he took two steps forward and looked inside the living room.

There was no sign of anyone, not a sound to be heard.

He walked in.

He was expecting the room to be in more of a mess than it was. There were drifts of fluff in the corners and dried-up orange peel on the glass table, but Jerry's oil paintings were still hanging on the walls. Per had given him a few books over the years, and they were untouched and neatly arranged on the bookshelf. His father had never taken the time to read.

To the left of the doorway stood a lacquered veneer chest of drawers, a reproduction of a piece by Georg Haupt, and that was anything but untouched. Per remembered it from his childhood; it had three drawers which were always locked – but they were open now.

Broken open. Someone had taken a screwdriver or chisel and hacked their way through the wood surrounding the black keyholes, then ripped out the locks. The papers and documents Jerry had kept in the drawers had been pulled out and strewn across the floor.

The bedroom was beyond the living room. The blinds were drawn; it was as dark and silent as the rest of the apartment. A painting of a naked woman with enormous rounded breasts hung above Jerry's water bed.

Per took three steps towards the doorway and listened again. He could see that the bed was unmade, with the duvet and pillows in a heap. But there was nobody in it.

The apartment was empty.

He turned and went slowly back downstairs.

Out on the street cars and buses were passing by, and an elderly man and woman were walking along arm in arm just a short distance away. Life was carrying on as normal, and Per tried to calm down. He went over to the car and opened the passenger door. His father looked at him. 'Prince, Pelle?'

Per shook his head. He stood by the car, staring over at the door of Jerry's apartment block. It remained closed.

'Jerry, when you left for Ryd last weekend, did you close the front door of your apartment?'

Jerry coughed and nodded.

'You closed it and locked it – are you quite sure?'

Jerry nodded firmly, but Per knew he had forgotten things before. Since the stroke it was almost routine that everything he had said and done the previous day was completely forgotten.

'The door was open when I went in, and a chest of drawers has been damaged . . . I think you've had a break-in. Unless you did it yourself?'

Jerry sat in silence, his head bowed.

Per had to make a decision. 'OK . . . let's go back up and see if anything's been stolen. Then we'd better contact the police.'

He leant down and helped his father out of the car. 'Jerry,' he said, 'did anyone else have a key to your apartment?'

Jerry got to his feet unsteadily and appeared to consider the question before replying with a single word. 'Bremer.'

35

Per reported the break-in to the police in Kristianstad, even though Jerry was unable to determine whether anything had actually been stolen from the chest of drawers or not.

'Jerry, what's missing?' he'd asked several times. 'What have they taken?'

But Jerry had simply stood there looking at the piles of documents, as if he no longer remembered what they were. When Per leafed through the papers that had been left behind they seemed to consist mostly of old rent bills and bank statements.

So where was everything else? Surely there ought to be contracts for all the models Jerry and Bremer had filmed over the years? Signed agreements where the young women certified that they weren't *too* young, and that they were doing this of their own free will?

He couldn't find anything like that, and looked at his father. 'Do you remember what you kept here, Jerry? Was it anything important?'

'Papers.'

'Important papers?'

'Doc—' Jerry stopped; the word was too difficult.

'Documents? From Morner Art?'

'Morner Art?' Jerry seemed to have forgotten the name of his company.

When Per called the police, all he could do was give them vague information about the break-in. They noted it down, but didn't come out to investigate.

'It's a bank holiday,' said the police officer. 'We have to prioritize emergencies. But thank you for reporting it; we'll keep our eyes open.'

At about nine o'clock, Per rang Nilla at the hospital to say goodnight.

'How are you feeling?'

'Not too bad.' Her voice was quiet but audible. 'A bit better than yesterday . . . I'm still on a drip, and I've had loads of injections.'

'Good,' Per said quickly. 'And I've found your lucky stone.'

'Have you? Where was it?'

'On your bed,' said Per, without going into detail. 'I'll bring it next time I come to see you. Any news?'

'No . . . except there are a couple of new people on the ward,' said Nilla. 'There's a boy called Emil.'

Her voice suddenly sounded more cheerful when she said his name, so Per asked, 'Is he the same age as you?'

'Nearly. He's fifteen.'

'Good. Ask him if he wants to play Ludo.'

Nilla laughed and changed the subject. 'Did you get my thought message tonight? At eight o'clock?'

'I think so . . . there were lots of pictures in my head, anyway.'

'So what was I thinking about, then? What did you see?'

Per looked out at the sky above the town and took a chance. 'Clouds?'

'*No.*'

'A sunset?'

'No.'

'Were you thinking about your friends?'

'No, I was thinking about bats.'

'Bats? Why?'

'They fly around outside the hospital in the evenings,' said Nilla. 'They flap across the sky like black rags.'

'Don't you watch the birds any more?'

'Yes, during the day. But at night when I can't get to sleep, I watch the bats.'

Per promised to come and visit her the next day, and they said goodbye.

It was a bit late to set off home by that stage, and Per's cottage was empty in any case, so he stayed over with Jerry.

Before he went to bed he fastened the security chain on the front door.

Staying overnight in the apartment in Kristianstad felt strange, but he had slept on the long leather sofa as a teenager, when Jerry was living in Malmö. As he settled down on it, the memories came flooding back.

His mother had often given him a talking-to before he went to stay with Jerry: 'If he's got some woman there you don't have to stay over, you can come home . . . or I'll come and fetch you. You don't have to put up with that sort of thing.'

'No, Mum.'

But of course his father had had a woman staying from time to time. Several, in fact. Per had often wondered if he had any undiscovered half-siblings somewhere in southern Sweden; it wouldn't have surprised him.

The door to Jerry's bedroom had been closed, but as Per lay on the sofa he had been able to hear his father and the women, of course. By that time he was a teenager and less innocent than when he met Regina, and he knew what Jerry did, but the nights were still a torment.

It doesn't matter, Per had thought. *Love isn't important.*

And now? Now he was thinking about Nilla and Jesper. And for a brief moment he actually saw Vendela Larsson's big eyes in the darkness before him.

Then he fell asleep.

When he woke up it was Monday morning – Easter Monday.

There was no glamour in Jerry's kitchen. The table was covered in brown grease marks. Dirty cups and plates were piled up on the draining board, and there was nothing but coffee and crispbread for breakfast. And Jerry's cigarettes, of course.

Per topped up his father's coffee cup and said, 'I'll be off soon, Jerry. I need to get back to Jesper and Nilla.'

Jerry looked up.

'But not you,' said Per. 'You're staying here. You'll be all right here, won't you?'

He was trying to be firm, but it wasn't working. He looked around the dirty kitchen, unable to decide what to do with his father.

Go home, he thought, looking at his reflection in the kitchen window. *He wouldn't have bothered with you if you were old and sick.*

But Per couldn't do it. It wasn't just his promise to his mother, or the fact that Jerry didn't eat properly or look after himself, and needed help – there was this business of the spare keys as well. This business of arson and a possible break-in.

If Jerry was going to stay here, Per would have to get the police to keep an eye on his apartment, and until then it didn't feel safe.

If Hans Bremer had had a key to the apartment, and if someone had stolen it from him and got in over Easter to steal something, then there was nothing to stop that person from coming back.

In the end Per took Jerry back to Öland with him, in spite of everything. He packed a case with clean clothes and locked the front door carefully, then father and son got back in the car and set off towards the Baltic.

Per kept his promise to stop in Kalmar and visit Nilla, but found her fast asleep. Her slumber seemed peaceful and deep. He sat for a while in silence beside her bed, watching her pale face and struggling with an urge to split himself into two parts: one that would stay here and keep watch over her around the clock; and one that would prefer to run away and never come back. Per loved his daughter, but to see her like this in a hospital room was unbearable. All he wanted was to get back in the car.

He could tell himself that helping Jerry was of more use. But the truth was that Per wasn't really being helpful, he was just a coward who couldn't face his daughter's suffering.

Afterwards, Per and Jerry continued to Öland. At least there were no grandchildren to take into account at the cottage this time. And hardly any neighbours, either. They got back to the quarry at about three o'clock, and Per could see that the Kurdin house was all closed up.

It looked as if the other neighbours, the Larssons, were still there. He remembered promising to go for a run with Vendela this evening, and realized he was actually looking forward to it.

As he helped Jerry into the cottage, Per asked, 'So what happens to Morner Art now – the company you and Bremer ran together?'

238

'Bremer,' said Jerry, shaking his head.

Per thought he understood. 'That's right, Hans Bremer is gone . . . so I expect you'll wind the company up now, once and for all?'

His father nodded.

'Was that what Markus Lukas wanted when he got in touch with you?' asked Per. 'Did he want you to stop making films?'

Jerry looked confused, and didn't reply.

'I can help you wind up Morner Art,' said Per. 'I can take care of the practicalities – contact the authorities, the bank and so on.'

Jerry still said nothing, but Per thought his chin made a small movement of assent. And he hoped – he really did hope – that this would be the end of Jerry's business.

No more magazines, no more films.

No more trips into the forest.

36

Once Max had set off on his short promotional tour, Vendela was alone in the house for the first time, and suddenly it seemed even bigger than before. Too big – the living room with its high ceiling and thick beams reminded her of Henry's barn. Her steps echoed emptily when she walked across the stone floor. But she had hung old Gerlof's Turk's head mat on the kitchen door, and smiled to herself each time she looked at it.

Aloysius was still there, of course, and was good company. And he was so well! It was just fantastic. When Max had gone, Ally got out of his basket and walked around the ground floor several times, without bumping into a single piece of furniture. And Vendela thought he was looking at her all the time now, without her needing to call him. She wasn't really surprised, because that was exactly what she had wished for.

And now she was going for a run up the coast with Per Mörner.

'Hi,' said Per when she opened the door.
'Hi,' said Vendela.
'Are you ready?'
'Absolutely.'

They set off from the quarry side by side, and soon fell into rhythm with one another, breathing together as they ran, keeping abreast of the setting sun.

A chill moved in from the sea, up across the shore and the rocks. The sun stained the sky dark red. They picked up speed as they reached the gravel track, and Vendela felt strong, keeping up the same fast pace as Per. She could hear his deep, steady breathing, and the proximity of his tall body gave her fresh energy; she felt as if she could run all the way to the neighbouring village of Långvik.

But after three or four kilometres Per turned and asked, 'Shall we head back?'

She could see that he was tired. 'Sure. We've come far enough.'

They stopped and rested up above the shore for a minute or so, looking out across the dark-blue Sound, with not a boat in sight. They didn't speak, but took a deep breath at almost the same moment. Then they set off towards the south, keeping up a steady pace.

They didn't start talking until they were back at the quarry.

'There's something I wanted to ask you,' said Per, getting his breath back. 'That business with the stone . . . my daughter's lucky stone from Iceland. How did you do it?'

'Me?' said Vendela, letting out a long breath. 'I didn't do anything.'

'But you knew where it was . . . on her bed.'

Vendela nodded. 'Sometimes you just get a feeling about things.' She wanted to change the subject, and asked, 'So has your family gone now?'

'My father's still here. My children have gone to Kalmar.'

'Me too . . . well, my husband. My little dog Aloysius

and I are still here. He stayed out of the way during the party on Wednesday, but he's around now. Would you like to meet him?'

'Sure.'

Per walked up to the house with her. She opened the door and took a last look around, east towards the alvar and west towards the shore.

'We live between the trolls and the elves,' she said.

'Do we?' said Per.

'My father always told me the trolls lived down in the quarry, and the elves lived out on the alvar. And when they met, they would fight until the blood flowed.'

'Really?'

'Yes, there are still traces of their battles down in the quarry. Traces of blood.'

'The place of blood, you mean?' said Per. 'Do you believe in that?'

He looked at her quizzically, and she laughed out loud. 'Maybe . . . but not in trolls.'

He was smiling now, as if they were sharing a joke. 'And what about elves?'

'Yes,' said Vendela; her smile suddenly disappeared. 'Perhaps they do exist. But they're friendly creatures – they help us.'

'Do they?'

'Yes.' And she went on without thinking, 'They were the ones who helped to find your daughter's lucky stone.'

'Really?' said Per.

'I asked them about it, and they showed me an image of where it would be.'

Per said nothing, but Vendela could see he was looking sideways at her. She shouldn't have babbled about the elves, but it was done now.

The silence was getting a little too long and awkward, so she turned around. 'Ally!'

After a few seconds she heard the sound of pattering feet as the greyish white poodle made his way cautiously towards the door.

'Hello,' said Per.

Ally raised his head, but was unable to focus his gaze on their guest. So that Per wouldn't notice anything, Vendela bent down and scratched the back of Ally's neck.

'Thanks for your company,' said Per behind her.

She turned to face him. 'Thank you. Shall we do it again tomorrow?'

A straight, direct question, and she hadn't even laughed nervously as she asked him.

Per looked slightly hesitant, then nodded.

When Vendela had closed the door behind Per, the telephone in the kitchen started to ring. She stayed in the hall with Ally; she had an idea of who it would be, and wasn't sure if she wanted to answer.

The piercing tone rang out twice, three times, four – and by the fifth ring she was over by the worktop picking up the receiver.

'Hello?'

'Where have you been?' said a male voice. 'I've called three times.'

It was Max, of course.

'Nowhere,' Vendela said quickly. 'Out on the alvar.'

'Out for a run?'

'Exactly.'

'Alone? Weren't you going to go for a run with our neighbour?'

Vendela didn't even remember mentioning it, but Max had remembered, and of course he had to bring it up. She couldn't understand his need to be in control. She waited a few seconds, then came up with a less than truthful response: 'I went on my own.'

'Is there anybody else left in the village?'

'I don't know . . . a few people, I expect. I've been in-doors most of the time.'

'OK . . . well, I rang anyway.'

Silence. She heard the sound of pattering feet, and Ally came into the kitchen. Vendela clicked her fingers and the poodle listened hard in order to find his way over to her.

'How's the tour going?' she asked.

'Not bad.'

'Many people?'

'Some. But they're not buying many books.'

'I'm sure it'll improve,' she said.

'Anything else?' he said quietly.

'Like what?'

'Have you taken any tablets today?'

'Only two,' said Vendela. 'One this morning and one after lunch.'

'Good,' said Max. 'I have to go now; I'm having dinner with the organizers.'

'OK. Sleep well.'

After she had put the phone down, Vendela wondered why she kept on lying about the tablets. She hadn't taken a single one for several days. Her running was much more important now.

37

After Easter, everything went back to normal in Gerlof's little garden, once his children and grandchildren had gone home.

The last of the dead leaves had fallen off the hazel bushes around the garden, and Gerlof could see small, busy shadows hopping about among the branches. They were bullfinches, newly arrived migrants who would either remain in the village for the whole summer, or just rest for a few days before continuing across the Baltic to Finland and Russia. He could hear them too – the chorus of the finches sounded like tinkling bells.

The temperature had risen by a few degrees; there was only a gentle breeze, and Gerlof could work on his model ships out on the lawn. John Hagman had given him an old, well-dried piece of mahogany that he was intending to use to build a full-rigged ship. They had had their glory days on the world's oceans long before he himself became a sea captain, but he had always loved them.

He could also carry on reading Ella's diaries in secret. From time to time he had found a note about her visitor.

*

5th August 1957

Plenty of fish this week. Last Thursday we had fried pike steaks from a fish Gerlof caught with a spear between the rocks on the shore, and this morning Andersson the carpenter gave me a perch.

And we had a crayfish party last Saturday night. But Gerlof was down in Borgholm at a meeting, so the girls and I had a party on our own.

The changeling seems to know when there's no one around. He's stayed away for a couple of weeks, but today he was standing by the stone wall when I came out, and I fetched him some milk and biscuits. He came over and I could smell him; the stench was worse than ever, I expect it's the heat. He needs a bath, I thought, why can't he have a bath? But the changeling just smiled and I pretended everything was all right.

As usual he didn't say a word, just munched away at the biscuits and drank his milk. And then he headed off towards the north again, without so much as a thank-you.

He's so timid and he jumps at the slightest sound, so I don't think he's supposed to be here. He wants to come and go without anyone seeing him. That's why I don't mention him, not to anyone.

Gerlof stopped reading. He looked over towards the village road in the north and thought about the fact that Ella's visitor had always come from that direction.

What lay to the north? In the fifties there had been a few farms and boathouses up there; apart from that, there was nothing but grass and bushes. And the quarry, of course. That was the closest, on the other side of the road.

He was going to start reading again, but the bell on

the gate heralded the arrival of a visitor; not the care service this time, but Per Mörner. He waved, and Gerlof waved back. They hadn't seen each other since the previous week, at the party.

'I'm back,' said Per, walking across the lawn.

'I didn't even know you'd been away,' said Gerlof. 'Did you take your father back to the mainland?'

'That was the idea,' Per said quietly, 'but one or two things got in the way . . . He's still here, I'm looking after him.'

He lowered his eyes as he spoke.

'Well, that's good,' said Gerlof. 'You'll be able to spend some time together.'

'Yes,' said Per, not looking particularly pleased at the prospect.

There was a short silence, then Per suddenly asked, 'By the way, do you know anything about the blood over in the quarry?'

'Traces of blood?' said Gerlof. 'I've never seen any.'

'Not traces of blood,' said Per. 'It's more like a red layer that you can see in the rock . . . Ernst used to talk about the place of blood.'

'Oh, that?' Gerlof laughed. 'Yes, that's what the quarry workers used to call it. But it's not blood, it's iron oxide. It was formed when Öland lay beneath the water, and the quarry was part of the sea bed. The sun shone down through the waters of the Baltic and the sea bed oxidized. Then the island rose from the waves and the iron oxide solidified and formed a layer of rock . . . It was before my time, of course, but that's what I've read.'

'But did the quarry workers believe it was blood?'

'No, no, but they had lots of names for the different strata within the rock.' Gerlof raised a hand and counted on his fingers: 'There was the hard layer on the top; that was full of cracks, and they just broke it off and shovelled it away. Then there was the sticky layer that was solid and difficult to quarry. After that they reached the good layer, where they found the best, finest limestone, and that was what they dug out and sold. And underneath that, in certain parts, was the place of blood.'

'Was the stone good down there?'

'No, quite the opposite,' said Gerlof. 'When they reached the place of blood they'd gone too far.'

Per nodded and said, 'So now I know. There's always a simple explanation.'

Gerlof glanced at Ella's diary, lying on the table. 'Well, usually.'

38

Per started working again on Tuesday.

'Good morning, my name is Per Mörner and I'm calling from Intereko, a company involved in market research. I wonder if you have time to answer a few questions?'

Even while he was reeling off the questions he was thinking about other things. He gave some thought to Vendela Larsson and her talk of trolls and elves. She was a bit strange, but he couldn't get her out of his mind.

The telephone on the kitchen table rang at about ten o'clock, when he had just finished his twelfth conversation about soap. The memory of the strange anonymous call after Easter made him hesitate, his hand hovering above the receiver, but in the end he picked it up.

A firm male voice spoke. 'Per Mörner?'

'Speaking.'

'This is Lars Marklund from the Växjö police. We've spoken before . . .'

'I remember.'

'Good; it's about the house fire in Ryd, of course. We'd really like to expand on the interview from that first evening.'

'You want to talk to me?'

'And your father.' It sounded as if Marklund was shuffling through some papers. 'Gerhard Mörner. When would be a convenient time for you?'

'I'm afraid there's not much to be gained from speaking to my father,' said Per.

'Is he ill?'

'He had a stroke last year. It's affected his speech; he can only remember odd words.'

'We'd still like to ask him a few questions. Is he at his home address?'

'No, he's here on Öland.'

'OK . . . we'll be in touch.'

'But what's it about?' asked Per. 'What do you want to know?'

'We just have a few more questions . . . The fire investigators have finished now.' He paused and added, 'And the post-mortems have been carried out.'

'So what have you found out?' said Per.

But Marklund had already hung up.

Jerry was still asleep, or at least he was still in bed. Per managed to get him up and persuaded him to get dressed. It seemed to take longer and longer every day; Jerry had no strength whatsoever in his left arm, and Per had to help him into his shirt.

'Breakfast time,' he said.

'Tired,' said Jerry.

Per left him at the kitchen table with coffee and sandwiches and went out into the sunshine and the clear, cold air to take another look at Ernst's workshop.

He opened the doors wide so that the light fell on the sculptures inside. It was a strange group – like a big troll family, or whatever it was supposed to be. And all around them, lining the walls, were Ernst's tools: chisels, hammers, axes and drills. A whole arsenal of tools.

If Jerry had had other interests earlier in life, sleep was his only interest now. He stayed in bed in the mornings, and after his late breakfast he wanted to go straight back there. But Per was having none of it; he made his father put on his coat and shoes, and took him over to the edge of the quarry.

'Look,' he said, pointing. 'Jesper and I are building a flight of steps . . . we can use them now, if we're careful.'

He held Jerry's arm firmly as they moved down the narrow ramp; there was just enough room for them to walk side by side, although some of the stones felt alarmingly wobbly beneath their feet. But the blocks remained in place.

'Not bad, eh?' said Per as they reached the bottom.

Jerry's only response was a cough. He looked around the wide gravelled space. 'Empty,' he said.

Per kept an eye on him, but started working on the steps again. The wheelbarrow was still there, and he filled it with gravel and pushed it over to the rock face so that he could unload it and start building up the ramp with his spade to make it more stable.

When he had emptied out five loads of gravel, he turned and looked at his father. 'What are you doing, Jerry?'

Jerry had gone to stand over by the nearest pile of gravel, with his back to Per. He was just standing there, his head bowed, and at first Per didn't realize what he was doing – until he noticed that Jerry was fiddling with his flies.

'No, Jerry!' he shouted.

His father turned his head. 'What?'

'You can't do that down here . . . You need to go back up to the house!'

But it was too late. He could only stand and watch until Jerry had finished and done up his zip.

The trolls don't like it if you spill liquid, thought Per. He went over and took his father by the arm. 'There's a toilet in the house, Jerry. Use it next time, please.'

Jerry looked at him uncomprehendingly, then suddenly he stiffened, looking past Per and out towards the sea. He blinked. 'Bremer's car,' he said.

'What?'

Jerry raised his good arm and pointed over towards the coast road, winding its way between the quarry and the sea.

Per turned and saw that a car had stopped. A dark-red car had driven far enough to allow a clear view across the whole of the quarry. He hadn't seen it arrive, but he was fairly sure the coast road had been empty when he and Jerry had walked down the steps.

He squinted at the car, which was almost directly in the path of the sun. 'Why do you think . . . what makes you think it's Bremer's car?'

Jerry didn't answer, but kept on staring at the car.

'OK. I'll go and have a word,' said Per.

He strode across the huge expanse of gravel. The car was still there, and as he drew closer he could see a man hunched over the wheel, looking down at him. A motionless figure that seemed to be wearing some sort of cap.

When he was about a hundred metres away from the coast road, the engine sprang into life.

'Hello!' Per shouted and waved, without any idea of who he was waving to, and increased his speed. 'Wait!' he shouted.

But the dark-red car began to move. It reversed, swung around and shot away to the south, and it was still too far away for him to be able to make out a number plate, or even what make of car it was.

The sound of the engine died away, and Per had to turn back. He was out of breath when he reached the eastern end of the quarry.

Jerry looked enquiringly at him. 'Bremer?'

'No.'

'Markus Lukas?'

Per shook his head, gasping for breath. No one from Jerry's world was allowed to come here. Per lived here, and so did Jesper and Nilla.

'I expect it was a tourist,' he said. 'Shall we try out the steps, then?'

Lars Marklund rang Per again at about three o'clock, when they were back in the cottage.

'I've had a look at my diary,' he said, 'and I was thinking that perhaps we could meet halfway . . . Could you and your father come to the police station in Kalmar at the end of this week?'

'OK.'

'So we could meet on Friday at two o'clock, for example?'

'Sure. But things are a bit up in the air at the moment, so I don't know . . . I might have to go to the hospital.'

'Is your father seriously ill at the moment, then?'

'No, it's not my father. It's my daughter.'

'I see. But could we say Friday anyway, and you can ring me if there's a problem?'

'Of course,' said Per. 'But can't you tell me why you want us to come in? Have you found something in the house?'

'One or two things.'

'Was the person upstairs Hans Bremer?'

Marklund hesitated. 'The bodies have been identified.'

'A man and a woman, according to the papers,' said

253

Per. 'And the fire was started deliberately, wasn't it?' There was no response from Marklund, so he went on. 'You don't have to say anything – I saw a leaking petrol can down in the studio. And the whole place stank of petrol.'

The silence continued, but eventually Marklund spoke. 'As I said, we would like to ask your father a few more questions about what he saw when he arrived at the house . . . and what you saw inside.'

'Are we suspected of anything?'

'No. Not you, at any rate. You didn't have time to set the fire.'

'So you suspect my father? Or Bremer?'

Marklund was silent again, and then he sighed. 'We don't suspect Bremer. He can't have attacked your father, or started the fire.'

'Why not?'

Marklund hesitated again, then said, 'Because Bremer's hands were tied behind his back when he died. And so were the woman's.'

39

'Bye Ally, won't be long!'

Vendela closed the door and walked across the gravel. She reached up towards the sky, stretching her body as she tried to grab the wispy clouds floating high above. Then she jogged over to the Mörners' cottage and saw Per's father sitting out on the patio, slumped in a sun lounger.

She knocked on the door. After a minute or so Per opened it a fraction, as if he was unsure who the caller might be. She thought he looked a bit uneasy, perhaps even afraid.

'Ready?' she said.

He looked at her. 'Were we supposed to be going for a run today as well?'

Vendela nodded quickly. 'That's what we said yesterday. Have you changed your mind?'

Their arrangement seemed to have come back to him now. 'No, I'm coming. I just need five minutes to get Jerry inside.'

It sounded as if he were talking about a pet, Vendela thought.

Ten minutes later, Per had woken his father and got him settled on the sofa indoors. Vendela could see that Jerry was still half asleep; his son placed a blanket over him and let him nod off again.

When Per had changed into his tracksuit and running shoes, they set off.

'Same route?'

'Fine by me,' said Vendela.

They didn't run as fast today, and the steadier tempo made it easier to talk.

'Didn't you want your father to be outside today?' asked Vendela.

'Yes, but not when I'm out,' said Per. 'I need to keep an eye on Jerry . . . he has a tendency to wander off.'

They carried on running, striding out and breathing evenly. It felt just as good as the last time. When they had left the buildings behind, Vendela turned to him and said, 'You never use the word "Dad".'

Per laughed, or he might have been panting. 'No. We did away with all that.' He took a deep breath and asked, 'What about you . . . did you always say "Dad"?'

'To Henry? Yes, but sometimes I said "Father" as well.'

'But you loved him?'

'I don't know,' said Vendela, looking over towards the quarry. 'He came down here every morning and came home every evening. I think he was much happier here than he was on the farm . . . he enjoyed quarrying and working with the reddest limestone of all.'

'You mean the stone from the place of blood?' said Per. 'I know what it is now.'

'What it *is*?'

'I know how it was formed.' He took a deep breath and went on, 'I was talking to Gerlof Davidsson, and he said it was a geological—'

Vendela interrupted him. 'I don't want to know.'

'Why not?'

'It takes something away . . . it takes away the magic.'

They didn't speak for a while; the only sounds were the crunch of their shoes on the ground and Per's deep breathing.

Vendela suddenly veered off to the east on impulse, on to one of the smaller gravel tracks leading up to the main road.

Per followed her. 'Where are you going?'

'I want to show you something,' she said, running on ahead.

She led him along the track leading to her childhood home, and stopped by the gate. It had been a week since her last visit. The grass had grown greener and more lush, but the house was empty. There was no Volvo parked outside. The happy family who lived there had gone home to the city.

Per had also stopped; he was taking deep breaths and looking around. 'What is this place?'

Vendela opened the gate and said, 'You can hear my childhood sighing in the trees here.'

'Oh?'

'This is where I grew up,' said Vendela, walking into the garden.

Per seemed to hesitate before following her. 'So what was it like, living here?' he said. 'Was it a good childhood?'

Vendela didn't answer for a moment; she didn't want to say too much. And she didn't want to think about the cows.

'It was a bit lonely,' she said eventually. 'I didn't have any friends nearby, they lived up in Marnäs. I had my father for company, and then I had . . .'

She fell silent and stopped in front of the overgrown foundations that showed where the little barn had stood.

Then she looked up at the house, at the middle

window upstairs, and for a moment she expected to see two staring eyes up there. A face behind the glass, a raised hand and a low laugh.

Come up and see me, Vendela.

But the room behind the glass was dark and empty.

Öland 1958

When the elves have made Fru Jansson so ill that she is unable to work for the remainder of the school year, the supply teacher, Fröken Ernstam, is allowed to stay with the class. Vendela likes her very much, and so do the rest of the pupils. She comes from Kalmar and has new ideas about teaching. She seems young and *modern*; sometimes she leaves her desk and walks around the classroom, and she refuses to play the pedal organ.

A week after she has taken over the class, Fröken Ernstam tells the class that they will be going on a spring trip to Borgholm next Friday; they will be visiting the harbour and the castle, but they will also have the opportunity to spend some time in the shops around the square. The trip will be a kind of encouragement, a treat before they begin preparing for the important end-of-year exams.

A buzz of anticipation runs through the classroom, but Vendela remains silent.

She can't go, of course. The cows have to be taken care of, and besides, everyone has to take two kronor for their train fare. It's not exactly a fortune, but she hasn't got it, and she has no intention of asking her father for extra money. She knows he hasn't got any, he's said so several times.

But within a week the issue of money for the trip is sorted out; on Tuesday she is able to borrow two fifty-öre pieces from her best friend Dagmar, and on Thursday – yet another miracle – she is walking home past Marnäs church when she suddenly spots a shiny two-kronor coin that someone has dropped on the gravel. So now she has enough money for the trip, and some to spare.

There is only one more problem: Rosa, Rosa and Rosa.

With the coins in her hand, she stops by the elf stone. She stands there, looking at the hollows in the stone.

They are empty, of course.

Vendela places a fifty-öre coin in one of the hollows and wishes that she might be spared the job of leading the cows home and milking them the next day. One day off a year – that's not too much to ask, surely?

She stays by the stone for a little while, gazing at the coin. Afterwards she can't remember what she was thinking about – maybe she wished for something else.

A better life, perhaps? Did she wish that she could get away from the farm, away from her father and the Invalid upstairs, away from the island? That she could escape to another world where she would have no duties, and where money wouldn't be a problem?

Vendela can't remember. She leaves the coin in the hollow and sets off across the grass without looking back.

She goes out to the meadow when she gets home, and the cows lift their heads when they see her. Rosa, Rosa and Rosa form a line and begin lumbering towards the gate, and Vendela lifts her stick. But she doesn't hit them today; her head is full of thoughts. She walks behind the cows, wondering how her wish will be granted.

That night she is woken by the cows bellowing in the darkness. They sound terrified, and a strange crackling noise is mingled with their cries.

Vendela sits up in bed; she can smell smoke. Through the blind she can see a flickering glow outside. A yellow light around the barn that just keeps on growing, making the rest of the yard melt into one with the dark forest. She hears feet thundering up the stairs, and a shout: 'The barn's on fire!'

It's Henry's voice. She hears his steps crossing the floor, then the door is flung open. 'It's on fire! Get out!'

Vendela gets out of bed, and Henry pulls and drags and carries her down the stairs and out into the cold night air. She ends up on the wet grass, looking around in confusion; that is when she sees that the barn is ablaze. The flames are forcing their way out through the walls, sending sparks whirling up into the night sky. The fire has already begun to lick at the gables.

Henry is standing over her, barefoot and wearing only his nightshirt. He turns away. 'I have to go and get Jan-Erik!'

He rushes back into the house.

'Jan-Erik?'

No reply.

The cows are still bellowing, louder and more long-drawn-out than she has ever heard – they can't get out.

The flames writhe across the ground, scrambling up the barn and colliding with each other beneath the roof like red breakers, and Vendela feels as if her legs are paralysed. She can't move. She sits there on the grass watching her father emerging from the house with a big bundle of blankets in his arms.

Henry drops the bundle on the grass.

Vendela can hear the sound of wheezing. Two arms

push the blankets aside, a face with white eyes appears, blinking, then a mouth with white teeth smiles at her.

The Invalid is sitting there on the grass, just a metre away from her. They sit and stare at one another, and all they can hear is the sound of creaking and cracking as the roof of the barn begins to collapse.

In the glow of the fire Vendela can see that the Invalid is not old at all. The Invalid is just a boy, perhaps five or six years older than she is. His legs are long and thin.

But he is sick. Vendela can hear that he has thick phlegm in his windpipe, and there is something wrong with his skin; his face is red and swollen even when the glow of the fire is not illuminating it, and he has long, bloody scratches on his cheeks and forehead, as if an animal has attacked him. The upper part of his body is also red and covered in sores. But he's still smiling.

Between two and three years – that's how long the Invalid has been living on the farm without Vendela knowing who he is. Can he talk? Does he understand Swedish?

'What's your name?'

He opens his mouth and laughs, but doesn't answer.

'My name's Vendela. What's yours?'

'Jan-Erik,' he says eventually, but his voice is so quiet and muted that she can barely hear it through the fire. He carries on laughing.

'Who are you?'

'Jan-Erik.'

Henry is still running around the yard, sometimes clearly visible in front of the flames, sometimes completely invisible in the darkness. When the fire reaches out and grabs hold of the gables of the house, he pumps a bucket full of water and goes upstairs to damp down the wood and beat out any sparks.

Vendela's paralysis eases, and she begins to move.

She does just one thing right tonight: she goes over to the hens' enclosure next to the barn and opens the rickety gate. The hens and chickens come flapping into the yard, tumbling over one another, followed by the cockerel. They gather in a dense huddle in the darkness, out of danger.

'Ring the fire brigade!' shouts Henry.

Vendela dashes into the kitchen and rings the fire brigade in Borgholm. She is put through to Kalmar, and it takes a long time to reach someone and explain where the fire is.

When she comes back outside, the Invalid is still sitting on the grass, and Henry is still running back and forth between the barn and the water pump.

But it's all too late. The fire is roaring through the loft and across the walls along the animals' stalls, and in the end Henry slows down. He takes a deep breath, one long, heavy sigh.

Vendela can only stand outside and listen as the bellowing from inside falls silent.

Cooked meat: the night is filled with the smell of charred beef.

Vendela can feel the heat of the fire, but she is still freezing cold. She doesn't want to stay out here.

'Father . . . are you coming inside?'

He doesn't seem to hear her at first, then he shakes his head and answers quietly. 'It's not the fire's fault.'

Vendela doesn't understand what he means.

After almost an hour the fire brigade turns up with two vehicles from Borgholm, but all they can do is prevent the fire from spreading. It is impossible to save the barn.

Several hours after midnight, when the fire-fighters have left but the yard is still thick with smoke, Henry is sitting out on the steps in the cold. He has carried the Invalid back to his room, but refuses to go inside. Vendela goes out to him one last time.

'Who's Jan-Erik, Dad?'

'Jan-Erik?' says Henry; he seems to consider the question before answering. 'Well, he's my son, of course . . . your brother.'

'My brother?'

He looks over his shoulder at her. 'Didn't I tell you?'

Vendela stares at him. She has hundreds of questions, but asks only one. 'Why doesn't he have to go to school?'

'He's not allowed,' says Henry. 'They said it would be a waste of effort. It's impossible to educate him.'

Then he reverts to staring into the darkness.

Vendela goes back inside and takes herself off to bed. She lies there as stiff as a board.

Perhaps Henry is up all night, because when he wakes his daughter at seven o'clock the next morning, he is still wearing the same clothes.

'School,' is all he says. Then he adds, 'I let you have a lie-in today . . . No need to do the milking any more.'

Only when Vendela hears his words does she become aware of the smell of smoke in the room, and then she remembers the fire during the night. Then she remembers the Invalid. Jan-Erik.

Henry stops in the doorway as he leaves the room. 'Don't you worry about what's going to happen. I've got the insurance policy and a receipt for the premium, so everything will be all right.'

Then Vendela remembers one last thing: the school trip is today. The class is going to Borgholm on the train.

She can go with them. She's got the money for the fare, after all, and the cows are no longer a problem.

*

An hour later she is walking across the empty alvar, but gives the elf stone a wide berth, keeping her eyes fixed firmly ahead. She doesn't want to see it any more, but the questions come anyway.

What did she actually wish for as she stood by the stone the previous day? She can barely grasp what she has done, and she doesn't want to think about what the elves have done for her.

The children gather, ready to set off for the railway station, all smiles and eager chatter. Vendela does not smile, and she speaks to no one. She can still smell the smoke in her nostrils.

She goes to Borgholm on the train with her class and sits in a carriage with Dagmar and the other girls, but she still feels as if she is back on the alvar. Utterly alone. And she recalls nothing of the visit to Borgholm; in the shadow of everything that happened during the night, the day simply slips away.

When she gets home after the school trip, three hours after the cows would have needed milking, the yard is full of people.

The police are there – two constables from Marnäs are walking around inspecting the site of the fire. The gable at one end of the house has been blackened by the fire, and the barn is gone. All that's left are the stone foundations. They look like a rectangular swimming pool full of ash, with charred planks of wood and roofing tiles sticking up out of the grey mess. There are three bodies lying beneath the covering of ash, their legs rigid, and the stench of burnt meat hangs over the whole yard.

Rosa, Rosa and Rosa. But Vendela doesn't want to think about their names at the moment.

The neighbours have also gathered. People from Stenvik and even further afield have come to look at the remains of Henry the widower's barn, and some of them have actually brought milk and sandwiches for the unfortunate family. Henry smiles and says thank you through gritted teeth, and Vendela bobs a curtsy, her cheeks burning. Then she creeps away. She goes into the empty kitchen and up the stairs, but when she tentatively tries the door of the Invalid's room, it is locked.

'Jan-Erik? It's Vendela.'

No reply, not even laughter. All is silent behind the door.

She goes back downstairs and looks out of the kitchen window.

One of the men who has come from Stenvik is tall and slim, and he is looking around with a thoughtful expression. He speaks sympathetically to her father, then stands by the barn when the police suddenly call Henry over.

Vendela watches through the window as her father shows them around the ruins and points out the dead cows.

The police carry on looking. Henry comes inside to Vendela, who is still gazing out of the window. She sees the tall man from Stenvik come over and speak to the police after a while, pointing towards the barn, then at something down on the ground.

The policemen listen and nod.

'I don't know what they're doing out there,' Henry mutters. 'They're cooking something up between them.' He looks at Vendela. 'You'll have to support me,' he says. 'If they start asking questions.'

'Questions?'

'If there's a problem. You'll do that, won't you? You'll support your father?'

Vendela nods.

In the twilight half an hour later the policemen make their way up the steps, bringing the smell of smoke into the kitchen with them. They flop down at the table and look at Henry.

'Tell us what you know, Fors,' says one of them.

'I don't know much.'

'How did it start?'

Henry places his hands on the kitchen table. 'I don't know, it just started. I'm always unlucky, always. There's something cursed about this place.'

'So the fire woke you up?'

One of the policemen is doing the talking, the other is just sitting in silence, staring at Henry.

He nods. 'At about midnight. And my daughter too.'

Vendela dare not even look at the police officers, her heart is pounding so hard it feels as if it's trying to burst out of her chest. This is the twilight hour, and the elves will be dancing in circles in the meadows.

'We think it started in two places,' says the talkative policeman.

'Oh yes?'

'Yes. In the east and west gable end. And that's rather peculiar, actually, because it has rained quite a bit. The ground is damp, after all.'

'Somebody lit candles there,' says the other one. 'We found lumps of wax in the mud.'

'Oh yes?' says Henry.

'And you could smell paraffin as well,' says the first policeman.

'That's right,' says the other one. 'I could.'

'Could we have a look at your shoes, Fors?'

'My shoes? What shoes?'

'All of them,' says the policeman. 'All the shoes and boots you own.'

Henry hesitates, but the officers escort him into the porch and go through all his shoes. They pick them up one by one, and Vendela can see them studying the soles.

'It could be this one,' says the first policeman, holding up a boot. 'What do you think?'

The other one nods. 'Yes, it's the same pattern.'

His colleague places the boot on the kitchen table and looks at Henry. 'Do you have any fuel in the house, Fors?'

'Fuel?'

'Paraffin, for example?'

'Well, I suppose it's possible . . .'

'A can?'

Vendela listens to her father and thinks about the fire wriggling along like a snake, as if it were seeking out a path across the ground and up the wall of the barn, as if it knew where it was going.

'A bottle,' Henry says quietly. 'There's probably a half-full bottle of paraffin around somewhere.'

The policemen nod.

'I think that's it,' says the first one to his colleague.

'Yes.'

There is a brief silence, but then Henry straightens his back, takes a deep breath and says just one word: 'No.'

They look at him in surprise as he goes on. 'That's not it. I had nothing to do with the fire. Anybody could have poured paraffin around. I was indoors all evening, until the fire started. My daughter here can confirm that, she'll give you her word of honour.'

Suddenly the men are looking at Vendela. Her whole body goes cold.

'That's right,' she says eventually, and begins to lie for all she is worth. 'Dad was indoors . . . He sleeps in the room next door to mine and I always hear when he goes outside, but he didn't go anywhere.'

Henry points at the boot on the kitchen table. 'And that's not mine.'

'It was in your porch,' says the first policeman. 'So who else would it belong to?'

Henry says nothing for a few seconds, then he goes over to the stairs. 'Come upstairs with me,' he says. 'I'd like to show you something.'

40

Gerlof did his best to collect empty bottles into which his little ships could sail – he had a glass of wine with his meal every night. But he had barely touched his model-making since Easter; he hadn't even started the full-rigged ship. Almost all his time was spent sleeping, sitting in the sun on the grass – and reading Ella's diaries.

He read them regularly, one page at a time, and then he sat and thought about them.

18th September 1957
I'm quite ashamed of myself – I haven't got round to writing much lately, but today's the day! A lot has happened; we went to Oskar Svensson's funeral in Kalmar, and I've had a birthday – I'm 42 now!

Last Sunday we were at my nephew Birger's confirmation in the church at Gärdslösa; it was very solemn, and Pastor Ek asked some difficult questions.

Gerlof caught the train down to his ship yesterday and set sail for Stockholm this morning; the girls have gone off to Långvik on their bikes, so I'm all alone in the cottage, which can be nice sometimes.

It's cloudy today and a stiff autumn breeze blew up over the Baltic this morning. I know that Gerlof can ride out a storm, but I pray to God that he will be safe. He will be on the ship for at least two months now.

I'm sitting out on the veranda as I write this. When the girls had gone I came out here and found something strange on the bottom step: there was a piece of jewellery lying on the stone. A brooch shaped like a rose; it looked like silver, but it can't be silver, can it? It's probably from the little changeling; I don't know what to do with it, it just doesn't feel right.

When Gerlof had finished reading, he thought for a while. Then he got up and went indoors.

He had kept Ella's yellow jewellery box all these years; it was in the chest of drawers in his room, under his old, faded ensign. He took it out, lifted the lid and stared down at a pile of bracelets, rings and earrings. And some brooches that needed cleaning. One of them was shaped like a rose, with a little red stone in the centre.

Gerlof picked it up carefully.

Had he ever seen Ella wearing it? He didn't think so.

41

Jerry and Marika were standing motionless in the hospital corridor, staring at one another.

Per was standing beside them, but he really wanted to be somewhere else. On the other side of the Sound, perhaps, out for a long run with Vendela Larsson. But now he was here.

He and Jerry had stepped out of the lift five minutes earlier, and his ex-wife had been waiting.

'Hello, Jerry,' Marika said quietly. 'How are you?'

Marika had met Jerry only once before, but that was a long time ago, the year before the twins were born. She had met Per's mother Anita several times by that stage and things had gone very well, and she insisted on meeting his father as well. So one weekend when they weren't far from Kristianstad, Per had driven into the centre and rung the doorbell of Jerry's apartment.

He had been hoping that no one would be at home.

But Jerry had opened the door dressed in a dark-blue silk dressing gown and leopard-print underpants, and had invited them in for lunch: toast with whitefish roe. Plenty of sparkling wine as well, of course. When they left he had given them the latest issues of *Babylon* and *Gomorrah* as a present – just to destroy the romance.

After that, Marika hadn't wanted to see Jerry again.

And now, fourteen years later, they were standing here face to face. Per wasn't sure if Jerry actually recognized his ex-wife. He was just staring at Marika, but then that was what he did with everybody these days.

'Jerry doesn't say much any more,' said Per. 'But apart from that he's doing pretty well. Aren't you, Jerry?'

His father merely nodded, still staring at Marika.

'Have you been in to see Nilla?' Per asked.

'Yes . . . she's feeling quite cheerful today. I have to go – the doctor wants to see me. Will you come with me?'

Per shook his head. He was frightened of hearing any news about Nilla. 'Not today.'

'It might be important,' said Marika.

'Every meeting about Nilla is important,' Per said quickly. 'I'll be back soon, but there's something Jerry and I have to do right now. That's important, too.'

'Can't you put it off?'

'No . . . We've got to go to a meeting.'

He didn't want to say it involved the police. Marika nodded, but she didn't look pleased.

'See you later,' said Per, heading into the ward.

Nilla was sitting cross-legged on her bed, drinking something out of a glass; she was dressed in her pyjamas, and her back was straight. She nodded at her father as he came in, but carried on drinking. Per looked at the strange, orange liquid in the glass and asked her, 'What are you drinking?'

'Carrot juice.'

'Did you buy it yourself?'

She took another swig and shook her head. 'Emil gave it to me . . . His mum makes it for him, and she adds all kinds of vitamins that are supposed to make him better. But he doesn't like it.'

'But you do?'

'It's OK . . . and at least it means he doesn't have to drink it.'

From outside they heard the sharp tone of a nurse as she asked a patient what he was doing in the corridor. The response was a barely audible mumble.

'I see. In that case we'll try a bed-pan,' said the nurse, and her footsteps tapped away down the corridor.

'Are you staying?' asked Nilla. 'Mum will be back soon, she's just gone to a meeting.'

He shook his head. 'I can't, Granddad's waiting for me.'

'What are you going to do?'

'We're . . . we're just going for a bit of a drive around Kalmar.'

He was lying to his daughter, just as he had lied to Marika.

Marika had gone when Per got back to the lifts. Jerry was sitting on a chair with his mobile to his ear. He ended the call before Per reached him.

'Who were you talking to?' Per asked on the way down in the lift. 'Did somebody ring you?'

Jerry peered out of the window. 'Bremer,' he said.

'He's dead, Jerry.'

'Bremer wanted to talk.'

'Did he?'

Per twisted Jerry's phone around and looked at the display: NUMBER WITHHELD again.

They went back to the car; Per sat down next to his father and started the engine. 'Do me a favour, Jerry,' he said. 'Don't tell the police Hans Bremer rang you. They might get the wrong idea about you.'

Jerry didn't reply. He remained silent for a little while as they drove through Kalmar, but as they were passing a little games shop with the windows painted over, he

274

followed it with his eyes. Then he opened his mouth and said two words Per didn't quite catch.

'What? What did you say, Jerry?'

'Moleng Noar.'

'Moleng . . . What's that?'

Jerry smiled to himself. 'Malmö.'

'Moleng Noar in Malmö?'

Jerry nodded.

'It sounds like a Chinese restaurant,' said Per. 'Or is it a person . . . a Chinese person you knew in Malmö?'

Jerry shook his head.

'Cindy,' he mumbled all of a sudden. 'Suzie, Christy, Debbie . . .'

'Was it a place where you used to meet girls in Malmö?'

His father merely nodded and smiled to himself; he didn't speak again as they drove through the town.

The police station in Kalmar was a large, yellow-brick building with narrow windows. It was just north of the town centre, and occupied half a block.

Jerry looked at the sign that said POLICE outside the entrance, and gave a start. He refused to move.

'It's fine,' Per said quietly. 'They just want to talk to us.'

He gave their names to the woman on reception and sat down with Jerry on a plastic-covered sofa. In front of them was a poster on the dangers of selling alcohol to those under-age, featuring the sorrowful eyes of a young girl and the words DO YOU KNOW WHAT YOUR DAUGHTER'S DOING TONIGHT?

Yes, I do, thought Per.

Lars Marklund, the inspector he had spoken to on the phone, came out after a few minutes. He was casually dressed in jeans and grey polo-neck sweater.

'Welcome,' he said, shaking hands. 'We thought we'd have a chat with you on your own first, Per. Then we'll bring Gerhard in later.' He glanced at Jerry. 'You can wait here for the time being, Gerhard.'

Jerry suddenly looked anxious. He tried to get up, but Per bent down to him. 'You just stay here, Jerry, it'll be fine . . . I'll be back soon.'

His father seemed to consider this, then he nodded.

Marklund led Per to a small, bare room containing nothing but a desk covered in various folders, and two chairs. 'Take a seat . . . So you're from Öland?'

Per sat down opposite him. 'That's right.'

'It's a beautiful place . . . I've always fancied a house on Öland. Is it expensive?'

'I should think it might be . . . I don't really know. I inherited my cottage.'

'Lucky you.' Marklund picked up a pen and looked at Per. 'OK . . . Can you just tell me in your own words exactly what you saw both outside and inside the house that day? Every detail is important.'

'About the fire, you mean?'

Per glanced down at the desk, and saw that Marklund was resting his elbow on some kind of technical report, and a sketch of the ground floor of Jerry's house. He could see arrows and crosses on the drawing, and the words FIRE STARTED DELIBERATELY IN FIVE PLACES! written in pencil.

'Absolutely, tell me all you can about the fire,' said Marklund. 'How you discovered it, when you made that discovery, exactly where you were in the house, whether you noticed any damage before the fire, and how you think the fire spread.'

Per took a deep breath, then started to explain how he had gone to Jerry's house to pick up his father, only to discover that he had been attacked with a knife. He told Marklund he had gone back into the house, up the stairs and into the smoke-filled room where the bed was on fire. He thought he had seen a man's body there, then heard a woman screaming from another room. And then the fire suddenly seemed to be getting closer from several different directions, and he had to jump out of the window.

The truth and nothing but the truth, as far as he could remember. It took about quarter of an hour.

'That's all I know,' he said when he had finished. 'I was inside the house, but I had nothing to do with starting the fire.'

'Nobody said you did,' said Marklund, making a note on his pad.

Per leant forward. 'But what have you found out? It must have been carefully set up, surely?'

Marklund didn't respond at first.

'Normally we wouldn't comment, but you did see a can of petrol with holes punched in it, and a car battery – what does that indicate?'

'Planning,' said Per.

Marklund nodded. 'The forensic team found remnants of paper near the places where the fires started . . . remnants of documents.'

Per thought about the open door to Jerry's apartment. 'They might have been contracts,' he said. 'For people who appeared in Jerry and Bremer's films and magazines. Have you spoken to any of them?'

'They're not that easy to find,' said Marklund. 'We haven't had much success so far.'

'No, they didn't use their real names,' said Per. 'Do you need any help? I could have a look for—'

The detective quickly shook his head. 'That's our job.'

Per raised his eyes wearily to the ceiling. Ungrateful sod.

'But we believe the dead woman was a former model,' said Marklund.

Per looked at him. 'Oh? What was her name?'

'We're not prepared to reveal her name at this stage.' Marklund made a note, then went on, 'Tell me about your father . . . How long has he been involved in this particular profession? And what did he do before that?'

'Jerry's never said much about it,' said Per. 'But I know his father was a vicar, and Jerry left home pretty early on and became a car dealer at the beginning of the fifties. I'm sure he was good at it . . . And a few years later he bought a postcard company and started printing erotic pictures. They sold well. Then in the sixties he launched his first magazine, *Babylon*; it was printed in Denmark and smuggled into Sweden aboard small motorboats.' He stopped, then added, 'But then porn became legal in Sweden at the beginning of the seventies. He formed a limited company and started employing people, and sold magazines all over Europe.'

'So that was the start of your father's glory days, if I can put it that way?' Marklund made another note before looking up. 'And the people he employed – what do you know about them?'

'Nothing. One guy who was around a lot was called Markus Lukas, but that sounds made up as well.'

'And Bremer? What do you know about Hans Bremer?'

'Not much.'

'Have you ever met him?'

Per shook his head. 'I only know bits and pieces that my father has mentioned over the years . . . they started working together at the end of the seventies, and Bremer lived in Malmö. Jerry said he was a fast, efficient worker, and he was very pleased with him.'

278

Marklund wrote this down, then said, 'We probably know a little bit more about Bremer than you do.'

'Like what?'

'I can't go into detail, but Bremer was involved in various things down in Malmö. The film business was just one of his many interests . . . We're busy looking into everything else at the moment.'

'So he was a gangster?'

'I didn't say that. So they got on well, your father and Bremer?'

'I think so, I mean they worked together for many years. And Jerry had gone to the house to meet Bremer before it caught fire.'

Marklund looked through his papers. 'But they'd quarrelled that day, hadn't they?'

'So Jerry says. He insists it was Bremer who cut him with the knife, if I've understood him correctly . . . but if Bremer was tied up and locked in, it must have been somebody else.'

'Did you see anyone else?'

Per hesitated. *Markus Lukas*, he thought. *Who else could it be?*

'I don't know . . . I thought I saw someone running off into the trees at the edge of the forest, just after the fire had broken out. There's a track, and tyre marks on the ground . . . I think.' He hesitated again, but went on, 'I got the idea that Bremer's car had been parked in the forest and someone drove off in it once the house was on fire.'

'Oh?' Marklund looked at his notes again. 'What makes you think Hans Bremer had a car?'

Per looked at him. 'He did, didn't he? He used to give my father a lift sometimes. Bremer must have picked him up at the bus station before the fire . . . By the way, have you found all his keys?'

Marklund checked his notes once more. 'His keys? Would he have had a lot of keys?'

'I don't know . . . But someone went into my father's apartment in Kristianstad while he was on Öland and broke into a chest of drawers. They were obviously looking for something. They'd been rifling through all Jerry's papers. We discovered it over Easter, and my father said that Bremer had a set of keys to his apartment. I did report it to the police.'

'A break-in?' Marklund made a note. 'I'd better check up on that.'

'Good,' said Per.

There was a brief silence. Marklund looked at the clock and said, 'Is there anything you'd like to add?'

Per thought about it. Part of him wanted to carry on talking, to tell Marklund he could still hear the woman's screams reverberating in his head, mingled with Regina's cries in the forest. But this wasn't a therapy session.

Then something occurred to him.

'One thing, perhaps . . . My father and I have had some strange phone calls since the fire.'

'From whom?'

'I don't know. They were anonymous calls.'

'OK, but sometimes it's possible to get the number anyway . . . We'll give it a try.'

Marklund made a few more notes, then nodded. 'Right, I think we're done here.' He looked at Per. 'Many thanks. Would you like to go and bring Gerhard in now?'

Per stood up. He thought about Nilla, and asked, 'How long will it take?'

'Not long . . . Twenty minutes, maybe?'

'OK . . . but Jerry doesn't talk much, as I told you.'

As he left the room he looked at his watch and

discovered that the interview had gone on for a good half-hour. Jerry had no doubt fallen asleep.

But when he got to reception his father was not fast asleep on the sofa; in fact, he wasn't there at all. The sofa was empty.

Per stared at it for a few seconds, then checked the toilets in the little cloakroom. They were also empty.

The woman on reception looked up as Per went over to her. 'The old man?' she replied. 'He left.'

'Left?'

'I think he spotted someone out in the street, and he went off.'

'When?'

'Not long ago. I'm not sure . . . maybe quarter of an hour ago?'

Per turned and was out of the police station in three strides.

He stood on the pavement looking around, blinking in the sunshine. A few cars went whizzing by along the street to his right, but there wasn't a soul in sight.

Jerry had disappeared.

42

Kalmar was a labyrinth. Per had always thought it was just the right size, and easy enough to find your way around, but right now the town seemed like a confusing tangle of streets and pavements.

There was no sign of Jerry anywhere.

Per dashed over to the wide junctions at either side of the police station, then ran all the way around the block, but there was nothing. He switched on his mobile and tried to call Jerry. No reply.

After that he gave up and went back to reception. Lars Marklund was waiting just inside the door. He looked at his watch and asked, 'Is there a problem?'

'My father's disappeared,' said Per, his heart in his mouth. 'I need to drive around and look for him.'

He turned away, but Marklund called after him, 'Hang on! You can't just go rushing off . . . Let's have a description.'

Per stopped and came back, forcing himself to calm down.

Marklund took out a notebook and together they ran through Jerry's appearance, height, and what he was wearing.

'Good,' said Marklund. 'We'll put out a call.'

Per hurried to the car. He started the engine, but didn't set off. He clutched the wheel like a lifebuoy and tried to think – where could Jerry go? To a bar? To the bus station?

It was pointless, he would just have to search at random.

He pulled away and started to search, block by block. He turned left, then left again, scanning the streets around the police station. He met several cars and saw groups of schoolchildren on their way home, and mothers with buggies, but there was no sign of Jerry.

He was heading north towards the motorway when his phone began to ring in his pocket. He slowed down and got it out. 'Hello?'

'Where have you been, Per? I've been calling you for ages.'

It was Marika. Per could feel his guilty conscience like a weight on his shoulders, but he kept on staring through the windscreen. 'With . . . I've been in a meeting.'

He still didn't want to tell her he'd been interviewed by the police, and Marika didn't ask any more questions. 'You have to come to the hospital,' she said.

'I haven't got time right now, Marika,' said Per, gazing around. Still no Jerry. 'I'll be there in a little while, but at the moment I have to—'

She interrupted him. 'I've been talking to Stenhammar.'

'Stenhammar?'

'Nilla's doctor, Per. Don't you remember?'

'Yes, of course . . . What did he say?'

There was silence on the other end of the phone.

'What is it, Marika?'

'It's a tumour,' she said quietly. 'A particular kind of tumour . . . It isn't growing quickly, but it has to be removed.'

Per slowed down and closed his eyes briefly. 'OK,' he said. 'But we knew that, didn't we?'

Marika's voice was still quiet. 'It's right next to the artery.'

Per didn't understand. 'Next to the artery?'

'Yes. It's wrapped itself around the main artery. The aorta.'

'What does that mean?'

Marika fell silent again, then spoke even more quietly. 'Nobody's prepared to operate.'

'But . . . they have to,' said Per.

Marika didn't reply.

'They *have* to,' said Per.

'Georg and I spent half an hour with Stenhammar. He's spoken to several vascular surgeons, but he says none of them is prepared to risk it.'

But they have to, thought Per. *Otherwise there's no hope.*

'Marika, I'm out in the car, there's something I have to do for Jerry . . . But I'll call you back soon.'

She started to say something, but he switched off the phone. He put his foot down. He had to find Jerry. He'd think about all the other stuff later, but first he had to find Jerry.

No hope for Nilla, he thought. *But there has to be hope.*

He gazed blankly out through the windscreen. Nilla . . .

But they have to operate, they just have to!

He was on his way out of the town now. He passed a petrol station, followed by a grassy area on both sides of the road, with a viaduct crossing over it. There were fewer cars here.

He had almost reached the motorway. Best turn back.

Per looked up at the viaduct, a hundred metres away, and on the other side of the barrier he saw a dark-coloured car. It had stopped on the carriageway. The passenger door opened, and someone got out.

An old man in a grey coat, stooping. Per suddenly realized it was Jerry.

The car started to reverse; Jerry stood still. He seemed to be looking around, lost and confused. Then he started shambling forwards.

Per braked and stopped the car; he'd found Jerry, but couldn't get to him. He was on the wrong carriageway. How could he get up on to the viaduct? The area was completely unfamiliar to him.

In the end he started to reverse. He was just about to do a U-turn and take the entry slip for the motorway, in defiance of the traffic regulations, when he saw that the car that had dropped Jerry off had stopped reversing. It was moving forwards instead.

Per realized it was picking up speed. It was a red car, he could see now – possibly a Ford Escort. Was it the car from the quarry? The driver was wearing a cap, and was nothing more than a dark shadow behind the wheel.

The car was coming up behind Jerry on the viaduct, but instead of slowing down and sticking to the middle of the road, it was speeding up.

Per was a hundred and fifty metres away, perhaps two hundred. He stopped the car, opened the door and yelled: 'Jerry!'

But Jerry kept on walking, his head lowered against the wind.

Per got out of the car and cupped his hands: 'Dad!'

Jerry seemed to hear him. He turned his head, but by that time the car behind him was no more than ten metres away. It didn't stop. On the contrary, the driver put his foot down.

Jerry looked like a rag doll as the car hit him.

The front of the car knocked his legs from underneath

him and lifted him off the ground. Per could only watch as Jerry's body flew up over the bonnet and was thrown forwards like a blurred shadow, his arms outstretched and his coat flapping.

His father spun around in the air and landed heavily.

'Jerry!'

The car had slowed down after the collision; Per could see that the windscreen was cracked.

He left the door of the Saab open and started to run up the slope, up towards the viaduct. His shoes slithered and skidded on the grass.

Jerry slowly raised his head from the Tarmac. He was bleeding, but still conscious. Then his head sank down again.

The car that had mown him down stopped by the side of the road ten or twelve metres ahead of him; Per saw the driver turn his head and look back, then the car sped away. Faster and faster.

It was a hit and run.

Per slipped again on the grass. He battled his way up the slope and fumbled in his pocket for his mobile – then remembered he'd left it in the car.

He jumped over the barrier and landed two metres away from Jerry, just as the car that had hit him joined the motorway.

Per bent over the body on the Tarmac. 'Jerry?'

So much blood. It was pouring from his nose and forehead, running between his broken teeth.

'Dad?'

His father's eyes were open, but his whole face was scraped raw, and there was no response. Per looked around in despair for someone who might help him.

The red car accelerated south and disappeared up the motorway. The last thing Per saw was water spurting over the windscreen.

43

'That was just the pits,' said Max. 'It was absolutely terrible.'

'Don't think about it,' said Vendela.

After she had settled Max in an armchair and poured him a whisky, she began to massage his neck and shoulders. She leant forward and said quietly, 'Max, there are those who are worse off than you.'

He took a slug of his whisky, closed his eyes and sighed. 'Yes, but there was the same level of incompetence wherever I went . . . Wrong directions, hotel rooms with hairs in the bath – and then the local radio station that had forgotten they'd booked me for an interview. They'd *forgotten*!' He shook his head. 'And every time I walked on to a new stage, there was a bloody spotlight shining straight into my eyes. I couldn't even *see* the audience!'

'Were there any good—' Vendela began, but Max interrupted her; he hadn't finished yet.

'And nothing but a dried-up sandwich before I was due on stage, even though my contract states that they're supposed to provide dinner. I didn't even get a glass of wine . . . Bread and water, that's what they expected me to get through an entire lecture on!'

'But what about the audiences?' Vendela asked. 'Lots of people turned up, didn't they?'

'About three hundred each night,' Max said quietly. 'I'd been hoping for five hundred . . . none of the venues was full.'

'But that's still a good number,' said Vendela, 'and it'll be even better when the book comes out.'

Max emptied his glass and stood up. 'Any post?'

'Just a few letters,' replied Vendela, following him into the kitchen.

She looked around for Aloysius, but the dog had hardly shown himself since his master came home. Ally could tell when Max was in a bad mood.

Max picked up the pile of post and started to flick through it. 'So what else has been happening here?'

'Not much,' said Vendela. 'I planted a bit more ivy at the front, and carried on with the lilac hedge. And I've planted three robinias at the back.'

'Good, they'll provide a good screen in time.'

'That's what I thought.'

Max picked up a note from the worktop. 'What's this?'

Vendela saw that he was holding up the note from Per Mörner.

'*Thanks a lot for the stone! . . . Per.*' Max read out. 'What stone? And who's Per?'

She stared back, not knowing what to say.

'It's from our neighbour,' she said eventually. 'You know, Per Mörner. His daughter had lost her lucky stone. I helped them to find it.'

'Oh? So where was it, then?'

'Outside their cottage,' said Vendela, unable to look Max in the eye.

It was a lie, but she couldn't tell him the truth; she couldn't tell him she had asked the elves for help.

288

'So you've been meeting our neighbour,' said Max. 'Is that why you haven't been answering the phone?'

Vendela blinked and didn't answer. What could she say?

'So what did you and Per do when you met up?'

'Nothing . . . not much,' Vendela said quickly. 'But he likes exercise, so we went out for a bit of a run. Up the coast.'

'I see,' Max said calmly and slowly. 'So you've been exercising together.'

'That's right.'

She clamped her teeth together to stop herself from laughing nervously.

44

Jerry and his granddaughter Nilla were both in Kalmar hospital now, but on different wards. Per spent all weekend shuttling between his father and daughter, sitting by their beds.

His steps were heavy as he made the journey – and each time he had to pass the maternity unit, with parents-to-be and new parents constantly coming and going. When they opened the door, the sound of bright voices and cheerful shouts from small children who had just become big brothers or sisters came pouring out, mingled with the thin cries of newborn babies.

Per hurried past as quickly as possible.

Nilla's ward was unbearably quiet. The nurses moved silently along the corridors and spoke to each other in muted voices.

Before Dr Stenhammar left for the weekend he had given Per and Marika a time and date for Nilla's operation: ten o'clock in the morning on 1 May. He was being optimistic; so far no vascular surgeon had agreed to carry out the operation.

Almost two weeks to go, Per thought. *Plenty of time.*

The blinds were drawn in her room. She was lying in bed with her lucky stone and her earphones.

He sat next to her, holding her hand. They talked quietly.

'They said they'd find someone,' she said. 'So I'm sure they will.'

'Of course they will,' said Per. 'And everything will work out fine . . . You'll be home soon.'

His smile felt stiff, but he hoped it looked reassuring.

'I'd better go and see Granddad,' he said.

'Say hello from me.'

She was more sympathetic than her mother. Since Per had cut Marika off when she called his mobile, she had hardly spoken to him. They had met just once, in the doorway of Nilla's room on Saturday, but she had barely glanced at him.

'Shame about Gerhard,' she said as she walked past. 'Hope he's OK.'

Do you really? Per directed the thought at her back as she went in to see Nilla, and the next moment felt thoroughly ashamed of himself.

Jerry didn't wake up.

His room was small, and the closed blinds transformed the sunshine outside into small glowing dots. Per sat in the darkness beside him during Saturday and Sunday, long hours when very little happened. The nurses came and went, changing his drip. They looked at him, patted his hand, and went out again.

Jerry had been sent for X-rays and put in plaster on Friday evening; half his face and his right arm and leg were covered in bandages. Those parts of his face that were visible were bruised and battered, but Per knew that the most serious bleeds were in the brain.

He had been moved from the emergency department to intensive care, and then to his own room off a ward.

This could have been interpreted as a positive sign, but in fact the opposite was true, as a nurse made clear to Per.

'Just don't expect any miracles,' was all she said.

Jerry had been moved to a room of his own because there wasn't much they could do. He lay in a torpor, muttering to himself and opening his eyes occasionally. He was asleep for most of the time.

Per sat by the bed, remembering that Jerry had failed to turn up when his mother Anita lay dying of kidney failure ten years earlier. He hadn't even phoned. Three days before her death he had sent a Get Well Soon card by post. Per had thrown it away without showing it to her.

Then he tried to remember when he had been closest to his father during the almost fifty years they had known one another. As a child? No. And not as an adult, either. He couldn't recall one single hour of closeness – so perhaps this was it.

I ought to say something about his life, Per thought. *I ought to tell him what I think of him. Get it all off my chest and then I'll feel better.*

But he said nothing. He just waited.

When he went down to get some lunch on Saturday he saw the headline in one of the evening papers in the little shop:

DOUBLE MURDER IN PORN STUDIO

So the news was out at last. Sex and violence in one headline – that was pure gold for the press. Per bought the paper, but didn't learn anything new. It simply said that the police were investigating an arson attack on a property owned by 'the notorious porn director Jerry Morner', and that two bodies had been found in the house. Next to the article a black and white picture from the seventies showed a smiling Jerry holding a copy of *Babylon* up to the camera. It didn't mention the fact that he was in hospital – merely that he was unavailable for comment.

Inspector Marklund turned up at the hospital at about three o'clock on Sunday afternoon, and Per met him outside the door of Jerry's room.

'I'm on my way back to Växjö,' Marklund said quietly. 'How is he? Has he said anything?'

'He hasn't come round yet . . . They think he's suffered brain damage.'

Marklund just nodded.

'Have you found the driver?' said Per.

'Not yet, but we're examining the motorway and we've found some tyre marks. The car must have been damaged, so we're checking garages too. And we're looking for witnesses.'

Per glanced towards Jerry's room. 'It must have been someone Jerry knew . . . I mean, he was getting out of the car when I spotted him. So he must have gone along with whoever it was of his own free will.'

'Did you recognize the driver?'

Per shook his head.

'Did you get the number?'

'I was too far away; the car was up above me on the bridge. I could see it was dark-red . . . I think I saw one like it driving past our cottage on Öland a few days ago.'

Marklund took out his notebook. 'Can you remember any details?'

'Not many . . . It was a Swedish number plate, and I think it was a Ford Escort, a few years old.' He looked wearily at the inspector. 'Is that any help?'

Marklund closed the notebook. 'You never know.'

But Per realized it was no help at all.

Jerry was sinking deeper and deeper into unconsciousness, but his eyes occasionally moved behind his eyelids. His breathing was shallow, and he mumbled disjointed words. They sounded like a long series of Swedish names, many of them women: 'Josefine, yes . . . Amanda . . . Charlotte? . . . Suzanne, what do you want?'

He never mentioned Per's mother Anita, nor Regina.

As the day passed, his breathing grew weaker and weaker, but in the midst of all the mumbling there were other names and words Per recognized: 'Bremer . . . Moleng Noar . . . and Markus Lukas, so ill . . .'

At about eight o'clock on Sunday evening, when Per had almost fallen asleep, Jerry suddenly looked at him with total clarity and whispered, 'Pelle?'

'I'm here,' said Per. 'There's nothing to worry about, Dad.'

'Good, Pelle . . . Good.' He fell silent.

Per leant closer. 'Who was it?' he asked. 'Who was driving the car?'

'Bremer.'

'It can't have been.'

But Jerry simply nodded, then closed his eyes again.

He passed away just after nine on Sunday evening, with a barely audible sigh. The wheezing Per had heard ever since he was a child stopped with a quiet exhalation, and his body gave up the struggle.

Per was sitting by the bed holding Jerry's hand when it happened, and he remained there when the room became utterly silent.

He sat there for several minutes. He tried to think of someone who needed to know that Jerry had gone, someone he ought to call – but he couldn't come up with a single person.

Eventually he went to look for a doctor.

45

Per got back to Casa Mörner an hour after midnight, once he had seen his father's body transferred to a trolley and wheeled away by a porter.

The last thing one of the night nurses had done in Jerry's room was to go over and open the window wide, the curtains fluttering as the cold night air swept in.

She turned to Per and gave him a brief, embarrassed smile. 'I usually open the window when they've gone,' she said. 'To let the soul out.'

Per nodded. He looked over at the window and could almost see Jerry's spirit drifting away through the night, like a shimmering silver ball outside the hospital. Would it sink down towards the ground, or float up to the stars?

He left Kalmar at half past midnight and drove slowly across the Öland bridge. As he drove north on the island he kept glancing in the rear-view mirror. A couple of times he saw headlights coming up behind him at high speed and gripped the wheel more tightly, but both cars overtook him.

Down by the quarry it was almost completely dark, with only a couple of outside lights showing over at the new houses. Per drove up to his little cottage, got out of the car and listened, but everywhere was quiet. The faint soughing of the wind, nothing else.

Then he heard the telephone ringing in the kitchen.

He began to walk slowly towards the house, and the phone continued to ring.

Markus Lukas, he thought. *You've killed Bremer and now you're hiding somewhere, wondering if you managed to kill my father.*

He unlocked the door and followed the sound into the kitchen. He looked at the telephone for a few seconds, then picked up the receiver. 'Hello?'

No one spoke; all he could hear was an echoing sound, and rhythmic cries in the background.

It was a recording, Per realized, and he had heard it before. On Maundy Thursday someone had rung up and played exactly the same thing in the middle of the day.

And now he recognized what he was listening to – a girl crying out. It was the soundtrack from one of Jerry's films.

He clutched the receiver tightly. 'Talk to me,' he said. 'Why are you doing this?'

There was no answer – the soundtrack continued. He listened and closed his eyes. 'You don't need to play that . . . Jerry's gone now,' he went on. 'You killed him.'

He held his breath and listened for some kind of response, but all he heard was the sound of the film for a few more seconds, then a click. The call was over.

He slowly replaced the receiver and saw his own pale face reflected in the kitchen window.

What was the message he had just been given? That this Markus Lukas intended to carry on? That he wasn't just pursuing Jerry for what he'd done, whatever that might be, but the whole Mörner family? The sins of the father passed on to the children and grandchildren . . .

297

He got up and went back out into the night. To Ernst's old workshop.

The trolls stared at him from the shelves lining the walls as he started to carry out Ernst's tools. Hammers, saws, chisels, sledgehammers and wooden clubs – plenty of excellent weapons. Under the light outside the cottage, Per could see that many of the tools were blunt and worn, but some were sharp. There was a big axe for chopping wood that looked lethal. He raised it with both hands.

You want revenge? You just come here then. Come here and see if I'm prepared to pay for something my father did . . .

He took his weapons inside, locked the door and distributed them through the different rooms. He placed the axe next to his bed. Then he turned off the light and lay in the darkness, staring up at the ceiling and thinking of Markus Lukas, the man whose face was turned away.

Eventually he fell asleep.

Four hours later the rising sun woke him. He raised his head, blinked and saw the big axe within reach on the floor. It all came flooding back.

His father had been murdered and his daughter was seriously ill.

The world was cold and empty.

He lay in bed for an hour or so but couldn't get back to sleep, and in the end he got up and had some breakfast. He looked at the telephone, but it remained silent.

After a while he picked up the receiver and made the necessary calls following the death of a relative: to a funeral director, to Jerry's bank, and to the priest at the church where the funeral would take place.

Then he sat and stared out of the window, waiting for

something to happen. But he had to occupy himself in the meantime. He took out his questionnaires.

He couldn't work at the moment, of course, he just didn't have the strength – so he started making up the answers. He filled in the forms himself, one after another. At first it was a slow process, but as time went by it became surprisingly easy to conjure up people who had seen an advert for a particular soap and were considering buying it. Some of them, like 'Peter from Karlstad' and 'Christina from Uppsala', were absolutely certain they would be making a purchase. They were convinced that this soap would give their life new meaning.

If Per hadn't been feeling so bad, he would have laughed.

Making up his own answers was much quicker, too – in just a few hours he had done three days' work. And his fear of Markus Lukas had begun to subside.

Afterwards he went into Jerry's bedroom and looked around. His father hadn't been there for long and had left few traces, not even his smell. A pair of scruffy flannel trousers was draped over the back of a chair, and Jerry's briefcase was still lying on the bed.

Per went over and opened it. He had hoped there might be something important inside, but he found nothing but some pills for high blood pressure and two small spring-loaded hand grippers that Jerry had been given to help rebuild his strength after the stroke.

And the old copy of *Babylon*, of course.

He opened the magazine and looked at the photo sequences. But he wasn't studying the young girls, just the man referred to in the caption as Markus Lukas, the man who never showed his face. In the pictures he looked about thirty; the magazine was twelve years old, so Markus Lukas must be in his forties now.

Per looked at the back of the man's head and tried to imagine Markus Lukas behind the wheel of a car. Was this the man who had killed his father?

Suddenly he saw something he hadn't noticed before: there was an arm sticking out in one of the pictures. It was pointing at the naked couple on the bed, and it was wearing two wristwatches. One gold, and one stainless steel.

It was Jerry's arm. Per looked at it for a long time.

The telephone rang twice on Monday evening. The first call was from a reporter on an evening paper who had somehow found out that Jerry was dead and that Per was his son. He'd heard that Jerry had died in a car accident 'in mysterious circumstances', and asked a long series of questions, but Per refused to give him any answers.

'Ring the police,' was his only response.

'Are you intending to take over?' asked the reporter. 'Are you going to run his porn empire from now on?'

'There is no empire,' said Per, and put the phone down.

The second call was from Marika.

'How are you feeling, Per?'

It sounded as if she really wanted to know.

He sighed. 'Oh, you know.' He paused. 'I'm sorry I haven't been spending much time with Nilla . . . Things will get better.'

Marika made no comment on that. 'I've got some news,' she said.

'Good news or bad news?'

'Good,' she said, but she didn't sound particularly optimistic. 'A vascular surgeon from Lund has been in touch, a friend of Dr Stenhammar. Apparently he's

300

prepared to operate around Nilla's aorta. He thinks it's "a challenge", so he wants to make an attempt.'

An attempt, thought Per, feeling a heavy, icy clump in his stomach.

'Good,' he said.

'He can't make any promises. Stenhammar said that several times.'

In some African countries children die like flies, thought Per. *Like flies. It will be nothing more than a notice in the paper.*

'Are you worried?'

'Of course I am, Marika.'

'So am I, but, I mean, I've got Georg . . . Do you want Jesper to come and stay with you for a while?'

'No,' Per said quietly. 'It's best if he stays with you.'

He glanced at his reflection in the dark kitchen window, at his tired, frightened eyes, and he knew that Jesper couldn't come back to the cottage. Not until the troll had been slain.

46

Summer is on its way, thought Gerlof. With all the flowers – wood anemones, poppies and butterfly orchids. And soon it would be lilac time.

It was a fresh, mild spring day, with just a week left until May. The thin soil on the island was moist but dried quickly in the sun, and Gerlof could smell in the air that all the stagnant water in the bogs and marshes around the village had begun to evaporate. Over the course of just a couple of weeks his lawn had gone from yellow to pale green, and had begun to thicken and flourish.

Spring was almost over for this year. In just a few weeks it would be summer – early summer, at least.

'Spring on Öland arrives with a bang and doesn't last for long,' as someone had written. But Gerlof was grateful that he had been able to sit here and watch it come and go from his front-row seat, out here on the lawn, and not from behind triple-glazed windows at the home in Marnäs.

Everything was quiet and peaceful. He had put out a chair for visitors, but no one had appeared over the past few days. John Hagman was down at his son's in Borgholm helping him redecorate the kitchen, and

Astrid Linder wasn't back from Spain yet. The whole of Stenvik had felt somehow empty this week, but Gerlof had seen Per Mörner's old car turn down the track leading to the quarry.

Gerlof hoped he would come over. He wasn't all that keen on the rich folk on the other side of the road, but he enjoyed talking to Per.

As Gerlof was sitting in his chair out on the lawn an hour or so later, Per actually turned up and pushed the gate open.

But his neighbour looked tired this Wednesday morning. He made his way slowly across the grass and with a brief greeting sat down.

'How are things?' Gerlof asked.

'Not so good.'

'Has something happened?'

Per looked down at the grass. 'My father's dead . . . He died in hospital on Sunday night.'

'What happened?'

'He got hit by a car.'

'Hit by a car?'

'A hit and run, in Kalmar.'

'An accident?'

'I don't think so.' Per sighed. 'It was a hit and run, but Jerry must have known the driver, because he persuaded my father to go with him to a deserted road. Then he just mowed him down and took off.'

'And who did it?'

'Who wanted to kill him? I don't know . . . A few things have happened recently, his studio burnt down a few weeks ago. It was deliberate, an arson attack.'

Gerlof nodded. 'So he wasn't popular?'

'Not particularly. Not even with me . . . I've often pretended I didn't have a father, especially when I was younger.' He smiled wryly. 'And now I don't.'

'Did he have any other children?'

'Not as far as I know.'

'Do you miss him?'

Per seemed to consider the question. 'The priest asked me that today when we were talking about the funeral. I didn't know what to say. It was quite difficult to love Jerry, but I wanted *him* to love *me* . . . It was important, for some reason.'

The garden was silent.

'My mother loved him,' Per went on quietly. 'Or maybe she didn't . . . but it was important to her that I kept in touch with Jerry. She wanted me to write and ring several times a year, when it was his birthday and so on. Jerry never contacted me . . . but after he'd had the stroke I obviously came in quite handy. He started calling me then.'

'This profession of his,' said Gerlof. 'Photographing men and women without any clothes on. Did it make him rich?'

Per looked down at his hands. 'In the past, I think . . . not lately. But the money used to come rolling in.'

'Money,' said Gerlof. 'It can, as St Paul wrote, make people do evil things . . .'

Per shook his head. 'I think it's all gone. Jerry had a great talent for raking money in, but he was just as good at getting rid of it. He hasn't had anything to do with magazines for several years, since before he had the stroke. In the end he couldn't even afford to run a car.'

'Jerry Morner,' said Gerlof. 'Was that his real name?'

'No, his name was Gerhard Mörner . . . But he decided he needed a new name when he started directing porn films. They all seem to do the same thing in the porn industry.'

'Hiding behind the name,' said Gerlof.

'Yes, unfortunately,' said Per, looking down at the grass. 'I'd really like to talk to people who knew Jerry, people who worked with him and are still alive, but even the police can't find anyone . . .'

Gerlof nodded thoughtfully. He remembered the magazine Jerry Morner had thrown on the table at the party, and said, 'I'll see what I can do.'

Per looked up. 'What *you* can . . .?'

'I shall do a little bit of research,' said Gerlof. 'What were those magazines called, the ones your father published?'

That same evening Gerlof rang John Hagman down in Borgholm. He chatted about this and that at first, as usual, but after a few minutes he got down to business.

'John, you once mentioned that your son had a pile of magazines under his bed, and he took them with him when he moved down to Borgholm. You described them, they were a particular kind of magazine. Do you remember?'

'I do,' said John. 'And he wasn't the least bit ashamed. I tried to talk to him, but he said all the lads read them.'

'Has Anders still got them?'

John sighed. He often sighed over his son. 'I expect he has, somewhere or other.'

'Do you think he might lend them to me?'

John remained silent for a few seconds. 'I can only ask.'

After quarter of an hour or so, John rang back. 'Yes, he's still got a few . . . and he can get hold of some more if you want them.'

'Where from?'

'He knows some junk shop in Kalmar that sells old magazines, everything you can think of.'

'Good,' said Gerlof. 'Tell him I'd be very grateful, if

he doesn't mind; I can pay for them. I'm trying to get hold of two particular magazines.'

'Which ones?'

'*Babylon* and *Gomorrah*.'

'That Jerry Morner's magazines?'

'Exactly.'

John didn't say anything for a little while.

'I'll have a word with Anders,' he said. 'But are you sure?'

'Sure?'

'Are you sure you want these magazines? I mean, I've seen some of the ones Anders had and they're extremely . . . extremely revealing.'

Embarrassed and excited, thought Gerlof.

'Yes, I imagine they are, John,' he said. 'But I don't suppose it's any worse than secretly reading someone else's diary.'

47

Five minutes after raising his voice to Vendela, Max came back into the living room speaking quietly, almost whispering. The fist he had shaken at her was now an outstretched hand pointing at himself, at his own chest, and he had turned into the understanding psychologist.

'I'm not angry with you, Vendela, you mustn't think that,' he said. He let out a long breath and added, 'I'm just a little bit disappointed. That's the way I feel at the moment.'

'I know, Max . . . There's nothing to worry about.'

After ten years, Vendela had learnt that his annoyance and jealousy went in cycles, and were always worse when he was coming to the end of a book.

She was making an effort to remain calm. It was Friday evening – and the eve of the feast of St Mark, an important day according to folklore.

'Max, I think I'm going to go out for a little run,' she said, 'then we can have a chat later.'

'Do you have to? If you stay at home we can—'

'Yes, it's for the best.'

Vendela went into the bathroom to change. She caught a glimpse of herself in the mirror: a tired soul, a hungry body, and lines of anxiety etched on her forehead. She thought about the tablets that could make her feel better, but she didn't even open the cabinet.

When she came out, Max was sitting in an armchair by the window with his Friday whisky, which was slightly bigger than his Thursday whisky. Aloysius was lying at the other end of the room, ears pricked towards his master.

Max lowered his glass and looked at her. 'Don't go for a run,' he said quietly. 'Can't you spend the evening at home?'

'I *will* be spending the evening at home, Max.' Vendela tied her shoelaces and straightened up. 'When I've been for a run. It'll only take half an hour . . .'

'Stay here.'

'No, I'll be back soon.'

Max knocked back his whisky and looked over at Aloysius. Then he stood up and took a couple of steps towards her. 'I'm going to start thinking about a new book this weekend.'

'Really? Already?' said Vendela. 'What's this one going to be about?'

'It's going to be called *Emotions to the Max*. Or perhaps even better, *Relationships to the Max*.' He smiled at her. 'Relationships are the most important thing of all, aren't they? Who we're with, what we do with them. You and me. You and me and other people. You and other people.'

'Me and other people . . . what are you talking about?'

'You and our neighbour in the little house on the prairie.' He nodded towards the north. 'You and Per Mörner, you've got a close relationship going on there.'

'Max, that's not true!'

He moved two steps closer. Vendela could see that his temples were shiny with sweat, as if the heat before a thunderstorm was building up inside his head. The lightning would strike at any moment.

'What's not true?' he said, wiping his fingers around his mouth. 'I mean, I've seen it with my own eyes.'

'We haven't done anything.'

'But you've been out for a run with him.'

'Well, yes, but—'

'And the grass on the prairie is dry now, I assume? Dry and soft? You can *lie down* on it, behind some stone wall?'

'Stop it, Max,' she said. 'That's enough.'

'Is it?'

'Yes. You sit there brooding about what I might be doing when I go out running, but that's because you're really thinking about something else altogether.'

'Like what?'

'You know exactly what I mean . . . You're thinking about Martin.'

'No!'

Max moved quickly towards her and Vendela backed away.

If I say the wrong thing now, he'll hit me, she thought.

'I'm going out, Max,' she said quietly, 'until you calm down.'

Her husband's shoulders dropped a fraction. 'You do that,' he said. 'You just go.'

Vendela ran. With long strides she ran away from the fairytale palace she had dreamed of once upon a time. Away from Max. She thought of turning off towards the Mörners' cottage and knocking on the door so that she could speak to a sensible person, but it looked as if it were all locked up. She hadn't seen Per or his father all week, and the Kurdin family was also away.

She took a wide swing to the west and headed for

the alvar. But this far south it was difficult to find her way; her route was frequently obstructed by stone walls she didn't recognize, or by thorny thickets and barbed wire, and it was a while before the landscape opened out ahead of her.

As the sun went down she could see that the alvar had begun to bloom. The yellowish-brown ground had absorbed the water and was now shaded dark blue with spiked speedwell, wild thyme and pasque flower, dotted with bright-yellow dandelions. Beautiful.

But there was a stillness among all the beauty that felt ominous. When Vendela stopped to catch her breath among all the flowers, she closed her eyes and wished all those around her a happy and peaceful St Mark's Eve. But she couldn't feel any warmth or benevolence flowing back in return. She couldn't see any pictures; there was only darkness.

The elves were not happy.

48

Gerlof was sitting on the lawn in the sunshine when Carina Wahlberg came to visit him on Friday afternoon. John Hagman had been over in the morning and given him a substantial pile of magazines – old copies of *Babylon* and *Gomorrah*, stained and torn, and he was just flicking through them.

Gerlof was holding the magazines with his fingertips; most of them didn't smell too good.

The doctor greeted him cheerily from the gate, and he waved to her. 'Afternoon, Doctor,' he said.

She smiled at him and came closer – but stopped dead when she saw the magazines. 'I came to check your hearing,' she said, looking down at the pile of magazines. 'I can see there's nothing wrong with your eyesight. Would you like me to come back another time?'

Gerlof shook his head. 'Come and sit down.'

'You look busy.'

He looked up from the magazine, not smiling. 'It's not what you think,' he said.

'I don't think anything.'

'Well, it's not like *that*, anyway. I'm eighty-three, and my last girlfriend, Maja up at the home, was about the same age, but she got too ill to spend time with me any more . . . I haven't looked at young girls in twenty-five years.' Gerlof gave this some thought, then added, 'Well, twenty at any rate.'

'So why are you looking at those magazines?' asked Dr Wahlberg.

'Because I have to.'

'Oh?'

'I'm conducting an investigation.'

'Of course you are.'

Dr Wahlberg came over and sat down. Gerlof flicked through the magazines, one after another, and kept talking. 'I'm trying to come up with something in particular to do with these girls, but I don't really know what I'm looking for. The whole thing just seems terribly sordid.'

Dr Wahlberg looked at the pictures, her expression anything but cheerful. 'Well, I can see one thing that's not good,' she said eventually, 'from my perspective.'

'What's that?'

'They're not using any protection.'

'Protection?'

'Contraceptives. The men should be wearing con-doms. But I suppose they never do in magazines like this.'

Gerlof looked at her. 'So you've seen them before?'

'I used to work as a school doctor. Young lads buy them and get completely the wrong idea; they think these fantasies are reality.'

Gerlof looked down at the pictures, nodding thought-fully. 'It's true, they're not using any protection . . . But you're wrong.'

'About what?'

'These aren't just fantasies,' said Gerlof. 'They're very real to those who are being photographed.'

312

Dr Wahlberg stood up. 'I'll go inside and sort out your tablets, Gerlof.' She turned away, then added, 'Let me give you a piece of good advice: throw those magazines away as soon as you can. I don't think you'd want your daughters to find them.'

'When I'm dead, you mean?'

The doctor wasn't smiling. 'When someone has died in their own house or in a care home,' she said, 'magazines like this often turn up, hidden under the mattress or in a drawer. It happens more often than you might think. And it's always upsetting when the person's child or grandchild finds them.'

Gerlof nodded. 'These aren't actually mine,' he said, 'but I'll certainly pass that on to the owner.'

When Dr Wahlberg had gone, Gerlof carried on leafing through *Babylon* and *Gomorrah*. There was no variation, just page after page of photos of blonde girls in different sexual positions – he was surprised how tedious it all seemed after a while. Sad and depressing. But he kept on looking.

He suddenly stopped at one of the pictures. It was a colour photo that looked like most of the others: a picture of one of the muscular men, naked among the desks in a little classroom. The man was with a young woman. According to the brief caption she was called Belinda, and was described as 'a naughty Swedish schoolgirl who has a lesson to learn'.

Gerlof was fairly sure her name wasn't Belinda. But he looked at the picture for a long time, eventually picking up his glasses and holding them close to the page, like a magnifying glass.

After a minute or so he put them down, got up slowly, and went inside to make a phone call, taking the magazine with him.

He rang Per Mörner on Ernst's old number, but there was no reply so he tried Per's mobile.

'Mörner.' He still sounded exhausted.

Gerlof cleared his throat. 'It's Gerlof – Gerlof Davidsson in Stenvik. Can you talk?'

'For a little while . . . I'm just on the way to visit my daughter in hospital. Has something happened?'

'Maybe,' said Gerlof. 'I've been looking at some of your father's magazines.'

'Oh? How did you get hold of them?'

'I have contacts,' said Gerlof, not wanting to mention John Hagman or his son by name.

'So what did you think?'

Gerlof picked up the copy of *Babylon* and looked at the front cover. 'Lots of blonde wigs and sad eyes,' he said. 'And it's all very seedy. Very seedy pictures.'

'I know,' said Per, sounding even more weary. 'But that's the way it is, and we men buy it.'

'I'm too old,' said Gerlof.

'I've never liked it,' said Per. 'Jerry was keen on pictures and films like that, but not me. Not at any age. But somebody buys them, after all.'

'And these men in the pictures, who are they?'

'Men?' said Per. 'There's only one man . . . his name is Markus Lukas. Or at least that's the name he uses.'

'No, there are different men. At least two. You never see their faces, but their bodies are different.'

'Oh?'

'And they don't use any protection, either. No condoms.'

'No, that's true. I suppose Jerry thought it wouldn't look right, it would look silly – you're very observant, Gerlof.'

Gerlof sighed. 'Why do they do it, these girls? Do you know?'

'Why? I can't answer that,' said Per. 'I don't suppose it makes them feel too good about themselves . . . but I don't know.'

He stopped, so Gerlof carried on, 'I've found one of them, anyway.'

'One of them?'

'One of the girls in one of the magazines. You did say you wanted to find someone to talk to.'

'You mean . . . you recognize one of the girls?'

'I recognized her sweater.'

'She's wearing a sweater?' said Per.

'It's thrown over a chair in the background,' said Gerlof. 'She comes from Kalmar, I think. I don't know her name, but you should be able to find her.'

49

Per was on his way to see Nilla, but had stopped in Borgholm and was just going into the library when Gerlof rang about his discovery in one of Jerry's magazines. It sounded promising, but Per was intending to search for Markus Lukas in the phone books in the library. The name wasn't listed in any of the books covering southern Sweden, so he started looking for the name Jerry had mentioned in the car, *Moleng Noar.*

The name sounded Asiatic, like a Chinese restaurant. He flicked through the Yellow Pages for Malmö, but couldn't find any restaurants with that name.

Hans Bremer had lived in Malmö, he remembered. He leafed through the section containing residential numbers, reached B and found *Bremer, Hans* with the address given as Terränggatan 10B.

He noted down the address, then went back to thinking about the name. *Moleng Noar.*

He picked up his pen and tried out different spellings:

Molang-noor
Mu-Lan Over
Moo Leng Noer

But it was no good, none of those names were in the phone book.

Or could it be a French name, a variation on Moulin Rouge, for example? He tried the French spelling: *Moulin Noir*. The black windmill.

He went back to the phone book, and this time he was in luck. There was actually an advert for the Moulin Noir; it was a night club in Malmö, open from two o'clock in the afternoon until four in the morning; SHOW EVERY HALF-HOUR, it said.

A sex club. It couldn't be anything else.

Had Jerry owned the club? He hadn't mentioned it to Per, but nothing would surprise him.

He wrote down the address. He would go to Malmö today, but first he would stop off at the hospital. Six days to go until the operation.

Per couldn't get in to see Nilla straight away; there were nurses with her taking samples for more tests. He had to sit and wait until they had finished.

The waiting room wasn't empty; there was one other person there. A woman of about sixty-five was sitting on the sofa opposite him with her head bowed, clutching a folded woollen sweater. It wasn't the first time he'd had to wait with someone else, and it was always awkward – each knowing why the other was sitting there, but neither having the strength or the inclination to acknowledge it.

They were relatives, and they were waiting for news. Perhaps the woman opposite him was taking a break from all the major and minor symptoms floating around the ward.

Per ought to sign himself off work on the grounds that he had a sick child to care for; if he'd had the strength, he would have done so. But Marika had said she was signed off work at the moment, and he didn't know if both parents could claim at the same time. There was bound to be some regulation about that. In the meantime he would just have to carry on making stuff up.

The woman suddenly looked at him. 'Are you Nilla's dad?'

Per nodded.

'I'm Emil's grandmother . . . he's talked about Nilla.' Her smile was slightly strained. 'It seems as if they've become quite good friends.'

'That's right . . .' In spite of the fact that he was afraid of the answer, he asked, 'How are things with Emil?'

The woman stopped smiling. 'They're not saying much . . . all we can do is wait.'

Per nodded again, but didn't say any more.

Everyone was waiting. There was nothing to say.

Eventually he was allowed in.

Nilla was lying in the darkness holding her lava stone; she raised a hand to wave at him. It was probably his imagination, but Per thought that the arms protruding from her hospital gown were thinner, that her chest had somehow collapsed.

'How's it going?'

'Not so bad.'

'Are you in any pain?'

Nilla looked down at the black stone. 'Not right now . . . not much.' She sighed. 'But I'm so tired of all the horrible stuff. Of the pain, of the doctors and nurses always wanting me to describe it. They keep on asking me where the pain is, and what it feels like. Is it a stabbing pain, or does it sting, or is it more like a cramp? It's like some kind of exam, and I'm no good at it.'

'It's not an exam,' said Per. 'You can answer however you want.'

'I know, but when I say the pain is like a black cloud up above me, growing and sucking up the white cloud I'm sitting on, they stop listening . . . it's too weird for them.'

They were both silent for a few moments.

'Nilla, I have to go away for a little while.'

'Go where? Is it to do with Granddad?'

Per shook his head. He still hadn't told Nilla her grandfather was dead. That could wait.

'I'm going down to Malmö . . . there's something I have to do. But I'll be back tomorrow night.'

50

It was just an ordinary weekend in the city when he reached Malmö. Cars crawling around the round-abouts, ferries setting sail for Denmark, people enjoying their leisure time as they walked by the water in the spring sunshine, pushing their baby buggies.

It had taken Per almost four hours to drive down from Kalmar. He reached the city centre at about three o'clock and parked a few blocks away from the central station, where the hourly parking charge was lower. Then he found his way to the back street where the Moulin Noir lay.

It wasn't a place that went out of its way to advertise its presence; there was just a small, cracked sign above the entrance with the words MOULIN NOIR – SEX SHOP & NIGHT CLUB. The windows were painted black and protected with iron bars – Per guessed that the anti-porn lobby would sometimes gather here with placards and rotten eggs. But at the moment the entire street was deserted.

He stopped a few metres from the door, where a white handwritten notice proclaimed OVER 18s ONLY! Despite the fact that he didn't know anyone in Malmö, he checked one more time to make sure nobody could see him.

Dirty old man, he thought. Then he straightened his back and went inside.

He found himself in a long, narrow shop, just as quiet and deserted as the street outside. The sharp, lemony smell of some kind of cleaning product hung in the air, but the vinyl floor still looked grubby. The shelves lining the walls were stocked with films and magazines wrapped in plastic, but there were no copies of *Babylon* or *Gomorrah*. The gap Jerry's defunct magazines had left in the market had been filled long ago by his colleagues.

On the glass counter at the far side of the room stood an old metal till, and behind it a woman was sitting on a tall bar stool filing her nails. She was about thirty, dressed in a tight black dress and high, shiny leather boots. Her eyes were black with kohl and her hair was long, red and glossy, but it looked like a wig. Per assumed that most things were fake in this establishment.

Behind the counter was a staircase leading down to the cellar, with a beaded curtain at the bottom. Per could hear the thump of music and a woman's long-drawn-out moans, but the tone was metallic and tinny, like a film soundtrack. It was almost exactly the same as the background noise he had heard on the telephone on two occasions, but he still didn't know who had called, or why.

Per went over to the woman. She put down the nail file and smiled at him.

'Hi,' he said.

'Hi there, darling. Would you like to go down into the den of debauchery?'

'Maybe. How much is it?'

'Five hundred.'

That was three hundred kronor more than Per had on him.

'Five hundred,' he said, 'just to get in?'

'Not just to get in, darling,' said the woman, smiling even more broadly. 'You get a big surprise down there!'

'Do I indeed. And is it worth five hundred?'

She winked at him. 'Men usually seem to think so.'

'Have you worked here long?'

'Quite a long time,' she said. 'Are you going to . . .'

'How long?'

He was trying to ask questions in the same firm tone as Lars Marklund, the police officer.

The woman stopped smiling. 'Six months. Are you going to pay?'

'Who owns this place?'

She shrugged her shoulders. 'Some guys.' She held out her hand with its long, red nails. 'Five hundred, please.'

Per took out his wallet to keep her interested, but didn't open it. 'I'd like to speak to one of the owners.'

The woman didn't respond.

Eventually he opened his wallet and took out the two hundred he had, along with a piece of paper. '*Ring me!*' he wrote underneath his telephone number, and signed it '*Per Mörner (Jerry Morner's son)*'.

He handed over the piece of paper and the two hundred-kronor notes. 'These are for you,' he said, 'and you don't even have to let me in. But give the note to one of the owners . . . the one who's been here the longest.'

The woman took the money, but looked bored to death again. 'I'll see . . . I don't know if he's coming in tonight.'

'Give it to him when he does come in,' said Per. 'Will you do that?'

'Sure.'

She quickly tucked the money away, then folded his message and put it next to the till. Then she adjusted her position on the high stool, titivated her hair, and appeared to forget that Per existed.

He took one step to the side, listened to the music and glanced at the staircase. He thought about Regina again, and got the idea that she was waiting for him in the cellar. Perhaps Jerry and Bremer were sitting down there too, two corpses with a cigar between their lips and a hand on her thigh. All he had to do was pay, and he could go and have a look.

But he turned away and went back outside.

A room in a cheap hotel by the motorway to the north of the city was waiting for him, but first of all he drove over to Terränggatan. It was a sudden impulse – he just wanted to see where Hans Bremer had lived.

Terränggatan was a gloomy place even in the spring sunshine, he thought. Number 10 was a grey five-storey building on an equally grey, cracked street. An old van with a trailer was parked outside, half-full of packing cases.

The name BREMER was still there at the entrance to 10B, and the door was open. The lock appeared to be broken.

There was an unpleasant smell in the echoing stairwell, as if someone had poured sour milk all over the floor. Per went up to the second floor. The door with Bremer's name on it was ajar, and he could hear banging and crashing from inside.

He opened the door and was assailed by an even nastier smell.

'Hello?' he called.

'What do you want?' a voice said wearily.

A middle-aged, grey-haired woman was standing in

323

the kitchen doorway watching him, her arms folded. Behind her a teenage boy wearing his baseball cap back to front was busy disconnecting an old TV and tying up the cables.

Per's head was suddenly empty – what did he actually want?

'Hi, I just thought I'd call in,' he said. 'I was a . . . a friend of Hans.'

The woman looked even more worn out. 'Oh? One of his drinking buddies, were you?'

'No,' said Per, and decided to stop lying. 'Actually, we weren't friends, but he used to work with my father. And I was in the area, so I thought I'd just come and see where he lived.'

The woman didn't appear to be listening to his explanations. She didn't invite him in, but turned and disappeared into the apartment, so he followed her and asked, 'Were you his wife? If so, may I offer my—'

'Hans never married,' the woman interrupted him. 'I'm Ingrid, his younger sister. New tenants are moving in at the end of the month, so we're just clearing the place out.'

There wasn't much to clear out, Per thought as he walked through the narrow hallway. There was no bed in the bedroom, just a mattress, and the yellow-painted walls were bare. Bremer seemed to have put all his time and energy into producing films and magazines with Jerry, and none into interior design.

His sister had gone into the kitchen and was packing cutlery and pans into a box. The kitchen was just as empty as the bedroom: a rickety table and two chairs over by the window, and a few postcards on the fridge, faded by the sun. There was no sign of any films or magazines – nothing that might have given away what Bremer did.

'Since you're here . . .'

He looked up to see Ingrid pointing at him.

'. . . you might as well give me a hand to empty the cupboards,' she said. 'Is that OK?'

'Well, no, I really ought to . . .'

'You can stay for a little while, surely? Then you can help Simon with the boxes.'

So Per found himself standing on a chair, gathering up plates and piling them in boxes. Up and down, up and down.

When he picked up a stack of soup bowls from the bottom shelf, he caught sight of a piece of yellow paper behind them. It was a little Post-it note that had presumably dried out and fallen off the inside of the cupboard door. There were four telephone numbers in shaky handwriting in pencil, each with a name in front of it:

Ingrid
Cash
Fountain
Danielle

The first number was Bremer's sister's, no doubt. One of the others should have been Jerry's, but he didn't recognize any of them.

'Finished?' said Ingrid behind him.

'Nearly.'

He slipped the note in his pocket and went back to the crockery.

When Per had finished in the kitchen, he started carrying boxes downstairs, and it turned out there was actually quite a lot of stuff in the apartment. It took almost an hour to get everything out.

Bremer's sister didn't say much while they were working, and neither did Per.

'Do you know how your brother died?' he asked

when they had finished and were standing out in the street in the sunshine.

Ingrid wiped her brow. 'The police said there was a fire . . . He'd gone to meet some dodgy character, and the house burnt down.'

'Was there a quarrel?'

'A quarrel? I don't think so. I imagine they were sitting around smoking and drinking . . . That's what Hans usually did.'

A small-time gangster, with a finger in lots of different pies – that was how the police had described Hans Bremer to Per. 'But . . . did he have any enemies?'

Bremer's sister shook her head. 'The police asked me the same question . . . No, he didn't have any enemies. But people did take advantage of him, I know that.'

'In what way?'

'He lent people money, he was always ready to help out . . . Hans was too kind, and he had no real friends, only drinking buddies. If you don't have any friends, you can't have any enemies, can you?'

Per wasn't at all sure about that, but he simply asked, 'Was one of his friends called Markus Lukas?'

'Markus Lukas? Not as far as I know.'

'I heard that Hans and Markus Lukas worked together . . . Your brother worked hard, didn't he?'

Ingrid shook her head again. 'Hans worked as little as possible. He always said he had plenty of money, but nothing ever came of it.'

Per nodded. He realized Bremer's sister hadn't had a clue what her brother did; he had lied to her.

Silence and lies. Business as usual when you were dealing with Jerry.

51

Max was bright red in the face; he looked as if a heart attack was imminent.

'He's thirteen years old, Vendela!'

'What does it matter how old he is, Max?'

'Thirteen! That's the equivalent of an eighty-year-old in human terms!'

'So? He's eighty years old and *healthy*!'

The argument between Max and Vendela on Monday evening had been exclusively about Aloysius and his health. They had argued about the same thing several times before, but their discussions always went round in circles, and they had tired of every other topic.

'He is *not* healthy!'

'He is, Max. He's up and about much more often, and he's walking better.'

'He's *blind*!'

When they had started to repeat themselves they had both given up and walked past each other across the echoing stone floor. Max had shut himself in his thinking room, and Vendela had chosen the kitchen. Aloysius had stayed out of the way during the quarrel, but had taken Vendela's side by padding after her and rubbing his nose against her legs.

This was not the right thing to do, she had said so to Max many times. You should never simply storm off after a quarrel without sorting it out. He had even included that particular piece of advice in one of his books.

Vendela wiped a few breadcrumbs from the stainless-steel worktop and sighed. They weren't going to get anywhere, she realized. They either had to give up, or go for counselling – but the problem was that Max was a trained psychologist, and always knew best. He refused to see other therapists; he didn't believe in them.

Vendella went into the bathroom, but didn't take a tranquillizer. She drank a glass of water, felt a little fuller and longed to be out on the alvar. She started to change into her tracksuit.

Five minutes later she was ready. She patted Aloysius and opened the front door. 'Won't be long!' she shouted.

There was no response from the thinking room.

She ran straight to the elf stone this Monday evening, with long strides and tightly clenched fists. She stumbled a few times on tussocks of grass and hidden stones, but stayed on her feet. At last she was there.

Vendela had no money or jewellery with her. She had nothing to offer the elves, but she wanted to be here anyway. She had run here four days in a row now; she didn't have to listen to Max out here.

She placed her palms flat on the stone and tried to relax. Loud voices reverberated inside her head, the memory of the quarrel. But this evening there was no solace to be found.

Things had got much worse since her last visit, and sorrow hung heavily over the kingdom of the elves. Vendela could see clear pictures in her head when she closed her eyes: the king of the elves sitting on his throne

328

weeping for his ailing queen, blue blood trickling from his eyes.

Vendela felt that no one had any time for her. She turned and ran westward once more.

When she got home, there were no lights on in the house. The Audi had gone, and the front door was locked. Max must have gone off somewhere, but the spare key was under one of the plant pots. Vendela unlocked the door and went inside.

'Hello?' she shouted.

The echo of her call died away, and there was no reply. Vendela hadn't expected an answer from Max, but why hadn't Aloysius barked, or come pattering across the floor?

'Ally?'

No response, but when she went into the kitchen she saw a note stuck on the fridge:

Gone home – taking Ally to the vet to get him checked over, will be in touch.
Love and kisses
Max

Vendela ripped down the note and threw it away.

She went around the house, looking in every room until she was certain Ally wasn't there. Then she sat down in the enormous living room and stared through the enormous windows, out on to the deserted quarry.

Max had gone back to Stockholm and taken their dog with him. There was nothing Vendela could do.

She closed her eyes.

She could hear the sound of a cow bell, and Jan-Erik's giggling laughter.

Öland 1958

Henry Fors has taken the boot with him and is leading the policemen up the stairs. Vendela sneaks silently behind them; she has a bad feeling.

'Come with me and I'll show you who owns this boot.'

He goes over to the only closed door and opens it without knocking.

'Here he is . . . my son Jan-Erik.'

Vendela watches the policemen follow Henry into the room. All three gather around the figure sitting on his blanket, dressed in the same dirty clothes he was wearing the previous evening. Jan-Erik tilts his head back and looks up at them. Then he giggles and turns his attention to Vendela. She wants to say something, but doesn't even open her mouth.

'Is he ill?' asks one of the policemen.

'Well, that's one way of putting it. He's retarded.' Henry is pointing at Jan-Erik as if he were exhibiting some kind of curious object. 'We've had him here for a couple of years now . . . He was in an institution before that, but I brought him home out of the goodness of my heart.' He pauses, then adds, 'That was probably a mistake.'

'So it's his boot?' says the first policeman.

'Indeed it is – I can prove it.'

Henry bends down, grabs hold of one of Jan-Erik's legs, stretches it out and puts on the boot. It seems to fit, even though Vendela knows perfectly well that it's her father's boot.

'That's all very well,' says the policeman, looking over at the wheelchair. 'But can he walk?'

'Oh yes,' says Henry. 'The doctor at the institution said that he *can* walk. But he only does it when nobody's looking.'

'Show us,' say the policemen.

Henry bends down and gets hold of Jan-Erik under the arms. 'Up you come.' Then he lifts him from the blanket in one movement.

Jan-Erik is still giggling. He is standing upright, with a thick sock on one foot and the boot on the other.

Henry gives him a shove. 'Go on now, boy. Off you go!'

Jan-Erik stands there for a few seconds, looking at the policemen. Then he takes a short step forward, followed by another.

'But why would he set fire to the place?'

'Why?' says Henry. 'Who knows? It doesn't make any sense . . . the lad's in a world of his own.'

The policemen look at each other, unsure what to do.

'What do you think – can his sort be taken to court?'

'No idea. How old is he, Fors?'

'Seventeen.'

'In that case it might be possible . . . We'll have to check.'

Vendela feels sick. She opens her mouth. 'No!'

They all stop dead and stare at her, and she has no option but to continue: 'It was my fault. It was me! I

331

hated the cows . . . I went out on to the alvar and wished that they would disappear. I asked . . .'

The elves, she thinks, but she dare not say it. That would probably make things even worse.

The policemen look surprised at first, then they smile at one another. One of them winks.

'I see crime runs in the family,' he says.

The policemen walk past Vendela and leave the room.

The house is very quiet once they have left. Henry doesn't say anything, and Vendela doesn't want to talk to him. The word must have got around about the policemen's suspicions, because the following day nobody comes to visit the Fors family – it even looks as if the neighbours are taking a detour so they don't have to walk past the farm and look at it.

The week after the fire there are more interviews with the police. Eventually it is decided that both Henry Fors and his son are under suspicion: Jan-Erik is accused of burning down the barn, and Henry of having kept quiet about his son's actions in order to claim the insurance money.

'It wasn't Jan-Erik,' Vendela says to her father. 'It was you.'

Henry shrugs his shoulders. 'It's better this way . . . I mean, your brother is retarded, they can't punish him.'

In spite of everything that has happened, Henry carries on working as a quarryman. He walks down to the coast with his head held high every morning, and comes home in the evening. Vendela dare not ask what he does there all day, because it's hardly likely that he has any customers by this stage.

Vendela herself carries on walking back and forth to school, but now the long trek and the hours she spends there are one long torment. She is no longer Vendela Fors, she is just one of 'that family who burnt down their own farm', and at break and lunchtime Dagmar Gran sits in a circle with the other girls in their class without even looking at Vendela.

After a couple of weeks of silent waiting, both Jan-Erik and Henry are summoned to the court in Borgholm where the case will be heard.

Henry puts on his black Sunday-best suit and combs his hair carefully. He gets out clean clothes for his son and goes upstairs.

He raises his voice. Vendela realizes that Jan-Erik is refusing to go. Eventually Henry comes downstairs carrying his son. Jan-Erik is clinging to his father.

'Right, we're off to catch the train,' says Henry.

Standing in the porch, Vendela notices that her brother is wearing a new shirt, but his face is just as dirty as it was before.

'Shouldn't Jan-Erik have a wash?'

'Yes, but they'll feel more sorry for him if he looks like this,' says Henry as he walks out of the door.

Vendela is left at home. She sits down in the kitchen and stares blankly into space.

Late that evening, Henry and Jan-Erik return with a verdict from the court: Henry will serve eight months in prison in Kalmar for insurance fraud. In addition, in view of Henry's current financial state, the farm and all its contents are to be sold at auction.

'That's just the way it goes,' he says when he has carried Jan-Erik upstairs and come back down to Vendela in the kitchen. 'Man proposes, God disposes. We just have to get used to it.'

He is smiling grimly at her across the kitchen table, as if the end of his farm is somehow good news.

'And Jan-Erik?' Vendela asks. 'Will he go to prison too?'

'No.'

'So he's free?'

Henry shakes his head. 'Things didn't turn out quite the way I'd hoped . . . he's going up to Norrland.'

'Norrland?'

'To a place called Salberga. It's a mental hospital for the socially maladjusted.'

'How long for?'

'I've no idea . . . Until they let him out, I suppose.'

The silence in the kitchen grows heavier and heavier, until eventually Vendela asks, 'And what about me?'

She is expecting to hear that she will be left alone in the house, but Henry says, 'You're going to Kalmar as well. You'll be living with your aunt and going to school there.'

'And what if I don't want to?'

'You have no choice,' says Henry.

Vendela says nothing. Did she stand by the elf stone and wish for this, wish that she could go and live in the town? Did she wish that everything would end like this?

She doesn't remember; she has wished for far too much.

The time comes when the little family is to be dispersed. Henry is to begin serving his sentence, Vendela will go to stay with her aunt, and Jan-Erik will be picked up in Kalmar by two care workers from Vänersborg. The day before is a Sunday in the middle of May, overcast and gloomy.

In the morning Henry packs a suitcase for himself and a rucksack for Jan-Erik. He makes coffee and drinks it. Then he sits in the kitchen staring silently at the rectangle of ash outside. Vendela sits opposite him, staring equally silently at her thin hands.

Her father is restless. He stands up at about ten o'clock and picks up the coffee pot, then seems to remember that he has already drunk his coffee. He turns to Vendela. 'I'm going to do some work . . . day of rest or no day of rest.'

'You're going to the quarry now?'

'Yes. I'll be back this evening,' says Henry, 'when your aunt and uncle arrive. They're taking the three of us to Kalmar.'

Then he sets off down towards the coast to work, perhaps for the last time. Vendela hears him start to sing a familiar old Öland song as he reaches the gate. The song gradually fades into the distance, and Vendela remains sitting in the kitchen, feeling like the loneliest person in the whole world.

But she has no intention of waiting for Aunt Margit and Uncle Sven. Once Henry has disappeared in the direction of the sea, she goes into his room, opens the cupboard and takes out the jewellery box.

The last large piece of her mother's jewellery that is left is a gold heart on a fine silver chain. Vendela puts it in her pocket. Then she goes upstairs. The only sound is a monotonous voice reading the weather forecast on the radio in Jan-Erik's room. Vendela opens the door without knocking.

He is lying on the floor on the bloodstained blanket, listening to the radio; he seems to be waiting for her. He smiles.

Vendela kneels down in front of him and looks into his sea-blue eyes. 'Father has gone, Jan-Erik,' she says, slowly and clearly. 'He's gone down to the quarry, where he works.'

Jan-Erik blinks.

'They're coming to fetch you, and me . . . but we're not going to wait for them. Do you understand?' Vendela points in the direction of the alvar. 'We're going to the elves.'

He smiles at her.

'Come on then.'

But Jan-Erik remains on his blanket, holding his arms up to her. He wants to be carried, she realizes. There is no hesitation in him, but she is aware of the acrid smell in the room, and holds up her finger.

'First you need a wash.'

She drags out the tin bath in the kitchen, pumps up several bucketfuls of water and warms it on the wood stove. Then she carries her brother downstairs. It's quite easy; he is not much more than skin and bone.

Jan-Erik giggles nervously as he lowers himself into the water. It is almost black after just a few minutes. Vendela lets him wash his body himself, but helps him with his face. She puts plenty of soap on a tea towel and rubs gently, washing away all the dried pus and congealed blood. Underneath there are scratches and self-inflicted wounds that have healed, but the skin looks healthier than she had expected. Jan-Erik is beginning to look human.

When he is dry, she cuts his nails. He doesn't seem to have any clean clothes of his own, so she borrows some of Henry's, turning up the sleeves and trouser legs to make them fit.

'Right, time to go.'

Vendela carries him out of the house and feels him rest his chin on her shoulder. She puts him down, then goes upstairs to fetch the wheelchair; they set off along the cow path.

She talks quietly to her brother. 'The elves will help us, Jan-Erik . . . It will be better when we're with them.'

Jan-Erik just smiles. He leans back in the chair and draws up his legs as she takes hold of the handles and pushes him along.

Vendela chooses the route through the trees so that no one will see them. She has walked here behind the cows so many times.

It is only when they are crossing the meadow and are several hundred metres from the house that it occurs to Vendela that she should have brought more than just a gift for the elves. She should have brought food and blankets as well, but it's too late now.

She pushes the wheelchair across the grass. The ground is damp, but the wheels are large and the chair makes slow but steady progress. They pass through the last gate and set out across the alvar.

Vendela is walking with her brother beneath the immense blue sky, heading for the strip of water in the distance. Between the huge lakes on the alvar, with the setting sun at her back. Making straight for the motionless juniper bushes.

'Nearly there,' she says.

She can see the elf stone; she leans forward and tenses her leg muscles to get up some speed over the last few hundred metres.

But then they come to a sudden halt. She has got too close to one of the meltwater lakes, where the grass is soaking wet and the soil is loose and muddy. The wheelchair is listing to the right. The big wheels have been sucked down into the mud, and they are stuck.

Jan-Erik remains sitting in the chair at first, but as Vendela heaves and tugs with no success, he lifts himself out of the seat and stands beside her. Vendela hopes he will start walking, but he doesn't move. He smiles as he watches her struggling with the wheelchair.

She gives up and leaves it where it is. Once more

she holds out her arms and picks up her brother, even though there is hardly any strength left in her own legs.

They set off again, heading for the circle of juniper bushes.

She hauls Jan-Erik the last few metres to the elf stone, little by little. While she is tense and sweating, the body she is holding is completely relaxed – he is resting his chin on her shoulder again.

They make their way in among the juniper bushes where the ground is dry and hard, and Vendela makes one last desperate effort to get Jan-Erik to the stone. He places his feet on the grass and walks the last few steps.

At last he is sitting with his back against the rough block.

Vendela looks at the top, and sees that all the hollows in the stone are empty.

The elves have been here, very recently.

She reaches into her pocket and feels the silver chain between her fingers. The last piece of her mother's jewellery. She places it in one of the hollows.

Take care of him, she thinks. *And of me. Make us healthy and free from sin.*

She breathes out. Then she sinks down on the grass next to her brother between the juniper bushes.

The wind soughs gently. They sit in silence side by side, and Vendela waits. Eventually the birds stop singing around them, one by one, and it grows colder and darker.

Nothing happens. No one comes. Jan-Erik doesn't move, but Vendela begins to shiver in her thin dress.

In the end, when the night has come and the air is bitterly cold, she cannot sit there any longer. She gets up and looks at her brother. 'Jan-Erik, we have to go . . . we need to fetch some food and warmer clothes.'

He smiles and holds up his arms, but she shakes her head. 'I can't. You'll have to walk.'

But he merely looks at her, and remains sitting by the stone.

Vendela starts to back away. She turns around. 'Wait here, Jan-Erik. I'll be back.'

52

The Krona grammar school in Kalmar was a collection of reddish-brown buildings extending over half a block. Per arrived there on his way back from Malmö about half an hour before lunchtime, while lessons were still going on. He walked down long, empty corridors and up a flight of stairs to the main office.

In the first room he found a young woman who was hardly likely to have been working there fifteen years earlier, but when she saw him she immediately asked, 'Can I help you?'

'Maybe,' said Per. 'I'm looking for a former pupil; I think she attended this school in the early eighties.'

'What's her name?'

'That's what I don't know. But I do have a picture of her . . .'

He showed her the photograph of the blonde girl Gerlof Davidsson had found in *Babylon* – but not the full-length nude shot. He had cut her face out of the magazine and stuck it on a piece of white paper.

'I've inherited an old cottage on Öland,' he went on, 'and this picture was in a cupboard with a diary and some letters and other papers. I'd really like to find her and return them.'

He looked at the woman to see if the series of lies was working. She looked closely at the picture and asked, 'So what makes you think she attended this school?'

Tell as few lies as possible, thought Per.

'Because . . . because there were other pictures of her with a school jumper from here.'

The last part was true, because Gerlof had spotted a jumper from the Krona school in the background of one of the pictures in *Babylon*. It was hanging over the back of a chair, apparently forgotten, with the name of the school and 1983–84 on it – one of the few signs in Jerry's world that the girls weren't just fantasy figures.

'OK,' said the woman, 'it's probably best if you speak to one of our Maths teachers, Karl Harju. He's been here since the seventies.'

She got up and escorted Per down the stairs to the empty corridors again, and led him to a classroom with the door closed. 'You can wait here, it's almost lunch-time.'

Per waited five minutes, then the door flew open and a motley collection of teenagers came pouring out, laughing and talking in loud voices as they disappeared down the corridor. He watched them go and realized that his own children would be just like that in only a few years.

Both his children.

A middle-aged man in a green cardigan was in the classroom, calmly wiping equations off the board; Per went and stood in the doorway. 'Karl Harju?'

'That would be me,' said the man in a Finland-Swedish accent.

'I wondered if you might be able to help me with something . . .'

Per walked in and ran through the same mixture of

truth and lies once again, and held out the picture from the magazine.

'Do you recognize her?' he said. 'I think she might have studied maths and sciences.'

The teacher looked at the picture with a frown. He nodded. 'I think her name was Lisa,' he said. 'Wait here.'

He got up and left the room, and after almost ten minutes he returned with a folder. 'They weren't on the computer system in those days,' he said. 'We ought to enter their details now, but . . .'

He opened the folder and took out a sheet of paper, and Per saw that it was an old class list.

'Yes, Lisa,' said the teacher. 'Lisa Wegner; she was a bit quiet, but she was a nice girl, and very pretty – well, you can see that from the picture. There was a group of girls in that class who were good friends – Lisa, Petra Blomberg, Ulrica Ternman and Madeleine Frick.'

Per could see that there were addresses and telephone numbers on the list, but of course they were fifteen years old.

'Could I possibly make a note of those?'

'I'll do you a photocopy,' said the teacher.

He handed the copy over to Per and asked, 'Do you happen to know what became of Lisa? It looks as though this photo has been cut out of a magazine . . .'

'Yes, it's from a monthly magazine,' said Per. 'So I expect she was a model, a photographic model, for a little while.'

'Well I never,' said Karl Harju. 'As a teacher I'm always interested to hear what becomes of our charges in later life.'

Per went back to the woman in the school office and asked if he could borrow the local telephone directory.

He found only one of the names of the four girls who had been friends at the school: there was an Ulrica Ternman in the area. The address was in Randhult, a village somewhere to the south of the town.

He made a note of the number, went back to his car and called it on his mobile.

'This is an answering machine,' said a male voice. 'You have reached Ulf, Hugo, Hanna and Ulrica. We're not at home right now, but if you'd like to leave a—'

Per was about to end the call when a woman's voice broke in. 'Hello?'

Per shifted closer to the wheel. 'Hello? Is that Ulrica Ternman?'

'Yes, who's calling?'

'My name is Per Mörner. You don't know me, but I'm looking for a woman called Lisa Wegner. I heard you were friends?'

The woman was silent, as if it took time to call up the name from her memory.

'Lisa? Yes, we were friends for a while when we were at school,' she said eventually, 'but we haven't kept in touch. She lives abroad.'

'And you don't have her phone number?'

'No, she became an au pair in Belgium or France, and married some guy down there, I think . . . but what do you want with her?'

'I think she used to work for my father, Jerry Morner.'

Silence once more.

'What did you say his name was?'

'Morner – Gerhard Morner, known as Jerry.'

Ulrica Ternman lowered her voice. 'You mean the man who published those . . . those magazines? He was your father?'

'That's right – *Babylon* and *Gomorrah*. Did you know him?'

'Well . . .'

'You did?' Suddenly Per understood, or thought he did, and said quickly, 'So you worked for Jerry too?'

There was silence at the other end of the phone, followed by a click as the connection was broken.

Per looked at his mobile. He waited fifteen seconds, then rang the number again.

The woman answered after four rings. Per took command, like the experienced telephone interviewer he was. 'Hi Ulrica, it's Per Mörner again . . . I think we were cut off.'

He thought he heard her sigh. 'What do you want?'

'I just want to ask a few questions, then I'll leave you in peace . . . Did you work for Jerry Morner?'

Ulrica sighed again. 'Just once,' she said. 'One weekend.'

Per gripped the phone more tightly. 'Ulrica, I'd really like to talk to you about all that.'

'But why?'

'Because . . . my father is dead.'

'Oh?'

'He died in a car accident. And . . . well, there were some things I never got to know about him, about what he did.'

'Really? So you weren't involved in any of that?'

'No,' said Per. 'But others were. Other men.'

'Yes, I know that,' Ulrica Ternman said wearily. 'But I don't think there's much I can tell you.'

'Could we try?'

She hesitated.

'OK,' she said eventually. 'You can come here tomorrow evening, as long as it's before seven.'

'Excellent. I live on Öland . . . Where exactly is Randhult?'

'Twenty-five kilometres south of Kalmar,' she said.

344

'It's signposted, and I live in the only brick-built house, next to a barn.'

'Thank you.'

Per had called in to see Nilla on his way back from Malmö that morning, but she had been asleep. He went again after his visit to the school.

Marika wasn't there, but Nilla was awake this time and on a drip, attached to the bed with a plastic tube going into her arm.

'Hi Dad,' she said quietly, but didn't move.

'How are you?'

'I'm . . . not so bad.'

'Are you in pain?'

'No, not much.'

'What is it, then? Are you feeling a bit lonely?'

Nilla seemed to hesitate, then she nodded.

Per thought about the horde of teenagers racing past him in the school corridor, and asked, 'Would you like to see some of your friends?'

Nilla didn't say anything.

'Some of your classmates, maybe? If you give them a call I could go and pick some of them up.'

Nilla didn't reply; she just smiled wearily and shook her head.

She was much quieter than when he had seen her on Saturday. Today she was indicating how she felt only through her smiles, usually just that same tired smile. Per almost stopped breathing each time he saw it. No thirteen-year-old should look so devoid of happiness.

'No,' she said eventually, turning to face the wall. 'I don't want to see them.'

'No?' said Per.

Nilla coughed and swallowed, then answered in a whisper, 'I don't want them to see me like this.'

The silence in the room became unbearable, until eventually Per realized his daughter had started to cry. He sat down next to the bed and placed a hand on her back. 'What's wrong, Nilla? Tell me and we'll fix it.'

The tears flowed as she started to tell him.

When he got home, Per put on his trainers and set off. He didn't give a damn where he was going, he just had to get out. He ran with the wind in his face along by the quarry, beside the sea and then away from it, increasing his speed all the time until his lungs were bursting and his thighs were aching.

He stopped on a rocky outcrop, gasping for breath and leaning forward into the wind. He wanted to throw up, but couldn't.

He kept on thinking about Nilla.

The rest of the school year was a write-off, he had realized that several weeks ago. The spring term was lost, but she would be back at school in the autumn. Back with her classmates.

She would be back.

That was the only thought in Per's head as he stood there. She would get better, she would come racing out of the classroom, out into the corridor with her friends. She would start playing basketball again and do her homework and go to school dances and organize parent-free parties.

She would move up to the grammar school and sneak in too late while Per pretended to be asleep. She would travel in Europe and learn new languages.

Nilla would go back to school, she would have a future. Her life existed only in the present right now, but soon she would get her future back. He would do anything to make sure that happened.

Save the children, he thought, and set off again.

He reached a moss-covered stone wall and followed it for a hundred metres or so before climbing over it. He was on the edge of the alvar. There was no water left out there now. The ground was dry and hard as he ran among the bushes.

It was a while before he realized that he was being followed – a rustling sound made him stop and look back. He could clearly hear someone running behind him, at almost the same pace.

Per stopped and held his breath; he thought about Markus Lukas, and crouched down. He was completely defenceless out here on the alvar – the axe and all his other weapons were back at the cottage.

A figure eventually appeared among the juniper bushes and caught sight of him, but everything was fine – it was Vendela Larsson. She was just as puffed as he was, and stopped a few metres away to catch her breath.

They looked at each other without speaking, both panting with exertion from their run. But Per saw a weariness that went beyond the purely physical when he met Vendela's eyes.

Eventually he straightened up and took a deep breath. 'My father is dead,' he said.

Vendela placed her hand on his cheek. 'I'm sorry,' she said.

Per nodded. 'And my daughter's friend Emil is dead too.'

Vendela said nothing; she left her hand where it was and looked inquiringly at Per. He went on: 'He died on Sunday night. He picked up an infection in hospital, and he was too weak to fight it . . . Nilla was in love with him, she cried when she told me what had happened. She just cried and cried, and I didn't know what to say.'

Vendela moved closer, holding out her arms.

Per didn't want her to hug him, she was so skinny and there was no love left in the world.

They stood motionless in the grass holding one another for several minutes. After a while Per could hear that they were breathing in time with one another. Long, deep breaths.

Eventually she let go of him, then she took a step back and turned her head. She nodded over towards the labyrinth of rocks and bushes.

'Come with me. There's something I want to show you.'

53

Vendela had called Max's mobile and the landline at their apartment in town a total of eight times on Monday evening, but he didn't answer until the ninth call. By that stage she was no longer capable of keeping her voice steady; she shouted down the phone, right across the water: 'Ally should be here, Max! Here on the island!'

'But right now he's here.'

'He doesn't feel well in town!'

'We'll see,' said Max. 'In any case, he's going to the vet first thing tomorrow morning; I've made an appointment. Then we can find out what's wrong with him.'

Vendela clutched the receiver tightly. 'He'll get well here. With *me*!'

'That's just your imagination.'

Max sounded calm and collected, but Vendela got even more angry when she heard how much he was enjoying having the upper hand. She lowered her voice. 'Bring him back here, Max. Come straight here after you've been to the vet.'

'Of course, we'll soon be back . . . And of course you can go off jogging in the meantime.'

Vendela realized what he was implying, and sighed.

'I'm on my own here, Max,' she said quietly. 'All the neighbours are away.'

'So you're keeping an eye on their comings and goings, then?'

Vendela didn't reply; this was pointless. 'Bring Ally back tomorrow,' she said, and hung up.

She stood by the window, staring out at the empty landscape. Something was complaining and screaming out there, and at first Vendela thought it was a child, but then she saw a gull flying south along the coast.

She was dizzy with rage and hunger, but she wouldn't eat yet. She would go out instead.

Quarter of an hour later, as she was setting off from the house, she noticed that Per Mörner's car was parked outside his cottage.

But she didn't stop, she ran towards the alvar with the sun on her back and her eyes fixed on a point far ahead in the distance. She became a machine, lifting her legs and pumping her arms and moving across the ground. She didn't achieve a sense of rhythm, but she ran fast.

Eventually she noticed that she wasn't alone. Another figure was moving through the bushes ahead of her.

Per Mörner. He was wearing the same blue tracksuit top, but was running in shorts this sunny evening.

Vendela increased her speed and gradually caught up with him. She didn't call out, but he stopped and turned around when she was about fifty metres away.

They stared at one another; by the time Vendela stopped she was completely out of breath and hadn't the strength to speak, and Per also looked totally exhausted.

It wasn't until a few moments later, when she had her arms around him, that Vendela decided to take Per to the elf stone. When she got her breath back the first thing she said was, 'Come with me. There's something I want to show you.'

And they set off again, running straight across the alvar. She could find her way between the bushes without even thinking about it now, and Per followed her. They ran in step and close together, as if they were helping one another.

Vendela didn't slow down until she saw the grove of juniper bushes. Per stopped and took deep breaths; he looked worn out.

'It's over here,' she said, leading the way.

They entered the dense ring of bushes, and Vendela saw the elf stone. As always, she speeded up as she approached it. For a brief moment she forgot that she wasn't alone, but Per followed her right up to the block of stone.

'A big stone,' he said.

'Yes, a big stone,' said Vendela. 'Have you never been here?'

He shook his head. 'But you have?'

She placed her hands on the stone, running her fingers around the empty hollows. 'Yes, many times. This is a very old place. I think people have been coming here through the ages to forget the rest of the world for a while.

Per looked around. 'It seems like a good place to do that.'

'A good place? I don't know . . . But time passes more slowly here. And you can sit here and pray.'

'Pray?'

Vendela nodded. 'Pray for help and good health.'

'God's healing power, you mean?' said Per.

'Something like that.'

She sat down on the grass with her back resting

against the stone. Per hesitated, then sat down beside her.

They rested for a while with their legs outstretched, watching as the setting sun stained the clouds dark red.

'Have you told your husband you're out here?' Per asked.

Vendela didn't answer at first. How much should she tell him?

'Max isn't at home,' she said eventually. 'He's taken our dog back to the city so the vet can check him over. And . . . we've had a row as well. I stood up to him, and he's not used to that. He gets frustrated.'

Per didn't say anything.

'But he'll soon come bouncing back, like a rubber ball . . . Max needs me.'

'In what way?'

'I help him with his books.'

'How? You mean you . . .'

'I make sure he finishes them.'

Per looked at her. 'Do *you* write his books?'

'Sometimes.' Vendela sighed. 'We work together. But Max thinks it's better and simpler if he's the one in the limelight, with his name on the cover as the author.'

'Better for him, anyway,' said Per. 'What do they call it when you lend your name to someone else who wants to remain anonymous?'

'I don't know . . . but then again, Max has nothing against being well known,' said Vendela. 'I prefer to remain invisible.'

She had always found it difficult to talk about her husband; it felt like a betrayal, but she went on, 'Max likes to be in the centre of things, and he has tremendous self-confidence. He's written a cookery book this spring, in spite of the fact that he can hardly even boil water . . . I wish I had just a fraction of that confidence in myself.'

352

She closed her eyes. 'I was in therapy for a while, seeing a psychologist. That's how I met Max.'

'He was your therapist?'

Vendela nodded. 'I fell in love with him and we got together, but he was given a warning by the psychology association. Therapists aren't allowed to seduce their patients – it's unethical.' She added, 'So Max got angry and decided to become a writer instead; he regarded it as his revenge on the association when his books became popular.'

They sat in silence for a little while.

'Why were you in therapy?' asked Per.

'I don't know . . . So that I could move on from a difficult childhood, isn't that usually the case?'

'Did you have a difficult childhood?'

'It wasn't great. My mother died when I was very young, and my father was in a dream world most of the time . . . And I had a brother, an older brother called Jan-Erik. We lived in the same house, but he didn't want to see me. His door was always closed. So I thought we had some kind of monster living upstairs.'

'But you got to know him eventually?'

'Yes, but he frightened me at first. He was mentally handicapped . . . retarded, as we said in those days. And he looked horrible.'

'Horrible?'

'Jan-Erik had allergies, just like me . . . but his were much worse. I think he had a mixture of different allergies, as well as asthma and sensitive skin. He had long nails that were hardly ever cut; they tore his skin when he scratched himself, and that led to infections.'

'It sounds horrendous,' said Per.

'It was, but there was no attempt to help a person like that back in the fifties. They were just hidden away.' She closed her eyes. 'And then he was convicted of setting fire to our barn, and the authorities decided to send him to a mental hospital on the mainland . . . Which meant he would end up among psychopaths and those who'd committed sex crimes. It was out of the question.'

'Out of the question?'

'I helped him to run away.'

She didn't say any more. They sat in silence again.

The setting sun had begun to nudge the trees over by the shore. Before long it would be pitch dark out here.

Per was lost in his own thoughts. After a while he looked over at the red clouds and said, 'There's no love or consideration in this world, only egotism . . . He taught me that at an early age. But when I grew up I tried to prove to him that it wasn't true.'

Vendela turned to look at him. 'Who are you talking about?'

'My father.'

Vendela reached out her hand and he took it. His hand was cold and almost as slender and bony as her own. 'And now Jerry's gone. And I'm frightened of what he's left me.'

'What has he left you?' asked Vendela.

'Bad memories. And a whole lot of problems.'

They sat there by the stone, still holding hands. The sun had disappeared and the sky was growing dark, but they carried on talking. Eventually they got to their feet.

They didn't say much on the way home, but Vendela stopped outside Per's cottage. She looked at him in the darkness. He opened his mouth, but didn't seem to know what to say or do. And Vendela didn't know either.

'This is where I live,' he said eventually, turning away.

Vendela stayed where she was for a minute or two,

wondering whether to go with him. What would he do then? What would she do? A range of possibilities extended before her like meandering rivers.

'Sleep well, Per.'

Vendela set off again – home to her own dark stone fortress.

54

Per was sitting at the kitchen table with the telephone in front of him, peering out of the window. There was no sign of any strange cars on the coast road. And there had been no anonymous phone calls over the past twenty-four hours. But he was still unable to relax this morning.

He had intended to work, but he just couldn't summon up any enthusiasm for making up yet more opinions on soap. Instead he made some other calls.

First of all he contacted Jerry's bank in Kristianstad to get an idea of the situation regarding his father's finances. The question was, would there be any money left for Per?

Apparently not. Twenty-two thousand kronor, that was what he managed to track down in Jerry's bank accounts. Plus a few shares in Volvo – which was ironic, as Jerry had always refused to drive Swedish cars. But there were no valuable works of art stashed away, no expensive wines or luxury cars.

Everything had gone. Morner Art was an empty company.

'Your father wasn't completely wiped out, but near

enough,' said the bank manager who was dealing with Jerry's estate.

'But he did have money at one stage, didn't he?'

'Oh yes, there was money in the company. But your father made a number of significant withdrawals in recent years. Of course, there's the property outside Ryd as well, but that's an insurance matter now . . . The estate will just about cover the funeral expenses, in my view.'

Well, at least that means we can bury him, thought Per.

He had suspected that he was unlikely to inherit very much from his father – nothing of value, anyway. He had certainly inherited other things.

'These withdrawals from the company . . . Was he paying himself a salary?'

'No,' said the bank manager, checking something on the computer. 'They were salary and pension payments to an employee . . . Hans Bremer.'

After the conversation, Per sat by the telephone thinking. Mostly about Hans Bremer. Why had Jerry given him so much money? And where had the money gone, in that case? Bremer's sister hadn't seen any sign of it, after all.

He suddenly remembered the little note he had found in Bremer's apartment. A note with four names on it.

His trousers were in the laundry basket, but the note was still in his pocket. He put in on the kitchen table in front of him and stared at the names: *Ingrid*, *Cash*, *Fountain* and *Danielle*, each followed by a telephone number.

Ingrid was Bremer's sister, so he didn't need to ring her, but he had no idea who the other three were. He chose the first one, the person Bremer called Cash. It looked like a mobile number.

Shouldn't he just let all this go?

Perhaps, but the alternative was to sit here thinking about tumours. He picked up the receiver.

The phone rang three times, then a man's voice answered decisively: 'Fall.'

'Good morning,' said Per. 'My name is Per Mörner.'

'Yes?'

'I'm ringing with regard to a person I think you might know.'

'Yes?'

'His name is Hans Bremer. Do you know him?'

There was silence at the other end of the phone for a few seconds, and Per could hear the faint sound of voices in the background, as if there were some kind of conference going on, before eventually the man answered. 'Bremer is dead.'

'I know that,' said Per. 'I'm just trying to find out more about him . . .'

'Why?'

'My father Jerry worked with him for a number of years, and I'd really like to know who he was. So you did know him then?'

He heard the background noise again for a few seconds, then the answer came: 'Yes.'

'And your name is Fall?'

'Yes . . . Thomas Fall.' The man still sounded hesitant. 'So how did you get hold of my number?'

Per explained, and when he mentioned the note he had found in Bremer's kitchen, Thomas Fall seemed to relax slightly.

'He'd written "Cash" next to your number,' Per went on. 'Any idea why he did that?'

Fall didn't speak for a few seconds, then he laughed. 'That's what he called me sometimes. I used to listen to a lot of Johnny Cash when I got to know him. The Man in Black.'

'Were you related to Bremer?'

'No,' said Fall. 'He was my photography tutor in Malmö. I did an evening course in the mid-seventies because I wanted to get into advertising, and Bremer was teaching at the college. He left the following year . . . Or perhaps I should just come straight out with it: he got the sack.'

'Do you know why?'

There was a short silence.

'He was a bit different. He was good with the students, but his teaching was a bit disorganized . . . and he was drinking a fair amount, even then.'

'Did you know he was involved in porn as well?' said Per. 'That he made porn films every spring and summer?'

Another pause at the other end of the line.

'Yes, I did know that,' Fall said eventually. 'He didn't exactly talk about it, but I found out after a while.'

'But you kept in touch with him?'

'Yes,' said Fall, 'but only to the extent that I rang occasionally to see how things were, and helped him out with the odd freelance job. I think Bremer was pretty lonely . . . he had no family of his own, just a sister.'

'Did he ever mention a man called Markus Lukas?'

Silence once more.

'I don't think so,' Fall said after a while. 'Not that I remember.'

Per was just wondering what else to ask when Fall went on, 'But he gave me a briefcase . . . I think I've still got it.'

'Bremer gave you a briefcase?'

'Yes, he left it here last year. He called round and he was pretty drunk; he asked me to look after it. I'm not really sure where it is now.'

'Have you got time to look?'

'Of course. I'll check in the loft.'

'Can I ring you back?' said Per.

'Sure,' said Fall, and added, 'Let me take your number as well.'

Per gave him both his mobile number and the landline number for the cottage, and thanked him for his help before hanging up.

I think Bremer was pretty lonely, Thomas Fall had said. Per thought so too.

He stretched his back, then rang the third number on Bremer's list, the one with 'Fountain' next to it. This time it took even longer for someone to answer; the phone rang eleven or twelve times before the receiver was picked up.

'Hello?'

It was a tired male voice. Canned laughter from a TV programme could be heard in the background.

'Hello,' said Per, 'is that Fountain?'

'Yes – who wants to know?'

'Excellent!' said Per. The laughter from the TV was so loud and the man was speaking so quietly that he almost found himself shouting. 'I got your number from Hans Bremer.'

'Right,' said the man. 'What do you need?'

'What do I need?' said Per, trying to think. 'Well . . . what have you got?'

'Not all that much at the moment,' said the man. 'I've got some ten-litre packs of Swedish schnapps and a couple of Polish vodka. Will that be enough?'

Per finally got it – Fountain supplied cheap, home-distilled illicit spirits.

'That's not really what I had in mind,' he said, and was about to hang up when the man said, 'Bremer was supposed to be settling up – do you know anything about that?'

'What do you mean?' asked Per, as the canned laughter grew even more hysterical.

'He said he was going to pay off his debts before the summer.'

'How much are we talking about?'

'Twenty thousand. Are you going to sort it out?'

'No,' said Per. 'And I shouldn't think Bremer will be sorting it out either.'

He hung up and called the last number on the list, which apparently belonged to someone called Danielle. It was a mobile number, but an automated message immediately cut in, informing him that the number was no longer in use. No other number was given.

That was it, then. He sat at the table thinking about Jerry's dead colleague.

Hans Bremer had led a double life. He seemed to have put all his energy into making porn films at the weekends, then had gone back home to Malmö to live a miserable, debt-ridden existence fuelled by booze.

Per picked up the phone again and rang the undertaker to discuss Jerry's funeral.

'Do you know how many people will be coming?' asked the funeral director. 'Approximately?'

'No. But probably not very many.'

He couldn't actually think of anybody who ought to be invited to the funeral. Jerry's relatives had broken off all contact with him long ago – or perhaps it was the other way round. All in all, he had probably been just as lonely as Bremer.

Then Per looked around and realized that he was sitting here in an empty house. His family wasn't here, and how many friends did he have? How many people would come to his funeral?

That wasn't something he ought to be thinking about right now.

Quarter of an hour later he drove away from the quarry, and couldn't help glancing over at Vendela's house. Lights were shining from the tall windows. He wondered what she was doing and whether her husband had come home yet, but didn't stop to find out.

Randhult wasn't a village like Stenvik; it was just a few farms scattered around in an agricultural landscape, half an hour by car along the motorway to the south of Kalmar. Ulrica Ternman had said she lived in the only brick-built house in the village, and it was easy to find. Per parked on the drive.

He heard a clattering noise as he was getting out of the car and saw a boy of about twelve trying out a radio-controlled jeep on the gravel. The boy looked up when he saw Per, but quickly turned his attention back to the car.

Per went up the steps and rang the bell, and a woman of about thirty-five opened the door. She was no blonde bimbo; she had short brown hair and was dressed in faded jeans and a black cotton top.

Per remembered what his father had said about Regina during the Easter weekend: *Got old, I suppose.* No doubt that was how Jerry had divided women up – into hot girls and old bags.

'Hi,' said Per, and introduced himself.

Ulrica Ternman nodded. 'Come in.'

She turned away and Per followed her into the hall-way.

'Is that your son outside?'

'Yes, that's Hugo,' she said. 'We also have a daughter called Hanna . . . My husband has taken her into town to her gymnastics class this evening. It's probably best if they're not at home.'

'Does he know you . . .'

Per was searching for the right words, and Ulrica Ternman looked tired.

'That I was a slag, you mean?'

'No, I mean . . .'

'I haven't mentioned the modelling,' she broke in. 'But Ulf knows I did plenty of stupid things when I was young, and so did he. Before he grew up.'

Per took off his jacket. 'And you remember Jerry, my father?'

She nodded. 'He was a bit different, a mixture of a teddy bear and a dirty old man . . . I never quite worked him out.'

'I don't think anybody did,' said Per.

She led him into a neat little kitchen and put some coffee on.

'So Jerry Morner is dead?'

'He died a few days ago.'

'And you want to know more about him?'

'Yes . . . but I think I really want to know more about the people he worked with,' said Per. 'He had a colleague called Hans Bremer . . .'

'Bremer, that's right,' said Ulrica. 'He was the younger one, he organized everything. And took the pictures.'

She didn't say any more; she just looked serious and seemed lost in thought, so Per asked, 'How did you end up working with my father?'

Ulrica gave a mirthless laugh. 'I don't really know,' she said. 'I didn't really do much thinking. You don't when you're nineteen, do you? You decide in a split second and just *go* for it . . . A boyfriend had dumped me that summer and gone off with another girl; I was angry and upset and furious with him, so this was meant to be some kind of revenge. I was going to send him a copy of the magazine, but I never got round to it,

363

in fact I never even got the magazine . . . Although I did get paid, of course, in cash.'

'Did you get a lot of money?'

'Fifteen hundred, I think. That was a lot of money when you were nineteen . . . I would have had to work at least a week in a nursing home to earn that much.'

'So how did you hear about the job?'

'There was a small ad asking for photographic models in one of the evening papers. Lisa Wegner had seen it, and mentioned it to me and Petra Blomberg. It was obvious what it was all about . . . You had to send in nude pictures, so we took a few photos of each other and sent them off to Malmö. And a couple of weeks later I got a call from someone who said his name was Hans.'

'Did he sound nice?'

'Not bad,' said Ulrica. 'He talked about how cool it would be. So Petra and I went down to Ryd together on the train. We spent most of the time giggling – it was a bit like an adventure, like running away with the circus.' She looked at Per and added, 'But without a band.'

Then she went on: 'When we came out of the station in Ryd there was another girl waiting there . . . She was much more provocatively dressed in tight jeans and a tight top, and she just glared at us. Then this guy Bremer came along in his car; he got out and smiled at us and said hello, and ushered us into the car. Sitting there in the back seat it all suddenly seemed much more serious; I stopped giggling, and when I looked at Petra she seemed really nervous.'

She looked down at the table.

'So what did Bremer say then?' Per asked.

'He spent most of the time talking to the girl in the front seat; it was obvious she was an old hand and had been there several times before. Cindy or Lindy,

364

he called her.' Ulrica smiled tiredly. 'I shouldn't think that was her name . . . both Petra and I were given new names in the magazine. Petra was called Candy and I was Suzy.'

'And the men were always called Markus Lukas, weren't they?'

Ulrica nodded. 'I suppose most things were fake in that industry . . . Anyway, we were driven out to the house – it felt as if we were deep in the forest – and as Bremer pulled up I realized that nobody knew where we were. That wasn't a very good feeling . . . and the house was big and dark, with thick curtains at the windows on the ground floor. It smelled of detergent, but I remember thinking that was probably just covering up a whole load of disgusting smells that you would start to notice if you stayed around for too long.'

'And Jerry, was he there?'

'Yes, he was there. He said hello and brought some papers over for me and Petra. We both signed some kind of contract, it said something along the lines that we were doing this voluntarily and weren't underage.'

'Did they check your ages?'

'No . . . Bremer asked how old we were when we rang up, I think, but nobody asked us for our passport or driving licence or anything like that.

'I don't know if it was so we could learn how things worked, but Petra and I were allowed to stay in the studio while Cindy/ Lindy was being photographed, with Bremer egging her on. She sat on the bed stroking herself and undressing for the camera. It was ridiculous sometimes, what she was doing. Shy yet wanton at the same time, somehow . . . as if there was a war going on inside her.'

She lowered her gaze to the floor.

'When I saw her I realized I could never make a career

of this, or even do it again . . . I just wanted to go home, even at that stage. But I still had my own photo session to do; it was impossible to back out. I just had to do it . . . I was to be photographed on a sofa. So I had to walk into the bright light, and we made a start. You didn't really have to move, just pose in different positions.' She paused. 'I was really nervous, but it was just routine for the others – all in a day's work.'

'Who was there?' Per asked.

'Bremer was standing between the spotlights; he was directing everything and telling me what to do, then there was a young lad who was the photographer, then this wiry, tattooed guy who was to do the shots on the sofa with me.'

'So what was Jerry doing while all this was going on?'

'Not much,' said Ulrica. 'He was probably standing to one side somewhere "adjusting his trousers" . . . that's what we used to say about the dirty old men who hung about near our school.'

Per could imagine Jerry doing exactly that.

'Then it was Petra's turn. She was after me, with this other guy who was also called Markus Lukas.'

'What do you remember about him?'

Ulrica thought about it.

'He was taller and a bit older, much more muscular,' she said. 'Taller and quieter, a bit bored maybe . . . it was obvious this was just a job to him. At least my Markus Lukas chatted, made the odd joke and tried to get me to relax. And he told me his real name afterwards. It was Tobias . . . Tobias Jesslin, and he was from Malmö.'

Per made a mental note of the name. A Markus Lukas called Tobias – another real name among all the false ones.

'Are you still in touch with Petra?' he asked.

Ulrica looked horrified. 'In touch?' she said.

'Have you got a number or an address? I'd really like to talk to her as well.'

'Petra's dead,' said Ulrica.

Per looked at her in surprise.

'She died at the beginning of the nineties. We'd lost touch by then, but I heard about it, and I saw the notice in the paper.'

'How did she die?'

'I think she was ill . . . It was just a rumour, but I think she had cancer.'

Per looked down into his coffee cup; that was a word he didn't want to hear. 'Very sad,' he said.

'Yes,' said Ulrica, 'and what happened to Madde was just as bad. Or even worse, actually.'

'Madde?'

'Madeleine Frick. She was another friend of mine from school. She moved to Stockholm after we left, but just a couple of years later she threw herself in front of a train.'

Per breathed in slowly and said quietly, 'Did she work with my father as well?'

Ulrica nodded. 'I think so . . . I never saw any pictures or films, of course, but when we met up that summer she told me she'd been out to Ryd and had done some filming too. "With the wiry guy or the tall one?" I asked her. "The tall one," she said. I didn't want to hear any more . . . that was the only time we talked about it.'

Per didn't say anything. Of the four girls he had found who had filmed with Jerry, two were dead.

Suddenly a door flew open in the hallway.

'Mum?' a boy's voice called out.

'Coming!'

Per looked at her and tried to come up with one last question. 'How do you feel about it now?'

'It's OK,' said Ulrica, getting up to rinse her coffee

367

cup. She looked at him. 'What's done is done . . . If you do stupid things when you're young, you regret it, and if you don't do anything stupid, you still regret it, sooner or later. Don't you agree?'

Yes, thought Per. *If you survive.*

But he didn't say anything.

As he drove away from the farm, he thought about Ulrica Ternman, then about Regina. What was he doing? He wanted to save girls who sometimes didn't want to be saved. He wanted to save them from his father.

Just before he reached the motorway, he pulled into a car park and rang Directory Enquiries. He found two people called Tobias Jesslin. One lived in Mora, the other in Karlskrona.

Karlskrona was closer to Kalmar, so he tried that number first. After three rings a girl's voice chirruped: 'Hello, this is Emilie!'

Per was taken aback, but asked for Tobias anyway.

'Daddy's not here,' said the girl. 'Do you want to talk to Mummy?'

Per hesitated. 'OK.'

There was a rattling sound, then a stressed female voice came on the line. 'Hello, this is Katarina.'

'Hi, my name's Per Mörner . . . I was hoping to speak to Tobias.'

'He's at work.'

'Where does he work?'

'Honolulu.'

'Sorry?'

'The Honolulu restaurant. Who are you?'

'I'm . . . I'm just an old friend. We haven't been in touch for a long time. This is the Tobias who used to live in Malmö, isn't it?'

The woman didn't say anything for a few seconds.

'Yes, he did live in Malmö.'

'Good,' said Per, 'I've probably got the right person then. When will he be home?'

'He finishes at eleven . . . but you could ring him at the Honolulu.'

'Or I could go there . . . what's the address?'

He made a note of it and rang off.

Then he thought it over. It was almost seven o'clock now, and it would probably take him about an hour to drive down to Karlskrona.

He made a decision, and got in the car. He would go and see Tobias Jesslin, who once upon a time had been called Markus Lukas.

55

Vendela spent the whole of Tuesday working on the new garden. Before lunch she planted ivy, box and a long row of elder saplings which would provide good foliage and shade when they had grown, and in the afternoon she hauled bags of compost and small limestone blocks and created three little flowerbeds. She could see in her mind's eye the rows of green leaves emerging in May, the stems growing strong in June, the big petals turning towards the sun.

The telephone in the house rang a few times, but she didn't answer. At about seven she went in and ran herself a hot bubble bath, ate a couple of pieces of crispbread for dinner, and stared out of the window. Over towards the little cottage to the north.

She didn't want to go for a run on the alvar this evening. She thought about going to see old Gerlof, but didn't want to disturb him. What she really wanted was to go over to Per Mörner and spend the rest of the evening sitting chatting to him, but his car wasn't there. So she sat there in her big empty house, waiting for her husband and her dog to come back.

They didn't come. At ten o'clock she went to bed.

*

Through the fog of sleep Vendela could hear a throbbing noise coming closer, then she was woken by the sound of someone unlocking the front door. She opened her eyes and saw from the clock by her bedside that it was quarter to eleven.

The light went on in the hallway and a strip of light fell across her bed.

'Hello?' called a man's voice.

It was Max.

'Hello . . .' she replied quietly, running a hand over her forehead.

'Hi darling!'

Max came into the bedroom, still wearing his padded jacket.

Vendela raised her head and looked around the floor. 'Where's Aloysius?'

'Here,' said Max, throwing something on the bed. 'It's done now.'

Vendela looked at him in confusion. 'What's done?'

Then she looked down at the bed and saw something small and narrow lying beside her, something strangely familiar. She reached out and picked it up.

It was a strip of leather. A dog collar.

She recognized the faint smell of Aloysius. It was his collar.

Max was still standing by the bed. 'I thought you might want that. As a memento.'

'Max, what have you done?'

He sat down on the edge of the bed. 'I'll tell you about it, if you want to know. It was very peaceful and I was holding him all the time . . . The vets know exactly what to do.'

Vendela just stared at him, but he carried on. 'First of all they gave him a tranquillizer, just like the ones you take sometimes. Then they injected an overdose

371

of anaesthetic into his front leg, and by that time—'

Vendela sat up. 'I don't want to hear it!'

She threw the covers aside and leapt out of bed, pushing past Max. She ran into the hallway, pulled on her coat and boots and hurtled out of the door. When she landed on the path the gravel flew up around her feet.

Away, she had to get away.

Suddenly the Audi was there in front of her and she fumbled with the door. It wasn't locked.

She got in the car and leant her head against the hardness of the wheel.

Then came the tears. Tears for Aloysius.

Ten years. She and Max had bought him when he was just a young dog, the autumn they got married. When they walked into the kennels to look for a dog he had wagged his tail and come running up to them, as if he had chosen them instead of vice versa, and he had been with Vendela every single day since then.

A shadow appeared next to the car.

'Vendela?' It was Max, tapping on the window. 'Come inside, then we can talk.'

'*Go away!*'

She flung open the door and clenched her fists, forcing Max to take a step backwards. Then she took the torch out of the glove compartment and got out of the car. 'Don't touch me!' she screamed.

He took two more steps backwards and she walked past him, heading for the gravel track.

'Where are you going, Vendela?'

She didn't answer – she just wanted to get away from her husband as quickly as possible, heading out into the cold and the darkness.

56

A bitterly cold wind was blowing in off the Baltic as Per got out of his car in front of the Honolulu restaurant. The air felt icy cold tonight, as if the winter had suddenly changed its mind and come back.

The restaurant was right by the water just outside the centre of Karlskrona, but it didn't look as though it boasted many Michelin stars. Two of the neon letters weren't working, so the sign above the entrance said HON LULU RE TAURANT.

He went into the warmth and took off his jacket. There were about thirty tables, only eight of which were occupied, but then it was Monday, after all. No doubt there would be plenty more customers in three days' time, on May Day.

He sat down at a table in a quiet spot by the window and picked up the menu; the choice was limited almost exclusively to pizza and hamburgers. When the waiter appeared, Per ordered a glass of water and a Honolulu burger with cheese.

He glanced covertly at the waiter as he took Per's order through to the kitchen. He was dark-haired and broad-shouldered like one of Jerry's models, but he looked about twenty-five, and was hardly likely to have been employed by Jerry ten years ago.

When he came back with the food fifteen minutes later, Per asked, 'Do you know Tobias Jesslin?'

The waiter put the plate of food down on the table. 'Tobias? Tobias the chef?'

'That's right, the chef,' Per said quickly. 'I'd really like to speak to him.'

The waiter looked dubious. 'Is it to do with the food?'

'No, it's nothing to do with the food.'

'Tobias is rushed off his feet at the moment.'

'But he'll be free later, won't he? Could you give him a note?'

The waiter hesitated, then nodded.

Per took an old receipt out of his wallet and quickly jotted down a message, similar to the one he had left at the Moulin Noir.

The waiter took the note and disappeared without a word. Per started to eat his burger, which was greasy and somewhat rubbery. He gazed out at the blackness of the sea as he chewed. The old cargo ships carrying limestone from Öland had sailed past out there, heading for Denmark and Norway.

When the plate was empty he sat there staring at the kitchen door. It remained closed.

The thought that Markus Lukas might be behind that door was making him nervous. After waiting for ten minutes he just had to do something. He got up, went into the empty foyer and called a mobile number he had rung earlier that day. It was answered immediately.

'Fall?'

'This is Per Mörner from Öland. I rang you this morning . . . about Hans Bremer?'

'Yes, I remember.'

Thomas Fall sounded tired, but Per went on anyway. 'I just wanted to check if you'd found that briefcase yet . . . Bremer's briefcase?'

'Yes . . . it was in the loft.'

'Great. Have you looked inside?'

Fall seemed hesitant, as if he were embarrassed. 'Yes . . . I did take a look, just a quick look. It's full of old magazines, and some kind of book manuscript.'

'Like a diary?'

'Maybe. I haven't read it.'

'Could I have a look at it?'

'Of course,' said Fall. He paused. 'Actually, you can have it. It's no use to me.'

'That would be great, although it's going to be a bit difficult for me to come and pick it up . . .'

Per was just working out how he could drop everything and drive all the way back down to Malmö again – he couldn't go so far away from Nilla right now – but Thomas Fall solved the problem.

'I'm driving up to Stockholm for the May Day celebrations, so I could take a detour to Öland and drop it off, if I can have your address.'

Per gave it to him and explained how to get to Stenvik. 'It's the third house along by the quarry,' he said. 'The smallest one.'

He switched off his mobile and went back to the table. The waiter removed his plate.

At half past nine the kitchen door opened and a man in chef's whites emerged. He came over to Per's table and held up the note. He didn't look put out or annoyed, just curious. 'Did you write this?' He spoke with a Skåne accent.

Per nodded, and the next question came:

'So you're Jerry Morner's son?'

'That's right. And you're Tobias?'

'Yep. I did a bit of work for your father before I became a chef.'

Tobias's face was sweaty, perhaps from the heat of cooking. But he looked Per in the eye, and didn't seem bothered in the least.

'I know,' said Per. 'Jerry called you Markus Lukas.'

Jesslin didn't say anything for a few seconds.

'Yes. But that's all finished now. There's hardly any Swedish porn these days . . . Practically all the films are made in the USA now, in California.'

'Could we have a chat anyway? I'm just curious about a few things to do with my father's activities.'

'Sure . . . We can go to the staff room.'

Jesslin turned back to the kitchen. Per put the money for his meal on the table and followed him.

The smell of cooking hung in the air around the stoves, but the tiled floor looked clean. Tobias Jesslin led the way to the back of the kitchen and into a small room with closed metal cupboards, a shower, and a chair with several tables. A window framed a view of the sea.

'Ulrica Ternman wanted me to say hello,' said Per when Jesslin had closed the door.

'Who?'

Jesslin sat down and took out a packet of cigarettes.

'One of the girls you filmed with,' said Per. 'She was the one who gave me your name.'

'Oh? I don't remember.' Jesslin lit a cigarette and blew the smoke up towards the ceiling. 'I don't even remember how many girls I filmed with . . . A hundred and twenty, maybe, or a hundred and fifty.'

Per realized he was supposed to look impressed, man to man. But all he said was, 'How does that feel?'

'How do you think?' Jesslin gave a little smile. 'A bit odd, like standing next to a conveyor belt as the girls

376

came rolling along . . . But that was years ago; I've settled down now.' He took a drag of his cigarette. 'So how's your dad these days?'

'Not too well.'

'No?'

'No. He's dead.'

'Really? What happened?'

'A car accident.'

Per was watching Jesslin closely, but his surprise seemed genuine.

'That's a shame,' he said. 'I liked Jerry, he was always himself. He was never ashamed of what he was doing.'

'How long were you employed by him?'

'Well, you say "employed" . . .' Jesslin said, blowing out a stream of smoke. 'I stood in front of the camera from time to time and got paid in cash.'

'Did you work at the Moulin Noir as well?'

Jesslin nodded. 'That was where Jerry found me. He saw me dancing, and said he could find me some work. Why not, I said. So he took me to a really good restaurant in Malmö, we had something to eat and drink and we chatted . . . and when we got to the coffee, this young, pretty girl turned up at our table and kissed Jerry on the cheek. Jerry asked for the bill and said, "OK kids, shall we get to work?" It was only then that I realized I was supposed to have sex that same afternoon with this girl, whose name I didn't even know.' He gave a brief laugh and added, 'Things moved fast in the porn industry – but you got used to it after a while.'

Per was listening, but he wasn't smiling. 'So how many other men called Markus Lukas were there?'

'A few that I know of . . . maybe two or three. There aren't that many guys who can manage it.'

'Manage what?' said Per.

Jesslin nodded towards his trousers. 'You know . . . getting it up to order, when the camera's rolling.'

'Did you know any of the others?'

'Only one. He came from the Moulin Noir too . . . his name was Daniel.'

'Daniel what?'

'Daniel Wellman.'

'How do you spell that?'

Jesslin spelled out the name and Per wrote it down. He hoped he was on the way to finding Markus Lukas the troll now.

'And you did a lot of filming together?'

'Sure, we went up to Jerry's studio in Småland every weekend.'

'It's gone now,' said Per.

'Gone?'

'The whole place burnt down a few weeks ago.'

'How come?'

'It was deliberate – arson,' said Per. 'Somebody had set some kind of timed incendiary devices in the house.'

Jesslin thought for a moment.

'That sounds like Bremer, he was fond of pyrotechnics . . . sometimes in the summer we filmed scenes in a clearing in the forest where he'd rigged up a whole load of petrol containers . . . we were supposed to lie there naked among all the smoke and flames. Bremer had a couple of buckets of water behind the camera just in case anything went wrong, but I was still scared shitless, lying there on a mattress stark bollock naked, surrounded by flames.' He smiled again. 'Have you met Bremer?'

'No,' said Per. 'And he's dead too. He died in the fire.'

'Oh?' said Jesslin, still smoking.

'Didn't you like Bremer?'

'Not particularly.'

'Why not?'

Jesslin looked over at the dark window, as if he were recalling difficult memories. 'I don't know . . . personal chemistry, I suppose. Bremer worked fast, and he was really hard on the girls. If they were in pain during filming and wanted to stop, he didn't give a damn. They just had to turn their faces away so the tears didn't show, and we'd carry on filming. Finishing the film was all that mattered to him.'

'To you too, I presume,' said Per. He thought again how little Ingrid knew about her brother. *Hans was too kind* . . .

'Of course, I was just as unfeeling as Bremer and Jerry after a while,' said Jesslin. 'I just wanted to get the filming done and go home. That job really did dull your perceptions.'

'And what about the girls who died?'

Jesslin looked at him. 'You mean Jessika Björk?'

'Jessika Björk?'

'She used to work at the Moulin Noir with me and Daniel,' said Jesslin. 'She was in several films with us – she called herself Gabrielle or something . . . but I heard from a friend that she died in a house fire a few weeks ago. Very sad – she was a lovely girl. And she wasn't very old – only about thirty.'

'In a house fire?' Per leant forward on his chair. 'And you say her name was Gabrielle . . . Could it have been Danielle?'

'Sure. Gabrielle or Danielle, I don't remember.'

'When did you last see her?'

'Oh, a long time ago . . . ten years maybe. We haven't spoken often either, we just rang each other now and again. I think Jessika and Daniel Wellman had more contact with one another.'

Per looked at him. Was it Jessika Björk's phone

379

number that had been on Bremer's Post-it note? Maybe, but if so, what did it mean? He felt tired and devoid of any ideas, as if he had a tumour somewhere that was sucking all the nourishment out of his body.

'I didn't know about Jessika,' Per said quietly, 'but Ulrica Ternman had two friends who used to do some work with Jerry and Bremer. They're both dead as well.'

'Oh?' said Jesslin. 'So there were more?'

Per leant forward again. 'Tobias,' he said. 'I have to find more people who worked with Jerry. Have you got an address for this other Markus Lukas?'

Jesslin stubbed out his cigarette and shook his head. 'We were never close friends,' he said. 'His name was Daniel Wellman and he lived in Malmö – that's all I know.'

'Have you got any pictures of him?'

'Pictures? There are plenty of pictures in the magazines.'

'Not of his face.'

Jesslin laughed and stood up. 'No, the face wasn't the important thing when it came to the guys . . . The girls had to look good, not us.'

Per got up too. He had been expecting the vague answers he had received about Markus Lukas, but he still felt disappointed.

Jesslin stopped in the doorway. 'But if you were to ask me if anyone wanted to get rid of Bremer,' he said, 'I'd probably say it was a knight in shining armour.'

'A what?'

'A boyfriend who's recently found out that Bremer filmed his girlfriend years ago. Someone who wants to play the knight in shining armour and protect her reputation.'

Per looked at him and thought about the cheerful voice that had answered on Jesslin's home number.

'So what about your reputation, now you're a father?'

'No problem,' Jesslin said quickly. 'It's always worse for the girls. They have more to lose if the past catches up with them.'

'And is that fair?'

'No,' said Jesslin, shrugging his shoulders. 'But it's the men who hold all the power in the porn industry. They're the clients, it's their money, their values. That's life.'

As Per left the Honolulu and got in the car he was thinking about reputations and values, and how Jerry had stood by the quarry the week before he died, pointing at Marie Kurdin and hinting that he knew her.

He started the car and set off on the long journey home.

57

Vendela was standing tall in front of the elf stone; she could feel evil gathering in the air above her. It was almost midnight, and there were only two days left until Walpurgis Night, when dark powers gathered together. They were at their strongest now.

She had switched on her small torch and placed it in front of her on the stone, the only light in the great darkness.

The spirits and demons, the dark kin of the elves, had woken from their long winter sleep. They had emerged from the deepest caves in the old lands surrounding the Baltic Sea, flown across the wide waters and circled over the solid granite of Blå Jungfrun out in the Sound before swooping in across the island, chasing the spring birds from the sky. They were looking down on this flat, narrow island, where the waves surged up over the long shores, and smiled at all the little creatures crawling around below them.

High above the alvar the spirits met to bring down more misery and death on mankind for another year.

Vendela closed her eyes.

And what could mankind do about it? Nothing, apart from lighting a few fires on Walpurgis Night, the eve of May Day. But the light of the fires soon died away, and after that all you could do was lock yourself in your house and hope that the windows would hold, and that the demons would choose some other family. But they never did. They always took those who were weakest, those who were most afraid, those who had the most locks on their doors and who prayed most fervently that they would be safe, that they would be left in peace.

Vendela raised her left hand and held it over the stone.

Her wedding ring glinted in the light of the torch. Max had bought it for her in Paris. It was difficult to remove; after ten years it had almost grown into her finger, but she managed it in the end. She held the ring up to the sky in her right hand for a few moments, then placed it carefully in one of the hollows in the stone. She looked at the ring, and knew that she would never touch it again.

Do what you like with him, she thought, *but promise me that he will disappear for ever.*

She closed her eyes.

More heart problems, that's a good idea. Give him a massive heart attack, far away from any doctors.

When she opened her eyes and turned away from the elf stone she could feel the hunger and tiredness gnawing away at her stomach. She had simply rushed blindly out of the house in the middle of the night. She had to lean on the stone for support, and she stood motionless, staring at the horizon until the dizziness passed. Then she picked up the torch, pointed it at the ground ahead of her, and set off across the grass. Once she had passed the juniper bushes she lengthened her stride.

She was feeling better now. She couldn't run in her boots, but she walked faster and faster, her footsteps drumming on the ground and the wind whistling past her ears.

Some nights I'm even more crazy than usual, she thought.

Above her she could hear the sound of huge wings.

She slunk back across the alvar and down towards the coast like a cat. The grass and the bushes didn't even touch her.

A few hundred metres from the quarry she switched off the torch; the batteries were almost spent.

Suddenly she saw another glow along the road. Car headlights. They slid slowly past her own house and stopped outside the Mörners' cottage. When the car's interior light came on she could see that Per was driving, and hurried over.

He got out of the car, his movements stiff, and as Vendela approached he turned; he looked anxious at first, but relaxed when he saw who it was.

'Vendela.'

She nodded. Without thinking about it, without the slightest hesitation, she held out her arms and went to him.

The night was suddenly warm.

Per put his arms around her, but only for a long hug.

Vendela let go of him eventually, with a deep sigh. 'Come with me,' she said quietly.

Per let out a long breath. 'I can't,' he said.

Vendela took his hand. 'It's fine.'

She pulled him gently towards the door, as if the cottage were hers and not his.

58

Per opened his eyes; it was morning. He was lying in his bed, and someone was lying next to him, fast asleep. It wasn't a dream.

But it was still a strange, dreamlike feeling to have Vendela Larsson beside him; since Marika left him he had slept alone every night.

When Vendela's breathing had finally grown calm and even in the darkness, he had lain there beside her with his eyes open. He had felt good, but he had still expected a visit.

A visit from Jerry.

That's what had always happened on the few occasions in the past when Per had slept next to a woman. He would gradually become aware of the heavy aroma of cigars in his nostrils, or he would sense that his father was standing in the shadows by the bed, grinning scornfully at his son.

But Jerry's spirit stayed away tonight.

They got up at about nine o'clock, and Per made coffee and toast. This morning there was suddenly a whole range of topics they just couldn't discuss, but the silence at the kitchen table was neither tense nor embarrassing. Per felt as he if knew Vendela well.

Then he had to go and visit Nilla at the hospital.

'Can I stay here for a while?' Vendela asked.

'Don't you want to go home?'

She looked down at the floor. 'I don't want to be there . . . I can't cope with seeing Max at the moment.'

'But we didn't do anything wrong,' said Per.

'We slept together,' said Vendela.

'We kept each other warm.'

'It doesn't matter what we did . . . not to Max.'

'See you soon,' she said a little while later as they stood in the hallway.

'Will you?' said Per.

She gave him a fleeting smile as he closed the front door.

He walked to the car and breathed out slowly.

What had happened? And was it so bad, whatever it might have been? It was Vendela's decision, and they had spent most of the time talking and sleeping, after all.

But Per's life had become messier, and he felt as if this would influence Nilla's chances in some way. Lengthen the odds.

Finding Markus Lukas would shorten them.

He took out his mobile and rang Directory Enquiries. A young woman asked how she could help.

'Daniel Wellman,' said Per, and spelled out the surname.

'Which area?'

'Malmö, I think.'

There was silence for a few seconds before she responded. 'There's no one there by that name.'

'What about the rest of the country, then?'

'No. There are a number of Wellmans, but no Daniel.'

*

Per thought about Vendela all the way to Kalmar.

As he stepped out of the lift by Nilla's ward, he met a couple about the same age as him, a man and a woman walking slowly along the corridor. They looked exhausted, their eyes downcast.

The man was carrying a small blue rucksack, and Per suddenly realized that the couple were the parents of Nilla's friend Emil. Presumably they had been to collect his things, and now they would be going home to an empty house.

Per's warm memories of Vendela melted away. He slowed down as he approached Emil's parents, but didn't speak to them – he couldn't say anything. When they passed him on their way to the lift, he just wanted to turn his face to the wall and close his eyes.

'Hi Nilla. How are you?'

'Terrible.'

Two days before her operation Nilla was in a foul mood; she wouldn't even smile at her father as he sat down beside her.

'You only come and see me because you have to.'

'No . . .'

'Because that's what you're *supposed* to do.'

'No,' said Per. 'There are lots of people I never go and see, all the time. But I want to see you.'

'Nobody wants to see a person who's ill,' said Nilla.

'That's not true,' said Per.

They sat in silence for a little while.

'Don't you feel well today?' he asked.

'I threw up last night, twice.'

'But you're a bit better today?'

'A bit,' said Nilla. 'But the nurses wake me up too early. They always wake us up at seven, even though nothing ever happens then. We get breakfast and our tablets at half past.'

'But seven's not that early, is it?' said Per. 'I mean, that's just the same as when you're going to school . . . when I was at secondary school I used to get up at quarter past six every morning to catch the bus.'

Nilla didn't appear to be listening.

'Mum's auntie was here this morning.'

'Auntie Ulla?'

'Yes,' said Nilla, 'and she said she was going to pray for me.' She looked past Per, her eyes fixed on the ceiling. 'I want you to play Nirvana's "All Apologies",' she said. 'The acoustic version.'

'Play? What do you mean, play?'

'In the church,' she said quietly.

Eventually he understood, and shook his head. 'We won't be playing anything.' He added, 'Because . . . because it won't be necessary.'

'But at the burial,' said Nilla. 'Will you play it then?'

He nodded.

'When your heart stops on the dance-floor in eighty years' time, I promise to play Nirvana.' He looked at his watch. 'Mum will be here soon, we've got a meeting with your surgeon. Have you met him?'

Nilla folded her arms over her chest. 'Mm. He was here last night . . . He smelled of smoke.'

Fifteen minutes later, Per and Marika were sitting in silence next to each other in front of a desk. There was a faint smell of tobacco.

Tomas Frisch, the vascular surgeon, came from Lund and was about the same age as Per. Frisch meant 'healthy' in German – that had to be a good sign, didn't it? He had tired eyes, but he was tanned and in spite of everything he seemed relaxed about the operation. He shook hands with both of them.

'It's not a routine procedure, not by any means,' he said, 'but you can trust us. We're all very experienced – it's an excellent team.'

Dr Frisch opened up a laptop and switched it on. He started to click through a series of images on the screen as he explained what would happen during the operation.

Per looked and listened, but didn't know what to say. He would have preferred to sit there leaning forward with his head in his hands.

Tomas Frisch was the pilot who was going to bring them all down safely. But he wasn't part of the plan – Dr Frisch was risking only his reputation if Nilla didn't make it. In that way, Per thought, a surgeon was less like a pilot and more like God.

'We know you'll do your best,' said Marika when the surgeon had finished.

'That's what we do every single day,' said Frisch.

He smiled and shook hands with them again. But as they left the room, Per was wondering what words of solace Emil's parents had heard from the doctors.

Per stayed with Nilla during lunch, but neither of them ate more than a couple of mouthfuls. When he said goodbye to her, Marika walked with him to the lift – something she had never done before. Perhaps all this desperate waiting had brought them a little closer to one another, he thought, even if there was still a long way to go.

'You'll be here in plenty of time?' said Marika.

'Of course.'

'So when will you get here?'

'As early as necessary.'

389

Marika looked at him. 'You don't want to come at all, do you?'

'No, who would?' Per met her gaze. 'But I will.'

The lift doors opened behind him. He leant forward to give his ex-wife a friendly hug, and she accepted it in silence.

She had changed her perfume, he noticed. Marika's body felt tired and fragile, and after a few seconds it began to shake. Per held her until she stopped crying, but he couldn't think of anything to say. There was no love there any longer. There was only tenderness.

He held Marika and thought of Vendela.

As he was walking through the hospital foyer, his vision blurred, he saw a boy wearing a black jacket and carrying a black rucksack coming towards him from the bus stop, his head bowed. He looked tired and fed up.

As the boy came closer he recognized his own son.

'Hi Jesper.' Per cleared his throat, fighting back the tears. 'Has school finished?'

Jesper nodded. 'I've come to see Nilla.'

'Good . . . she'll be pleased. Her operation is the day after tomorrow; we've just had a meeting with the doctor who's going to make her better. He's very good.'

Jesper nodded without speaking. He took a couple of steps past Per, then stopped and asked, 'Did you and Granddad carry on with the steps?'

'The steps?' said Per. Then he remembered their building project in the quarry. 'We did – they're almost finished.'

'Good,' said Jesper. He hesitated, then added, 'It was me that wrecked them.'

'You mean . . . when they fell down?'

Jesper stared at the ground. 'I was trying to carry on

with them by myself and finish them when you went to fetch Granddad . . . but the whole thing collapsed.'

'I see. It doesn't matter . . . but you're lucky the stones didn't fall on top of you.' He laughed and went on, 'I thought it was the trolls who had knocked the steps down. After all, they do live in the quarry, according to our neighbour Gerlof.'

Jesper was looking at him as if he was crazy.

'It was a joke,' said Per. He went on quickly as if Jerry were still alive, 'But next time you come to Öland we'll finish them off. Nilla will be able to help too, when she gets home.'

He stressed the word *when*, and looked into his son's eyes to try to share the hope he still felt.

'OK.'

Jesper allowed his father to hug him without giving any indication of whether he believed Nilla would get better or not. Then he adjusted his rucksack and went into the hospital.

Per's mobile rang as he was getting into the car. A bright, friendly female voice announced, 'Hello, this is Rebecka from the funeral director's office. We've got two possible dates for the ceremony.'

'Ceremony? What ceremony?'

'The funeral of Gerhard Mörner,' said the woman. 'Tuesday, May twelfth or Thursday, May fourteenth – a spring funeral. Two o'clock in the afternoon on both days. Which would suit you best?'

'I don't know.' Per made an effort to pull himself together. 'Thursday, maybe.'

'Excellent,' said the woman. 'In that case I'll book the fourteenth. Have a nice weekend.'

59

Vendela had been unfaithful. Physically and mentally. Both were just as bad.

When she got home after spending the night with Per Mörner, she went out to do some work in the garden, creating order on the new plot.

She thought constantly about what had happened. What had she done? She had spent the night with Per, lying close beside him as they touched one another and whispered secrets.

She had behaved *exactly* as Max had suspected.

But *she* wasn't the one who had quarrelled and taken off with Ally. Vendela had always been there for Max when it came to his books and everything else. For once she had done something selfish; it hadn't been planned and she didn't know what would happen from now on. But she had *no* intention of feeling guilty.

She didn't remember falling asleep with Per, but they must have done, because she woke up from a peaceful darkness in the morning and looked into Per's eyes. She remembered where she was, and didn't regret a thing.

She didn't feel in the least uncomfortable about staying for breakfast, and there were no awkward silences. Per talked quietly about his daughter, and the operation that would save her life. He knew she would make it, he just knew it, and Vendela nodded seriously. Of course. Of course everything would be fine.

'I have to go into Kalmar,' he said after breakfast. 'To the hospital.'

Vendela understood, but didn't want to go home. 'Can I stay here for a while?'

'Don't you want to go home?'

She looked down at the floor and thought about her wedding ring in the hollow on the elf stone. 'I don't want to be there . . . I can't cope with seeing Max at the moment.'

'But we didn't do anything wrong,' said Per.

'We slept together,' said Vendela.

'We kept each other warm.'

But Vendela knew that didn't matter.

When Per had gone she went into the living room and sat down on the sofa. On the other side of the room, next to the television, was an old wooden chest with a scornfully grinning troll, a knight on a horse, and a weeping fairy princess carved on the front. Vendela looked at it for a long time.

From time to time she got up to look over at her own house, and towards lunchtime she saw Max come out of the front door. She couldn't tell what mood he was in from this distance, but he went straight to the car and drove off.

His heart was still beating, then.

But still Vendela didn't go home. She sat down in the spring sunshine out on Per's veranda, her face turned towards the empty sea.

An hour or so later she heard the sound of a car engine. It seemed to stop over at her house. Was Max back? Perhaps, but the windbreak was in the way and she had no intention of getting up to have a look.

It was only when she had made herself a modest lunch of salad and eaten it that she glanced through the window to the south once more.

There was no car outside her house. If Max had been back, he had gone off somewhere again.

Suddenly the telephone in the kitchen rang, and Vendela jumped. It might have been Per, but she didn't dare answer it, and it stopped after six rings.

What was Max up to? Why come back and then go off again?'

She was surprised that he was still in good health. But presumably her wedding ring was still lying on the stone.

That was when she realized she had actually wished her husband dead. The previous night she had stood by the stone and asked the elves to *kill* him.

It was now two o'clock, and she decided to go home. She wanted to talk to Max and find out what he had done.

There was no welcoming bark as she opened the front door; the house was silent. But Vendela was aware of a different smell in the house, the overwhelming perfume of flowers. And when she walked into the main living room she saw that the floor was virtually covered in flowers: bouquets of roses, tulips and white lilies, along with local spring flowers like wood anemones and wild thyme. Max seemed to have dug out every single vase they had in the house, along with every glass and mug. The dark-grey stone rooms were filled with splashes of red, yellow, green and lilac.

Vendela wandered slowly through the scented rooms. After a minute or so her nose began to itch, then it started to run. Her allergy was back, and it was Max's fault. In his own way he wanted to ask her forgiveness for Ally's death, but the flowers just made her feel worse than ever, both physically and mentally.

The house felt like a chapel of rest. All that was missing was a little coffin, just about a metre long.

Max, thought Vendela, *why must you always go over the top?*

The proofs of the cookery book were waiting for her on the worktop, but she didn't want to look at them.

She sat down and thought about Max, and then about Per Mörner. She couldn't ring either of them, but suddenly she remembered a man she could get in touch with.

It took a while to find the number, but once she found it she called straight away. The phone rang five or six times before he answered, his voice firm.

'Adam Luft.'

'Hello, it's Vendela here.'

'Who?'

'Vendela Larsson . . . I came on one of your courses, *Meeting the Elves.*'

'Oh, that one,' said Adam. 'That was quite some time ago.'

'Five years,' said Vendela. 'I was just wondering if I could ask you a question?'

'That course isn't running any more,' he interrupted. 'Not enough applicants. I'm working on astral travel for the soul these days.'

'Astral . . . what?'

'You ought to try it, it's brilliant.' Adam's voice became more intense as he went on, 'We're learning how to get the soul to leave the body . . . to travel through time and space. And I've still got places available on courses this summer – shall I put your name down?'

'No thanks,' said Vendela, and put the phone down.

There was no one else she could talk to now, and she was too restless to stay in the house.

Shortly after six she pulled on an extra pair of trousers, a woollen jumper and a thick padded jacket and went into the bathroom. To the medicine cabinet.

She had nothing of value with her as she left the house; she hadn't even taken her mobile.

When she reached the gravel track she saw the lights of a car approaching along the village road. Was Max on his way back?

Vendela walked faster. As so many times before, she headed north from the quarry and turned off towards the alvar. She thought about her wedding ring and knew that this particular gift to the elves had been a rash mistake. She couldn't wish Max dead, whatever he might have done to Ally, so she had to get the ring back.

She didn't run, she was too tired and hungry for that, but she strode towards the north-west until she saw the dense grove of juniper bushes.

She walked slowly up to the elf stone and looked at the top. The old coins were still lying there, but there was nothing else.

Her wedding ring had gone.

They had been here.

Vendela stood motionless next to the stone, her head lowered. The spring evening was cold and the darkness was on its way, but she hadn't the strength to move.

Öland 1958

Vendela is running across the alvar, competing with the setting sun. But it all feels so hopeless – not only must she find someone she can trust, she must also persuade that person to accompany her back to the kingdom of the elves and help Jan-Erik home. If she can't find any-one she must collect food and blankets from the farm, then she and her older brother will have to spend the night out on the alvar – unless she can persuade him to get up and try to walk.

She must hurry – everything depends on it.

On the way back her progress is constantly hindered by all the water, by all the lakes of meltwater spread across the grass, reflecting the sky. She has to go around them, sometimes to the left, sometimes to the right, and when the sun slips behind thick cloud it is difficult to remember exactly where she is.

She has also lost track of the time, she has no watch.

The blood is pounding in Vendela's ears. She scrapes her legs on bushes and small rocks, her leaky boots sink down into the grass and suck up the water, but she doesn't slow down.

She runs and runs, she doesn't stop until a wall built of big round stones looms up in front of her. The wall is almost up to her chest, and she can't see the end of it in either direction. She doesn't recognize it – where is she? The sky is overcast, and she is no longer sure which direction she is supposed to be going in.

In the end she turns away from the wall and runs in the opposite direction, but now she can't find her way back to the stone. The paths between the lakes are like a labyrinth, she is utterly disorientated in this watery world.

Vendela's spring clothes are damp with sweat; she is cold and starting to feel hungry. She wants to slip her small fingers into the reassuring hand of some adult, but there is no one. Everything is silent. She keeps on moving, and when she gets tired of walking around the meltwater she begins to wade through the lakes instead. Most of them are not very deep, and her boots are soaking wet anyway.

Eventually she sees a stone wall a couple of hundred metres away. She approaches it slowly, looks at it and measures its height against her body; she is convinced it's the same wall she was standing next to a little while ago. She has gone round in a circle on the alvar.

Vendela just cannot take another step, and sinks down next to the wall. She shuts her eyes and keeps them closed for a long time before opening them.

She sees shadows around her. Pale shadows. They shouldn't be there, but she can see them. And as they slip towards her she realizes the elves are coming. They have been to the stone to fetch Jan-Erik, and now they are coming for her.

And Vendela wants them to take her, she reaches out her hand to them.

'Come,' she whispers.

But the misty shapes slip away, they do not want

to play with her, and gradually their contours fade. Eventually they disappear completely.

'Hello?'

She can hear shouts in the darkness.

'Hello? Hellooo?'

Vendela opens her eyes. She is lying beside a stone wall, and she's very, very cold.

'I'm here!' she shouts.

She doesn't know if anyone can hear her, but the shouts are coming closer. Swishing footsteps move through the grass, dark figures take shape. Vendela sees a woman in a cape and a man in a hat and coat. She recognizes them.

'Vendela, what are you doing out here? We've been looking for you!' Aunt Margit takes hold of her frozen hands and helps her up.

She looks around. It is almost completely dark out on the alvar now.

'Let's get you home and make you a hot drink,' says Margit. 'Then we'll set off for Kalmar.'

She and Sven start walking, but Vendela cannot go with them. 'No,' she says. 'We can't go!'

Sven keeps moving, but Aunt Margit stops. 'What do you mean?'

Vendela points. 'I left Jan-Erik by the stone.'

Her aunt just stares at her, and Vendela has to explain that Henry has gone down to the quarry, and that she has dragged her brother out on to the alvar. She runs up and grabs her aunt by the arm. 'We have to go and get him,' she says. 'Come on!'

Her aunt and uncle follow slowly, and this time Vendela somehow finds her way along the paths between the silver mirrors made of water. They reach the stone among the juniper bushes as the twilight deepens to dark grey.

But it's too late. There is no sign of Jan-Erik, and the silver chain Vendela placed on the elf stone has also disappeared.

Only the wheelchair is still there, stuck in the mud.

The three of them stand there for a while shouting across the alvar, but there is no reply. It is almost pitch dark now.

'Time to go home,' says Uncle Sven.

Margit nods. Vendela feels the panic rising, but cannot protest.

Her aunt and uncle take the wheelchair back to the farm. They push it through the garden and put it in the tool shed. Vendela is sitting in the kitchen when they come back. The house feels very cold.

The kitchen clock is ticking.

Suddenly they hear the sound of heavy boots out on the steps.

The front door opens and Henry walks into the little porch. His breathing is heavy and he seems very tired; he stops in the doorway when he sees his sister and brother-in-law in the kitchen. He says nothing, and doesn't remove his peaked cap.

Margit and Sven don't say anything either; it is Vendela who speaks first.

'Dad . . . where's Jan-Erik? Have you seen him?'

'Jan-Erik?' says Henry, as if he can barely recall the name. 'He's gone.'

'Gone?' asks Vendela. 'Gone where?'

There is a brief silence in the kitchen, then her aunt chips in: 'Did he go up to the station?'

Henry won't look at his daughter; he looks at the floor and nods. 'That's right . . . Jan-Erik has gone on the train. He was heading for Borgholm, then the mainland.'

'You mean . . . he's run away?' says Sven.

'Yes. And I couldn't stop him . . . He's seventeen years old.' Henry looks up. 'Shall we make a move, then?'

No one says anything; everyone seems to be thinking of Henry's destination. The prison.

He goes into his room and comes back with his bag.

'Well, we'd better make a start on locking the house up,' says Aunt Margit.

Vendela goes to her room and packs her bags in silence.

Suddenly she hears a scream from downstairs. Her aunt shouts at the top of her voice: 'It's empty! Everything's gone, every single thing!'

When Vendela gets down to the kitchen, her mother's jewellery box is standing open on the table, and Aunt Margit is as white as a sheet. She has lowered her voice, but she is just as angry. 'Jan-Erik has stolen all his mother's jewellery,' she says. 'Did you see him do it, Vendela?'

Vendela shakes her head in silence. Her father is standing next to his sister, looking even more gloomy. 'I should have locked it away.'

He gazes blankly at Vendela; she lowers her eyes and goes back to her room to fetch her bags. She knows that Jan-Erik did not take the jewellery, and she doesn't believe he has run away on the train. She was the one who left him, not vice versa.

He sat on the grass and waited until he realized she wasn't coming back. Only then did he get up and walk away from the stone.

Jan-Erik has gone to the elves. That's what must have happened. He has gone to the world behind the mist, where the sun always shines.

*

When they reach Kalmar an hour later, Henry gets out with his bag in front of the well-lit entrance to the prison.

'Thanks for the lift,' is all he says.

He turns up his collar, grips his bag firmly and leaves Vendela without a word. He walks up to the guard at the gates and doesn't look back.

Time passes. When Jan-Erik doesn't arrive at the station for his journey to the mental hospital, the police are informed, but a retarded teenager on the run isn't a major issue. The police have other priorities, and he is never found. It is as if Vendela's older brother has been swallowed up by the ground.

Time passes, and the little farm belonging to the Fors family is sold that summer.

Time passes, and Vendela does not visit her father in prison, not once.

When he finally comes out he is a much subdued man. Late in the autumn he returns to Öland and settles in Borgholm, where he is less well known than in his home village. Henry becomes a labourer, lives in one room with no cooking facilities, and muddles along somehow.

By this stage Vendela is settled in Kalmar and doesn't want to go back to Öland. She has a whole new life with Margit and Sven. Soon the children in her class at school forget that she comes from the island, and stop teasing her. Her aunt and uncle have no children of their own, and they are very fond of Vendela.

Everything works out for the best.

She is given new clothes, a red bicycle and a record player.

She is given almost everything she asks for, and no longer has to wish for things.

She grows up, passes her exams and meets a nice man who owns a restaurant. They have a daughter.

The memories of Öland slowly fade away, and Vendela hardly ever takes the ferry across the Sound to see her father. His little room is always littered with empty spirit bottles, and they have nothing to say to each other when she does visit.

After Henry's death at the end of the sixties, she has no reason to go back. She no longer has any family left on the island – just a collection of graves in the churchyard. In her room she has a few objects made from beautifully polished limestone which she inherited from her father, along with an empty jewellery box.

It is not until she is in her forties, when her marriage to Martin is over and she has married Max Larsson, that Vendela begins to think about her childhood on Öland, and to feel a desire to return there.

And a growing urge to follow her brother to the elves.

60

I don't want any more jewellery! Ella had written.

Gerlof had reached the last entries in his wife's diaries from the fifties. Only four and half pages left to read now.

The book ended in the spring of 1958, and the final pages were filled with closely written text. Ella's handwriting had become anxious and untidy, and Gerlof hesitated before putting on his glasses. But eventually he began to read:

Today is 21st April 1958, but I hardly know how to begin writing. Something awful has happened, and Gerlof isn't here. He set off north towards Stockholm on his cargo boat the day before yesterday, and he was supposed to be back today. But last night he rang and said that he and John couldn't get away from the capital because of the wind, and were moored at the quay down below City Hall. There's a gale blowing up the Swedish coast, almost storm force, but it hasn't reached the island. It's just cloudy and cold here; the electric heaters are on all day.

The girls went off on their bikes late yesterday

afternoon to go to the cinema in the community hall. So I was left alone in the cottage. The whole village felt deserted.

The sun had started to go down and I was sitting sewing when I heard a faint noise from the veranda. It wasn't a knock, like when the neighbours come to call, just a kind of scraping against the door, so I put down my sewing and went to have a look. There was no sign of anyone, but when I looked more closely I noticed a piece of jewellery lying on one of the steps.

It was a gold heart on a silver chain, and I picked it up . . . but it didn't make me the least bit happy, because I knew where it had come from. And I was tired of it, tired of these gifts I hadn't asked for.

'I don't want any more jewellery!' I yelled out across the pasture. 'You can come and take it all back!'

There was no reply, but after a while there was a movement behind the juniper bushes beyond our land. And then the changeling stepped out in the tall grass and simply stood there, and I hardly recognized him, because his face was clean and his hair had been combed, and he looked really neat and tidy. He was smiling and giggling, and we looked at one another.

I held out the necklace, not really knowing what else to say. I just didn't want it. So I opened my mouth, but the changeling suddenly turned and hurried away into the darkness between the bushes.

I put my shoes on, and hurried after him.

Did the changeling know he was being followed? I didn't call out, but he seemed to be waiting for me to catch him up. He wasn't exactly running, more like lumbering along, and I caught glimpses of

405

his pale shirt and red skin among the bushes. He crossed the road quickly, like a cat, and moved into the shadows by the stone wall; it was obvious he was used to keeping out of sight. He was heading northwards as quickly as he could. But the grass hadn't yet grown long and lush in the pasture, and I was almost able to keep up with him.

It took a while for me to work out that he was on his way to the quarry. Why would he want to go there? But he increased his speed, and we emerged on the gravel up above the rock face.

I could hear singing from over by the shore, and I recognized the words; a man was singing an Öland sea shanty for all he was worth among the piles of stone.

The changeling slowed down, then turned and looked at me. I held the silver chain high above my head and showed it to him, but he ignored it. He listened to the song coming from over by the sea, then he set off again at full speed.

The quarry was almost empty, apart from one solitary man way up high. He was the one who was singing – a quarryman who had built himself a little shelter from the wind, or a semicircular wall up by the northern rock face. Only his head and shoulders were visible above the stones.

The changeling ran straight towards the man, and I saw that it was Henry Fors. I was surprised, I had heard about his troubles and thought he didn't want to work any more. But there he stood, sheltered from the wind as he polished away at some kind of sculpture, just as if nothing had happened.

Then everything happened so quickly I couldn't keep up. The changeling ran along the top of the quarry, and when Henry saw him he stopped singing. He yelled something, but I didn't hear what it was.

The changeling held out his arms and kept on running at full speed towards Henry's little wall. He ran straight into it and knocked it down. The stones rattled and clattered around his legs.

Henry yelled again: 'No!' And then a name, Hans-Erik or Jan-Erik. The changeling was yelling too, but it was more like shouts of joy.

I stopped and lowered my eyes. Henry carried on yelling, and still the falling stones rattled and crashed.

I think they had a fight, the man and the boy. And I think the last thing that happened was that one of them was thrown or fell down into the quarry, but I didn't want to see any more.

I turned around and ran.

All I could think of as I ran along the village road was that Henry knew what the changeling was called. They knew one another.

He had come from the north. Had he come from Henry's farm? Henry had a retarded son who had burnt down his barn – that was the gossip I'd heard recently.

When I got back home I sat down on the steps with the necklace in my hand, weeping because I had been too afraid and too much of a coward to help the boy in some way.

Then I dried my tears and went inside to wait for my girls and Gerlof to come home.

I wouldn't tell anyone what had happened. It was Henry's burden, and his son's. I had been stupid enough already, accepting and keeping all the changeling's gifts, jewellery that was not mine and never would be.

Ella's diary ended there, with just a few blank lines left on the very last page. Gerlof lowered the book, ashamed that he had ever opened it.

He sat there on the lawn, trying to remember how things had been when he got home a few days later, after the storm had abated. Had he noticed that anything had happened? No, Ella had never said much about what went on in the village during the weeks when he was away, and he probably hadn't asked many questions either. He had been too preoccupied with thoughts of loading up the boat with her cargo before his next voyage to Stockholm.

Ella's changeling had fought with Henry Fors. It must have been his son. Gerlof had never seen him, but he had heard the same stories as Ella: that Henry had a mentally handicapped son and had blamed him for burning down the barn. Perhaps entirely without justification.

At any rate, they had had unfinished business when they met in the quarry that last evening. Some kind of outburst had led to the boy disappearing without a trace, and to Henry's eventual collapse, from which he never recovered.

And it was all Gerlof's fault. He should never have spoken to the police.

61

Per was sitting in his cottage watching the sun set over the quarry. One and a half days left until Nilla's operation.

He had gone out earlier in the evening armed with a spade and crowbar and tried to do some work on the steps, but hadn't had the strength left in him to haul the blocks up to the top of the slope. Jesper hadn't managed to finish the steps on his own, and Per couldn't do it either. He managed to get only two more steps in place; when the third block tumbled back down on to the gravel, he gave up and went inside.

He sat down in the living room, feeling utterly exhausted.

Thirty-six hours, that was two thousand, one hundred and sixty minutes, he worked out. What was he going to do with all that time? Should he go for a run? He hadn't been running since his last outing with Vendela, but he just couldn't summon up the energy this evening.

He switched on the television, but there was some kind of children's programme on, and he quickly turned it off.

Silence. The sun was slipping away and the shadows were growing.

Suddenly the phone in the kitchen rang, and Per jumped.

Bad news? He was certain it would be, whoever was calling, but he went and answered it anyway.

A hoarse male voice spoke. 'Per Mörner?'

'Yes?'

He didn't recognize the voice, and the man didn't introduce himself.

'Nina said you wanted to talk to me,' he said. 'I own the Moulin Noir.'

Per remembered the note he had left at the club in Malmö. 'I did, yes,' he said, attempting to gather his thoughts. 'Thanks for ringing. I just wanted to ask you something about my father . . . Jerry Morner.'

'Oh, how is Jerry these days?'

Per had to explain – yet again – that he had lost his father.

'Shit, I'm sorry to hear that,' said the man. 'Didn't his studio burn down as well?'

'Yes, the weekend before Easter,' said Per. He went on quickly, 'But Jerry mentioned the Moulin Noir several times before he died, which made me a little bit curious about the place.'

The man on the phone sounded tired. 'A little bit curious . . . You were here last week, weren't you – what did you think?'

'Well . . . I didn't actually go downstairs,' said Per, 'but the girl on the till said there was a big surprise waiting down there. Is that true?'

The man laughed. 'The big surprise is that there is no surprise,' he said. 'Businessmen come in late at night flashing the plastic, thinking they're going to be able to screw a load of blondes, but the Moulin Noir isn't a brothel.'

'So what is it, then?'

'It's a dance club . . . Although to be fair, the dancers are all girls, and they don't wear any clothes. The men sit and watch. And lust after them.'

Men are good at that, thought Per.

'Did my father own the Moulin Noir?'

'No.'

'But he was involved in the club?'

'No, I wouldn't say that. We did work with Jerry to a certain extent; we used to advertise in his magazines, and Jerry often came here to check out our girls and guys. A few of them did some work for him as well.'

'Guys? So you had male dancers at the club?'

'For a while . . . Bodybuilders covered in baby oil who danced with the girls and had simulated sex with them. But not any more. There are much stricter regulations about what you can do on stage in Sweden these days, so now we just have girls.'

'But these male dancers – was one of them called Daniel Wellman?'

'Yes,' said the man. 'He used to work for us.'

'The same guy who did some filming for my father?'

'That's right. Daniel Wellman. He was only with us for about six months, but he worked for Jerry for several years.'

'With a new name,' said Per, reaching for a pen and a piece of paper. 'Markus Lukas, wasn't it?'

'That's what he called himself,' said the man.

'It was Jerry who named them,' said Per. 'All the guys were called Markus Lukas.'

'Everybody gets a new name,' said the man. 'It's a form of protection.'

There was a brief pause.

'Do you know how I can get hold of Daniel?' said Per. 'Can I ring him?'

The man laughed again, a weary laugh. 'That might be tricky.'

'In what way?'

'He's in the same place as Jerry.'

Per stared at his pen, poised over the piece of paper. 'Markus Lukas is *dead*? Are you sure?'

'I'm afraid so . . . Daniel was looking really rough the last time I saw him. Then he rang me several times during the last year wanting money, but he could hardly speak. He was depressed and angry. He wanted someone to blame. He talked a lot about Hans Bremer . . . Bremer had told Daniel to keep quiet.'

Bremer again, thought Per. 'I think Markus Lukas was after my father as well,' he said.

'It wouldn't surprise me . . . Towards the end he was begging money from everyone he knew. Then he stopped calling.'

'So what did he die of?' asked Per, expecting to hear the word *cancer*.

'Nobody knew, people thought he was on heroin . . . but last year I bumped into one of the girls who had worked with him at the club and with Jerry, and she told me he'd died a couple of months earlier. She'd been to get herself checked out after that, but she was fine.'

'Checked out?' said Per. 'Checked out for what?'

'She wanted to make sure she was clean.' The man paused, then went on, 'I don't know where Daniel picked up the infection, but he thought it was with Jerry and Bremer. He said he was going to sue them.'

'Infection?' said Per.

'His blood was infected. It happens from time to time in this industry. Daniel died of AIDS.'

62

Per slept until nine on the morning of April the thirtieth, but his head was still heavy when he woke up. He could hear the ticking of the wall clock in the kitchen and looked out of the window with a sense of being trapped beneath an immense sky.

Twenty-four hours to go.

It was a grey, windy morning on Öland. He wondered how he was going to get through the day, make the time pass as quickly as possible. He wanted to press fast forward so that Nilla's operation would be over.

He had one more important call to make, to Lars Marklund, which he did at about ten o'clock.

Marklund had nothing new to say about the investigation into Jerry's death, but at least Per was able to tell him that he had found 'Markus Lukas', and that his name was Daniel Wellman. He also told him that Wellman had been infected with HIV, and had passed away the previous year.

Marklund didn't say anything for a few seconds. 'So you think Wellman was HIV-positive when he was making these films? And that the girls got infected?'

'I don't know,' said Per; in his mind's eye he could see a procession of young girls disappearing into a

413

dark forest. 'But the risk has to be significant, surely . . .
I was talking to another of Jerry's male models a
couple of days ago, and he reckoned he'd been with
over a hundred women in the studio with my father
and Hans Bremer. I'm sure Daniel Wellman had been
with a similar number. And always without protection.'

Marklund remained silent again.

'A high-risk individual,' he said eventually. 'We need
to track down these girls.'

'I've got a few names,' said Per. 'Some are alive, and
some are dead.'

'Did your father and Bremer know about this . . . did
they know Wellman was infected while he was filming?'

'I don't know,' said Per. 'Jerry never mentioned it.'

'And now it's too late to ask them,' said Marklund.

He seemed to be keying something in on his computer.

'I've found a Daniel Wellman in Malmö,' he said,
then added, 'But you're right, he died in February last
year.'

Per caught sight of Bremer's yellow Post-it note, which
he had put beside the telephone. *Danielle*, he thought.
'Can I check a disconnected phone number with you?'

'No problem.'

Per read out the numbers next to Danielle's name,
and asked, 'Could you check whose number that was?'

There was a long pause on the other end of the phone.

'I don't need to check . . . It's already part of our investigation.'

'So whose number was it, then?'

'Her name was Jessika Björk.'

'Wasn't she the one who died in the fire?' said Per.
'Along with Bremer?'

414

'How do you know that?' asked Marklund after a moment. 'How did you get hold of her name?'

'I found a note with her number on it in Bremer's apartment,' said Per. 'Jessika must have worked for him and Jerry. They called her Danielle.'

'Not recently,' said Marklund. 'We've spoken to her friends . . . They said she'd given up that kind of thing seven or eight years ago.'

'So why did Bremer have her mobile number written down? And what was she doing with him in Jerry's house?'

'Yes, well . . . we're working on it,' said Marklund. 'Thanks for your help. I'll be in touch if anything comes up, but we'll take care of this from now on. You can relax and enjoy the spring on Öland. You will do that, won't you, Per?'

'Absolutely.'

Twenty-three hours to go.

Per had lunch, then went out into the fresh air. There were small tears in the cloud cover above the village, showing fragments of blue.

He walked slowly past Vendela's house, but the Audi was gone and the curtains were closed at the big windows. A car was parked at the other house for the first time in a while – the Kurdin family was evidently back.

Markus Lukas, Jessika, Jerry, Hans Bremer . . .

The names of the dead would not let him go. He went for a long walk south along the coast road, until the Tarmac ran out and the dirt track began. The only buildings out here were small stone boathouses above the shore. The water was calm, and there wasn't a soul in sight.

What did Jerry know?

Per didn't really want to think about that question. Had his father known about Daniel Wellman's condition, but let him carry on filming with the girls anyway? Had Bremer known?

He walked along the coast for almost an hour before looking at his watch and thinking of Nilla.

Ten past one. Less than twenty-one hours left.

He turned back towards the village. By the campsite he saw a poster advertising the fact that Walpurgis Night would be celebrated that evening with a bonfire and a sing-song down by the sea. He noticed there was already a substantial pile of twigs and branches on the shore ready for the fire.

Just before he reached the quarry he turned off to the right along the village road and opened Gerlof Davidsson's garden gate. It was only a week since they had seen each other, but a great deal had happened since then.

Gerlof was sitting in his chair on the lawn with a blanket over his knees and a tray on the table in front of him. There was also an old notebook on the table. The grass needed cutting, but Per was too tired to offer to do it.

Gerlof looked up and nodded at him. 'Nice to see you,' he said. 'I was just wondering when you might turn up again.

Per sat down. 'I've been away quite a bit,' he said. 'But everyone seems to be back this weekend.'

'That's right,' said Gerlof. 'Is there a bonfire tonight?'

'I think so,' said Per. 'It looks as if the local council are setting fire to a few twigs and having a bit of a sing-song down on the shore.'

'Setting fire to a few twigs?' said Gerlof. 'Let me tell you what we used to do here in the village. We collected all the old tar barrels that had split during the winter, and piled them up in a great big heap. Right on the top we put a new barrel full of tar . . . then we set fire to the whole thing! The tar in the top barrel melted and ran down into all the others, and we ended up with a bonfire that rose up towards the sky like a white pillar. It could be seen all the way from the mainland, and it drove away all the evil spirits.'

'Those were the days,' said Per.

Gerlof didn't say anything, so Per asked, 'Is everything all right, Gerlof?'

'Not really. How about you?'

Per shook his head. 'But maybe it will be . . . The doctors are going to cure my daughter tomorrow morning.'

'That's good,' said Gerlof. 'You mean she's going to have an operation?'

Per nodded silently, feeling the blood pounding in his throat. Why was he sitting here? Why wasn't he at the hospital with Nilla?'

Because he was a coward.

'Markus Lukas is dead,' he said.

'Sorry? Who's dead?' said Gerlof.

Per started to tell the story, and it all came pouring out. He told Gerlof about Markus Lukas, whose real name was Daniel Wellman, a male model who had been HIV-positive and had rung Jerry and Bremer asking for money. Per had misunderstood Jerry's fear of Markus Lukas; he had never been dangerous, just ill. And now he was dead.

So who had set the incendiary devices in the film studio, killing Hans Bremer and Jessika Björk? Who had taken Bremer's keys and got into Jerry's apartment? And who had killed Jerry?'

Gerlof listened, but eventually he held up his hand. 'There's nothing I can say about all that.'

'No?' said Per.

Gerlof hesitated, then went on: 'I've always puzzled over riddles and mysteries . . . tried to solve them. But it never ends well.'

'What do you mean?' said Per. 'Surely solving something can't do any harm?'

Gerlof looked down at the diary on the table. 'There was another mysterious fire not far from here forty years ago,' he said, 'at a farm to the north of Stenvik. A barn with cattle inside it was burnt to the ground. I was here at the cottage when it happened, and like everybody else in the village I went up to have a look. But I got suspicious, because there was the smell of paraffin all around the barn. And when I bent down I could see strange footprints left in the mud by a boot, with a big notch in the heel from a nail that had been badly hammered in. So I realized that the boot that had left the prints must have been repaired by Shoe-Paulsson.'

'Shoe-Paulsson?'

'He was a particularly bad shoemaker who lived in the village,' said Gerlof. 'So I mentioned it to the police, who found the owner of the boot and arrested him.'

'So who was it?' asked Per.

'It was the farmer who owned the place.' Gerlof nodded over towards the quarry. 'Henry Fors . . . the father of our neighbour, Vendela Larsson.'

'Vendela's father?'

'Yes. He blamed it all on his son, but I think it was Henry. It's funny, but arsonists almost always operate on their own patch. They almost always set fire to places they know.'

Per remembered Vendela's sad expression when she was showing him around her childhood home a couple of weeks earlier. *It was lonely here*, she had said.

'But why do you regret telling the police, Gerlof?' he said. 'I mean, pyromaniacs have to be stopped.'

'Yes, I know . . . but it destroyed the family. It broke Henry completely.'

Per nodded without saying anything; he understood. But here they were talking about misery and death again; he got to his feet. 'I'll be off to the hospital soon.'

It was a sudden impulse, but it felt right. He would drive down and spend the whole evening and night with Nilla, even if Marika and her new husband were there. He wasn't going to be afraid any more.

'I'll be thinking of you tomorrow,' said Gerlof. 'And your daughter, of course.'

'Thank you.'

Per turned and left the garden.

He was intending to go home, but a few metres from the gravel track by the quarry he came across Christer Kurdin, planting a tree. He had dug a hole in the lawn, and was busy filling in around the roots.

He straightened up and took a couple of steps towards Per. 'I heard about Gerhard, your father . . . that he'd died. Was it a car accident?'

Per stopped. 'Yes, he died in Kalmar . . . Is that an apple tree?'

'No, a plum.'

'Right.'

Per was about to move on, but Kurdin held his gaze. 'Would you like to come in for a while?'

Per thought about it, and nodded. He followed Kurdin up the path, glancing at his watch. It was five to three, and the hands kept moving on, tick tock.

'So you're here over the holiday weekend?' he said as they reached the house.

'Yes,' said Christer Kurdin. 'We're going home on Sunday . . . this will be our last visit before the summer.'

They were in a narrow hallway leading into a large living room.

419

Per looked around. There wasn't much in the way of furniture or ornaments, but there was plenty of electronic equipment, telephones and speakers. Black and grey cables snaked across the floor along the walls. On one table there were two large computer monitors. It seemed that either Kurdin or his wife was heavily involved in music as well, because under one of the windows was an oblong table with rows of dials and switches – a mixing desk.

'Would you like a cup of coffee?'

'No, I'm fine, thanks.'

Near the windows looking out towards the quarry was a black leather sofa behind a low coffee table made of stone. Per sat down.

'How about a beer?'

'That would be good.'

Per remembered he had just decided to drive to the hospital this evening, but one beer probably wouldn't do any harm.

Christer went into the kitchen and came back with two glasses of lager.

'Cheers.'

'Cheers.'

Per took a couple of swigs, put down his glass and wondered what to say. 'Have you been married long?' he asked.

'Marie and I? No, not very long. Two years, just about. But we've been together for five.'

'So where do you actually live? Stockholm?'

'No, Gothenburg. I went to university there, to the Chalmers Institute, and that's where my company is. But I come from Varberg originally.'

'And your wife?'

'She's from Malmö.'

They drank their lager in silence. Per took another

swig; it was quite strong, and the alcohol settled like a warm blanket over his anxiety about the following day. 'What do you think of Max Larsson?' he asked. 'Just between ourselves?'

Christer Kurdin pulled a face. 'Larsson? I think he's one of those people who has to be right all the time. He won't give up until everybody agrees with him. Didn't you notice how subdued his wife was?'

Per didn't respond to that; instead he asked, 'Have you read any of his books?'

'No,' said Christer, 'but I've seen how many he's churned out, so I can imagine what kind of advice you'd get from them.'

'Bad advice, you mean?'

'Simplistic, at any rate,' said Christer. 'Reading a psychology book isn't going to make you a good person. You need life experience for that – plenty of trial and error.'

Per nodded, and at that moment the front door opened. Marie Kurdin came into the hallway with their baby in a sling across her stomach.

'Hello?' she called out. 'Anyone home?'

She hadn't noticed Per, but Christer Kurdin got up quickly and went over to her. 'Hi darling,' he said. 'We've got a visitor.' He seemed relieved to see her, as if he'd been waiting for an interruption to a difficult conversation. But if he didn't like Per, why had he bothered to invite him in? 'It's our neighbour, Per Mörner.'

'Oh?'

Per clearly saw Marie Kurdin's smile briefly disappear.

Christer kissed his wife, who kissed him back, but Per thought they were both moving awkwardly. He had the impression they were playing roles for his benefit.

'Did you find everything, darling?'

'I think so . . . I got candles too.'

'Good.'

Per picked up his glass and looked at them. Marie and Christer Kurdin and their baby, the happy family in their luxury home. Was he envious of them?

Marie nodded at Per in passing as she disappeared into one of the bedrooms with the baby in her arms.

Jerry had pointed at Marie. *Filmed her*, he had said.

Christer Kurdin sat down again and smiled at Per across the table.

Per didn't smile back; he was searching for the right words to say. 'Did you know my father?' he asked.

Kurdin shook his head. 'Why do you ask?'

Per looked down into his glass, which was almost empty, and said, 'He was known as Jerry Morner, but when we met today you referred to him by his real name, Gerhard.'

'Did I?'

Per looked at him. 'Have you been phoning me?'

Christer Kurdin didn't reply.

'Someone's been calling me,' Per said slowly. 'It started after the party . . . Someone's been calling and playing something that could be the soundtrack from one of Jerry's films.'

Kurdin still said nothing; he just stared at Per for a few seconds before turning and calling over his shoulder, 'Darling?'

'Yes?' replied his wife.

'Could you come here for a moment?'

Marie Kurdin's heels tapped across the floor as she came back into the living room. 'What is it?'

'He knows,' said Christer Kurdin.

His wife didn't speak, but she looked Per in the eye.

'Did you do some filming with Jerry and Markus Lukas?' Per asked.

422

Marie shook her head. 'Of course not.'

She didn't say any more, but Christer Kurdin lifted his chin. 'Her younger sister did.'

'Sara,' Marie said quietly. 'She was in one of their films when she was only eighteen . . . and she fought it with antiretroviral drugs, but she died three years ago. She knew she'd been infected during filming and she told me, but she refused to tell anyone else. She was too ashamed.'

Per understood. 'So you rang my father . . . to remind him.'

'I recognized him at the party,' said Marie. 'I knew who he was when he got out that magazine.'

Per couldn't look her in the eye; he lowered his gaze. 'He did actually say that he recognized you too. You must have been alike . . . you and Sara.'

Marie didn't reply.

He looked into his glass. What was in the beer? It seemed cloudy – had Kurdin put something in his glass when he poured it in the kitchen?

Did Christer Kurdin own a red Ford?

Had he lured Jerry to a deserted road in Kalmar?

Per put his glass down carefully on the table and got to his feet, very slowly. He wanted to ask more questions, but his head was spinning.

'Must you go?' said Christer Kurdin.

Per nodded; he thought he could hear girls' voices echoing in the back of his mind. 'Yes . . . I have to go home.'

They looked at him and he felt ridiculous, but the girls were screaming inside his head now and Jerry was in there too, whispering and telling him to leave.

He took a step away from the sofa in the direction of the hallway, then one more. It was fine, he could move. It felt like being back in Jerry's film studio, in the

423

middle of all the smoke and heat and the smell of burnt human flesh.

Arsonists almost always operate on their own patch, Gerlof had said. So it must have been Jerry who burnt down his own studio. Or Hans Bremer. Or maybe Per himself, the lost son.

The last thing he did was to turn around in the hallway and raise his voice: 'I don't think Jerry . . . I don't think he knew anything. He didn't know Markus Lukas was infected. And I'm sorry, I didn't know, but they're all dead now . . .'

He was babbling, and closed his mouth. Christer and Marie Kurdin were standing side by side, still watching him, but he couldn't look them in the eye. He could only manage one more word: 'Sorry.'

He fumbled with the front door handle and eventually managed to get out.

63

The elves didn't come back to their stone.

It had been a cold night for Vendela out on the alvar, but she had curled up inside layers of winter clothes, and had got through it somehow. She had even slept for a few hours, stretched out on the soft grass with the elf stone sheltering her from the wind. Hunger had gnawed at her stomach, but she had coped with that too.

The situation with regard to Max was much worse.

The elves had taken the wedding ring from the stone, and now it was too late for Vendela to retract her wish.

Max was already dead, she was sure of it. She could see it all in her mind's eye across the alvar: the heart attack striking his chest like a hammer blow. Perhaps it had happened the previous evening, when he was back home sitting at his thinking desk among all the funeral flowers.

Bang, and his heart just stopped. His body slumped forward across the desk and lay there, his head twisted to one side. There was nothing to be done about it now, but Vendela still didn't want to go home. She didn't want to find her husband in his thinking room.

The elves had gone. But still she waited by the stone, hour after hour.

At some point in the middle of the day, she wasn't sure exactly when, she heard a rustling noise in the bushes a few metres away and a hare hopped past the stone. It turned to look at Vendela for a few seconds before it disappeared.

A couple of hours later she saw two people some distance away to the west, a man and a woman. They were walking side by side across the grass wearing red windproof jackets and sturdy boots. Neither of them looked in her direction.

Perhaps she was invisible. She wasn't hungry or thirsty now, she needed nothing.

No, that was wrong, there was one thing she needed.

She reached into her pocket and felt the bottle of tablets.

They were the Danish tablets, the strong ones that made her feel calm and weightless. She had only taken three or four since she came to the island, so the bottle was almost full.

She picked up one of the small tablets and closed her eyes as she put it in her mouth. There was no water, but it was easy to swallow.

After quarter of an hour she hadn't noticed any effects, so she took another tablet. And then two more at the same time.

When she had taken fourteen tablets she thought she'd better stop – after all, she didn't want to kill herself. She just wanted to relax and see the elves. And it looked as if they were on their way, because a white mist was creeping around the bushes.

She put the lid back on the bottle and slipped it into her pocket.

It was ten to four. She had been sitting here by the stone almost all day; soon it would be evening.

Vendela leaned back, feeling her pulse beating more and more slowly.

She suddenly remembered that it was Walpurgis Night. The evil spirits had left the alvar, at least for the time being. But the elves were still here.

The white mist quickly settled around her. It blocked out the sunlight, but suddenly she saw a small figure emerge from the juniper bushes.

It was a young boy. He walked across the grass between the drifting veils of mist, and Vendela knew where he had come from.

The boy stopped in front of a juniper bush and looked at her. Vendela smiled and held out her hands, because now she recognized him.

'Come here, Jan-Erik.'

The boy hesitated for a moment, then he came over to her. He stood by the stone and placed his cool hands on her shoulders. Vendela closed her eyes and relaxed.

When she looked up again a bright, warm gateway had opened up in the grass in front of her. There was no sign of any birds, but she could hear their song echoing beneath the sky.

She stood up and walked through the gateway, hand in hand with Jan-Erik.

She didn't look back. When the last of the mist had disappeared the yellow sunshine returned, and all the grey, earthly things were gone.

64

'Mörner!' a voice shouted from over by the quarry.

Per turned and saw that it was Max Larsson. He must have just come out of his house, because the front door was wide open. He was striding down the garden path, waving at Per.

Per stopped, despite the fact that he really wanted to get home. He could still feel the effects of the beer he had drunk with Christer Kurdin, and hoped he wouldn't start swaying on his feet.

'Where's my wife?' asked Max Larsson. He had stopped just a metre or so away.

'Your wife?'

'Vendela. Have you seen her?'

Per shook his head. 'Not today.'

He didn't care about Max Larsson, he had more important things to think about. But Max kept staring at him, as if he were weighing Per's answer on some internal set of scales. 'You've been spending time together,' he said. 'Haven't you?'

'Yes,' said Per. 'I saw her yesterday.'

He had no intention of telling Max what they had talked about, or what they had done. It was up to Vendela to tell him if she wanted to.

Max was still staring at him, but his expression was more uncertain now. 'She must have gone somewhere,' he said, looking around. 'I tried calling her from town, but she didn't answer. Her mobile's on the kitchen table.'

'Maybe she's gone shopping,' said Per.

'She can't have,' said Larsson. 'She hasn't got a car.'

Per took a step towards home. 'Perhaps she's just gone for a walk,' he said. 'I'll keep an eye open for her.'

'Good,' said Larsson. 'I'll drive down the coast . . . see if I can find her.' And then he added, with a certain amount of hesitation, 'Thanks for your help.'

Per nodded and left him. He felt quite sober now. The effects of the beer had subsided, and the idea that Kurdin might have put some kind of drug in it suddenly seemed utterly ridiculous. He was paranoid – and it was Jerry's fault. Jerry had thought people were out to get him for years, and he had evidently managed to pass this on to his son.

He walked quickly back to his empty cottage and unlocked the door. When he got inside, he switched on most of the lights to chase away the shadows.

It was quarter past four. Eighteen hours to go until Nilla's operation.

He took a deep breath and sat down at the kitchen table to call her.

'Hi, it's Dad.'

'Hi.'

She sounded subdued but calm. Per could hear music playing in the background. Nirvana, presumably.

'How are you feeling?'

'Good.'

'What are you up to?'

'Reading,' she said. 'And waiting.'

'I know. It'll be good when it's all over, won't it?'

'Yes.'

429

They chatted for quarter of an hour, and after a while Nilla seemed to be feeling a little better. Per felt calmer too. Nilla told him that Marika was at the hospital, and had been there all day.

'I'm coming over this evening,' he said.

'When?'

'Soon . . . in a few hours.'

'I might be asleep by then.' Nilla gave a tired laugh. 'They're going to wake me up early in the morning . . . I have to wash myself with some kind of spirit. Disfect my whole body.'

Disinfect, thought Per, but he didn't correct her.

'See you soon,' he said.

When he had hung up and was moving across to the cooker to start making dinner, he saw something black crawling slowly across the floor. It was a big blowfly, the first one this spring – at least the first one he had seen. It looked as if it had just woken up; it was moving very slowly and listlessly.

Per could easily have killed it, and for that very reason he scooped it up on a piece of paper and let it out through the kitchen window. It managed to get its wings working and disappeared across the quarry, without bothering to say thank you.

After dinner Per sat in the kitchen listening to the ticking of the clock and thinking about Vendela Larsson.

Where was she?

Of course, he knew where Vendela might have gone – back to her childhood. She could have run to the little farm, or out to the big stone on the alvar. Perhaps Max Larsson was searching there, always supposing he knew about those places. Did he?

Per tried ringing the Larsson house, but there was no reply.

It was quarter past five now. He could always take a look over at the farm himself before he set off for Kalmar, while it was still light. Running always made him feel better.

He got up, pulled on his running shoes and a tracksuit top and went outside. The air was fresh and chilly, and made him feel stone cold sober. And he was, wasn't he?

He looked south towards the Larsson house. The big Audi was gone, and the house was in darkness.

The lights were on in the Kurdins' house, but Per didn't want to think about that family at the moment.

He could hear a distant rattling sound, like pistol shots. Some kids letting off bangers down by the shore.

Per didn't run, but strode off along the track heading north-east. At first he followed the route leading away from the coast, then turned on to a smaller gravel track and eventually reached the farm.

The grass was even greener now and made the whole place look like some kind of Swedish summer idyll, but as he walked up the path he saw the outline of the stone foundations to his left. Now he knew why Vendela had stopped to look at it when she was showing him round. The rectangle on the ground was the remains of the barn that had burnt down.

The grass was slightly shorter and yellower there, or perhaps it was just his imagination.

Arsonists almost always operate on their own patch.

Per thought about Hans Bremer, who had enjoyed pyrotechnics, and who had been the person who knew the film studio outside Ryd best, along with Jerry. If anyone had had the time and opportunity to rig up incendiary devices in the house, it was Bremer. But Bremer's hands had been tied behind his back, according to the police. And he had died in the fire – even if Jerry

431

had carried on talking about his companion as if he were alive. Bremer had called him, Jerry insisted, and Bremer had been driving the car that had knocked him down in Kalmar.

Per hadn't taken him seriously; after all, his father was ill and confused. But was it definitely Bremer's body that had been found in the burnt-out house?

It had to be. His sister had confirmed it, and the police were hardly likely to have made a mistake. They had dental records, fingerprints and DNA analysis these days.

He went up to the house and knocked on the door. The family who owned the place were at home, and the woman who opened the door remembered Vendela.

'Yes, she was here a few weeks ago . . . she said she lived here when she was little. But that's the only time I've seen her.'

Per nodded and carried on, climbing over a moss-covered stone wall and heading out on to the alvar. It was completely dry now; the ground was covered with all the long-suffering little herbs and flowers that were able to root in the thin soil.

Spring had taken over the island, and he hadn't even noticed.

Despite the dry weather he didn't see a single rambler out there; they had probably all gone home to celebrate May Day. All he could hear was the faint soughing of the wind and the sound of distant birdsong. A white-throat, perhaps, or a blackcap? Per was hopeless when it came to birdsong.

He increased his speed. There was nobody to ask, and he could only hope that he was running in the right direction, towards the great stone that belonged to the elves.

65

Per thought he must be somewhere in the middle of the narrow island now. He had moved quickly along the tracks among the undergrowth for a kilometre or so, then set his sights on a clump of trees on the horizon and begun to run.

After ten minutes he was hot and out of breath. There was no sign of the elf stone, but when he looked to the north he spotted a group of juniper bushes that looked familiar. They were a few hundred metres away in a circular grove, and he headed in that direction.

When he got there he could just see the top of a large block of stone, and recognized its angular shape. He had reached the place Vendela had shown him.

The sun had emerged from the clouds and its evening glow shone over to the west. It made the shadows of the bushes extend like long black ribbons across the grass. He made his way through the thicket and stopped.

The stone rose up in the glade in front of him, and there was someone standing on the grass beside it. A slender figure who didn't reach the top of the stone.

It was a boy, wearing jeans and blue jacket. He turned to face Per, and seemed to be smiling.

Per looked at him and blinked several times, but the

boy was no illusion, he was still there, and Per could see that he was holding a little wooden box in his hand. He was perhaps nine or ten years old.

'Hi,' said Per.

The boy said nothing.

Per moved one step closer. 'What's your name?'

The boy didn't respond to that either.

'What are you doing here?'

The boy opened his mouth and looked sideways. 'I live over there.'

He pointed somewhere behind him, towards the north-east. Per couldn't see any buildings, or indeed any sign of human habitation, but if there were houses they were probably hidden by the trees.

'Are you all on your own here?'

The boy shook his head and took a step away from the stone. 'I've turned her on her side,' he said. 'That's what you're supposed to do.'

That was when Per spotted Vendela.

She was lying with her eyes closed behind the boy, half hidden by the stone and with her hands joined in front of her face. She was wearing a hat and a bulky padded jacket, and looked as if she were just resting.

Per quickly went over and bent down to her. 'Vendela?'

When he shook her shoulders he realized she wasn't sleeping. She was unconscious; he could see scraps of food gleaming among the grass, and there was a sour smell emanating from her open mouth. She had been sick.

'Vendela?'

No response.

The boy was still standing a couple of metres away, watching with interest as Per attempted to revive her. It wasn't working.

Per straightened up. He had his mobile with him, but an ambulance would never find its way out here. He looked at the boy. 'We have to help Vendela . . . she's ill,' he said. 'Do you know if there's a road near here?'

The boy nodded and turned away. Per bent down, managed to get his arms under Vendela's back and picked her up. Her body was thin and limp; he could easily carry her.

They left the stone and headed eastwards in silence, with the sun at their backs. The boy was still carrying the wooden box, but after fifty metres he stopped by a particular juniper bush and pushed it in beneath the lowest branches.

'This is my hiding place,' he said.

Per nodded and noticed that there were some magazines tucked under the bush as well. Only comics, thank goodness.

'Come on,' he said.

His arms were beginning to ache, and he kept on walking so that he wouldn't lose the rhythm. The boy caught up with him and led the way eastwards through the undergrowth.

After a few hundred metres he became aware of a swishing sound. He recognized the sound of a car driving past, and realized they were close to the main road – much closer than he had thought.

As the trees and bushes thinned out, he saw a pair of headlights flickering past only fifty metres away. He staggered on with Vendela in his arms; he didn't know how much longer he could go on carrying her.

'Vendela?'

She was still breathing and opened her eyes for a few seconds, but didn't seem to recognize him. She mumbled something in response, then she was gone again.

He took a firmer hold of her body and carried her the last few metres to the road.

There were no cars in sight, but there was a bus stop about a hundred metres away. He made his way there and laid her down on the wooden bench in the shelter before taking out his mobile and calling the emergency services. He explained what had happened, but when he had finished the call and looked up, he was alone with Vendela.

The boy had disappeared.

It took half an hour for the ambulance to reach the bus stop, and in the meantime Per tried to keep Vendela warm and to bring her round. He wrapped his tracksuit top around her, and by the time the ambulance finally pulled in by the bus stop she had opened her eyes and kept them open for several minutes before closing them again. Her breathing was faint but steady in the chill evening air.

The paramedics came over with their emergency kit and bent over Vendela; they took off her jacket and checked her blood pressure. Per stepped back.

'We'll be taking her to Kalmar,' one of them said.

Vendela had become a patient, Per realized, just like Nilla.

'Is she going to be all right?'

'I'm sure she is. Are you her husband?'

'No . . . just a friend. I'll try to get hold of him.'

Ten minutes later the ambulance set off towards the bridge leading to the mainland, and Per breathed a sigh of relief.

He took Vendela's padded jacket with him as he headed back down the gravel track and then along the path leading out on to the alvar.

At the end of the path the boy was waiting for him. He had pulled his wooden box out of the bushes and was sitting on it.

Per stopped by the juniper bushes. 'They've taken her to hospital in the ambulance . . . Thanks for your help.'

The boy didn't reply. It was almost twilight on the alvar, so Per asked, 'Are you OK to find your way home?'

The boy nodded.

'Good.' Per was about to go on his way when something occurred to him, and he asked, 'What's the box for?'

The boy didn't say anything at first. He seemed to be thinking it over, then he decided he could trust Per.

'I'll show you.'

He got to his feet and picked up the box. It had no bottom, and hidden in the grass underneath it was an old rusty biscuit tin. The boy removed the lid and showed Per what was inside.

'I need the box to reach the top of the stone,' he said. 'There's nearly always something new up there.'

Per saw that the tin was half full of coins and small pieces of silver jewellery.

And on top lay a shiny wedding ring.

66

That evening Gerlof was sitting in his garden with a blanket over his legs. He thought he could hear the sound of distant sirens from the main road. Ambulance, fire engine or police?

Probably an ambulance. Somebody at the home in Marnäs who had had a heart attack, perhaps? No doubt he would read about it in the paper sooner or later.

He had gone back to his chair out on the lawn after dinner, and didn't want to go inside. It was Walpurgis Night, after all, the high point of spring, the night when every student in Sweden went out to welcome in the month of May. You couldn't just sit indoors.

The sky was beginning to grow darker, and a breeze rustled through the tree tops above him. The birds around the garden fell silent, one by one. When the sun had gone down it would be a cold evening; there might even be a touch of frost during the night. It wasn't really the weather to be sitting outside; he would go in soon and watch the news on TV.

Gerlof refused to ponder on riddles and mysteries these days, as he had told Per Mörner, but the ideas came anyway. He had been incurably fixated on puzzling out mysteries since childhood, and now he was sitting here with the diary thinking about Ella's changeling, who must have been Henry Fors's son.

But where had he gone? He had been running north towards the sea when Ella saw him that last evening, but what had happened when he reached Henry at the edge of the quarry?

A quarrel, followed by a killing? Or an accident? In which case, if the boy was dead, he was probably buried beneath one of the piles of reject stone.

If Gerlof's legs had been healthy and ten years younger, he would have got up out of his chair that very minute and gone straight to the quarry to start searching. But his body was too old and stiff, and after all he wasn't absolutely certain that Henry had hidden his son's body there.

And where would he search, given the amount of reject stone there was?

Gerlof suddenly realized he was no longer fixated on his own death; he hadn't really thought about his forthcoming demise since Easter. He had been too busy. Ella's diaries had helped him in that respect. Or perhaps it was the new neighbours and their problems that had made him forget his own.

He shivered in his chair, despite the blanket. It had grown noticeably colder as the evening drew in, and he got to his feet.

He could hear the sound of a car on the village road. More and more cars had been passing along there in the last few weeks, most of them driving far too fast for the narrow road – but this one sounded as if it were moving very slowly. He heard it brake and stop, but the engine kept on running, strangely enough.

Gerlof was expecting to see a visitor at the garden gate, but no one appeared.

He waited for a few more minutes, then made his way

towards the sound of the engine, leaning on his stick for support. He felt slightly wobbly on the grass, but kept his balance.

When he reached the gate he saw a car had stopped on the road; a man in a cap was sitting behind the wheel holding something in his hand.

Gerlof didn't recognize him. An early tourist? He grabbed hold of the gatepost and stood there just a few metres from the road, but the man didn't appear to have noticed him. In the end Gerlof cupped his hands around his mouth. 'Do you need any help?'

He hadn't shouted loudly, but the man turned his head and caught sight of him. He looked surprised, almost caught out somehow.

Gerlof suddenly saw that the object the man was holding was a plastic bottle. A litre bottle containing some kind of red liquid, which he was mixing with a fluid from a smaller glass container. There were strings of some sort attached to the bottle.

'Are you lost?' he called out.

The driver shook his head, then put down the bottle and grabbed the wheel with his left hand. Gerlof saw something glint on his wrist.

The man quickly put the car in gear with his right hand, and it moved away.

Gerlof stayed where he was, watching it disappear in the direction of the sea. It slowed down when it reached the coast road and turned right, heading north towards the quarry.

He let go of the gatepost, leant on his stick and managed to turn around without falling over. He headed back towards his chair, but stopped a few metres away and thought about what the man in the car might have been up to.

He wasn't happy about what he had just seen. In fact,

the situation was so bad that the evening seemed to have grown even colder.

He set off again, but towards the cottage this time. He managed to haul himself up the steps with the help of the iron railing, and went into the living room. He could still remember the telephone number for Ernst's cottage, and keyed it in with a trembling finger.

The phone rang out twelve times, but neither Per Mörner nor anyone else answered.

Gerlof put the phone down. He blinked and assessed the situation.

Eighty-three years old, with rheumatism and hearing difficulties. And the first butterflies he had seen this year had been a yellow one and a black one.

Things could go well, or they could just as easily go very badly.

Gerlof didn't know if he could manage it, but he just had to get himself over to the quarry to see if Per needed any help.

67

As Per made his way back towards the coast, the shadows across the alvar were even longer than before. The sun hovered in front of him like a gold disc in a narrow blue strip between the clouds and the horizon.

He was very tired. The last thing he had done up by the road was to call Max Larsson and explain that he had found Vendela unconscious out on the alvar, but that she had come round and was on her way to the hospital in Kalmar. After that he had set off home, heading west.

Less than fourteen hours to go.

He thought about it when he got back to the spot where he had come across Vendela and the boy keeping watch beside her – back by the dense thicket of juniper bushes and the big rock in the centre.

The elf stone.

He had lingered for a while. This was where he and Vendela had sat a few evenings earlier, exchanging secrets. He had told her things about himself and his father that he hadn't told anyone else, and she had told him that she was the one who wrote most of Max's books.

Max has nothing against being well known, but I prefer to remain invisible, Vendela had said.

Per had remained by the stone for a few minutes, looking at the empty hollows in its surface. Then he had taken out his wallet and placed a note in one of them, with a few coins on top.

Wishful thinking.

He knew what he was doing, but he couldn't help seeing Nilla's face in his mind's eye as he let go of the coins. He couldn't help making a wish as he stood there by the stone – offering money and praying for a miracle.

He heard a rustling noise from somewhere in the bushes.

He looked around, suddenly afraid that he was being watched. And he was. A pointed, russet-coloured face was staring at him. At first he thought it was a dog with big ears, but then he realized it was a fox. It stood stock still for a few seconds, then it wheeled around and disappeared.

Per set off again, walking away from the stone.

The sun had almost set by the time he got back to Stenvik. There was a breeze blowing off the sea, and he could hear distant sounds from the southern end of the village. Laughter and cheerful shouts. People had begun to gather down on the shore to light the bonfire and to celebrate the end of winter and the coming of spring.

He was just too tired to go down there. He walked up the path to the cottage, took out his keys and unlocked the door. The smell of Vendela lingered in her jacket as he hung it up in the hallway. He went into the kitchen and put some water on to make vegetable soup before driving to see Nilla.

The note he had found in Hans Bremer's kitchen was still lying by the phone, and he glanced over at it as he chopped some carrots. He looked at the last name:

Danielle, whose real name had been Jessika Björk, as it turned out.

Jessika and Hans Bremer had been in touch, despite the fact that she hadn't worked for him for many years. Why? And why had someone murdered them?

The water was boiling. He added a stock cube, some herbs and the vegetables, and when the soup was ready he ate it at the kitchen table, still pondering.

Arsonists almost always operate on their own patch, Gerlof had said.

Jerry and Bremer knew the studio in Ryd better than anyone else. But neither of them could have rigged up and set off the incendiary devices in the house. Jerry was too old and too ill, and Bremer had been lying upstairs with his hands tied behind his back.

Per pushed his soup bowl to one side and looked over at the window. The sun had gone down by now, but a bright light suddenly fell across the cottage.

A dark-coloured car was driving along the coast road.

Was it a Ford?

He reached for the phone just as the car braked and turned off into the shadows by the quarry. It moved slowly down the track with its lights on, and stopped on the gravel at the bottom. Then it just stayed there.

Per picked up the phone and keyed in a number on the mainland.

A man's voice answered: 'Ulf.'

'Could I speak to Ulrica, please?'

'Who's calling?'

'Per Mörner.'

'I'll just check . . .'

There was a noise at the other end of the phone, and at the same time he saw the car door open down in the quarry. He heard Ulrica Ternman's voice in his ear: 'Hello?'

'Hi, it's Per Mörner again. Do you remember me?'

There was a brief silence before she answered quietly, 'I don't want to talk to you.'

'I know,' Per said quickly, 'but I've just got one quick question.'

'About what?' said Ulrica Ternman, still speaking very quietly.

'I was just wondering what Hans Bremer looked like.'

'Bremer? I suppose he was . . . quite ordinary. He looked a bit like you, actually.'

'Oh? But he was older than me, I presume?'

'Younger.'

'Much younger?'

'I thought he was old at the time, but then I was a teenager . . . I suppose he would have been about thirty.'

'Thirty?'

The driver was getting out of the car now. Per couldn't see his face; it was too far away, and he was wearing a cap. The man looked around the quarry, glanced over at the houses, then got back in the car. He seemed to be waiting for something.

'If Hans Bremer was thirty when you saw him in the studio,' Per went on, 'then he would have been about forty-five when he died in the fire. But that can't be right. Hans Bremer had a younger sister, and she's older than me.'

'Oh? I really have to go now.'

'Wait, Ulrica . . . I just want to say one thing. I've just worked it out: the director who took pictures of you and your friends *wasn't* Hans Bremer.'

'He said that was his name.'

'Yes,' said Per. 'But if there's one thing I've learnt recently, it's that *nobody* in the sex industry uses their own name. Everybody wants to be anonymous, don't

445

they? Even my father changed his name, from Gerhard Mörner to Jerry Morner.'

She didn't respond, so he carried on, 'Someone had simply borrowed Hans Bremer's name, paid him money so that they could call themselves Hans Bremer and avoid dirtying their own name.'

'So I'm dirty, is that what you're saying?' snapped Ulrica Ternman.

'No, I didn't mean—'

But she had already hung up.

Per sighed and looked at the phone, but didn't call back. He glanced down at the car in the quarry one last time. Then he left the kitchen.

On his way into the hallway he saw the old axe lying in the bedroom, and went to pick it up. He pulled on his jacket and went out into the cold once more. He walked along the side of the cottage with the axe in his right hand, but suddenly he thought he could hear someone wheezing in the shadows.

'Jerry?'

He turned his head quickly, but of course it was just his imagination. There was no sign of anyone by the cottage.

The car was still parked down in the quarry. It was seventy or eighty metres away from him, between two heaps of stone. It was a Ford, but if it was the same car that had killed Jerry, there were no traces of the collision. The bodywork looked as if it had been recently cleaned.

Per thought he knew why the driver was still sitting in the car; he was waiting for darkness to fall.

The trolls come out at night, he thought.

He stopped at the top of the rock face and heard the sound of the engine being switched off. Silence fell, then the window opened and the driver stuck his head out. 'Hello?' he shouted.

446

'Hello,' said Per.

'Is this Stenvik?' The voice sounded lost.

'It is!' replied Per, gripping the axe more firmly.

The driver's door opened again, and the man stepped out on to the gravel. 'Are you Per Mörner?' he called out.

'I am. Who are you?'

'Thomas Fall from Malmö!' the man replied. He held out a large object that he was carrying. 'I just came to drop this off on the way to Stockholm. You did say you wanted it . . .'

Per nodded. 'Excellent, that's great. But you took a bit of a wrong turning, Thomas.'

'Did I? But you said you lived by the quarry.'

'Right idea, wrong track.' Per pointed over his shoulder towards the cottage. 'We live above the quarry, up there.'

'OK . . . Well, anyway, this is Bremer's briefcase!'

Per pointed at the steps and shouted, 'I'll come down!'

He made his way cautiously down the wobbly blocks of stone to the gravel at the bottom. It was a few degrees colder here in the quarry, as usual.

The car was still in the same place with its headlights on. They dazzled Per, and turned Thomas Fall into a black figure in a cap, walking towards him with a briefcase in his left hand and a bunch of keys in his right. He was rattling the keys nervously, but he was holding out the briefcase. 'Here it is.'

Per looked at Fall and clutched the handle of the axe. 'Put it down.'

'What?'

'You can put it down in front of you.'

Fall looked at him. 'What's that in your hand?' he asked.

'An axe.'

Thomas Fall took two steps towards him, but didn't put the briefcase down. Or the bunch of keys.

'Are those Bremer's keys as well?' Per asked.

Fall didn't reply; he had stopped ten or twelve paces away from Per. It was still impossible to see his face clearly. Per pointed at the briefcase. 'I don't think that belongs to Bremer. I think it's yours, but I suspect it amounts to the same thing. You *were* Hans Bremer, weren't you? You borrowed his name when you worked with my father.'

Fall seemed to be listening; he didn't move.

'I think Jessika Björk tracked you down. I think she found Hans Bremer's apartment so that she could talk to him about her friend Daniel, who became infected with HIV while he was filming under the name Markus Lukas. But when Bremer opened the door, Jessika didn't recognize him. She saw a different, older Bremer from the one who'd been there when she was filming. And my father didn't know or work with this Hans Bremer at all.'

Fall said nothing, so Per continued, 'So the real Bremer admitted to Jessika that someone else had paid him money to use his name and that this man had started working in the porn industry. The real Bremer told her the truth about you. And then Markus Lukas got really sick, and Jessika Björk eventually tracked you down, demanding money to keep quiet. You had to burn down the studio to silence them both for good so that "Bremer" could disappear and become Thomas Fall again.'

Fall remained silent for a few seconds. Then he un-did the straps on the briefcase, and answered in a quiet voice, 'You're right. I worked for your father for several years and he knew me as Hans Bremer. I emptied his bank accounts after he had the stroke . . . But I had a right to that money.' He looked up at Per. 'He was my father too . . . We're brothers, you and I.'

Per blinked and lowered the axe. 'Brothers?' He stared at Fall, who was slowly slipping his hand into the briefcase.

'That's right – half-brothers, anyway. Jerry was only with my mother for one summer at the end of the fifties, but that was enough . . . He never recognized me and I didn't say anything either, but I think he was happier with me than he was with you, Per. He didn't know I hated him.'

Per listened as he gazed at Thomas Fall, trying to make out his face beneath the cap. Were they alike?

Then came the attack.

It happened fast. Dazzled by the headlights, Per couldn't really see what Fall was doing, except that he opened up the briefcase and twisted something with his hand.

There was a sudden crackle from the case, and Fall hurled it at Per. It spun around and began to leak yellow flames, spreading fire all around. Per stepped backwards, but not quickly enough. Some kind of liquid was pouring out of the briefcase, sticking to his arm and burning fiercely with a hot, searing brightness.

His left arm was burning, and so was his hand. A clear, white fire, but although he could feel the heat, it didn't hurt.

Per dropped the axe and staggered backwards; at the same time he heard footsteps running across the gravel, then the sound of a door slamming shut. The car engine started up.

The liquid splashing down on to the gravel split into long, red arms reaching out for him, but he turned away and they couldn't get hold of him.

Thomas Fall floored the accelerator and Per tried desperately to put out the sticky fire on his skin.

There was no water in the quarry any more, only dry stone, so he hurled himself to the ground, rolling over and over in an attempt to douse the flames. With his right hand he dug down into the gravel, scooping it over his arm, over the yellow flames flickering along his sleeve. But it kept on burning, eating into the fabric and working its way inwards.

Then came the pain.

Don't pass out, he thought. But his arm was throbbing and he was aware of the heat and the stench of it, the acrid smell of burnt skin. Thin, dark sheets seemed to be drifting down through the air around him. But he kept on scooping the gravel over his arm, and eventually both the flames and the glowing heat were extinguished.

He suddenly realized that the sound of the car engine was much louder; it was very close to him.

Per looked up, but only had time to see that Fall's car was heading straight for him; he got up and moved to one side, but everything happened much too quickly. He couldn't get out of the way.

The front right-hand side of the car caught him and lifted him into the air. His face hit the windscreen; he heard the thud and felt the crunch before he landed on the ground at the side of the car. His left foot and ribcage took the worst of the impact with the ground, but his head also received another blow and he lost consciousness in silent darkness for a few seconds.

Then he was awake again, curled up on the hard rock. Slowly he got to his knees, feeling the cold wind against his body and rivulets of warmth on his face as the blood flowed. A split eyebrow, or possibly a broken nose.

The car shot backwards in the darkness, and he heard a door slam shut.

Footsteps crunched towards him over the gravel. Thomas Fall stopped and lifted something in the air. When Per looked up he could see it was a can of petrol.

The surprise is that it isn't a surprise at all.

He couldn't move. He was on his knees, his ribs were broken and he was surprised at the tepid warmth of the petrol being poured over him. Compared with the cold evening air the liquid could almost be called hot, and it made his skin burn and smart as it ran down over the cuts in his face.

There was a calm, rhythmic glugging sound as the plastic container was emptied. Then the sound stopped and the empty container was thrown to one side.

He was in the middle of a large puddle, his clothes sodden. He was dizzy from the blow to his head, and the petrol fumes were making the world blurred and unclear.

Supporting himself on his hands, he tried to lift his knees from the ground. But it was difficult to focus, and Thomas Fall was no more than a shadow against the dark-red evening sky.

Like a troll, thought Per. His half-brother looked exactly like a troll.

'Walpurgis Night,' said Fall. 'People will be lighting fires all over the island tonight.'

Then he took something out of his jacket pocket, something small that made a faint rattling noise.

It was a box of matches.

Per suddenly thought of something he could do – he could beg for mercy. Brother to brother.

And for Nilla's sake, too. How many hours to go now?

He opened his mouth. 'I'll keep your secret,' he whispered.

His half-brother didn't reply. He opened the box and took out a match. Then he closed the box, held the match between his fingers and struck it.

There was a faint crackle and the match was burning just a metre or so in front of Per's eyes, and in the darkness of the quarry the glow was so bright that everything else disappeared.

He closed his eyes and waited.

68

How far was it to Per Mörner's cottage over by the quarry? Seven hundred and fifty metres perhaps, or even eight hundred. Gerlof remembered that his friend Ernst had put up a beautifully polished sign by the road: CRAFT WORK IN STONE 1 KILOMETRE, but it wasn't quite that far. He consoled himself with that thought once he had managed to get across the road safely.

It wasn't far at all.

Gerlof knew every centimetre of this narrow, bumpy track; he had walked up and down it countless times on his visits to Ernst, but it was six or seven years since he had last walked over to the cottage. He had been about seventy-five then, more or less healthy and almost young.

With his aching legs and hips he was able to take only small, cautious steps, which made the journey seem endless. The track curved around the quarry, and way ahead in the distance Gerlof could see the gravelled area in front of Ernst's cottage.

Could he really walk that far? He had managed the first hundred metres, but his body was aching and his legs were trembling. His only consolation was that he had put on his winter coat before setting off; it was buttoned up to the top, and kept his back and shoulders warm.

He didn't know what time it was, but the sun was low over the Sound now. It would soon be gone. The wind had got up and was making his eyes smart. He blinked away the tears and battled on.

After a few minutes he passed the first of the luxury homes. Kurdin, that was the name of the family. He couldn't see anyone, but there were lights showing in a couple of the tall windows. He considered turning off and ringing their doorbell, but gritted his teeth and kept on going.

He was still managing to keep his balance with the aid of his stick, although his knees had started to stiffen up.

He was too far away from the quarry to be able to look over the edge and check if the car he had seen had pulled in at the bottom. But he strongly suspected that the driver had been on his way there to meet Per Mörner.

What could Gerlof do when he got there? Wave his stick at the car and try to frighten the man away?

He didn't know. Perhaps he should have called the police instead of setting off to find Per – but then all he had to go on was a bad feeling, and that was hardly likely to get the police to send a car out to northern Öland.

Now he was passing the second new house, where Vendela Larsson had organized a get-together for the neighbours at Easter. There were no lights on anywhere.

He stopped at the end of the Larssons' drive to catch his breath, longing for his wheelchair. Still three hundred metres to go to Per's cottage, or maybe four hundred.

One step at a time.

He still couldn't see anyone around the quarry, but

the old Saab was parked outside the cottage. So Per was home, unless he'd gone out for a walk.

A sturdy wooden bench would have been useful at this point, but there wasn't even a rock to sit on here by the track. He just had to keep battling on. He could hear the wind in his ears, and perhaps something else – the sound of a car engine idling?

When he was two hundred metres from Per Mörner's cottage, the sun began to slip down into the Sound. The fiery glow was silently consumed by the horizon, leaving a burning sky in the west that was gradually beginning to darken.

As soon as the sun had disappeared, the night began to creep in across the coast. The quarry was filled with a grey gloom.

Gerlof wanted to hurry on, but his strength was almost gone.

After a hundred metres he had to stop and lean on his stick once again, and that was when he heard a dull roar.

It came from the quarry. He took a couple more steps, and saw a bright glow down below.

A new sun flared up briefly in the darkness down at the bottom of the quarry, yellowish-white and much brighter than the first, and a rumbling echo rolled up over the rock face. Something had exploded among the piles of stone.

He breathed in the cold air and started to move towards the edge as quickly as he could. A car engine revved. He heard someone shouting down below, and a few seconds later came the acrid smell of burning petrol.

69

Per blinked, waiting for Thomas Fall to toss the match into the shining pool of petrol. He could simply flick it away with his thumb and forefinger, then take a step back to watch the conflagration.

But Fall was much more cautious than that. He leant forward slowly, lowering the match towards the pool.

Per saw the flame twirl and grow – and then, at the last moment, a slightly stronger puff of wind from the sea blew it out. A glowing point lingered for a second, then disappeared.

I ought to get up and make a run for it, thought Per. *Or knock him down. After all, I can do a bit of judo, I ought to knock him down.*

But he couldn't get up, he was too badly hurt. He had severe burns on his arm, and the rest of his body just felt numb. He was not aware of any pain in his broken ribs; he felt nothing.

Fall didn't seem annoyed that the flame had gone out; he quickly dropped the match and took out a new one. No, in fact he'd taken out three, Per realized – he put them together and struck them.

He heard the crackling noise again, louder this time. The flame that sprang to life was three times stronger than the last one, and burnt more brightly. Per sat on the ground with his head pounding, still thinking about judo. He had sat in this position in the training centre in Kalmar, his knees resting on a thin, soft mat, and he remembered how he had learnt to relax and focus on moving through the space. A fluid movement – throwing himself forwards, rolling to one side, falling backwards.

Backwards. He could try to fall backwards.

Now Fall was bending down towards the edge of the pool of petrol, and at the same moment Per gathered all his strength and threw himself backwards in a somersault. He relaxed as he fell, arched his back, turned his head to one side and tried to make his body into a soft arc, rolling away from the flame and the petrol.

Fall had dropped the match. The fumes dancing just above the ground ignited first, then the entire pool began to burn with a dull *puff!* and a glow that lit up the rock face all around.

For a brief moment Per found himself on his back at the edge of the pool of fire with his shoes pointing up at the sky, then he completed the backward somersault as his legs hit the ground and he felt a stab of pain bury itself in his ribs.

But he was away from the fire. He had rolled backwards away from the pool of fire, and his petrol-sodden clothes were still only wet, not burning.

Good, keep going, he thought. *Get out of the way.*

His ribcage was throbbing and aching, but still he tried to get up. He put his right hand down on the gravel and managed to push himself up.

Behind him the flames continued to dance.

He had to try to get away, but where could he go? He was trapped in a giant punchbowl, with walls of rock several metres high all around him; between him and the track leading out of the quarry were Thomas Fall and his car.

A wide, jagged shadow loomed before him in the darkness beyond the fire, forty or fifty metres away. Per realized it was the nearest heap of reject stone, where he and Jesper had found the oblong blocks for the steps. It was perhaps two metres high, like a little round fortress on the bottom of the quarry – he could hide there.

He began to drag himself towards it. When he had gone some twenty metres, Per glanced behind him, but he could no longer see Thomas Fall in the glow of the fire. The burning petrol had begun to die down, but was still glowing and smouldering on the ground. The wind was spreading the billowing smoke, forming a grey curtain in the centre of the quarry – and somewhere behind it he heard the sound of a car engine starting up. The headlights swung around as if the car were searching for him.

Per increased his speed, and seconds before the lights found him he hurled himself down behind the heap of stone.

He clung to the dry blocks of limestone and tried to keep his head down.

The headlights swept past; the car seemed to be driving around in circles in an attempt to find Per. The engine was revving in a low gear, reverberating between the rock faces like a growling prehistoric monster.

Per took a deep breath of cold air and saw a faint glow down towards the coast in the south; he didn't know what it was at first, but realized it must be a bonfire. They were burning all over the island this Walpurgis Night, and anyone who happened to see flames shooting up in the quarry wouldn't give them a second thought. He couldn't count on any help.

Thomas Fall was still driving around in ever increasing

circles. Sooner or later, Per would be discovered.

Where was the axe? It had disappeared in the darkness.

Per looked over at the rock face and the steps leading up to his cottage, to a telephone and to all of Ernst's tools. A hundred metres away, perhaps. It wasn't far, but there was nothing to hide behind on the way there.

The beam of the headlights suddenly swept over him, and stopped. The engine roared and Per realized he had been spotted.

The car waited a few seconds, then shot forward. It ought to brake soon, but instead it was speeding straight towards the pile. Per clung on tightly and tried to scramble higher up, but his hands slipped on the blocks of stone. His ribs banged into something hard, and he gritted his teeth.

Fall braked at the last minute, but the bumper crashed into the stones just below Per's legs. The impact made the entire pile wobble, and Per was surrounded by clattering and rattling as lumps of stone came loose and tumbled down the sides.

The car reversed about ten metres, and he knew it would soon shoot forward at full speed again.

He had no intention of waiting; he jumped down and began to run. Straight out into the open, heading for the stone steps. He just had to ignore the pain in his ribcage if he wanted to survive. He limped along as quickly as he could, but the car headlights picked him out. He could see his own shadow growing and dancing along across the ground.

The engine started revving behind him.

The steps were still fifty metres away, and Per wasn't going to make it. He veered off towards the nearest rock face. The sheer wall was three or four metres high here; there was no way he could climb up it, but if he stayed put he would at least have a certain amount of protection – Fall was hardly likely to crash the car straight into the rock face.

In the beam of the headlights he saw the clumps of red in the rock. The place of blood.

He reached the rock face, pressed himself against it and tried to catch his breath. The car was still revving behind him, but Fall seemed to be hesitating. Then he swung the car around in a semi-circle, pulled in as close to the rock face as he could some twenty metres away, and headed straight for Per.

Per's protection was gone, and all he could do was run towards the stone steps.

He heard a shout above the roar of the engine, and looked up as he ran.

Someone was standing at the top of the quarry – a tall, stooping figure leaning on a stick. It was old Gerlof. He was standing right on the edge, and Per saw him raise the stick.

Per kept on going. The car behind him had picked up speed; he didn't know how near it was, but it was sticking close to the rock face, and Per had no means of escape. All he could do was keep on running. He was aware of some kind of movement in the air above him, Gerlof seemed to be waving, but Per didn't have time to look. His heart was pounding, his chest was aching, he was on the point of collapse.

The car roared behind him and he reached desperately for the steps just ten metres away, but when he realized he wasn't going to get there he took two long strides and hurled himself sideways, into the darkness. He rolled over and tried to tuck his legs beneath him.

A second later the car swept past him close to the rock face; the left-hand wheels missed his feet by just a few centimetres.

Per closed his eyes and heard the car brake violently. The gravel sprayed up around the tyres and the right-hand side scraped along the rock, then he heard a deafening crash and the screech of metal. Stones rained down on the bodywork.

He opened his eyes.

Thomas Fall had crashed into the flight of steps. One of the headlights had gone out on impact, but the rear lights were still glowing, like two red eyes in the darkness.

Per could see that the entire flight of steps was beginning to collapse. The limestone blocks he had so carefully piled up teetered for a few seconds like long bricks, then they began to fall, smashing on to the car and crushing the bonnet and front windscreen.

The ground beneath him shook as the uppermost blocks crashed down between him and the car. He closed his eyes again and waited until everything was quiet.

The whining engine coughed and died, and suddenly there was total silence. Per breathed out and opened his eyes. The closest block of stone was just half a metre from his legs.

Slowly he got to his feet and looked at the mangled car. The roof had been crushed and the side windows were broken; he couldn't see any sign of movement inside.

70

There was a cold wind blowing when Per reached the top of the quarry.

'I could see he wasn't going to brake,' said Gerlof. 'He was going to run over you, so I threw my stick at the car.'

Per wiped the blood from his split eyebrow and looked at Gerlof in the darkness. They were standing motionless just a metre apart on the edge of the quarry.

'Did you hit it?' he asked.

'I hit the windscreen, I think, so it might have distracted him . . . then the car crashed into the steps.'

Per nodded without speaking, and turned to look down into the quarry. The rear lights and one headlight were still glowing. A chaotic pile of gravel and blocks of stone covered the front of the car and hid the driver's seat from view.

The flickering glow of flames could be seen from the shore to the south, and the wind carried the faint sound of singing and music and happy laughter.

When the steps had collapsed, Per had tried to lift the blocks of stone off the car, but he didn't have the strength. His ribs hurt too much. He had made his way slowly up the gravel track leading out of the quarry, then all the way around the edge to where Gerlof stood waiting.

He looked at Per and asked quietly, 'How are you feeling?'

Per tried to work it out, then held up his burnt fingers. 'OK, except for my hand. I think I've probably broken a couple of ribs too, and I've got some cuts and bruises. And I might have concussion . . . Apart from that, I'm fine.'

'It could have been worse.'

'Yes.' Per looked down at the car; the lights seemed fainter now. 'He had some kind of home-made fire bomb, just like when he burnt down the studio. He was going to set fire to me at first . . . then he tried to mow me down with the car.'

'That was Hans Bremer,' said Gerlof.

'No, it wasn't Bremer . . . that was the man who murdered Bremer. His name is Fall, Thomas Fall. He just borrowed Bremer's name. My father never knew the real Hans Bremer, the man who died in his studio.'

Per tried to remember whether Thomas Fall had said what he did. Was he in advertising? Whatever it was, he didn't want to be associated with porn. He wanted the money, but not the reputation that went with it. And eventually, when Jerry was ill and Markus Lukas was dead and Jessika knew too much, and the real Hans Bremer was asking for more money, it was time to lure Jerry, Bremer and Jessika to the studio, burn the place down and get clean away.

Per looked at Gerlof. 'And you spotted him.'

'I saw him sitting in his car out on the road,' said Gerlof. 'He was pouring some kind of liquid into a bottle . . . and then there were the watches.'

'Watches?'

'He was wearing two watches on the same wrist,

one stainless steel and one gold, just like your father. I thought that was strange . . . so I wanted to see where he went.'

Per let out a long breath. 'I never saw him clearly . . . Did we look alike, Thomas Fall and I?'

'Alike? What do you mean?'

'He said we were half-brothers.'

Per turned his back on the quarry; he didn't want to look down at the car any longer. He was covered in blood, dirty, burnt and battered, and his clothes still stank of petrol. It was his turn to go to hospital.

'We need to ring for some help,' he said. 'We'd better go inside.'

He set off slowly towards his cottage, but when he looked around he realized that Gerlof was still standing on the edge of the quarry, his head drooping. He met Per's gaze and blinked slowly, his expression confused, and when he finally spoke his voice was very weak.

'I don't know if I can manage without my stick. I feel a bit . . .' Gerlof fell silent and swayed.

Per moved fast. His whole chest hurt as his ribs scraped against one another, but he didn't hesitate. He took three long strides and grabbed hold of Gerlof before he fell over the edge.

71

Life was a dream to Vendela, but only for short periods. Mostly it was an extended state of torpor without images or memories, occasionally interrupted by faint, echoing voices around her, or shadows lifting her body and pulling at her arms. She simply allowed it all to happen, she just slept and slept.

Eventually she woke up and reached for Aloysius – but stopped herself and blinked. Where was she?

She was lying on her back in a hospital bed, staring up at a white ceiling. She didn't recognize it.

The walls in the room were bare and painted yellow, with strips of sunlight seeping in through venetian blinds. After a few minutes she looked around and realized she was alone. Alone in a hospital room on a sunny spring day. It seemed to be around the middle of the day, and she must have slept for a long time, but she was still incredibly tired.

'Hello?' she called out.

No response.

A small, transparent plastic bag was hanging from a metal stand next to her bed. There was a tube attached to the bottom of the bag, and when Vendela followed it with her eyes she realized it ended in a canula inserted into her left arm.

A drip. She was on a drip.

She remembered the tablets. She remembered that she had gone out to the elf stone one last time, with sorrow and ice in her soul. She had taken the tablets with her, she had sat down by the stone and opened the bottle . . .

She had wanted to feel calmer, but she had probably taken too many tablets.

I must have been really ill, she thought. *Ill and sad . . . Am I well and happy now?*

She sat up slowly in bed, but felt dizzy and waited for it to pass before swinging her legs over the side. Then she waited for another minute or two, and eventually got to her feet.

She stood still, taking deep breaths. Her nose wasn't blocked; her spring allergy had gone.

There was a pair of slippers waiting for her by the wall, with a red cotton dressing gown on top of them. She put them on, then wheeled the drip stand along with her as she started to shuffle across the floor. The door of her room was ajar, and she pulled it open.

She wanted to call out again, but there was no one there.

The corridor outside her room was long, well-lit and completely deserted. There was a glass door with the word EXIT on it, but it looked very heavy; she didn't think she'd be able to open it. So she went in the opposite direction, further into the ward.

The long corridor led to a small day room with sofas and chairs. There was a TV on the wall; it was switched on, but the volume was low. There was some kind of race going on, with people running through a maze and shouting to one another.

There was only one person in the room, gazing at the TV screen – a powerfully built man wearing a brown polo-neck sweater. Suddenly Vendela realized it was Max.

He turned his head and caught sight of her. He got up. 'Hi, you're . . . you're up and about.'

Vendela stared at him. 'Where are we?'

'In Kalmar . . . in the hospital.'

She nodded, still staring at him.

Max looked tired too, but he was alive. Vendela had been certain he was dead, she remembered that – she had stood by the elf stone wishing that his heart would simply give up and stop beating. She had sacrificed her wedding ring for the fulfilment of her wish.

Why hadn't it happened?

Presumably because there were no elves to grant people's wishes. She stopped with her drip stand by her side, five metres from her husband. She had walked no more than ten metres, but her legs were trembling.

'Max . . . what day is it?'

'Day? It's Friday – the first of May.'

'Is there no one else here?' said Vendela. 'No nurses?'

'Not many. It is a holiday, after all.'

Max didn't look pleased at the thought that it was the first of May. Vendela remembered he had always hated that particular day.

'But I can go and get somebody,' he went on quickly. 'Is there something you need?'

'No.'

They stood in silence, looking at one another.

'What happened?' she said. 'I remember I was out on the alvar . . . did somebody find me?'

Max nodded. 'Our neighbour from the cottage, Per Mörner. He called the ambulance.'

There was another pause before Max continued, 'He

ended up needing some attention as well . . . He was hit by a car down in the village. Apparently somebody was trying to run him over.'

'Who?' said Vendela. 'Per?'

Max nodded again. 'So he's here in the hospital as well . . . But he's going to be OK, according to the nurses. And his daughter's in here too. She had her operation this morning.'

'Is she all right now?' asked Vendela.

'I don't know . . . you can never really tell, can you? Evidently it was a tricky operation, but it went well.' Max hesitated, then added, 'And how . . . how are you feeling?'

'Fine. A bit tired . . . but I'm fine.'

She could see that Max didn't believe her, and why should he? In the end she had done exactly what he was afraid of, and swallowed goodness knows how many tablets.

Yes, she had been ill, but Vendela knew that the darkness had passed – for now.

'I have to go,' she said.

She took hold of the drip stand and turned around, slowly and carefully.

'Do you need to sit down? I can . . .'

'No, Max. I have to go and lie down again.'

And she set off. The door of her room seemed a very long way off.

'Can we talk?' said Max behind her.

'Not now.'

'Where's your ring?' he asked. 'You weren't wearing your wedding ring when they brought you in . . .'

Vendela stopped. Slowly she twisted around, a quarter of a turn. 'I'm sorry,' she said. 'But I threw it away.'

'Why did you do that?'

'Because it was worthless.'

Vendela didn't say any more, she just set off down the corridor again. She was afraid that Max would call out or come running after her, but he didn't.

When she had almost reached the door of her room, she stopped and looked back one last time.

Max was still in the day room. He had slumped down on his chair, and was leaning forward with his hands on his knees.

Vendela stood and watched him for a moment, then went into her room. She lay down on the bed and stared at the ceiling.

She no longer believed in the power of the elves. And yet, in their own way, they seemed to have granted her wish when it came to Max's heart.

EPILOGUE

There was a breeze blowing from inland, and it carried with it the scent of some kind of blossom. Cherry, perhaps – or had that already finished flowering? Per didn't know.

Nor did he know if it was summer on Öland now, or still spring. Early summer, probably. At any rate it was Saturday, 23 May, and almost everywhere in the village was green. The quarry was still grey and almost barren, but even there thin blades of grass had started to show through the gravel. On the heaps of stone, small bushes were sprouting fresh new leaves.

He looked around and thought about how life sometimes seemed to have gone for good, and yet it always came back eventually.

The stone steps had not been rebuilt. They had been removed, and not a trace remained. When Thomas Fall's body had been recovered and the police had taken away his crushed car at the beginning of May, Per had decided that he didn't need a short cut down to the shore, so he and Jesper had spent a weekend carrying the blocks back to where they came from and spreading the gravel.

Jesper and John Hagman were shovelling gravel and

moving blocks of stone again in the quarry today, but not to build a new set of steps.

'It was there,' Jesper had said when Gerlof asked him exactly where he had found the fragment of bone during the Easter weekend. He had pointed to the largest pile of reject stone at the bottom of the quarry – the same pile Per had clung to when Thomas Fall was chasing him. So that was where they were digging.

Per was standing up above them in the garden, busy with a project of his own. He had dragged an old three-legged metal barbecue over to the edge of the quarry and was burning old leaves and papers. It was going quite well, in spite of the bandage around his arm.

The leaves were from the garden, and the papers had belonged to his father. They were the contracts of employment Thomas Fall had stolen when he broke into Jerry's apartment in Kristianstad – almost two hundred contracts that Fall had taken home with him and kept, for some reason. The police had found them when they searched the house, and copied all the names and addresses. Then the public prosecutor had returned them to Per, who was now the legal owner.

He stood by the fire, flicking through the papers one last time. So many made-up names.

Danielle, Cindy, Savannah, Amber, Jenna, Violet, Chrissy, Marilyn, Tammy . . .

A series of dream girls. But their real names and addresses were there too, neatly printed beneath the dotted line on which the models had signed to say that they had willingly agreed to be photographed. And when he had leafed through the old contracts the previous evening, he had found one name in particular: *Regina.*

He had looked at that sheet of paper for a long time.

Regina's real name had been Maria Svensson. It

was a very common name, of course, and no doubt the address was an old one, but her personal identity number was written down too. It ought to be quite easy to find her.

'What are you thinking about, Dad?'

Per turned around and saw Nilla, sitting in her wheelchair on the veranda. 'Guess.'

'I can't . . . My head's completely empty.'

'Is it now?' He smiled. 'So's mine.'

Gerlof was sitting next to Nilla. There was a gap of seventy years between them, but they seemed to be happy sitting side by side in their respective wheelchairs. They were both worn out and a little fragile, but would be fine when the summer came.

Nilla and Jesper knew that their grandfather was dead now, but neither of them had attended his funeral the previous week. Per had been the only representative of the Mörner family.

There had been few flowers on Jerry's coffin, and the chapel had been almost empty. A couple of cousins had turned up, and then there was a priest and a churchwarden – and a woman of about sixty-five, dressed in black, who had sat on her own right at the back and left quickly as soon as the ceremony was over. But before that she had written her name in the chapel's visitors' book, and when Per was alone with the coffin he had gone over to have a look at it.

Susanne Fall, the woman had written.

Was she Thomas's mother, saying goodbye?

If Jerry had been Thomas Fall's father, he hadn't known about it. Susanne hadn't told him, but she must have told her son. So Thomas had grown up in the shadow of his notorious father, but unlike Per he had chosen to go and work for him – in secret. Unbeknown to Jerry, he had borrowed the identity of his alcoholic photography tutor Hans Bremer, and had sought employment as a cameraman and director with Morner Art. And he had done very well in the loveless world his father had created.

Thomas had become the son Per had refused to be. But it had ended with a burnt-out studio and a murdered father.

Jerry was dead and buried now, but his granddaughter Nilla was well and had a long life ahead of her – Per had no choice but to believe that on this sunny day.

'So how are you?' Gerlof suddenly asked, looking at him intently. 'Have you started working again?'

Per shook his head. 'I'm looking for a job.'

'Oh? Have you given up the market research?'

'They terminated my employment . . . they said I'd been making stuff up.'

He looked over at the Larssons' house. He knew Vendela was there. He hadn't seen her since she came out of hospital a week ago, but her daughter had been to visit, and Per had seen Vendela taking her new dog out a few times. A terrier.

The Kurdins' house was all closed up. Per hadn't seen them since the first of May, but no doubt they would be back for midsummer.

And Max Larsson? His cookery book wasn't due out until August, but he had already started publicizing it. Per had seen him on various TV programmes over the last week, talking about his eating habits – but there had been no sign of him at the house by the quarry for a long time. He and Vendela seemed to have separated for good.

John Hagman was waving and shouting. They had found something in the pile of stone.

'What is it?' Per yelled.

'Bones,' John replied.

John and Jesper reached into the hollow they had dug out and started to uncover what looked like human remains.

Per ran down to where they were digging and quickly moved Jesper out of the way. Gerlof slowly wheeled his chair down to join them.

'Who do you think it is?' Per asked.

'It's Henry Fors's son,' Gerlof replied. 'Henry killed him to save him being sent into care.'

'Did he? How do you know?'

'I'm ashamed to say I read about it in my wife's diary.'

Per carefully began to cover the remains with stones again. 'Unless he went off with the elves,' he replied, thinking of the boy he had met out on the alvar.

'That's always a possibility,' said Gerlof. 'I think we'll let him be . . . It isn't necessary to know everything in this world.'

Per closed his eyes, feeling the heat from the sky reflected by all the stones. He picked up a smooth piece of stone from the makeshift grave and turned his back on the quarry.

Then he wheeled Gerlof back up to the cottage and placed the last contracts of employment – including Regina's – on the burning coals. It flared up and burnt just as well as all the rest.

When the fire began to die down he turned to Gerlof and Nilla. 'I won't be long,' he said. 'I'm just going to give this stone to Vendela Larsson.'

'In that case I've got something for her as well,' said Gerlof, picking up something he had on his knee.

It was a large white envelope. As Per took it he heard something rattling inside.

'What is it?'

'A few pieces of jewellery,' said Gerlof. 'You can give them to Vendela.'

Per didn't ask any more questions. He went past his cottage and out on to the gravel track, then turned off towards the Larssons' house and walked up to the front door. He rang the bell, the envelope and the polished piece of stone in his hand.

The thick walls of the house rose above him. As the bell died away he could hear a dog barking excitedly somewhere inside, but no one opened the door.

He rang again. Then he took a step backwards out into the sunshine, feeling the warmth and the breeze on the back of his neck.

The May sunshine makes both the trolls and the elves disappear, he thought. *They burst like soap bubbles. Only human beings remain, for a little while. We are a brief song beneath the sky, laughter in the wind that ends in a sigh. Then we too are gone.*

In front of Per the latch was suddenly turned, and the door opened.

AUTHOR'S NOTE

There are many quarries along the coast of Öland where the trolls (or *trullen*, as my great-uncle Axel Gerlofsson called them) used to get the blame once upon a time if something broke or was stolen. On the alvar there are also elf stones from the Bronze Age where people still place coins or other gifts for the elves. Courses on how to meet elemental beings such as elves have been run in Sweden, but not, as far as I know, on Öland or Gotland, and the places where the quarry and the elf stone are located in *The Quarry* are freely invented by me, as are all the characters and companies in the novel.

Two excellent non-fiction books which influenced the writing of this novel were *Flickan och skulden* (*Guilt and the Girl*) by Katarina Wennstam, which deals among other things with sexual morals and double standards, and *Porr – en bästsäljande historia* (*Porn – a Bestselling History*) by Mattias Andersson, which is a detailed analysis of the Swedish sex industry.

Johan Theorin

JOHAN THEORIN

Read the rest of the haunting **Öland** series . . .

Echoes From the Dead

Winner of the CWA Best Debut Crime Novel 2009

CAN YOU EVER come to terms with a missing child? Julia Davidsson has not. Her five-year-old son disappeared twenty years previously on the Swedish island of Öland. No trace of him has ever been found

Until his shoe arrives in the post. It has been sent to Julia's father, a retired sea-captain still living on the island. Soon he and Julia are piecing together fragments of the past: fragments that point inexorably to a local man called Nils Kant, known to delight in the pain of others. But Nils Kant died during the 1960s. So who is the stranger seen wandering across the fields as darkness falls?

It soon becomes clear that someone wants to stop Julia's search for the truth. And that he's much, much closer than she thinks . . .

'Evocative and haunting, with a subtle sense of menace that grows with each page'
Simon Beckett, AUTHOR OF *THE CHEMISTRY OF DEATH*

'An impressive debut novel . . . Theorin's excellence in conveying bleak atmosphere is matched by his insight into sensitive family relationships'
THE TIMES

The Darkest Room

*Winner of the Best Swedish Crime Novel Award and Glass
Key Award for Best Nordic Crime Novel, 2008*

*'For several hours I believed that my daughter had drowned
and my wife was alive, when in fact the reverse was true.'*

IT IS BITTER MID-WINTER when Katrine and Joakim Westin
move with their children into the old manor house at Eel
Point on the Swedish island of Öland. But their new home is
no remote idyll. Just days later, Katrine is found drowned off
the rocks nearby.

While Joakim struggles to keep his sanity, Tilda Davidsson
– a young policewoman fresh out of college – becomes
convinced that Katrine was murdered.

Then, on Christmas Eve, a blizzard hits Eel Point. Isolated by
the snow, Joakim does not know that visitors – as unwelcome
as they are terrifying – are making their way towards him.

For this is the darkest night of the year, the night when the
living meet the dead . . .

*'A powerful study of grief, loss and vulnerability, with a
commendably earth-bound solution'*
Laura Wilson, GUARDIAN

*'A nerve-jangling set-up . . . this latest tale of crime in a cold
climate summons up a haunting sense of human frailty'*
METRO

COMING SOON . . .

A BRAND NEW THRILLER SET IN SWEDEN

The Asylum
Johan Theorin

Dear Ivan, is it possible to write a love letter to someone you have never met? I've only seen your picture in the newspapers, below those terrible, screaming headlines. There is something about the look in your eyes, so calm and wise and yet so penetrating. I would like you to be able to look at me in reality too. I would love to meet you . . .

A DARK UNDERGROUND passage leads from the Dell nursery to Saint Patricia's asylum. Only the children are allowed through. They are visiting their parents . . . who happen to be some of the most dangerous psychopaths in the country.

Jan, a new employee at the nursery, is a loner with secrets he tries desperately to hide. Why is he so obsessed with a female inmate? And what happened during that outing in the forest nine years ago, when a young boy went missing?

AUTUMN 2012